THE FIELD OF WRONG DOING

LILI ST.GERMAIN

Published by:
Level 4 Press, Inc.
13518 Jamul Drive
Jamul, CA 91935
www.level4press.com

Library of Congress Control Number: 2020944864
ISBN: 978-1-64630-496-7
eBook ISBN: 978-1-64630-497-4

Printed in USA

Other books by Lili St. Germain

ALEX BLACK
OPERATION PHOENIX
THE KING'S GAMBIT

"Will you walk into my parlor?" said the Spider to the Fly,
"'Tis the prettiest little parlor that ever you did spy;
The way into my parlor is up a winding stair,
And I have many curious things to show you when you are there."
"Oh no, no," said the Fly, "to ask me is in vain;
For who goes up your winding stair can ne'er come down again."

— **Mary Howitt**

You would think when you bury someone deep enough in the ground, you'd be able to keep them hidden. Smooth your shovel over fresh-tilled soil, compact it under your boots, and pray nobody ever digs there.

But dirt doesn't let you forget what lies beneath it. It keeps settling, leaving a hollow in the earth, a dip in the landscape that reminds you of the horror encased within. A hollow that demands to be filled until it rises up instead of curving down. You give it one body, then two, and still it hungers for more.

Lie down, Death whispers, greedy in its want, a faint rasp carried on a summer breeze.

Join me.

THE GIRL IN THE CREEK

Leo

It's not every morning you drink dead girl juice.

Wait. Let me explain.

It was the dog barking that woke me. Rox was our built-in security system, not that we had anything of real value to steal.

Technically, the five acres of rock and dirt that backed on to Gun Creek was owned by the State of Nevada. But in a dying town like ours, they didn't exactly have a use for it.

The mayor of Gun Creek had been friends with my grandfather before he passed, so he turned a blind eye to the double-wide and assorted makeshift dwellings my family called home.

The fact that my mother also dabbled in meth production and small-time drug dealing made me realize, eventually, that the mayor's eyes were being turned not with compassion, but with favors from mommy dearest.

I couldn't think about that, though. My mother was a fuck-up who'd had too many kids with a somewhat questionable number of different daddies, but she was the only mother I had. I didn't want to think about some greasy guy in a cheap suit putting his chubby hands on her.

"Rox!" I hissed at the dog through the narrow window, mindful not to wake my girlfriend. The sun wasn't even up yet.

Beside me, Cassie breathed long and even, her chest rising and falling in time. Her hair covered her face, her expression weary even in sleep. I kept telling her she worked too much, but she just laughed and told me the more she worked the faster we'd be out of this town. It was one of the reasons I loved her so much.

We'd both been raised to believe that we'd never get out of Gun Creek, but Cassie was smart. She had that spark inside that matched mine. That's how I knew, unequivocally, that we'd be the ones who got away.

It was peaceful inside my room. I'd built it myself when I was twelve from an old shipping container somebody had dumped on our property. It leaked in the winter and there were gaps where the corrugated steel sheets attached to the ground. I had filled the gaps with expanding foam as best I could, but sometimes the mice still chewed through. My dog made quick meals of them if that happened. I didn't mind the mice. They were less intrusive than my mother in her rotting trailer up near the road.

Rubbing sleep from my eyes, I walked as quietly as possible from my bedroom to the kitchen. Loose definitions for one long, narrow space separated by a hanging bed sheet.

I'd been having a dream when Rox's bark woke me, but I couldn't remember it. I just knew I felt antsy, and I needed to go and shut the goddamned dog up before Ma came down and started yelling.

I went to the makeshift sink, a metal bowl with a hole cut in the bottom that I'd plumbed in myself. It drew water directly from our well, so I didn't need to pump water manually to make it flow. I even had a shower with heating that I'd made from old PVC piping and plastic sheeting, lifted from Lawrence's Auto Repair, the garage where I fixed cars after school for cash. That had come later when I'd decided that, if Cassie was sleeping over, she should be able to wash up without having to go up to my mom's trailer to do it.

I turned the tap on at the sink and filled an old jam jar. My eyes itched—the pollen was off the charts and fucking brutal in the spring.

I set the jar down and splashed cool water on my face. The pipes inside the well made the water smell of metal sometimes, and today especially so. Eyes itching considerably less, I turned off the water and reached for my jar.

I took an extra-long drink. I can still taste it now, all these years later. Straightaway I knew that something wasn't right. The taste of rot and pennies filled my mouth, and I almost gagged.

What the . . . ?

I held the clear jar up to the thin streak of sunlight coming through a crack in my homemade curtains. The water was a dirty rust color, still transparent, but stained like someone had taken a dropper of red ink and squeezed it into the liquid.

I looked at the small mirror I'd hung above the basin. My face looked kind of dirty, too. I grabbed an old T-shirt and wiped my face dry as best I could, Rox's barking reaching fever pitch.

The fucking dog. The fucking well. Fucking *all of it.* I was so tired of living with shit that didn't work properly, trash pieced together from more trash. When people looked at us, I knew that's what they saw— pieced-together trash.

When I left Gun Creek, I was getting Cassie and me a real house. One with rooms and curtains and a real bathroom. A house without wheels underneath, without foam to seal up the fucking gaps. A house with a proper front door painted her favorite color, blue.

Winter might have been months gone but the mornings here still chilled your bones. I hopped into a pair of jeans and threw on a hoodie, unlocking and opening the door as quietly as I could. It creaked in response. I made a mental note to get oil for the hinges.

Rox wagged her tail, curling her body sideways as she made her way toward me, her head and back end pointing at me as she did her dog version of an excited crab walk.

"Hey, girl," I murmured, putting my palm out for her. She licked it, right in the center, and when she pulled her pink tongue away the skin there turned cold.

"What's up, Rox?" I asked quietly, scratching behind her ear. Rox was a mutt, motley-colored and missing one eye, but sharp as a tack. She whined a little, running off in the direction of the well.

I had to check the damned thing anyway. Might as well follow her lead. I backed up a few steps, slipping inside to grab a flashlight from the ledge I'd built next to the door. Stupid well was always clogging up. That's the thing about living illegally on land you don't own—water isn't exactly an automatic thing to come by, even when you're right near a creek.

I picked my way down the stony sand path that led to the well, the dirty taste still in my mouth. I zipped my hoodie up over my chilled skin as I walked, my feet complaining loudly. *Should've worn my boots*, I thought, but I was too lazy to turn back.

I was three steps away from the well when I heard a twig snap behind me. I jumped, turning quickly, gripping my Maglite tightly.

Oh. Damn. I saw Cass, shielding her emerald-green eyes from the flashlight I was shining in her direction, wearing my old snow jacket on top of the oversized football jersey of mine she insisted on sleeping in. She'd slipped her feet into my boots, far too big for her, so when she walked she had to kind of drag her feet.

"Hey," I said softly. Sometimes it made my chest hurt when I thought about how much I loved her. Especially in the morning, when she was tired and warm and bleary-eyed.

"Come back to bed," she murmured, her voice still full of sleep.

She looked fucking adorable. I didn't want to be out fixing the well. I wanted to be back in bed with her.

I walked over to her, Rox momentarily forgotten. "The well's backed up again," I said, planting a kiss on her cheek. She turned her face, going for the lips, but I leaned back, covering my mouth.

"No," I said, jerking my thumb back toward the well. "I'm pretty sure I just drank dead mouse water." I didn't mention that it was probably something bigger than a mouse. Girls hate stuff like that.

"Eww," Cass said, wrinkling her nose. "Brush your teeth before you get the plague or something."

I laughed, turning back to the well. Fifty feet or so and I was there, bracing myself and holding my breath as I lifted up the lid. The water had been fine the day before, so the dead thing must have been pretty recent.

I folded the heavy wooden lid back on its hinge and peered inside. The sides of the well were made from stone, and cold, stale air rose up to greet my face. I shivered, my flashlight landing on something large and unmoving as Cass came to a standstill beside me.

Shit.

It wasn't a mouse. It wasn't a raccoon, either. It might be a fucking dog. A small calf. I thought of my younger brothers, little band of shitheads they could be, and wondered what accident they'd tried to hide in the well.

'Course, when you were six or seven years old, you didn't understand that by killing animals from neighboring farms, you were marking yourself as a potential serial killer. The triplets we called them, because there were three of them. Matty was five, Richie was six, and Beau was seven. They loved to break shit, kill shit, steal shit, and then lie about it.

My mom excelled at breeding. She'd really hit her stride when she met the triplets' father and banged out three in as many years before he OD'd in her bed and she left his corpse tangled in her bedsheets for three days thinking he was asleep.

My mom was fucking crazy.

Hence having my own makeshift room, as far away from her as I could get.

"It's something big," I said to Cass.

Her cheery demeanor quieted a little. When we were talking about things stuck down wells, big was more serious than small. "You think—"

I knew what she was thinking. Her mind always went to the worst possibility.

"Nah," I said, shaking my head. "Definitely not. Not big enough. I bet you anything those little shitheads killed something and threw it down here."

Cassie opened her mouth to say something and then closed it again. "You can shower at my house?" she said then. Her tone said she was trying to be helpful, as though we could just shut the well and be done with it.

I was the oldest. I was the man of the house. It was my responsibility.

"We need water," I said. "They all need water."

"You want me to try lowering you down?" she asked dubiously. I shook my head. We both knew she was too small to bear my weight.

"Get Pike," I said, flicking the flashlight off. "I can climb down there okay, but he needs to hoist me back up."

She nodded, standing on her tiptoes to kiss my cheek. I remembered again that I'd washed my face with the dirty water. Gross. After I fixed this, I was going to run the water clear and have a scalding hot shower for, like, three hours.

"Be careful," Cass murmured. "You know what—just wait. I'll get Pike and we can both lower you down with the rope. Last thing we need is you breaking an ankle before football finals."

Cass was going to get out of Gun Creek based on her smarts, and I was going to get out based on my athletic abilities. Old Tanner Bentley may not have gifted my brother and I with money or any kind of upbringing. However, he had passed down to me his ability to smash anyone I was up against in football. Cass and I were scholarship bound, baby. We were on our way.

I stood there for a moment as I watched her disappear up to the main trailer. I was impatient, my major downfall in life.

I should have waited like she said, but I couldn't be bothered. I would climb down, bracing my bare feet against the rock walls like I'd done countless times as a kid. I'd fix the problem, save the day, and then they'd bring me back up in a few minutes. Hot showers for all.

And after I was clean, after I'd scrubbed my skin and my teeth clean, I'd take Cassie into the shower with me.

I swung a leg over the lip of the well and got a good grip with my hands. Then I inched one leg down, the flashlight under one arm and my feet better than any rock-climbing shoe as I shinnied into the dark.

The problem wasn't getting into the well, because the rocks were relatively dry up top near the surface. It was getting out, because once you were down to the bottom, the rocks became smooth and wet, and it was impossible to gain purchase against them.

Once you were in the well, you were in.

Still, how bad could it be? Whatever was down there smelled, so it was dead, and therefore it couldn't hurt me. That was the logic I applied, anyway.

I gripped my feet against the rocks, my heart rate accelerating as I got closer to the dark lump at the bottom. Whatever it was floated against one wall, so I made my way down the opposite wall and winced when my feet touched freezing cold water. It came up to my ankles, sloshing about as I kept the flashlight gripped tightly under my arm. If I dropped it, I'd be screwed.

The smell down there wasn't as bad for some reason. It was as if the water had absorbed some of the scent and the rest had risen, bilious gases searching for freedom outside the confines of the narrow stone walls. But despite the smell improving, the feeling in my stomach only got worse.

My skin crawled as I tried not to think about what was in the water, my teeth clenched tight as I braced my bare feet on the bottom of the well and took the flashlight in hand, aiming it at the mysterious lump.

For a moment, I couldn't figure out what I was looking at. Dark hair. Blood. A dog? I'd been expecting a dog. Those fucking brothers of mine had killed a dog before, last summer, slit the poor Labrador's throat and dumped it in the creek.

The thing in front of me wasn't a dog.

It was a girl.

Or—half of a girl, cut from under one shoulder to over the other hip, the top half of her staring eternally forward with milky-blue eyes while parts of things that had once been inside her seeped out of the spot where she'd been brutally split.

I screamed.

I dropped the fucking flashlight.

I kept screaming.

Not just because of the girl. Not just because she'd been butchered, her lower half nowhere to be seen. But because I wondered, briefly, if I was standing on the rest of her body parts. Her legs. Where the fuck were her legs?

I screamed until it felt like my throat would bleed. I screamed for Cassie, for Pike, for Jesus, and for God . . . I didn't believe in the last two, but my subconscious didn't care about that minor detail.

JESUSCHRISTOHMYGODCASSIEPIKE.

Over and over again.

I think I even called for my mother.

Cassie's face finally appeared above me. She was so high up I could barely make out her expression. "What is it?" she called out. "Leo, what is it?"

Beside her, I saw Pike, lowering the rope down. Too slow. Too fucking slow and I was stuck next to the dead girl and I was still screaming.

I started to hyperventilate.

"Karen!" I screamed. "It's fucking *Karen*!"

I saw Pike speed up, heard Cassie gasp loudly.

Karen was a girl we went to school with.

Karen had been missing for almost a week.

Everybody thought Karen had run away or been swept up in a trucker's rig, or just plain gone and died somewhere nobody knew about. The police were searching for her, but you could tell it was kind of a half-hearted thing.

Because girls like Karen went missing, but they weren't always missed. Girls like Karen were trouble, and she had been *in* trouble. With drugs. With stealing. With sex.

Karen was the girl who'd given hand jobs to the entire male side of our class by the time she was thirteen.

Karen was the girl who'd already had three abortions.

Karen was trouble. Karen was *in* trouble.

But Karen wasn't in trouble anymore.

Because Karen was fucking *dead*.

"Pike, get that fucking rope down here, man, hurry!" I begged.

I know I'd said the smell wasn't so bad in the well, but that was before I'd seen what the smell was. Now, it crawled inside my nostrils. It laid a home on my tongue. It burrowed into my cheeks.

And then I remembered that I'd drank the water.

I'd drank dead Karen water. Dead girl juice.

I gagged violently, one hand up against the wall. I was terrified— of what, I'm not sure. She was already dead, after all. She was hardly going to hurt me.

Something brushed against my face and I yelled again, jerking my head away. My heart leaped when I saw the rope, a crudely fashioned bar attached to it to wrap your legs around while you got hoisted up or down.

I grabbed that rope for dear life. "Pull me up!" I yelled. The rope started to jerk almost immediately as Pike wound it up above. Relief flooded my body, right through to the marrow in my bones, and I closed my eyes momentarily as I took a proper breath.

But the rope was frayed, and I was too heavy. I wasn't a kid anymore; I was six-foot-five and growing like a weed, my once-skinny body now filled out with lean muscle. For all intents and purposes, I was a man, and the rope Pike offered me would hold a small child, at best.

The rope snapped.

I fell.

The fall ended just as quickly as it had begun when I slammed face-first into what was left of Karen. I screamed without opening my mouth, my eyes level with hers, seeing a tiny worm making a hole in her face to burrow into.

Her eyes had some kind of cloudy film over them, like my grandfather's eyes when he'd developed cataracts, as if she were watching me through the dirty windows of the beyond. I pushed away, heaving my body up and sticking to the opposite wall.

My eyes slowly adjusted to the dark at the bottom of the well, Karen's face coming into grainy focus. I stared at the milky blue-white of her dead eyes until the sheriff arrived and hoisted me out with a winch.

Something changed in me while I was down there. Some part of me died with Karen, sucked out of me and into her unseeing eyes. I still remember now, years later, the way I laughed at Cassie before I went over to the well. How light I felt. How easy it was to breathe.

I don't laugh much anymore.

Once I was finally at the surface, I ran as far away from the well as I could get. Cass tried to touch me, but I pushed her away, pushed Pike away, falling to my hands and knees in the dirt, the sight of that body on a constant loop inside my head. Karen. Dead. Her blood in the fucking water.

Her blood inside me.

I stuck a finger down my throat and gagged. Nothing came up. Fuck, no. I wasn't going to go on until I had the water that I'd drank *out* of my body.

I stuck two fingers down, farther, and threw up all over the grass. That strange, metallic taste returned to my mouth, masked by bitter stomach acid.

Dead girl juice. It took me months before I stopped tasting her in my mouth.

A bunch of kids found the other half of her floating in Gun Creek a few hours later.

My friend Chase Thomas was one of the kids who saw her lower parts, wedged underneath a grille in the water intake pipe that fed the whole town, legs dancing lazily in the current.

For a long time afterward, people were talking about how strange it was that Chase and I had found a half of Karen each.

How convenient.

Almost like they thought we killed her.

Cassie

'd only seen a dead person once before. My grandfather. Even then, it was after the funeral home had done their magic, embalmed him, taken away the pale death, and made him look like he was simply sleeping. White-haired and fragile, he was like a life-sized china doll, laid neatly in his coffin with his fishing hat and thick-rimmed glasses. It was only when I touched his hand that I felt his death. So, to me, death was cold. Death was waxen cheeks and liver spots, gray hair and wrinkled skin.

But when I saw Karen—or what was left of her, that part of her—death stopped being cold. Death became a savage thing; it became fresh and cloying and violent.

Death became our living nightmare.

Leo, he had it the worst. For weeks, he couldn't drink anything without gagging. Said all he could taste was Karen. The only thing that could wash her away was whiskey or vodka, any spirit that burned as it went down.

So he drank, and he stayed in his room, and for weeks he couldn't even look me in the eye, let alone touch me.

I still loved him. I *always* loved him. But Leo Bentley was never the same sweet boy after he came out of that well.

THE GIRL IN
THE WINDOW

CHAPTER ONE

Cassie

— *Now* —

I am a girl with a darkness inside me.

Carefully placed. Cleverly concealed.

A darkness that could devour you.

One hand on a cold pane of glass, watching the snow fall outside. It's pitch-black out here, far away from bright city lights. You can't see a goddamned thing. You can only feel fingers digging into your hips, hot and insistent, a tug of hair, a smack of skin, and the snowflakes as they fall through the weak pool of light that the porch provides below. And the pain. He's not gentle when he uses me to satisfy his want.

I think he likes it like this, up on the bed, against the window, as if somebody might see. But nobody could ever possibly see. It's too dark. No streetlights. No houses for a clear half-mile in every direction.

Just us, and the silence, and the darkness.

And the snowflakes, steady as they fall, through that yellow beam below.

You could never count them all. One blink and you'd miss some. One sharp stab of pain that drives your face into the mattress, and you'd miss plenty.

And that's the point, I suppose. You keep counting. You watch the snow fall, and you count every snowflake your eyes can catch until it's finally over.

The darkness wasn't always there. I was bright and shiny once. There was no tarnish at my edges, no very bad thing that existed inside me. I had a mother, and a boyfriend, and a life. I was loved. I had plans and goals and aspirations.

One moment and they were all gone.

I know what you'll think after you hear my story.

You'll think I went mad when I saw Leo being burned alive, or when I gazed down at my comatose mother in the hospital after, as words like *brain swelling* and *direct-impact collision* drifted through the air, meant for me but headed somewhere beyond.

Or maybe, maybe, you'll think it was during that first time, on the kitchen floor, a tangle of limbs, palm pressed against desperate lips, fingers squeezing wrists until it felt like they would snap.

And every time I'll tell you, you are wrong. That even as I cried in the aftermath of his sudden interest in me, I still was a girl without a coal-black heart.

I can tell you the exact moment the darkness burrowed in to stay. I imagine it like some filthy worm, coming up from the earth, chewing a neat circle in my skin and wriggling in. Finding that hollow space beneath my heart, in my rib cage, and curling up. Sated. Satisfied. Warm. I feel it sometimes when I'm frightened, and my heart won't slow down. It beats like crazy, like a machine gun with the trigger locked on. I can't breathe. My vision tunnels. In those moments, I imagine the worm, how happy it must be, how comfortable within my fragile chest.

It's strange how you know something has happened, even if you can't remember it.

When you wake up in your bed, and the sheets beneath you are wet, and you haven't wet the bed since you were little, a three-year-old girl who started to cry because she'd slept through instead of getting up and going to the bathroom.

Eighteen years old, naked, and laying in a cold wet spot, with damp thighs and a bitter taste on your tongue. The taste of a medication you took once after your dad died and you started having nightmares that kept you awake. The bitter pill that your mother crushed into a glass of milk for you, the one that knocked you under and held you there in a chokehold, so that you could still see the nightmares in your sleep but could no longer wake up from them. It was terrifying then, and it's terrifying now. It's in your mouth and in your nostrils and down the back of your throat and all you can remember is a low voice that says, *Finish your milk, Cassandra.*

You have been drugged.

Somebody has undressed you, tucked you into your bed, and they have used you. They have left something inside you.

A darkness. A coiled, buzzing midnight that becomes all you've ever known.

You don't like it at first. It frightens you.

The darkness is where nightmares come to life.

But after time goes by, you start to feel differently.

You begin to realize that the darkness you've been given is not a burden, but a gift.

CHAPTER TWO

Cassie

— Eight Years Ago —

've never felt rain like the rain we had that night.

It didn't fall from the sky so much as it drove into the earth, each drop an individual missile that indented the ground and turned firm-packed dirt to mud. It bit at your skin like tiny stinging bullets, if you were stupid—or unlucky—enough to be caught out in the deluge.

It's imprinted in my mind as if it's still happening now.

Truck lights flashed past on the interstate on their way through our tiny town, in and out of Gun Creek in thirty seconds. The town was barely that; a few thousand people in the middle of nowhere, scattered around a strip mall that boasted a tired-looking diner, a tiny convenience store, a rusty old auto repair garage, and a police station just big enough to squeeze the town's sheriff and deputy inside.

I worked at the diner after school and on weekends; we always had plenty of customers at Dana's Grill, but nobody ever stayed longer than a meal and a bathroom stop. The truck stop out front lay empty most nights, the once-bustling rest area in the road usurped by a fancier one up the highway fifty miles or so, with its shiny gas station and fast-flow gasoline pumps and sealed parking lot for the trucks to pull in for the night.

The diner was the most alive part of our town, and it was still dying.

It was storming, not unusual for that time of year, but the business it brought us was incredible. Dana's Grill was heaving; I couldn't remember the last time I'd had to seat customers at the bar while I cleared off tables. I had overheard a couple earlier talking about some flooding north of Gun Creek, and I guessed the shiny new rest stop had been cut off by the downpour.

I was handing change to a table of truck drivers when I heard the sound. It was dampened by the unrelenting rain, the water almost delaying the sound waves from breaching the diner.

A loud bang. The sickening screech of metal twisting, accordioning in on itself like a can being crushed underfoot. Every head in the diner swiveled to look outside, just as a crack of lightning lit up the world in an eerie blue-white flash that lasted but a fraction of a second.

A midnight-blue Mustang with a custom-painted white racing stripe down the middle. I looked just in time to see it smashing through the rusted guardrail that ran along the edge of the bridge into town. An entire diner full of people watched, slack-jawed and unmoving as the rail groaned and gave way, the car hurtling into oblivion below.

It hit something, hard. What did it hit? Not a tree. There weren't any on this stretch of highway, save for a few dying lemon trees that somebody planted out the front of Dana's Grill years ago and left to try and survive in the blistering hot summers and fatally cold winters that make up our little spot in northern Nevada.

Whispers began to flow through the diner before the car had even crashed to a stop in the shallow bedrock below. An accident? Somebody call nine-one-one. What's going on? The creek was somewhat frozen at this time of year, but no doubt the force of the car would bust straight through any ice and into the freezing water below.

I dropped the change onto the table, missing the guy's large, oil-stained hand completely. Coins rolled in ten different directions, and the guy glared at me, clearly unimpressed.

I wasn't paying attention to him, though. I was staring at what I thought I'd just seen—what I'd definitely heard—waiting for another crack of lightning to show me I was imagining things.

"Hey, you okay?" one of the truckers asked me. He was wearing one of those baseball caps, the peak so low I could barely see the whites of his eyes as they reflected my horrified expression.

My mouth was dry. It wasn't his car. I just spoke to him.

"My boyfriend drives a Mustang," I said slowly. An odd taste filled my mouth, and it was a moment before I realized I'd bitten the inside of my cheek hard enough to draw blood.

"Oh, hell," the guy said, putting a hand on my shoulder as a set of headlights rolled through the rain on the highway, stopping in front of the warped guardrail, illuminating it in full detail. The car that had gone over was nowhere to be seen. Oh, God.

I snapped out of my inertia. Tearing my apron off, I dropped it, sprinting for the front doors.

"Cass?" A voice sounded from my right. Hands fell upon my arms, a face leaning down into mine that I knew but couldn't place, even though I saw it every day.

"Cassie!" the face yelled, and suddenly, two light-brown eyes sprang into focus.

"It could be Leo," I said to the face with the eyes.

Those eyes scrunched up in confusion. "What?"

I needed for him to let go of me. I needed to get to the car down in the creek bed to tell myself it wasn't Leo. That it was anyone except Leo.

"The car!" I yelled, shaking myself free. "It's a Mustang. Let go of me!"

Chase Thomas. That was his name. The quarterback of Gun Creek High's football team. The little kid who pulled a chunk of my hair out in kindergarten. He was seventeen, like me. His eyes went wide as he let me go, and then I was smacking my shoulder against the heavy double doors at the entrance to Dana's, leaping off the front steps, and almost breaking my neck as I landed on icy asphalt. My teeth started chattering almost immediately. It was almost freezing that night, and the rain was turning yesterday's snowdrifts into pale, gray sludge.

My Skechers sank into the muddy snow, and I fell over a couple of times. I was getting closer, inch by painstaking inch. The wind whipped my hair around my face, matted blond strands sticking to my lips and teeth as I kept running and falling. Running and falling and getting back up.

Almost there.

I didn't even look for oncoming cars as I ran across the highway and up to Gun Creek. The banks of the creek were rocky and I slipped in my sneakers. I barely felt the cold, my focus so narrowed in on the Mustang that had smashed over the bridge and landed fifteen feet below on a pile of icy bedrock, submerged only partially in the water. One of its red taillights flickered weakly, on and off, a sign of life from the otherwise motionless vehicle. Nobody was moving inside. The radio was still playing, but I couldn't place the song. It all sounded like static to me as I tried to pick my way through snow and ice.

"Cassie!" A voice sounded from the bridge above. I didn't even look back. I couldn't. I had to get to the car and tell everyone it wasn't Leo inside. "Get the hell away from there!"

I scrambled over the last of the rock and onto frozen creek bed. I was almost at the car when flames started to spread inside.

"No!" I yelled, the wind buffeting any noise that might have come out of my mouth, literally making me choke on my own words as cold air slammed into my lungs. I coughed, water streaming from my eyes, tiny icicles already forming on my eyelashes.

I knew this car. I'd driven this car more times than I could count. Midnight-blue, with a white racing stripe. I'd held its parts in my hands, their oily black lifeblood smeared over my skin, and watched as Leo put it back together over a few years.

It's not him.

We lived in a small town, and when it wasn't football season, there was very little to do. Our favorite pastime was sneaking out to have sex, careful little rabbits we were, and having a car made that so much easier. Hence our rebuilding of the old Mustang wreck that Leo's father had somehow acquired but never gotten to fixing. That car was going to take us to our new place after we finished school. It was going to take us to Vegas so we could get married the weekend he turned eighteen. It was going to take our first baby home from the hospital in ten years when we were settled and ready to start a family. We might've been young and stupid, but Leo Bentley and I already knew where life was taking us. Life was a midnight-blue Mustang, and it was going places. Places that weren't Gun Creek.

I was thirty feet from the car when I saw the arm of a letterman's jacket hanging limply out the window.

And I knew, without a doubt, that the boy I'd wanted to marry since I was twelve years old was trapped, bleeding and unconscious, in a car that was being devoured by flames.

"Cassie!" I heard a voice to my left, barely audible over the wind. The voice sounded familiar. Damon King was—is—the town sheriff. He was also my mother's new husband. He was a nice guy. They'd been married for a couple months when the accident happened. *He'll help,* I remember thinking, my teeth chattering so hard I imagined them smashing into pieces that I'd have to spit into the snow. *Damon. He'll get Leo out.*

He didn't. He ran down the embankment, his sturdy boots and sheriff's uniform much more weather-appropriate than my flimsy shirt and sneakers. I watched him, assuming he'd go straight to Leo's door, but instead he climbed over icy rocks and disappeared around the passenger side of the Mustang.

What the hell?

"Leo!" I screamed, my words lost in the wind. It was cold and my throat hurt and I didn't know what to do. Instinct told me to run away from the car, but love was stronger. Love was foolish as it pulled me to the car like a moth to a flame—ha, a flame, a fucking bonfire now, strangely comforting as its warmth took the edge off my frozen state. Something about the fire snapped me out of my dream-like fog. I looked around and saw nobody. Nobody wanted to risk coming too close in case the car blew up. But me? They'd have to drag me away because I'd burn sooner than leave Leo to die.

I surveyed the car, my breath bubbling up in my chest as I struggled to stay calm. I had to save him. I had one small thing going for me—the fire was raging much harder on the passenger side of the car. I could see Leo's right arm being licked by the flames, but so far his body and face were out of their path.

I stepped into the freezing water and waded over to the driver's side of the car. The car was at an angle and partially submerged in the creek, the water line barely below Leo's open window. The driver's door was pinned against a large boulder; there was no way to open it.

I would have to pull him through the open window. I lay down on the boulder, gasping as icy water seeped through my clothes. I reached my hands into the car window and realized that I'd have to crawl through the window and across Leo to undo his belt. It meant I had to put my hand in the flames. White-hot pain seared every nerve ending I had and some I wasn't aware existed. It burned hot enough to choke me, but I couldn't pull away until Leo was safe.

With the pain and the smoke, I started coughing almost as soon as my head was in the car window. I couldn't bear to look too closely at Leo, not yet. If he died . . . No. I refused to even think like that.

Operating on adrenaline, high on smoke fumes, I was about thirty seconds from passing out when a hand locked around my ankle and pulled. "Cassie!" Damon yelled. "Get back!"

I kicked my mother's husband square in the face as hard as I could and resumed my rescue operation. *Please don't die.* Hand in the fire, I undid the seatbelt pinning Leo and hooked my hands under his arms. *Don't fucking die on me, not here, not like this.*

Somehow, I managed to pull a two-hundred-pound linebacker out of a burning car and away from the wreckage, dousing his burns in ice water. I made it to the rocky shore, thankful for the slippery ice for once as it helped me to pull Leo's lifeless body along, just in time to cover my face. Something exploded—probably the fuel tank—and showered the creek in pieces of burning metal.

Shaking, wet, and on the verge of hypothermia, I pulled Leo into my lap, surveying the damage. He was burned badly along his right arm and part of his neck, but the flames had spared his face. His dark blond hair was matted with blood, little bits of glass stuck in the shaggy strands. I slapped his cheek softly, my fingers numb slabs of meat. "Hey," I rasped, quietly at first, then a louder, more insistent yell. "Hey!"

Just open your eyes. Just show me those eyes of yours. I pried open his left eye with my fingertips, my stomach twisting painfully as I saw his pinprick-sized pupil almost swallowed up by dark green iris.

"Leo, please wake up," I begged.

He didn't wake up. An ambulance arrived on the bridge, then another. Damon was back, his face ashen, bright blue eyes bloodshot, a streak of blood painting his left nostril down to his lips. I did that.

"I don't need an ambulance," I said to him, as the paramedics pried my fingers away from Leo and lifted him onto a stretcher.

He said something I didn't quite catch, something like *other*, pointing to the other side of the embankment where a second team of paramedics was taking a stretcher, and that's when I understood. My vision narrowed to two tunnels, and all I could see was my stepfather's solemn eyes and the fire as I deciphered his words. He wasn't saying *other*.

He was saying *mother*.

My mother had been in the car. In the passenger seat. In the fire. There'd been a party at the high school to celebrate the football team getting into the finals. My mom had been there, since Damon helped coach the team after work and on weekends. Leo, I surmised, must have been giving her a ride home. It was less than a mile from the school to our house. Yet somehow, in less than a mile, they had driven off a bridge instead.

I watched in horror as the paramedics rushed my mother past me. She looked dead. Her lips were blue, half her face was melted like a wax crayon left too long in the sun, and the paramedics were yelling at each other over her still form. One of her legs hung off the stretcher at a strange right angle and blood flowed like muddy rivers out of her mouth and nose, carving tributaries through her burnt flesh.

People were talking to me. I guessed they were asking which ambulance I wanted to travel in. As if in slow motion, I looked between the two vehicles with their flashing lights and bright red sides. The two people I loved most in the world.

I opened my mouth to speak. Closed it again. I couldn't hear anymore. Everything was a staccato hiss, everything the sound of the rain as it hit the rocks I stood teetering on. The world tilted suddenly as my legs disappeared beneath me, I heard a loud *thwack* as the back of my head hit a sharp rock, and then nothing.

Later, in the sterile white of the hospital hallway, I started to hear things again. Two rooms, side by side, where teams of doctors worked on the two people I loved most in the world.

I started to hear things I did not want to hear.

My mother was in a coma.

She was almost certainly going to die.

My boyfriend was awake.

He had burns on his arm and a concussion.

My boyfriend was holding his hands out; wrists suddenly handcuffed to the stretcher he was sitting up on.

Leo. The guy I was going to marry.

This was all his fault.

The cop shifted to the side after cuffing Leo, and he spotted me in the hallway. "I'm sorry," he mouthed, his eyes glassy and red.

I looked down at my own arm, bandaged from the burns, and wished I'd left him in his car while the flames took over.

"It should have been you," I said loudly, my hand burning with pain from where the fire had licked at me. "It should have been fucking *you*."

And so I sat, bleary-eyed, next to Damon on a row of hard hospital chairs. He held an ice pack to my bleeding skull, the stubble on his sharp jaw growing well past a five-o'clock shadow, and we waited. I felt his blue eyes burn into me as we silently lingered, and I couldn't tell if they were alight with concern, or blame.

There was so much waiting. For news, good or bad. At that point, we still didn't know if my mom would make it out of surgery.

I fell asleep on the chairs, concussed and still wearing my Dana's Grill uniform, a hot pink shirt and navy-blue skirt. I'd taken my sweater off—the sleeves ruined from the fire—and while I slept somebody had wrapped me in one of those emergency tinfoil blankets and covered me with Damon's dark green SHERIFF jacket. I woke up with a start, muffled words piercing my exhaustion as the back of my skull lanced with pain and I felt fresh blood seep through my matted hair. I needed stitches, but I refused to let anyone near me until I'd heard about my mother's surgery.

"I think we should speak in private," the doctor was saying to Damon, eyeing me with one of those pity looks that I became so accustomed to in the aftermath of the crash. Everyone was so fucking pitying, it was nauseating.

"No," I said, sitting up suddenly. I sounded drunk from the Percocet they'd given me. "You can't leave me by myself."

Damon squeezed my hand. "It's okay," he said to the doctor. "She's old enough."

The doctor ushered us into a blank room. Bare walls, bare floors, nothing except three hard plastic chairs and a wooden crucifix hanging on the wall, crooked. Where was the furniture? This was like an interrogation room, not a place of refuge. The only thing to focus on was Jesus's face, contorted with agony, crucified for a lopsided eternity.

I sat in one of the hard chairs. Damon paced.

"Sheriff," the doctor urged. "Please. Sit down. You're both exhausted."

Damon turned and gave him a look so scathing, he took a step back. Pride blossomed in my chest at my stepfather's outrage. *We're in this together,* I remember thinking.

We hadn't always gotten along, Damon and I. My mother had often been a mediator between the two of us when he first moved into our house. But now, we were a single unit. We would pray for my mother to wake, together. Such was the power of our love for her.

"Sheriff—"

"Damon."

"—Damon. Your wife was gravely injured. Did she often ride without a seatbelt?"

Not, does she. *Did* she.

As if she were already dead.

"What?" Damon choked, his bright blue eyes pooling with tears. "No, she always wears her belt."

I was too shocked to process the information properly. My mom was thirty-eight years old. She couldn't be dying.

"Is she going to be okay? Is she dead?" I asked, hope overriding the reality written all over the doctor's infuriatingly kind face.

"She's alive. The machines are keeping her body functioning. Her brain sustained what we believe to be irreparable injury." A pause. "I'm so sorry."

Good news and bad news all wrapped up in one neat little statement that took the air from my lungs. Your mother is alive. *Punch.* She might as well be dead. *Punch.*

"Are you sure?" Damon asked.

I reached for his hand again, his palm damp with sweat, his fingers crushing mine as he squeezed.

The doctor looked at me apprehensively. "The swelling makes it impossible to tell precisely right now . . ." He trailed off. He cleared his throat, adding in a half-whisper, "It doesn't look good."

My mind spun as I tried to process what was happening. Beside me, Damon was doing the same. He scrubbed his hand across his jaw, his stare vacant. How could this happen to us? "I am so very sorry," the doctor repeated. I wanted to throw up. My hand burned where Damon was gripping it. I'd been burned by the flames, and now his touch was like agony.

I stopped hearing things at that point. I focused every ounce of my attention on the pain in my fingers, the burned skin that was being crushed by Damon's stronghold. It was an odd comfort, the way the pain distracted me.

It can't get worse, I kept thinking. *It can't get worse than this.*

I was wrong.

The next morning, I remember Gun Creek's deputy sheriff leading Leo away in handcuffs. *How could a hallway be so long?* It seemed to stretch on forever. Damon pulled me tighter to him, his arm slung over my shoulder, and I sagged into his side. We both watched on, dazed and battle-weary. They walked and walked until they were pinpoints, and then they were gone.

It's my fault, I would say to myself, over and over. As I held my mom's hand in the ICU, her face already starting to hollow with death. She was still hanging on, and they'd said any brain swelling needed to go down before an accurate prognosis could be given, but she was already gone.

I know that now, picking that memory out of my brain, folding it over, tearing off the waxy film of denial and hope that marred my view at the time. I don't have that now, and I can tell you that my mother, God rest her soul, exited her body at the moment Leo's car plowed into the creek and her untethered body smashed into the front dash.

I'd argued with Leo before I left for work that afternoon. Had yelled at him for something trivial before I stormed off and drove away, leaving him with balled fists and that horrible longing, that thirst in his eyes that had never really gone away since Karen. I don't even remember what we fought about now. It was something ridiculous, for sure, minor enough that I can't even recall.

So I made him angry, he got drunk, climbed into his car, and drove that car through a safety barrier, into a creek, with my mother riding shotgun.

CHAPTER THREE

Leo

— Now —

L ovelock Prison, ironically, doesn't contain a lot of love.

At least, not the kind of loving I'm looking for. Some of the men here have been in prison for decades—multiple. They've long since compromised on what they stick their dicks into.

Not me. I might not be the most built guy compared to some of the other prisoners here, but I am quick on my feet. My grandfather taught me how to rumble when I was a kid before he died, and I've never lost a fight yet.

Which is handy in a place like this. Because I like my asshole untouched very much.

"Bentley!" a guard barks from the cell door. I roll my eyes, sliding off the lower bunk in my cell and getting to my feet. I share this cell with three other guys on the sixth floor of Lovelock, and it's no accident that I have the best bed, the most cigarettes, and have never been touched by another male prisoner.

My fellow prisoners learned my name the day I arrived here, just shy of eight years ago. Some motherfucker tried to make me his bitch. I took his eye out with my toothbrush. One-eyed Al we call him now. People at Lovelock know the name Leo Bentley, and they don't fuck with me.

I saunter up to the guard, taking the cigarette from behind my ear as I do. We aren't supposed to smoke here, but rules are made to be broken, right? The fucking guards here are just as bad as the inmates. Worse, in some cases.

Martinez, one of the less abrasive male guards, waves an unsealed envelope through the small hole in the door. My heart leaps into my chest for a moment.

Is it from Cassie? Did she finally respond to one of the letters I've been writing her while I've been stuck in this hellhole?

But then I see the official typed font on the front of the envelope and my hope fades. Of course, it's not from her. It's probably about my parole board hearing. I'm not expecting miracles. When you drive off a bridge with the wife of a sheriff in your car and basically kill her, even though she's not technically dead, people don't take too kindly to your good behavior record. Mine's flawless. Nobody ever snitched on me for Al's missing eye, and he claimed it was self-inflicted. I don't think he wanted to rat on me in case I took the other one while he wasn't looking. Ha! Jesus. My sense of humor is terrible.

"Good behavior," Martinez says, rolling his eyes. "Good one, Bentley. You sure fooled them."

I grip the envelope tightly in my hand. "Huh?"

Martinez lifts his chin toward the sleeve in my hand. "Early release for good behavior. You got somewhere to go, boy?" It's ironic that he calls me a boy, because I'm twenty-five years old now, and I haven't been a boy for a very long time. Hard time makes you grow up. If you're not a man when you enter prison, you'll sure as hell be one by the time you get out.

"Uh . . ." I can't string a sentence together. I feel like I've just had the shit knocked out of me. As I tear the letter open and scan down the print, I can barely understand what it says. It could be written in Chinese, for all I know. Not because I can't read—I was a straight-A student in high school, even though I was a little prick to my teachers—but because I can't believe what Martinez has just said.

I'm finally leaving this shithole.

I've been granted parole.

Cassie. For a moment, I imagine seeing her again. Kissing her. Fucking her in the backseat of my car, sucking on her neck as she makes those little sighs of pleasure beneath me. The way her eyes used to light up whenever she saw me.

Then I remember her in the hospital, the last time I saw her before they arrested me and dumped my sorry ass in jail. Her eyes didn't light up for me as our gazes met over her comatose mother. Jesus, Cassie, if you knew how fucking sorry I was, for everything.

Saturday, I'm out of here. In three days.

Part of me feels like I'm not ready. Even though I want out of this hellhole, the problem is where I'm going after this. I'm almost considering stabbing somebody in here just so I don't have to go back to Gun Creek and face Cassie and Sheriff King.

Guard Ramsay is sitting across from me, a fifty-something weed of a guy with thick glasses perched on his nose and liver spots on his hands. He looks as bad as I feel, and that's saying something.

This place'll break you if you let it, or if they keep you here for long enough. My sentence for felony DUI causing injury was nineteen years, so the fact they're paroling me now is a fucking miracle. I haven't even served half my sentence.

As far as luck goes, I'm pretty much all out, but the one glimmer of hope in my case was the fact that, even though my dumb, drugged-out ass plowed off the road and into the creek at high speed, with an unrestrained passenger, I had a clean record. No priors.

Sheriff King pushed and pushed the courts to give me the maximum sentence, and I don't blame the guy. Technically I killed his wife, but she's still locked in some vegetative state where she can't eat or speak or do anything. She can't even kill herself to escape what I did to her. She's just a bag of bones now, bedsores and bedpans, because I was dumb enough to get behind the wheel, drunk and high, and fly down the highway.

Guard Ramsay clears his throat, looking at me over the Coke-bottle-thick glasses he's wearing as he takes a bite of his sandwich and chews. "You got something on your mind, boy?"

I shake my head. "No, sir."

He leans back in his chair and takes his glasses off, rubbing the bridge of his nose. He looks dead tired. He's old for his age. Old and worn out from being in a place like this. His sandwich smells like greasy, old lunch meat.

"Have you read through the conditions of your parole?" he asks.

I nod, rubbing my hand across my face. The razors in here are always fucking blunt. There's no point shaving when you're still left with a five-o'clock shadow, but by the same token, if you don't shave every day you end up with a bushy fucking beard on your face. Nobody wants any more hair than absolutely necessary here. I've seen guys with pieces of scalp missing because they wouldn't give up their cigarettes and someone decided to rip their hair out of their skull.

"You go home. You get a job. You check in with the sheriff's department every week. And if you don't, son, your ass is gonna be back in that cell so damn fast, you'll think you dreamed getting out of this shithole."

I nod, clenching and unclenching my fist.

"Most people in your position would be a damn sight more excited right about now," Ramsay says.

I shrug. "Most people didn't kill the sheriff's wife."

The blood drains from Ramsay's face as he glances down at the papers in front of him. "Says here you're in for DUI and bodily harm. Not murder."

"Wasn't murder. And she's not dead. Not yet anyway."

"What the hell kind of statement is that, boy? You threatening that she might die if you go home? You got a grudge against this woman?"

I sigh, scuffing my sneaker along the worn linoleum floor. Somebody has written RAMSAY IS A CUNT on the floor in marker. Obviously, he didn't read my files to know what happened with Cassie's mom. Nobody ever reads the files.

"No threats, sir. She's in a delicate state, is all."

Ramsay flips a manila folder open and reads something in front of him. I turn my head to try and see, but he closes it. "A persistent vegetable state," he says.

"Vegetative," I correct him before I can think.

He glares at me over his glasses. "That's what I said. You got ears full of wax, boy?"

"Yes, sir," I say.

He leans back in his chair, studying me for a long moment. I'm itching from sitting in this chair and I need to piss, but I bear the time silently and wait for the guy to speak.

"Tell me what happened."

I nod. "It was a car accident. I was—"

Truth is, I don't remember the accident. Not one bit. All I remember is drinking a couple beers after the football game. Blacking out. The hideous sounds of twisting metal and sirens. And then waking up in a hospital in Reno, handcuffed to the metal bed rails, a cop standing guard at my door. The doctors said it might take time for the memory to return, if it ever did.

It's been eight years now, and I still don't remember why the fuck I got behind the wheel of that car and drove. My dad was an alcoholic. He died of liver failure when I was ten. My ma still loves the hard stuff. Must be in the genes to drink 'til our destruction.

I don't remember the accident, but I do remember the aftermath and I kind of wish I didn't.

"You were what?" Ramsay prompts, snapping me out of my flashback.

"I was . . . drinking, sir. I should never have been driving, but I was seventeen years old and I was an idiot." A complete motherfucking idiot, I want to say, but Ramsay doesn't like swearing.

Ramsay's mouth forms a hard line as he surveys me. "No drinking, no drugs, and definitely no driving a car. You find a job, you go to work, you go home, you don't touch a single drop of alcohol, and you keep your ass out of here. Is that clear?"

I nod. "Yes, sir."

"You need me to arrange an ankle monitor to keep you from the drink?"

I shake my head quickly. "No, sir. I've got no interest in drinking anything."

"You'll have to submit for random drug and alcohol tests as the sheriff's department deems."

"Yes, sir."

"Bentley. Keep your nose clean, son."

"I will, sir."

"This is your second chance at an honest life. Don't piss it away by being weak."

I nod. I won't.

"What the hell were you thinking, getting behind the wheel with that much junk in your blood?" He's referring to the massive dose of Oxy that was simmering in my veins when I most likely nodded off at the wheel.

"I don't know. I can't remember."

He rocks back on his chair, pensive. "You know you don't belong here," he says. I don't answer him because I don't know. Once upon a time I was cocky enough to think I'd be the one who broke the cycle, shattered the mold, but not now.

He gestures to the door. "You can go."

I chew the inside of my cheek as I stand up, repeating the words inside my head as I walk back to my cell. As I try to figure out how eleven more years of being here just got shortened to seventy-two hours.

CHAPTER FOUR

Cassie

— Now —

C*rack.*

Someone claps their hands together; the sharp smack of skin on skin jolts me out of my deep sleep.

I open my eyes and cringe at the harsh white light that comes in through the window. It's snowing. It's bright. People think snow equals cold, but when the sun reflects off of it at the right angle, it can burn your skin to cinders.

There is something burning me, just by coincidence. Not the bright reflection of snow. I blink my eyes rapidly, trying to make the blur in front of me form into something other than a blur.

A pair of blue eyes. A frown.

Damon. My stepfather, standing in my bedroom doorway, raking a hand through neatly trimmed brown hair.

I suck in a breath and sit up with a start, my head spinning. I'm wearing an oversized T-shirt that smells faintly like the guy I fucked last night; and in front of me, my stepfather's eyebrows rise in disapproval.

"Good morning," he says, equal parts amusement and disdain. His jaw strains with something akin to irritation. "You're finally awake, party animal."

I rub my eye with the heel of my palm. I feel smashed, worn, like I've been run over. My entire body feels achy and dull, my head stuffed full of wool, and somewhere at the edges of my memory, I remember swallowing pills, the taste of their bitter residue still faint on my tongue. *Jesus.* My wrists ache, faint bruises ringing them. I hold my right hand in my left, counting the five fingertip-shaped bruises that punctuate my pale skin. Four on one side, one on the other. Four fingers and a thumb. I wonder how I'd explain them. If anyone will ask. Most likely, nobody would even notice the way my skin has been marked as large, hot hands held me tight and still.

Damon clears his throat pointedly. I forget my wrist and look back to see he's fully dressed for work, the gold star affixed to his sheriff's uniform glinting in the light. He's clean-shaven and smells like pine needles and mint, his cologne drifting over to me from where he stands in my bedroom doorway. I catch a glimpse of that boyish innocence beneath his stress lines, his worrisome demeanor. I wonder what he's worrying about today. It's always something with him.

"What time is it?" I ask. My voice comes out low, hoarse. Did I drink last night? The taste of stale whiskey lingers in my mouth, confirming my suspicions, and I have to stifle the overwhelming urge to scrape my tongue with a corner of the bed sheets. Just picturing the bottle of Jack makes my stomach twist. Don't puke. Do-not-puke.

"Almost eight."

Almost eight? Shit! I lift the covers to get out of bed; my underwear's gone. I freeze, setting the blanket back over my thighs. I see him glance at my lap, what looks like suspicion sparking in his blue eyes. He takes a step toward the bed, and for one horrific split second, I imagine he is going to rip the blankets off me and see what I am—or rather, what I'm not—wearing. And if that happens, he'll flip his shit.

Fate decides to intervene, though. *Thank you, universe.* I hear the static buzz of a two-way radio, and Deputy Chris McCallister's voice sounds in the kitchen downstairs. Damon hears it, too, freezing mid-step.

We continue to stare-off, his curious eyes pitted against mine, as the radio crackles to life again. The voice more urgent. *"Sheriff King, do you copy?"*

"Downstairs in five, Cass," Damon says with an air of reluctance, giving my lap one final glance before he turns and leaves. A moment later, I'm out of bed and pulling fresh panties over my bare legs, my skin rising in gooseflesh to greet the frigid air. Gun Creek is the coldest place in Nevada, and it only gets colder after Thanksgiving. Soon, the pass forms ice and it'll be dangerous to drive on, just like it is every year.

Just like the year of the accident.

Coffee. I need coffee.

I locate my pajama bottoms, stuffed down into my blankets as if they were kicked off in a hurry. Kicked or pulled, it's all the same. I'm sore down there, and although I can't remember much of the act itself, I've got a fairly good idea about what happened. It was quiet, but it definitely wasn't gentle.

I traipse downstairs, the tight feeling in my chest expanding with every step. Running late is a cardinal sin, according to my stepfather. Everything must be perfect. Everything must be on time. All the time. He frets if things are out of order. If things are messy. If things are not just so. I am a creature who is always messy, always out of order, never on time.

The staircase stops at the entrance to our kitchen. We've got one of the bigger—and older—houses in Gun Creek, one of the original gold mining ranches. Every window is large, rectangular, and frames a picture of mountains and empty tundra and snow.

It's beautiful to look out there if you're in a good mood. If you're not, it's utterly desolate, miles of blank space waiting to swallow up your soul.

I'm not in a good mood.

"Hey, daydreamer," Damon says, breaking my thoughts. He's sipping coffee from an old Mickey Mouse mug my grandfather bought for me when I was eleven and we went to Disneyland. Something stabs me in the gut. I wish he wouldn't touch that mug. That's my fucking mug. Leo's in prison and my mom is in a coma, and now I can't even drink coffee out of the mug my dead grandfather gave me. My gray mood, always balanced on a knife's edge, turns black, and I grit my teeth together as anger stirs in my gut.

I never used to be prone to rage, but I'm not the girl I used to be before all of this.

"I made you cereal." He pulls out a chair and points to it. "We've got ten minutes." I do as I'm told, acting every inch the sullen step-daughter. He tells me all the time that I need to curb my attitude, but my attitude is just about the last piece of me that's still hanging on. After the accident, after Leo got locked up and Mom was just . . . gone, I had a lot more . . . salt. I was feisty. I threw tantrums. In public.

You should be nicer to Damon, more than one person has said to me. *He's doing the right thing, taking care of you all these years while your mother's been sick.* Fuck those people. My mother isn't sick—she's dying. I'm twenty-five years old with a brain-dead mother and a wait-ressing gig at the local diner. I've got nothing. And I don't give a fuck about being nice.

Damon sits across from me, pointedly eyeing my unbrushed rat's nest of blond hair and my bare cheeks. His hair, by contrast, though short, is neatly combed, his badge shined, his shirt pressed.

"You look like shit, sweetheart," he says casually.

I dig my spoon into the bowl and suppress a gag. The last thing I want to eat is something full of milk and sugar. My churning stomach needs dry toast, or saltine crackers, or preferably nothing at all.

"You smell like a fucking pine forest," I mutter around a mouthful of Froot Loops. Damon's aftershave situation definitely isn't helping my stomach. I stare down at the brightly colored cereal in my bowl and imagine myself down a well, or floating in a lake, just like Karen. I don't know why I'm thinking of Karen now, nine years after she turned up in Leo's well.

"Don't swear at me," he says, his eyes narrowing. "It's not ladylike."

Getting drunk-fucked in the middle of the night and not being able to remember is pretty unladylike, too, but I don't mention that. My life would be pretty miserable if I started talking about that. I throw my spoon down after two mouthfuls and stand up, in search of coffee. The pot's been brewed a while ago, and the thick, brown liquid inside is lukewarm at best, but it's better than nothing. I take another mug out of the cupboard and set it down on the sink, watching a moose wander by outside as I pour my liquid crack cocaine and take a sip.

"You're losing weight again," Damon says, interrupting my daydreaming and moose-watching. His voice softens. "You know I worry when you don't eat."

He wants me to keep eating. I sit back on my chair with great reluctance, washing cereal down with giant mouthfuls of coffee, even though I'm fairly sure what I'm eating is completely devoid of nutritional value. I drink two cups of caffeine, just to get through my breakfast, all the while being watched carefully by Damon's bright blue eyes. Another thing he frets about. Plates with food left on them and girls who don't eat enough. He told me once how he was never allowed cereal as a kid. How he never had enough food. How I should appreciate him buying it for me. If he knew that I throw up almost everything that passes my lips—with the exception of alcohol, of course—he would be very upset, indeed.

"Thanksgiving's next week," Damon says. "Did you get the turkey organized like I asked?"

I nod. I'm lying. I haven't. I will. Damon's a traditional guy, wants the roast turkey and all the trimmings. I hate turkey. To be truthful, I hate food in general. The little I do eat to keep up appearances I purge as soon as I can. It's comforting to be in control of some part of my life; and besides, the thinner I am, the less tits and ass I have, the less attention I get from the male population. I'm almost androgynous, with cheekbones that could cut glass. Except for the long hair I can't bear to part with and my tits that, while small, refuse to disappear entirely no matter how hard I restrict my calorie intake.

"Pick up the prescription from the pharmacy?"

"Yup." I left it on the hallway table, like always.

"Did you get the wood chopped?"

My stomach twists nervously. *Damn.* All week I've been walking around in a state of semi-anxiety, knowing I've forgotten something. "I'm planning on doing it tonight," I say quickly. "I was busy with the shopping."

Damon's face turns from dispassionate to frustrated. "You're useless," he mutters.

"Really." I roll my eyes.

"Cassie. You can't even get out of bed in the morning without being reminded. You're like a child. A retarded child."

"You're supposed to say 'intellectually challenged.' It's more PC."

He slams his palm down onto the table, hard enough that my cereal bowl dances. "Do you know how goddamn hard I work to keep this house paid up? To keep your mother's nursing bills paid up? To buy fucking prescriptions so that shit keeps her alive?"

I swallow cold coffee, unmoved by Damon's martyr speech. I work just as hard as him, turning tables, pulling double shifts whenever I can, pouring every cent I earn into Mom's medical care, the bills, this falling-down house. So I don't care about poor Damon.

For the first time this morning, I notice his face is puffed out on one side, and there's a small cut above his right eye.

"What happened to you?" I ask.

He glares at me.

"Get dressed," he says, making a choking sound after he drains his last inch of coffee. "Machine's broken again."

"I'm pretty sure it's the operator," I say, leaning over to the counter and lifting the lid on the coffee maker, slamming it down again so it locks properly. After a moment, dark black coffee starts to flow into the pot underneath. "There."

Damon stares at me, unimpressed. "Hurry. Up. Or I'll take you to work as you are." He gestures to my pajamas.

"I bet the customers would love that," I reply, pushing my chair back and standing. I jump as a hand curls around my upper arm and yanks me so my upper half is bent across the table.

"That's not funny," Damon grinds out, his face inches from mine. "You want everyone thinking you're the town whore?"

"No," I say softly.

His hand squeezes tighter. "You know what happens to girls who act like whores?"

"Yeah," I say, meeting his steely gaze. "I'm thinking it's pretty similar to what happens to girls like Karen."

"Karen?"

"Murdered Karen," I clarify.

"I know which Karen," he snaps, rubbing his hand along his jaw. "Why the hell would you bring that poor girl up after all these years?"

I shrug. "I don't know. She's the first town whore that came to mind. Unless you count Mom before she got knocked up with me."

He doesn't say anything for a beat. Then, apparently done, Damon drops his grip and I hurry upstairs.

In my room, I drag on jeans and a clean, long-sleeved work shirt, scraping my long blond waves up in a messy ponytail. Function takes place over form in winter, at least for me. I don't have the energy for all that bullshit preening and careful wardrobe selection that some other girls do. Girls like Karen Brainard. They put so much effort in and look where it gets them. Taken. Raped. Murdered.

In the bathroom, I don't bother with makeup. Makeup draws attention, and the last thing I want is for anybody to look at me too closely.

Some days I feel like I'm made of glass, my clothes and my hair and my downturned eyes the only things that stop the light from getting in, from showing the world what's happening within me. Who's touched me. Who's been inside me.

Nobody can ever know the things I've done.

Besides, I'm barely making it through the days without the added burdens of mascara and blush.

I brush my teeth listlessly, my brain smashing relentlessly inside my skull—I wish I could remember what pills I took last night.

I really don't need to add liver failure to my list of this year's achievements, but I think if I have to go to work with this noise inside my head, I might pass out before the lunch rush even begins.

I spit toothpaste out, grateful that at least the cereal taste has been burned away by mint-flavored chemicals, and find a bottle of aspirin in my top drawer. I shake a pile of the tiny white pills into my palm and toss them into my mouth, swallowing them dry. I catch sight of myself in the mirror, all hard angles and sour expression, the light smattering of freckles across the bridge of my nose the only thing that colors my lily-white skin. We don't exactly get an abundance of sun up here in winter.

"Let's wrap it up!" Damon yells from downstairs.

My head throbs on cue. I take my iPhone from the charger beside my bed and see missed calls from the diner, a worried text. Whatever. I'll be there soon enough.

Steeling myself, I give one last glance to the face in the mirror, slap a knitted cap over my hair, and take the stairs two at a time, flying past Damon and to the front door. I grab my bag from the coat hook and sling it over my shoulder, eager to get out of this house and away from this nightmare for a few hours.

I try the door. Locked.

My stomach sinks.

"Cassie," Damon says behind me. "Aren't you forgetting something? Sleeping in doesn't excuse you from chores."

I'm tired. I'm so, so tired. I'm twenty-five years old and I'm just as hollow as the woman down the hall, the one whose body carried me for nine months, the one whose body no longer carries anything—not even her soul.

Still facing the door, I swallow back an argument.

I drop my backpack off my shoulder and turn to face him.

"Sometimes I think you'd let her starve if it weren't for me reminding you." Damon hands me the liquid nutrition prescription and I take a deep breath, holding it between my palms as I approach the respiring corpse. Maybe he's right. Maybe I would let her starve. Anything's got to be more humane than keeping her alive all these years when she really should have died in that creek.

CHAPTER FIVE

Cassie

Damon finally lets me leave the house fifteen minutes later, once I've injected the liquid nutrition mix into Mom's feed bag and finished everything up just the way he likes.

He took my house keys off me right after Mom's accident, and I spend my days either locked in or locked out. Him controlling the keys means I can't punch out early and walk home in the middle of the day before he's finished his shift. I did that a couple times before he caught on, and now he's got the place locked down like Fort Knox. And before you do a double take and start counting on your fingers, yes, you read that right: I'm a twenty-five-year-old woman with less power over her life than most teenagers.

No wonder I spend my afternoons daydreaming about how long it would take to murder my family and take off.

"Can you take me to the store later?" I ask Damon as we drive over the bridge, *bumpbump, bumpbump,* past the shiny section of guardrail that was replaced after the crash, and pull up in front of Dana's Grill. It's beyond ironic that I work at the same place where the accident happened. That I get to relive it every time I happen to look out the window and let my eyes fall upon the highway.

He rolls his eyes. "We'll see."

My heart sinks until it's a lead weight in the bottom of my stomach. "We'll see" means "no" most of the time.

"I need to get the turkey," I say flatly.

He throws the car into park and turns to me, his sheriff's badge glinting in my peripheral vision. How he keeps that fucking thing so shiny, I'll never know. He certainly doesn't get me to polish it, surprisingly. It's gleaming like a goddamned Academy Award. A proclamation of power. *I own this town.* And he damn well does.

"Thought you took care of the turkey."

I shake my head. "I forgot."

He takes a deep breath and exhales. He's pissed. I see his fingers curl around the black steering wheel and squeeze. His knuckles turn pinkish-red in the cold, not white like I expect. "You forgot last night because you started drinking at midday."

"My shift finished early yesterday. What was I meant to do?"

I immediately regret lying about the turkey. It won't end well.

"What were you supposed to do?" he repeats. "Hmm, let's see. Maybe get some food for Thanksgiving so we don't starve? We have guests coming."

I snort. "We have your asshole brother coming."

Damon frowns. "You know he's your only family aside from me."

Damon's brother is a fucking creep. "He's not my family." I almost add, *Neither are you.*

He looks at me for a long moment. "Sometimes I don't know what to do with you," he says finally.

"You get the fucking food if you want it so bad," I reply, staring at the diner's front doors.

"You really want to do this, Cassandra?"

"No," I say. He called me Cassandra. Fuck. Should've just gone to the store yesterday.

"I'm sorry, what?" He cocks his head and puts a hand up to his ear. "I didn't catch that."

"No," I say, more forcefully this time.

"You're an ungrateful little bitch," he says angrily.

"Go fuck yourself," I snap. Before Damon can lock me in the car, I quickly open my door and slide out.

"I'm not finished with you," he says, waving his finger at me.

"Go rescue a kitten from a tree or whatever it is you country cops do," I reply, slamming the door as hard as I can. I lug my backpack over one shoulder, watching Damon's car drive away, growing smaller and smaller until I can't see it at all. I glance at the police station, on the same row of buildings as the diner, and wonder where he's gone since not there.

What did she ever see in him? Oh, yeah. The face. The eyes. Guy's a catch. Until you catch him and realize you're stuck with the sorry bastard. *Thanks, Mom.*

I take a deep breath of winter air, the cold burning my lungs. It feels good. I'm heading into the diner when I see a familiar face staring at me from a piece-of-shit Honda three slots down from where Damon pulled in.

I don't know whether to smile or run, so I do neither. Instead, I head toward the car before nerves can send me scurrying in the opposite direction.

The eyes that were staring at me don't look away, but they change. Withdraw. Guess he wasn't expecting me to come over to his car, after all.

"Pike," I say. "You still live here?"

It's Pike, Leo's oldest little brother. Irish twins, their mom called them because of how close their birthdays are—ten and a half months, to be exact. Leo's mom didn't mess around back in the day. She was born in Gun Creek, had half a dozen more kids after Leo was born on her sixteenth birthday, and she'll probably die in her double-wide one day when she smokes too much meth and blows a crater in the middle of her trailer. Most of her older children have scattered, buckshot as far and wide from Gun Creek as possible. The little ones are still with her, as far as I know.

Pike flicks his long fringe out of his eyes. He's a pale, goth version of Leo, night and day but unmistakably brothers.

"Nah. I moved to Reno a while back. I'm just working a job."

Oh. He's dealing. I spy a battered Nike backpack on the passenger seat. There's an excellent chance it's full of drugs. I don't judge him. His mom, sure. She's fucking deplorable. All these kids and she never could take care of them. But Pike? He's just doing what he has to do to get by. When you start life in this place, your options are limited.

"Have you heard from Leo?" My throat constricts as I push the words out into existence; it almost aches to mention his name. Leo. It's a name your mouth really has to work for. It's not easy, like Pike or Cassie. With Leo, you have to use your tongue, your teeth, your lips, your cheeks.

Pike shifts in his seat; I notice he's not dressed properly for the cold. Like, at all. He's wearing jeans slung loosely over his skinny hips, a T-shirt (in this weather?), a thin cotton zip-up hoodie you'd wear on a cool summer night.

"Aren't you cold, Pike? Jesus. It's barely freezing out."

Pike looks me up and down from behind his black fringe, tossing it out of his view again. *Just cut the damn thing*, I want to tell him. But I don't. He wants to be the seventh member of Panic! at the Disco, I'm hardly going to stop him.

"Sheriff told me not to talk to you about Leo," Pike mutters at my midsection.

Something sharp pierces my chest and burrows its way in. I feel like I've had the air sucked out of my lungs. "What? What do you mean?"

Pike's face looks stricken. "Whatever, Cassie, I gotta go. Mom's waiting for me."

"Oh, well, you wouldn't want to keep your momma waiting, would you?"

He goes to roll his window up and I catch his sleeve. He stares at my hand like it's a cockroach before he shrugs me off angrily. "You think you're the only one affected by what happened? Leo's the one person in our family who had a fucking job, Cassie. The only one who had his shit together. So, yeah, Mom's waiting for me to bring her fucking groceries for her fucking kids because she spent all her money on fucking dope. Nice seeing you."

I feel the color drain from my face. "I'm sorry—" I start, but he cuts me off.

"They're gonna cut her power off next week if I don't find some money. So unless you want to pay me to call Leo and ask how he's been, don't interrupt me."

I would pay him if I had any money. I *would*.

He rolls the window up and starts the car, looking anywhere but at me.

I curl my hands up by my sides, the violence simmering at my fingertips something I can barely keep a lid on, wanting nothing more than to slam my fists into the hood of his car until he relents and tells me something about Leo. Anything. Does he ask for me? Does he think about me? Does he still love me, even though I'm unlovable, even though I've become the worst human being I could possibly be?

I don't ask him anything, though. I don't scream or use my fists or beg. Because there's nobody in the world that could answer the questions in my head. *Will I ever see him again?*

The judge gave him nineteen years, so—I doubt it.

I turn and trudge across gray-sludge snow to the front doors of the diner. Everything I do is on autopilot these days.

I go into the staff bathroom and make myself throw up stale coffee and cereal before I pull my hair into a more respectable topknot, my skin pallid under the bare bulb overhead, the whites of my eyes tinged yellow. And the veins. Jesus, I look stoned—a map of tiny burst blood vessels that traces the map of my terrible diet and my affection for alcohol.

I linger in the bathroom longer than I normally would, chewing mints to mask my vomit breath because today is going to be a shit show. I already know it, and positive thinking isn't going to help me out of this bind.

The holidays are not kind to people like me who never made it out of town. They're ripe for unwelcome reminders of what could have been. They bring with them husbands and wives and fat babies that smell of sweet milk and diaper cream.

They pull into the parking lot of the Grill in gleaming rental cars because they've flown in because they had to move that far away to forget how desolate this place is. What they've since tinged with nostalgia and rose-tinted memory—I grew up in the cutest little place!—is the empty present for the rest of us.

Visit the past briefly and go back to your shiny new life, but this *is* my life, and when the others who were planted here, the ones I grew up beside, the ones I was better than, look at me with an edge of discomfort in their eyes, it takes every bit of willpower I possess to not scratch their eyes out with my chipped fingernails. My high school best friend visits every year with her rapidly growing brood and her giant diamond wedding rings, but the pity in her eyes is worse than any of the things she has that I don't. I pray like hell that I don't run into her. It's like rubbing salt in a gunshot wound every time I see her perfect little life.

Grow where you're planted, the saying goes, but everything withers and dies here in winter. Even in summer, it's winter for me. It's been winter for eight years. I have long since shed my petals and burrowed beneath the layer of snow that smothers this place.

My mom was big into the law of attraction. She had all those *The Secret* books, the DVDs, the notebooks. She was a self-proclaimed self-help junkie before that shit was mainstream. She always told me that focusing on something makes it come true. But I've been focusing on getting out of Gun Creek for probably ten years now, and I'm still here. My manifesting game is strong, though, because it seems I've attracted the very thing I didn't want to deal with today.

Mother*fucker.*

Shelly Rutherford and Chase Thomas. They're in a booth in my section, in the back, away from the front windows. It's quieter there and the tables turn over less, so I earn less, but at least I don't have to look at the highway every time I serve somebody.

Shelly was head cheerleader in our graduating class; Chase was the quarterback, second in skill only to Leo. Shelly's still beautiful, tanned and slim without being painfully thin, the only sign of weight on her body a gigantic baby belly that looks like it's about to pop right here in the diner. Chase chats to her and rubs her belly affectionately as their three daughters, all less than five years old, jump on the booth seats and throw sugar packets everywhere.

I have to see them every time they come back into town, but usually I'm better at hiding. Usually, there is more staff on duty to take their table, every time they come home with a brand-new baby and a great big rental car and the diamond rock on her hand so big, it's obscene. I see his hand on her stomach and I can't look anymore. Which is hard because it's at that moment that Shelly sees me.

Her eyes go wide with shock before the pity settles into them. *Fuck you, bitch.* "Cassie," she says, pushing Chase's hand away and arranging her pretty face into a smile just for me. "It's so good to see you. How are you?"

My best friend. She's a stranger, now.

I smile, hoping the mint is doing its job and my vomit breath isn't noticeable. "I'm good," I lie, glancing at Chase, who offers his own plastic smile and a wave. "I'm really good."

We make small talk before I take their orders; Shelly is a natural at being able to speak to anybody. She always was. She was my best friend from kindergarten all through school; apart from her annual visits back to her family, we haven't spoken since the day she moved out of town six years ago to follow Chase to the college Leo and I had picked.

"How's your mom?" Shelly asks.

"She's doing much better," I lie. "Her doctors say she could wake up any day now."

Shelly glances at Chase; they might think I don't notice the invisible words that flow between them, but I'm all about invisible words. They think I'm lying.

The *ding* from the kitchen saves me. "I'll be right back," I say, smoothing my apron as I walk to the pass and grab a bunch of plates.

While I'm waiting for Eddy, the cook, to finish plating up a Dana's Big Breakfast, Amanda, the owner's daughter, joins me at the pass. Amanda is a registered nurse, a few years younger than my mom, and she only covers shifts at the diner when her parents, Dana and Bill, are traveling or unwell. She's pretty, with red hair that falls in loose curls down her back, a smattering of freckles across her pale face, and big, pale-blue eyes that like to linger on my stepfather when he comes to pick me up from my shift. Or when she comes to our house. She does a couple shifts a week as Mom's home-care nurse, bathing her, moving her to avoid bedsores, and making sure her meds are all adjusted correctly to keep her out of pain. I've seen how little Damon pays her—all he can afford, according to him—and I'm pretty sure she only does it because she and my mother used to be close. Plus, she likes my stepfather. She always manages to be getting off shift as he's arriving to pick me up, or dropping things at the house close to dinnertime.

The police station is a few hundred yards away from the diner, which makes it convenient for Damon. He's here a lot, more than he needs to be. With the meth problem in this town, he and Deputy McCallister should be everywhere. I know where Nurse Amanda wants him. In her bed. She's also a woman of morals, even at the ripe age of thirty-nine, and I know she doesn't want to move onto my mother's turf until she's in the ground. She's been exceedingly patient. My mother's been on the verge of dying for eight years now.

Nobody wants to be the whore that sleeps with a woman's husband while she's comatose and having a machine breathe for her, but also, nobody else would wait so long. She's kind of lovely, and kind of pathetic.

She's talking, but I'm not listening to what she's saying. Instead, I'm making a list in my head of all the things I need to buy for Thanksgiving dinner:

Yams
Turkey
Cranberry sauce

How the hell do I make cranberry sauce?

"Cassie," Amanda's voice cuts through my Thanksgiving meal planning.

I stop daydreaming and look up, not answering. I've figured out that what people hate more than anything is an awkward silence, and if I don't rush to fill it, someone else inevitably will. She searches my face, her expression one of concern more than anger.

"Are you feeling okay?"

I clear my throat and take the plates from the pass. "I'm fine."

I set my face to resting bitch, surveying her calmly, and she almost seems to do a double take.

I have that effect on people these days.

"Oka-ay," she says, breaking our stare-off. I win again. I always do. I learned from the best.

My toes are cold. I didn't dress in enough layers this morning, and my head is pounding from all the alcohol I drank last night. I bide the rest of my shift as patiently as I can, wondering if Leo gets to eat turkey on Thanksgiving.

I doubt it. Even for someone in prison, it seems unfair. But then, I suppose, my mom won't be eating Thanksgiving dinner either. She'll be fed through a tube, she'll breathe through a tube, shit through a tube, and, eventually, we'll take all those tubes away so the poor woman can finally die.

I don't know why I care about anything in Leo's life. Why I'm drawn to Pike. Why I'm so pissed off that he won't give me anything. Because I should forget the boy I loved ever existed.

I am a horrible person. Because even though Leo's the reason my mother is waiting to die, I'd still do anything to feel his fingers touching me one more time.

The kitchen bell rings. My head throbs. I collect more plates, dispense them at more tables, run into Amanda again.

"Cassie," she says. "You have two tables waiting on water and bread. Do you need a hand?"

She's nicer to me than I deserve. Her eyes are wide with genuine concern. "I have a headache," I say, glancing at the highway. "Have you got any aspirin?"

She looks worried. "Cassie, you always have a headache. Have you been to a doctor?" She leans in a little. "Have you been eating? Sleeping?"

She reaches out, pressing the back of her hand against my forehead softly. I flinch at the sudden jolt of sympathetic skin on mine, an unfamiliar sensation. She sees me react and pulls her hand away slowly, letting it fall at her side.

"I'm worried about you, Cassie," she says. "This isn't an easy time of year . . ." She trails off, searching my face.

"Please don't." I swallow back the hard tennis ball lodged in my throat. I'm not going to start crying now just because somebody cares. She's just doing her job. I mean, if I hang myself in the bathroom while everyone else is out here, it's going to fall on her. She doesn't care enough for it to make a difference to me.

Her eyes fall to the bruises on my wrist. I don't want to talk about that.

"I just need aspirin," I say firmly.

"You know, there are people who can help you," she says.

I can't help the smirk that forms on my mouth. Amanda looks horrified.

"You think this is funny?" she asks, her cheeks turning red.

I shrug. "Kind of. Do you have aspirin, or do I need to walk over to the store?" If I could get my hands on some of those codeine pills Pike used to have—

"Here." She reaches into her own apron and pulls out a bottle of aspirin, shaking several pills into my palm. "You'll get a stomach ulcer if you keep eating these like candy," she warns, but there's no strength in her words.

"Thank you," I say, tossing the pills back and swallowing them dry. I smile at her, but she doesn't return the gesture.

It's because my smile doesn't reach my eyes anymore. It's just a meaningless gesture, muscles pulling skin up over my skull.

"Table eight and thirteen," she says, pushing two glasses of water into my hands. For someone who was so concerned five minutes ago, suddenly she doesn't want to look at me. I get it. It's the same reason I want to cover all the reflective surfaces in our house.

I wouldn't look at Cassie Carlino if she weren't staring back at me, accusingly, in every mirror.

I fought with Leo. He crashed his car with my mother.

The weight of my sins is a burden that breaks me every time I have to look at my own face.

I take the water and baskets of bread to the tables and wait patiently for the aspirin to start bubbling in my veins.

When it's my turn to take a break, I go into the bathroom and pull up Shelly's Instagram account on my iPhone; it's not hard to find her. She checked into the diner thirteen minutes ago, a selfie of her and her precious little family. I dig further. They live in Miami. Chase plays football for the team Leo was being scouted for before the accident. I already know all of this. I scroll through photos of her lounging by a pool, her stomach bigger than the rest of her body. There are photos of her daughters eating ice cream, of her fucking lifestyle blog, the baby football jersey she's hung over her impending arrival's crib. My skin feels hot and prickly as I imagine them all getting into a terrible accident and dying, the entire family, because this was the life I was meant to have with Leo. I hate her. I hate them all. I wonder if she believes that she deserves the things she has, *hashtag sofuckingblessed*, or if she knows that she's the consolation prize. I hit the button on my phone that will give me a notification every time she posts something. What can I say? I don't need to eat real food, because I'm a glutton for self-punishment instead.

When I come out of the bathroom, they're still there. I bring them their dessert, plates of pie and ice cream balanced up and down my arms. Chase is glaring at Shelly.

"Cassie," she says, taking my hand and squeezing it after I've dropped their plates in front of each of them. "We're having a get-together next Saturday afternoon. Just a few people. You should come."

"Unless you're busy," Chase says quickly. I glance at him. He's deeply, deeply uncomfortable with the thought of me being anywhere near him. Maybe because he fucked me up against a set of bleachers three times in one night while Shelly was at cheer camp and after Leo went to prison. Or maybe it was the time I sucked his dick in a closet at a party and swallowed because Shelly thought fellatio was *gross*.

"Sure," I say, squeezing Shelly's hand back. "I'd love to."

I look at Chase, smiling as I lick my lips. He pretends to break up an imaginary fight between two of his daughters. Of course, I'll be there. He doesn't get to forget me that easily.

I watch their table from the safety of the kitchen pass as they finish dessert. Mid-morning, just as they've finally packed up all their children to leave, a trio of high school girls bursts into the diner.

Chase's little sister Jennifer is among the threesome. She works the evening shift for pocket money; not that she needs it. Her family is loaded. I read on *Business Insider* that Chase's net worth is fifteen million dollars. She'd be lucky to earn fifteen dollars in tips here, but

I guess she is young and beautiful and sultry in a Lana Del Rey–esque way. I watch as she squeals in delight and picks up one of the toddlers, while her two friends stand by patiently and eye-fuck her football star brother. Everybody always wants the celebrities. Not me. Every time I let Chase Thomas fuck me up against the locker room wall, on the nights Shelly worked in this very diner and I pretended I was at home, he could barely last long enough to get the condom on.

CHAPTER SIX

Cassie

After the shift from hell finishes, Damon picks me up. We get the frozen turkey for next week and drive home in silence. He seems to have something on his mind because he's gripping that steering wheel again like it's somebody's neck he wants to snap.

After I pack away the groceries, I wander into Mom's room, a makeshift assortment of furniture and windows that used to be our den. We'd never be able to get her hospital bed up the narrow staircase, and besides, I think Damon prefers that she's away from him.

I give Mom her liquid nutrition through her feeding tube and then I clean the equipment in the kitchen sink. When I go back in, Damon's already there. He's pulled an old armchair up to the far side of her bed, the TV on low, sports playing as the background soundtrack to cover the silence and the way Mom's chest rattles when she breathes.

He does this. He has some sixth sense that tells him when I'm about to talk to Mom, and he makes sure he's included. I ignore him, taking up a spot on the edge of the bed and laying my ear ever-so-gently to her chest.

"It's snowing outside," I whisper, my eyes itching as I hear my mother's heart beat slowly inside her rail-thin chest. *Won't you please wake up?*

I lie to her as I paint bright pink polish onto her fingernails. I tell her I'm getting a new haircut. I tell her I saw Chase and Shelly at the diner. I tell her that I'm happy, because even though most of the time I wish she would die, I don't want her to die thinking about how horribly sad her daughter is.

Even though it doesn't matter, and it's impossible, and she's probably not even in there anymore: I don't want her to know what a fucking mess I turned out to be.

Damon glances at me from the other side of the bed. He's lounging back in his chair, his feet crossed at the ankles and resting on the edge of the bed. The chatter of a football game hums around us, or maybe it's baseball. I have no idea who's playing what game, and I don't care. He turns back to the screen, completely unaffected by the sight of the comatose woman between us. He never says anything to Mom. His wife.

"You shouldn't lie to your poor mother, Cassandra," he says absently, popping a Milk Dud into his mouth and chewing enthusiastically as one of the teams scores a goal, or a point, or whatever. I wish he wasn't here. I wish he was never here.

"Why don't you talk to her, then?" I ask him bitterly. "Why don't you tell her the truth?"

He snaps his gaze to me, the game forgotten.

"And let your mother know what an epic disappointment her only child turned out to be?" he asks coldly.

"What about her husband?" I challenge. "I think disappointment is an inadequate word, don't you?"

And then he says the words that punch me in the gut. "Teresa would still be here if it weren't for you, Cassandra." His words cold, his tone measured, my mother's name like a bullet he's just fired. "If it weren't for you and your deadbeat fucking boyfriend, she'd still be *her*, instead of this bag of bones you insist we hang out with."

My throat starts to burn with sadness, with crushing guilt. He's right. I never used to believe him when he told me it was my fault Leo ran off the road that night, but it must have been. If I hadn't fought with Leo, he wouldn't have stormed out. He wouldn't have been driving when he'd been drinking all afternoon. He wouldn't have taken the pills. We wouldn't be here. I slide off the bed and go back to the kitchen. I really should spend more time with my mother, but there's really only so much you can say to a person who won't wake up.

I'm dicing potatoes when I hear a knock on the front door. Adrenaline spikes in my stomach and then moves out like a stealth ninja, bleeding into every cell of my being until the knife is shaking in my grip. Nobody visits us. Only Damon's brother, Ray, and he's not due here until tomorrow. I have a brief flash of panic as I imagine Shelly standing at the threshold, full of fresh fucking pity, or maybe Amanda, coming to check on me.

I busy myself with the potatoes, letting my breath go in relief as I hear Chris's voice in the hall. Of course, nobody's coming to check up on me. Thank God for that.

Damon enters the kitchen, Chris trailing after him. Boyish even though we're the same age, he always looks like he's just seen something unpleasant. Or maybe that's just because when I see him, he's looking at me? Either way, he's an odd choice for a small-town cop. I imagine him as an accountant . . . or a vampire. He's pale and lanky and when I fucked him during senior year, he wanted me to bite him really hard, like hard enough to make him bleed. It was kind of weird and totally hot at the same time.

He looks uncomfortable, like he doesn't want to be here. "Hey," I smile, looking up at him at the same time that I slice through the tip of my finger.

"Fuck!" I mutter under my breath, looking down at my clumsiness. Yup, I've sliced my index finger, and it's deep. I suck my finger, meeting Damon's glare. He just looks at the knife, then me, shaking his head as he disappears into the garage.

"Are you okay?" Chris asks.

"I'm fine." I wave him off, talking through a mouthful of blood. "You working overtime?"

Damn, this cut is deep. Too deep to be sucking on it and hoping it'll stop bleeding. Yuck. I grab a dish towel and wrap it around my hand, opening drawers along the kitchen counter in search of a first-aid kit.

"Just picking something up," Chris says.

I nod in acknowledgment, walking past him. I've remembered where the bandages are. I pad down the hallway on bare feet and into my mother's room, my finger starting to throb. "You doing anything special for Thanksgiving?" I call out to Chris, rummaging through a drawer beside Mom's bed. My headache from this morning has finally abated and I'm feeling a little better—hence, the small talk. Chris appears in the doorway, stopping at the line where the polished wood floor butts up against brown carpet. "Just the usual family stuff," he says, casting a glance at Mom.

"You can come in," I say, waving him in as I open another drawer. "She won't bite." Then I remember biting him and I try not to laugh. It's worse when I look up at him and see him biting his lip, too, clearly on my wavelength. His hands are stuffed into his jeans pockets and he looks like he can't wait to get the fuck out of here.

So when he steps closer to me and offers his help, I'm kind of stunned. He can see me fumbling with the package of Band-Aids and holds his hand out. "Here. They've all got these damn tamper-proof seals these days."

Wordlessly, I hand him the package and he opens it easily. "There," he says, unpeeling a Band-Aid and holding it out to me.

"Thanks," I reply, nestling my bleeding wound on the small white padding inside the bandage and letting him wrap the sticky plastic around my finger. It's about the nicest thing anyone's done for me in a long time.

"Can I ask you something, Cass?" Chris says suddenly.

I meet his gaze. "Of course."

He's so serious I'm almost anxious for him. "Why don't you put your mom in a nursing home? I mean, you could go have a life. Away from here. Away from Gun Creek." He glances back at her like he doesn't want her to hear, which is ridiculous since she can't hear a damn thing in her state. "I'm sorry," he adds quickly. "That's a terrible thing to ask someone."

I shake my head. Is this the first genuine conversation I've had with a human being outside of Damon in years? Yeah. It is.

"It's okay," I reply. "It's not terrible at all. When we brought her home from the hospital after the accident, it was for palliative care. They said she'd go quickly. I've thought about the nursing home thing a lot."

"So why don't you do it?" he presses.

I smile wanly as I look at my mother. She was so beautiful, once. "Because she'd die in there. It'd break her heart and she'd die alone, and I would have to live knowing that I killed my own mother."

We go back out to the kitchen and Chris hovers awkwardly. Everybody is awkward in this house except its inhabitants. It's like when you step over the threshold all the air in your lungs is vacuumed out, and you're walking around and drowning at the same time, until you can get outside and cough and take deep lungfuls of cold winter air and thank God you don't have to live here.

I pick up the knife and rinse it under the faucet, then resume my chopping. Damon clatters about in the garage. Chris paces. I chop. Blood seeps through my flimsy Band-Aid. I watch him pace.

Chris is a nice boy. Well, he's a man now, isn't he? A nice, regular guy. Single. I size him up for a moment, wondering how quickly I could go back down into the den and kill my mother. It's not like she's alive anyway, right? One sweep across her throat and she might finally find some peace. And that'd just leave Damon.

I could take him by surprise, slide the blade into his midsection before he even notices I've murdered her. Then I could go and get into Chris's deputy's car and we could go and have dinner with his family while mine start to decompose here.

I mean, not that I'd ever do that.

"Cassie," Damon says. I look up from where I've been staring at the knife in my hand.

Chris is gone. I hear his car in the driveway. I've zoned out again; I do that a lot these days.

"Cassie," Damon repeats, his tone sharper this time. He takes the knife from me and sets it down. "You're bleeding all over the food."

The Band-Aid was useless; the potatoes need to be trashed. I wrap another dish towel around my hand and let Damon guide me to the sink. He takes the towel away and holds my hand under running water, washing away the blood so he can get a better look at my self-inflicted wound. It's deep. It's disgusting. The water stings, but I don't say a word.

"We need to get you a doctor," Damon says. Under his breath, he mutters, "*Jesus Christ*. This is deep. You need stitches."

I glance at the knife on the counter and wonder how far away Chris is now.

CHAPTER SEVEN

Leo

They don't serve nachos at Lovelock.

But they do serve them at Dana's Grill. Gooey, thick cheese, so yellow it's almost orange. Dana's homemade salsa, fresh guacamole . . . almost like a sexual experience when the waitress slides them in front of me. All of my senses are on high alert, tucked into a back booth of the diner with a baseball cap pulled low so nobody I know will see me. I should be at home, but I don't have to check in with the sheriff's department until Monday morning, and I know it'll be a shit show as soon as Ma sees me. So I'm taking the scenic route home, from the Greyhound bus stop outside the diner to Ma's property a mile down the road. And I'm taking my fucking time.

I'm hyperaware of my surroundings—the hiss of the fluorescent lights overhead; intermittent beeps and sizzles in the kitchen, food on, food off; the ding of the service bell that tells the waitresses when food is up and ready to be served. It's so dark in here even with the overhead lights and the bar lamps that hang over every table. So dark compared to a white-washed prison cell. The seat is soft underneath me, so soft that my back starts to ache. I'm not used to being comfortable. I'm not used to being alone like this.

I like being alone, and at the same time, it's terrifying. Nobody telling me when to eat. When to shower. When to sleep. Just me and the cup of black coffee in front of me, and now the nachos so sexy I almost come in my pants when I see them. They're placed in front of me by a pale, slender arm, and I follow that arm to its owner as if in slow motion.

A pretty girl stands at the end of my booth. She can't be more than seventeen, but she's got the body of a woman. Tits that strain against her bright pink Dana's Grill shirt; the buttons at her sternum struggling to contain them. Lips painted in a gloss with specks of glitter in it. Big brown doe-eyes that look amused when the path my gaze is making finally meets hers.

"More coffee?"

I laugh under my breath. "I know you."

She smiles as she pours more coffee into my mug, her nose wrinkling up when she does. "You're in Gun Creek. Pretty sure you know everyone, Leo Bentley. Welcome home."

She's Chase's little sister. "Jenny. Christ, last time I saw you, you were, what—ten?"

Shit. I've been checking out the girl I used to babysit when she was in diapers. "Eight, I think," she replies. "I just turned sixteen."

"Really?" My dick is hard as granite under the table. It hasn't been inside a woman in eight years. I should not be looking at a sixteen-year-old and getting a hard-on, but then I looked at the nachos on the menu and got a hard-on. So I'm going to try and forgive myself. And then find someone age-appropriate to fuck as soon as possible. I already feel sorry for whoever that girl's going to be because I'm either going to last ten seconds, or I'm going to fuck her so hard she sees stars.

Cassie and I used to sneak out to the fields and have sex, and then look for shooting stars after as we fumbled our clothes back on and caught our breath. Then I ruined everything.

Suddenly I'm not so turned on anymore.

I pick up a corn chip and bring it to my mouth as Jennifer looks around conspiratorially. She puts her coffee pot down on the edge of the table and slides into the booth across from me. "I'm surprised you're here," she says. "You know Cassie still works here, right?"

The hairs on my arms stand up on end, like someone's Tasered me, and I look around the diner as I try to shrink down in my seat without her noticing.

"Don't worry, she works the morning shift," Jennifer says, taking an upside-down mug from next to the sugar packets and pouring herself a cup of coffee.

"Aren't you supposed to be working?" I ask her, watching as she dumps three sugars in her coffee and stirs.

"Aren't you supposed to be at home?" she asks in response. I grimace, not knowing what to say, wishing she'd go away now so I can shove these fucking nachos in my face instead of politely nibbling them like I am now.

"How's your brother?" I ask between mouthfuls.

"Rich and annoying," Jennifer says, waving her hand dismissively. "He married Shelly, you know. They've got three daughters and she's pregnant *again*. They keep saying they want to keep it a surprise, but everyone knows they're just going to keep going until they have a boy. Which means this next baby has to be a girl."

Speaking to a teenage girl after eight years of male conversation, peppered with the occasional yard chat with a female prison guard, is jarring. I can practically see the cogs moving in her brain, but they're whirring too fast for me to focus on. I've forgotten how much girls like to talk.

"They might have a boy," I say, pushing my nachos away and sipping on my coffee. It's strong and incredibly bitter.

Jennifer raises her perfectly manicured eyebrows. "If you want something that much, you're never going to get it," she says, sliding back out of the booth and grabbing her coffee pot, her mug forgotten. "It's just the way the world works." She tips her chin toward the rucksack on the seat next to me, all of my worldly possessions from prison and a hundred dollars from the gate. "How are you getting home?" she asks. "Pike picking you up?"

"Pike lives in Vegas now," I reply. "Or maybe it's Reno."

"Huh," Jennifer says. "He's got that side bangs thing going on, right?" She grabs a section of her bangs and imitates the extreme hairstyle my brother has had since our senior year. He visited me in Lovelock, like, three months ago, and he still had the fucking thing. Jennifer pretends to flick hair out of her eyes with an exaggerated head toss, and I laugh. "Yeah, that's my brother."

She nods. "He was here this afternoon, getting coffee to go. He's got those extenders in his ears. His earlobes are, like, basically touching his shoulders or whatever. He looks like a homeless Criss Angel."

"He's in town?" I didn't tell him I was coming home. He must be visiting Mom. What a good son.

Jennifer shrugs. "Yeah. You need a lift home? I get off at ten."

I look at the clock on the wall above her head. It's nine-forty-five. "That's nice, but—"

"Leo. I drive right past your house. I won't even stop the car if it makes you feel better. I'll just open the door and you can jump out while I'm rolling."

I open my mouth to protest, but—it is fucking cold outside.

"A ride would be nice," I say, with difficulty. "Thank you."

I catch sight of a trucker glaring at me from across the diner. I know him. Lou Potts. Owns all the transport rigs around these parts. I've fixed his trucks countless times. Well, I used to. Something about the way he's trying to kill me with his eyes tells me that he won't be hiring me again anytime soon.

Jennifer follows my gaze, looking over her shoulder at Lou. "What's his problem?" she whispers, turning back to me.

"Me," I say, draining my coffee and letting her fill it again. "His problem is me."

"Why?" Jennifer asks. "What did you do?"

She's too young to hate me for the accident and too pubescent to care about anything else except lip gloss and shopping at the mall with her friends. Or whatever the fuck it is sixteen-year-old girls do. As I recall, Cassie enjoyed outdoor sex and baking when she was sixteen, but she was always different than other girls. Kind of why I loved her so much.

Love her so much. Still. Even though I haven't seen her in eight years.

At ten on the dot, Jennifer comes back to my table. "It's on me. Keep your money," she says, picking up the folded note I've left under the saltshaker. I grab her wrist as she's stuffing the crumpled twenty into my pocket.

"Jennifer, you're in high school. Keep your money. Save up for spring break or something."

"I drive an eighty-thousand-dollar Range Rover, Leo," she replies, sticking up her perfectly polished middle finger at me. "And my manicure cost more than your nachos."

I cough. "If that's the case, why the fuck are you working here for minimum wage?"

Her smile falls ever so slightly, but I see it. She looks around before tapping her nose. "Ever tried coke?" she asks. "It's really fun until your parents find out and cut off all your access to money."

I frown. "Where on earth does one find coke in a place like this?"

Jennifer snort-giggles at that. "Seriously? Oh, God, you are serious. Ask your brother."

Of course. I should have known. My brother, the drug dealer.

I thank Jennifer for the meal and for the three extra doggy bags full of cherry pie that she hands me on our way out. I doubt my mom would have stocked the fridge—she doesn't even know I'm coming home—so I stop arguing and take the favor. I know she feels sorry for me. But at least she doesn't want to rip my fucking throat out like Lou who stares at us as we leave the diner, as I slide into the Range Rover's electronically warmed passenger seat, and as we drive off down the highway.

I almost expect to feel something when we cross the bridge. I see the shiny section where they replaced the guardrail that I busted through on my way down. The creek below is flanked by shadows, far too dark to make it out, but I know it'll be frozen over. It was frozen over when I crashed.

I don't remember getting in the car, or going off the bridge, but I do remember the freezing cold water as it seeped inside. I remember the flames on my arm. I remember Teresa King's face as she screamed. As she burned.

"Are you excited?" Jennifer asks, piercing my garish daydream.

"Excited?"

"About going home. About seeing your family."

I laugh under my breath. "Sure. I guess."

"Did you forget how to have a conversation in prison?" Jennifer asks pointedly. Shit. Guilt slams into me, shame. This girl who hasn't seen me since she was in grade school gave me food, a ride home, and no judgment, and I'm not even making polite conversation with her.

"I'm sorry," I say. "I am so fucking rude."

"You're not," she says quickly.

"No, I am. You're right. I kind of did forget how to have a conversation."

She shrugs. "That's okay. Makes sense, I guess."

We drive in silence the rest of the way. Something about the way Jennifer has aged so rapidly in the past eight years has woken me the fuck up—in prison, time has no meaning. Nobody grows or is born. Nobody is ever a child. You go there and you live each day the same as the last, and sometimes you stay so long you die there.

Not me. I'm not ever going back. I'll die before I go back.

Jennifer pulls on to the shoulder in front of our property, watching quietly as I grab my backpack and the bag of food.

"Thanks for the ride," I say, opening my door.

"I guess I'll see you at the house sometime," Jennifer replies. "My brother's home. You should come around and see us, Leo. He'd like that."

I slide out of the car and turn around, smiling at her. "Yeah, me, too. Drive home safe, okay?"

She nods, and it's only as I'm closing the door that I realize how fucking ridiculous that sounds, coming from the mouth of a man who just served eight years in prison for driving the opposite of safe.

I stand on the side of the road and watch her taillights as she drives away.

CHAPTER EIGHT

Leo

As soon as I get home, I almost wish I were back in prison.

The moment I trudge down to my "room," my makeshift shipping container, my feet sinking into the thick snow blanketing everything, I'm greeted by what sounds like two people fucking each other to death.

Animals. Of course, it makes sense that anyone of age in our house would use my room for some privacy instead of trying to fuck in the trailer, paper-thin walls stifling nothing. Of course. While I was away, they've turned my room into a goddamned brothel.

I just about rip the door off the hinges, I'm that furious, my brother's name on my lips. I mean, it's either Pike or my mom using this room, and I can't even think about it being Mom.

So what I see breaks my fucking heart and makes me want to commit murder all at the same time.

"What the fuck is this!?" I yell, my voice filling the small room. It stinks like sweat and sex and pot in here. Everything is as I left it—the bed, the sink, clothes hanging on a piece of rope strung up in the corner.

My baby sister, naked and bouncing on top of some guy I vaguely recognize, is the thing I didn't leave here. Hannah is fourteen, and as if that weren't bad enough, she's slow. Special, I call her. My mom drank too much when she was pregnant with her and she's mentally the age of a preschooler. The last time I saw her, she was six years old, and in all the time I've been in prison, she's never mentally progressed. At least, that's what Pike told me.

And now she's fourteen, she's on top of some guy, and he's making this noise with his hands on her big belly. Her big *pregnant* belly.

I see red. I'm pretty sure I'm about to set a record for how quickly someone can get arrested for brutal fucking murder after being let out on parole. I charge at them, Hannah's face breaking into a smile as she sees me. "Leo!" she says, reaching for me. I dodge her, grabbing the stunned guy by the neck and literally dragging him out from underneath my sister. I throw him onto the ground, kicking him in the ribs as hard as I can, and the guy looks like he's about to have a goddamn heart attack.

"Derek?!" I say. Derek Jackson is one of my mom's sometime boyfriends and occasional business partners when they do a cook together. He was hanging around like a bad fucking smell when I was arrested.

"Jesus Christ," I seethe, putting my boot on Derek's throat when he tries to get up. "Does my mother know about this?"

"Don't hurt him!" Hannah interjects.

"Get dressed, Hannah. Get dressed now!" I find a pile of clothes on the floor and throw them at my baby sister; I don't even know if they're hers, but I don't care.

"Man, just pass me my pants—" Derek says, choking when I step harder on his windpipe.

"Did I say you could talk, fucker?" I ask him. "Just give me a reason. Just give me a reason to break your fucking neck."

"You dressed?" I say to Hannah, without taking my eyes off Derek. The dude looks completely fucked up—he's missing half his teeth, no doubt thanks to all the ice he smokes, and his eyes are so bloodshot it looks like somebody burned them with a blowtorch.

"Yeah," Hannah says. I glance at her, fighting the urge to roll my eyes. She's wearing an oversized checked shirt that definitely isn't hers, a pair of men's boxer shorts, and slippers. Apart from the fact that she'll freeze outside like that, none of the clothes are hers. I focus my attention back on Derek, who is staring at Hannah.

"Don't look at my sister," I snap, pulsing my foot against his throat so that he chokes painfully. "You aren't ever going to see her again, you hear me?"

"Leo," Hannah whines.

"You know she's not right, don't you?" My eyes fucking bore into his. "You know she's slow. You've basically been screwing around with a kid from the first grade. You got a *child* pregnant, you fucking pedophile."

Something changes in Derek's eyes.

"You got something to say?" I challenge him, lifting up my boot so he can talk.

"She's a young woman!" Derek protests, holding his throat. "Look at her. Your mama gave us her blessing, so fuck you, Leo Bentley."

"Fuck *me*?" I repeat. "Fuck *you*." I smash my fist into his face, adrenaline surging through me as my blow finds purchase. I want to kill him. I hit him again and again, only stopping because Hannah is screaming out enough to alert the entire town. If the sheriff turns up, he'll no doubt take great pleasure in hauling my ass back to Lovelock.

"Get out," I spit, pointing at the door as I stare Derek down.

"My clothes—"

"Get new ones," I interject. "Get out before I rip your dick off."

"I didn't knock nobody up," Derek says defiantly, his face a bloody pulp. "Don't you come asking for no money for that bastard, Leo Bentley. That there ain't my kid. She was already like that when I started up with her."

I pick up one of my football trophies and lug it at his head. I'm an excellent aim, and I flinch a little when it hits him square in the temple. Blood explodes from his face. Fuck. That really could have killed him.

"Get out!" I yell.

He runs outside, naked except for his boots, cupping his cock and balls in his hands as he runs through the snow to his pickup. He gets in and starts the car up, tearing off as I stare at my little sister.

"You're mean," Hannah says, pouting a little.

"Hannah," I say quietly, scrubbing my hand across my chin as I try to figure this out. "How far along are you? How many weeks?"

She looks dumbfounded.

"Jesus Christ," I mutter. "Have you been to the doctor? Has anyone taken you to check on the baby?"

She shakes her head. "Mama says she will when her check comes in."

I let out a noise that's half-sigh, half-growl. I've been hearing that same excuse my whole life. "Where are your clothes, Hannah?"

"None of my clothes fit me," she says, resting her hands on her belly. "I'm too fat. Pike gave me some of his stuff."

I'm about to snap. Anger surges through me, and guilt. This happened because I wasn't here.

"I told Pike to watch you," I say to Hannah. She's already distracted by something else, a game she's playing with herself. It's what she does when she feels threatened. Retreats inside her head and won't look anyone in the eye.

"Hannah," I implore her. "I'm sorry I yelled, honey. I thought he was hurting you."

Her lower lip is trembling. Goddamn it. This is on me. This is all on me.

"Come on," I say, putting a hand on her shoulder. I don't want to touch her after she's been with that guy, but she's my sister. "Hannah, I'm sorry. Please talk to me."

She looks up at me, her eyes filled with tears, and I'm relieved. At least she's making eye contact. "You never came back," she says. "You told me you'd be right back."

"When?"

"When you went to the party," she replies. "I've been waiting for you. You've been gone for so long, all the leaves fell off the trees and the snow came back. You've never been away that long, Leo."

Oh, my God, she's talking about the night of the accident. Eight years ago.

"You've been waiting for me?" I ask, a hard lump forming in my throat.

She nods. "I was scared without you here," she says.

I can actually feel my heart breaking into pieces. "Come here," I say, drawing her into a hug. Her baby belly between us. My baby sister with a fucking baby of her own. "I'm here now. I'm not leaving again."

I start to think up ways to kill our mother for letting this happen.

It's this town. There's something in the water, even after the dead-girl blood's been washed away. It's some poison, some toxin that seeps into everyone.

This town will suck the life out of you.

I get Hannah dressed in some of my warmer clothes, give her my thick snow jacket and some sweatpants that have a drawstring she can tie up under her protruding stomach. I'll have to go to the thrift store in Tonopah and buy her some new things so she doesn't have to go around holding her pants up to stop them from falling down. I mean, she's already pregnant, so she can't get knocked up again, but still. I can't even think about the rest. She's going to have a baby. I'm not even sure what that means. Will the state let her keep it? I mean, she's got a file as thick as my fist. We all do. I wonder if Mom's avoided taking her to the doctor because she's afraid they'll take Hannah—and the baby—away.

Probably she's just a lazy bitch, knowing my mom.

The heat isn't working that well in my room, so I take Hannah back up to Mom's trailer. I hold her hand as we walk through the snow, bitter wind biting at my cheeks. As I walk, I glimpse Cassie's house. I've been purposely avoiding looking that way, but Hannah has distracted me, and before I know it I'm stopped in my tracks, staring. If I had a pair of binoculars, I'd be able to see straight into Cassie's kitchen.

Into her bedroom. She used to write me messages and stick them in her window back in the day.

"I miss Cassie," Hannah says, tugging on my hand. "Can we please go visit her now that you're home?"

I grind my teeth as I try to think of a suitable response.

"Leo?"

"No," I say, resuming my brisk pace, half-dragging Hannah behind me. "Cassie and I aren't friends anymore."

The trailer's exactly as I remember, only smaller. It feels tiny, no doubt because my family has grown bigger in my absence. My mom sits on the torn leather couch like some kind of royalty on her throne, smoking a cigarette as she watches the television intently, and two brand-new baby brothers somebody forgot to tell me about play with Legos at her feet. They're two and three years old at best, and the quietest kids I've ever seen. Pike's already told me that the triplets—Matty, Richie, and Beau, who were barely in grade school when I went to prison—are living with their paternal grandmother in Reno after my mother failed to send them to school for almost a year. I glance at these new little boys again and wonder if she's given them NyQuil to calm them down. That's what our batshit mother used to do when Pike and I were going stir-crazy inside in winter. Give us each a dose of medicine to calm us down before she got her own "medicine" sorted.

"Mom."

"Oh, hey," she says, glancing away from the TV for a second. "Welcome home. They give you gate money?"

I chuckle, shaking my head. That's a record, even for her. Normally she'd try to sweet talk me before asking for money.

"Hey, Mom," I reply. "Missed you, too."

She rolls her eyes. "Don't be like that. I need to buy food for the boys."

"What happened to Hannah?" I ask her, ignoring her question.

She shrugs, blowing cigarette smoke over my brothers' heads as they play quietly. She's older than I remember. Her mouth is smaller, the corners of her eyes more lined. She's barely forty and she looks sixty.

"Mom," I say, more forcefully this time. "Hannah's pregnant."

She looks at me like I'm dumb as shit. "You're kidding."

Sarcastic bitch. "She's fourteen."

"I know that."

Hannah breaks away from me, going for a Lego on the ground. "Hey," I say, pulling her back gently. "Go wash up first."

For once, she doesn't argue. A few moments later I hear the shower turn on and Hannah starts singing a song from *The Little Mermaid*.

I don't move from my spot next to the TV. I stare at my mom, imagining laser beams shooting out of my eyes and burning holes in her face. Anger in my veins. I always think of the pasta sauce I used to make with Grandma when I'm angry. It had to simmer for hours before it was done. That's how my rage works. It simmers for hours, and then I'm fucking done.

I'll wait. As long as it takes, I'll wait for my mom to bite.

"What?" she says, lighting a new cigarette, the old one burned down to the filter and abandoned in the overflowing coffee mug she's using as a makeshift ashtray.

"Did you know what she was doing down in my room?"

She coughs. "I'm sorry, did she mess your room up sometime in the last ten years, baby?"

Sarcastic bitch.

"Eight years," I correct her.

Bitch doesn't respond.

"I don't care about the mess, Ma," I say through gritted teeth. "I care about walking in on my fourteen-year-old sister being used as a plaything by some guy you used to date."

"She's almost fifteen," Ma says, flicking a bit of tobacco from her lip. "I was sixteen when I had you."

"Mom!" I yell. "She's not almost fifteen! She's intellectually fucking disabled." The "thanks to you" part is silent, but strongly implied.

She stands up, furious. "How dare you!" she cries. "Coming in here after all these years and yelling at me! I'm trying to watch my show!"

I respond by yanking the TV's power cord out of the wall socket.

"Leo . . ." my mother growls.

"Mother," I reply. I really didn't mean to come back and upset her. But then Hannah happened.

"Have you got food? A turkey for Thanksgiving?"

"That depends," she says. "You got gate money for me? Turkey ain't cheap."

I snort-laugh. "How much money you think they give you at the gate? Not enough to spring for a fucking turkey to feed six people. Six and a half, if we're being accurate."

Her eyes narrow to slits, and I know she doesn't believe me. "Derek got two hundred dollars and a bus ticket to anywhere in the country after he got out," she says.

I shrug. "Yeah, well, Derek was in prison in California, Mom. In Nevada, they don't give you two hundred dollars."

She taps ash on the floor, digesting that. "Well, how much?" she asks.

I shake my head. "I'm not giving you money so you can go and shoot it up your arm."

She's about to launch a tirade against me when a horn beeps outside. I know that noise. Short and sharp, two beeps. Mayor Carter is here. Hannah's biological father, though he'd never admit it, and he definitely won't come in and see the daughter who has no idea her daddy is the town mayor. Fucking prick. Probably getting one in before he has to spend Thanksgiving with his poor, unsuspecting wife and their six teacup poodles.

"What the fuck's he doing here?" I ask.

My mom looks me up and down. "Dropping off some money, since my own son can't spot me twenty dollars."

"Whatever."

She glares at me as she brushes past, the boys following. They're stir-crazy, no doubt. "Stay here!" she snaps at them. "I'll be back in a minute."

The boys go back to their Legos. I wonder if she's just drugged them or if she's started beating them, as well. At this point, nothing would surprise me.

Mom shrugs into her own winter coat and slams the door behind her. A few seconds pass and then I hear a car door slam, followed by the sound of an engine tearing off at high speed.

I stand there for a moment, staring at the closed door, waiting for her to come back inside. I count to five inside my head, just like I've been taught. I do that five times over and she's still not back inside, so I open the front door and step out onto the stoop, scanning the yard.

She's gone. I can see the rear end of the smart black Town Car she's gotten into as it crests the ridge at the top of the hill and disappears.

"Fuck," I mutter under my breath, turning to go back inside. Less than five minutes and she's taken off. That *is* a record.

"Derek says you shouldn't say *fuck*," Hannah says. She's been standing right behind me, and I almost knocked her over when I turned.

"Shit, Hannah," I say, one hand on my chest. "You scared the hell out of me."

"You shouldn't say *shit* or *hell* either," she says, her face serious. Her hair is soaking wet from the shower and I'm afraid if I don't get her inside soon, it'll start to form icicles.

"Let's forget about Derek," I say, putting my hand in the small of Hannah's back and guiding her into the trailer. "Let's pretend we never met him."

Hannah wrinkles up her nose at me, but she doesn't argue.

"Pike!" I yell. I don't need to go looking for my brother; his piece of shit car is out front, so he's in this trailer somewhere.

He appears a moment later, eyes red, smelling like dirty bong water. "Hey. You're back."

He's gotten weirder while I've been away. He's got a giant tongue piercing that looks like a ball of metal rolling around his mouth, and he's dyed his blond hair jet black.

"You auditioning for My Chemical Romance?" I ask, punching him lightly on the shoulder. I'm not sure whether to laugh or be fucking disturbed that my younger brother looks like an emo.

He frowns, a lip piercing glinting in the harsh light.

"Hannah's pregnant," I say.

"No shit," Pike replies, looking bored.

I fight the urge to throw him up against the wall and throttle him; I'd break the wall before I did any damage to him, and now we don't have Derek to fix it.

"I told you to watch her while I was gone," I say to my brother. He looks at the floor, with embarrassment or anger, I can't tell.

Maybe both.

"I've been in Reno," he mutters. "Selling a little. Mom's checks stopped coming."

I raise my eyebrows so high they almost hit the fucking roof. Not that that'd take much; I can barely stand straight without hitting the ceiling in this tiny shithole.

"They stopped coming, or she spent them?" I ask.

Pike shrugs. "It's all the same, right? Either way, I had to pay the bills since you were gone. Keep the heat on. Feed these kids."

I take a step back and decide that maybe Pike doesn't need the living shit beaten out of him, after all. I take a twenty-dollar bill out of my jeans pocket, the twenty Jennifer insisted I keep, and hand it to Pike.

"What's this for?" he asks, holding the money like it's diseased.

"Thanksgiving dinner."

"Thanksgiving dinner," Pike repeats, sounding unimpressed.

"Yeah. I missed it last year. And the seven years before that. I need you to go to the store tomorrow and get some things."

He looks dubious. "We don't celebrate shit like Thanksgiving."

"We do now!" I snap. "First thing in the morning. Go to the store."

"And get what?"

I let out a long breath. My head hurts already and I've been back in Gun Creek a matter of hours. Prison was easier than this. "Get some chicken pieces. Look for the ones with the sticker. They're always fine a few days past the date. Some yams. Cauliflower or broccoli, whatever's cheaper. Milk. Cheese—a small package, that shit isn't cheap. Cranberry sauce if you can afford it. Make sure it adds up right before you take it all to the register."

I take out a second twenty as another thought strikes me. "Prenatal vitamins. Get the biggest bottle you can afford. Where's the dog?" Pike looks uneasy, and for a moment my heart sinks. "Please don't tell me she's dead," I say.

He shakes his head quickly. "No. We didn't have money for dog food, and Cassie kept feeding her. She stays up there most of the time at the Carlino place."

The mention of Cassie stabs me like an ice pick to my heart; it takes every ounce of willpower not to physically grab at my chest to stop it from hurting. I'm glad Rox is with her. A dog is good protection, among other things, since I haven't been there for her.

"How is she?" I ask, hungering for something. Some crumb of news, of intel on the girl I still love so much it's killing me inside.

Pike shrugs. "She's different," he says. "We're all different since you went away."

Well, I don't know what to say to that. I nod, rubbing at my eyes. I'm exhausted. I say goodbye to Pike and trudge back through the dirty snow to my room. It's the last place I want to be after what I saw, but I'll end up killing my mother if I spend one more minute in that goddamn trailer. I rip the sex-stained sheets from the bed and throw them outside in the snow, turn the mattress over, and try to sleep.

Pike goes off to the store the next morning; I think he's relieved more than anything to have someone else take charge. I pile my little brothers into the bath, then find them each a change of clothes without holes. When Pike finally gets back with the ingredients and a quarter to spare, I make Hannah take three of the big oval-shaped vitamins with a glass of the milk. Even though it's technically a week early, I cook Thanksgiving dinner for my siblings, trailer style, and Mom doesn't come back for days.

Once everyone is finally taken care of—clean, dressed, warm, fed—I leave them in the trailer and trudge through dirty snow down to my room. The place is trashed. I may have slept in the bed last night—or laid awake trying to sleep—but now I need to make the place habitable again. I spend hours getting everything back in order. Even though it's freezing outside I open up the door and the little makeshift window to air the place out, get fresh sheets, and wipe down dust-choked surfaces with a clean rag. After I'm done, I sit in the middle of the bed in my warmest jacket and smoke half a pack of cigarettes to try and paint over the other smells in here, the ones that don't belong to me, and, finally, it starts to feel like my room again. My house. This is my place in the world and I've reclaimed it. Nobody else can have it. Tomorrow I'll get a new padlock for the door and hide the key.

Before I turn in for the night I go down to the well. I can still taste Karen if I close my eyes, and now I don't even have alcohol to dull the edges. In prison, I had four walls and three cellmates to keep me company. In prison, I didn't dream of Karen. Now, here, in the frozen dark, it's just me and the ghost of the girl I found dead all those years ago.

The well has a new cover. It looks sturdy, and it's locked. I pull at the shiny padlock to test its strength. It's not opening without some serious bolt cutters, and that brings me some relief. I smoke a bunch of cigarettes and stare at Karen's final resting place, hopeful that her ghost stays trapped in the well and is unable to come visit me like it used to every night when I closed my eyes.

When I can't feel my toes anymore, and my cigarette packet is empty, I go back to my room.

At first, I think I'm seeing things. That I was wrong. That Karen's ghost is still here, sitting on my newly made bed waiting to pick up where we left off in my nightmares.

But the girl on my bed is not a ghost. She is real. Alive. Made from flesh and bone and shiny strawberry lip gloss.

"Jennifer," I say, leaning against the doorframe and waiting for her to speak, to offer some explanation as to why she's here.

"Leo," she replies.

CHAPTER NINE

Leo

Nobody says anything for a beat.

"It's cold," Jennifer says. "You should shut the door."

I step inside and I shut the door. I don't think about Karen. I don't think about Cassie. All I can think about is what I'd like to do to the sixteen-year-old girl sitting on the edge of my bed.

"What do you want?" I ask her.

She smiles. Shrugs her narrow shoulders. Parts her knees ever so slightly. I notice everything, every movement, every facial expression. I've been starved for eight years. I am hungry. She needs to leave, *now*.

"Do I have to want something?" she asks. "Can't a girl just drop in?"

I scrub my hand across my chin. It's sharp with new growth; I need to shave. "Does your father know you're here?"

She laughs, sliding off the bed and stepping toward me. The sound of her laughter fills up the room until it feels like it might explode. She's too bright, too shiny.

"My father's on a business trip," she whispers.

She's so close, I could reach out and wrap my hands around her throat.

She traces my bottom lip with her index finger, and I almost come in my jeans just at her flesh touching mine. Bad, bad Leo. I'm twenty-five. This girl is sixteen. I used to babysit her.

She's touching me, so I figure it's only fair if I touch her back. I place my hand at the base of her throat, just above the spot where her tits press together inside her shirt, my thumb against the hollow in her neck. "What do you want?" I repeat slowly.

She motions for me to come closer. I bend down so she can whisper into my ear. Her breath tickles as she tells me all the things she can't look me in the eye and say aloud.

I visit Jennifer every evening at the diner; she seems to like the attention, and I could use the distraction. I make sure to turn up just before her shift ends, and she gives me a ride home every night. The first night she came over we ended up talking for hours. My mouth hurt by the end, every sense on high alert. I was a gentleman. I didn't lay a hand on her again, not after she started to talk. She's in trouble. A lot of trouble. I think it eased her mind to be able to confess to somebody who pretty much wrote the book on trouble in this town.

I mean, there's not a thing I can do to help the girl. Not unless she tells me who got her into this mess in the first place. "That's the problem with men," she'd said to me when I urged her to give me the name of the guy blackmailing her. "They always jump straight to problem-solving. Men always want to fix everybody."

"You don't want to be fixed?" I'd asked her.

"I can fix myself," she'd replied. "I just need somebody to understand."

I don't understand. Her predicament is something I've never experienced. But I can listen. I listen to her talk as she drives me home in her shiny new car every night, and it makes me feel less of a fuck-up. I mean, she hasn't killed anyone. But she's planning to. And that's why we've found each other. I am a killer and she is ready to spill blood. She is a welcome diversion from my sins, and I am a makeshift altar for her to lay her own sins upon. Because when I'm with Jennifer, I don't think about Cassie Carlino. I don't think of Karen Brainard. And, most especially, I don't think of Teresa King and the way she burned beside me in that car.

The night Jennifer Thomas disappears is like all the rest. I go to the diner. Order nachos and a Coke. I'm surprised Jennifer is working. It's Thanksgiving, and the place is deserted. Even Amanda is nowhere to be seen.

"Working on Thanksgiving?" I ask Jennifer, as she slides my food in front of me.

She shrugs, that glitter lip gloss catching the light as she moves. "It's just another day, isn't it?"

I nod.

"Besides," she says, "it pisses my dad off that I'm not at home. I asked for this shift."

At ten, I help her turn out all the lights. I wait beside her as she locks the front doors of the diner, feeling vaguely worried about the fact that somebody had left a sixteen-year-old cheerleader alone to lock up this late at night. I note the lack of video surveillance, the remote location, the fact that everyone is tucked safely inside their houses while Jennifer is alone with a convicted criminal in the dead of night.

Jennifer offers me a ride home, which I accept. Except, instead of driving me straight home like she has done for the past six nights in a row, she pulls her Range Rover off the road into an uncleared section of pine trees that tower over us. The track is narrow and winding and she doesn't answer me when I ask her where she's taking us.

She stops in a small clearing and cuts the lights. The engine is still running. Bits of snow fall outside, slow and bloated in their trajectory toward the ground. Jennifer's hands are small as they grip the steering wheel; her eyes lit up by the red illumination of the dashboard, making her look almost demonic.

"What are we doing here?" I ask her.

"I don't want to go home," she says, staring straight ahead.

"Fair enough," I reply. I watch her as she struggles to find words. She squirms in her heated leather seat, her nails shiny and perfect, her shoulders sagging under the weight of something I cannot see.

"Do you think I'm pretty?" she asks me in a tiny voice, and she sounds so mouse-like and weak that I almost laugh.

"Do I think you're pretty?" I echo, feeling a smirk cut its way across my face. "Jennifer, you're so pretty I could die just from looking at you."

She rolls her eyes. "You think I'm stupid. You're just here because you feel sorry for me, Leo."

I shake my head. "I don't think you're stupid. And I'm not here because I feel sorry for you."

She swallows thickly; I can see the pulse beat nervously in her throat. "Then why are you here?"

"Well, I guess I'm here right now because you just drove us off the road and into the woods."

"You know what I mean."

Do I, though? I sigh. "Because you're the only person in this town worth talking to who will even look at me."

She bites her lip and I have the sudden, piercing urge inside my skull to wrap my hands around her throat and drag her onto my lap. That's some messed up shit. She's sixteen. Six. TEEN. I'm repeating the number in my head over and over, willing my dick to settle down. I can feel the throb of wanting her in my cock, in the thunderous rush of blood that makes my heart hit my ribcage like the firing of a gun—*bang, bang, bang*. My need eclipses my rationality. *So what if she's sixteen? She drove into this fucking clearing and licked her lips and asked me if I thought she was pretty.*

"Why have you been back to the diner every single night, just as I'm about to get off my shift?"

"Umm," I try. "It's the only decent place in town?"

She narrows her eyes at me and there's a fire inside her pupils; it might be below freezing outside, but it's a billion degrees in here. We're already fogging up the windows with our breath, and I haven't even laid a finger on her.

"Liar," she says. "I want the real reason."

You're about to get the real reason, sweetheart. I grip the armrest. I grip it so hard my fingernails ache.

"I'm here because I'm a bad guy, Jennifer."

"And?"

"Because you're so pretty I can't think about anybody else. Because I want to do things to you . . . that would probably frighten you. Things that might hurt you."

Her cheeks are flush; her breathing quickens. I haven't even touched her, and she's already excited. Or scared. Or both. I want to reach between her thighs and see if it's lust I'm reading on her face.

"What kinds of things?" she asks.

I cover my face with my hands.

"What kinds of things?" she repeats, a hand on my shoulder.

I let my hands fall into my lap and fix my stare on this girl who should be home with her family, not out here in the dark in the woods and snow with a criminal. I watch in awe as she slides her seat back and reaches her hands up underneath her skirt, tugging a pair of panties down her legs and unhooking them from her heels. She can't look at me as she hands me a pair of baby-blue silk panties with a bow on the front. I grip the underwear in my fist so tight I could tear it to shreds with a single pull, but I don't rip it. I find the damp spot of arousal in the center of the material and bring it up to my face. I close my eyes. I breathe Jennifer in.

I shouldn't be here. Not with her. Not like this. I will get out of the car, I decide. I will walk home. I will not touch this girl.

But then, "I promise I won't tell anyone," she whispers.

Fuck.

I grab her. I drown out her shocked moan with my mouth. I move my lips along her jaw, down to her slender neck as I undress her with my prison-rough palms. I drag her across the car, into my lap, pulling her to me as I dig my fingers into her arms hard enough to leave bruises. There are things in the way—my seatbelt, my pants—but I fumble my way through like a teenage boy losing his virginity. I may as well be; eight years is a long time to abstain. She's so wet and I'm so beyond ready that when I'm finally inside her, I barely last thirty seconds.

The second time is better. She's a loud one, and in the end I have to put my hand over her mouth to drown her out. She doesn't seem to mind. Some girls like it rough, and it seems like Jennifer Thomas is one of them.

Somewhere in the back of my mind I know I should stop. That this has already gone way too far. That I might be hurting her. She's too young, too innocent, and I am a terrible man.

It's only after when I'm looking at the dazed expression on her face, the hickeys I've left on her neck, the bruises blossoming on her spread thighs, that I understand what I have done.

By then, it's too late.

The night Jennifer Thomas disappears is like all the rest.

Apart from the way it ends.

CHAPTER TEN

Cassie

Damon's brother, Ray, comes over for dinner every Thursday night. And since Thanksgiving is on a Thursday, we're lucky enough to be graced by his presence. It's a two-hour trip from Reno in good traffic. He must really miss his brother to come all this way for some conversation and a few beers every week.

I don't like Ray. There is something about him that gives me the creeps. He's ordinary enough if you're not looking too hard. He's stockier than Damon, his arms tanned from outdoor work, his large hands rough and leathery. His nose is too big for his round face, but his wide mouth and dark eyebrows almost balance it out. I've never asked, because I don't care, but he looks like he has Italian heritage. Which is odd, because Damon—blue-eyed, pale-skinned, with light brown hair—looks nothing like that. Even their facial features don't match. Damon's cheekbones are higher, his nose straight and smaller than Ray's.

Ray has a face that should seem approachable, and I suppose it is, until you get too close. Something about the way his dark eyes linger on me for too long whenever we're in the same room makes my skin itch. So much so that I make sure we're never left alone together.

I serve dinner and everything seems to be okay. Damon's in a strangely quiet mood, but Ray's presence sometimes has that effect on him. I half listen to their conversation as they talk about the weather and Ray's job. He can be pretty funny when he tells stories about the casino where he works security. I make sure to laugh at the appropriate points in the conversation to keep from pissing anybody off. Life with people is just one big act for me these days.

After dinner, I'm exhausted. I've eaten far more than normal, just shoveled in turkey and potato casserole mindlessly while Ray talked and talked. Usually it's just Damon and me, and we talk about other things, and I'm too busy talking to binge eat half a turkey. I desperately need to empty my stomach.

I go upstairs and vomit up as much as I can, and then I clear the table and wash and dry every dish, and they're still talking at the table. Damon looks distracted, and I can't help wondering if he's bored by Ray, too. I sit back at the table, the damp dish towel in my hands.

Damon raises his eyebrows at me as if to say, "Are you okay?" I nod. "I'm tired," I announce to the table, as soon as there's a gap wide enough in the conversation to interrupt. "Mind if I turn in?"

"Go," Damon murmurs, standing at the same time as me. "Sleep in tomorrow. I'll fix breakfast."

Dr. Jekyll is being nice to me, for now. I wonder if that mood will last long enough for me to sleep in, or if he'll conveniently forget what he said and berate me for being lazy in the morning.

I'm too tired to think about it. I say good night, get a super awkward hug and cheek kiss from Ray (shudder), and then I pass out upstairs, face down across my bed, without even so much as taking my shoes off.

I'm awakened by a creaking noise. I've been sleeping deeply, so deeply that I have drool on my cheek. I sit up with a start, wiping my face as a shadow moves in the slightly cracked doorway.

"Damon?"

The door swings open, and illuminated in the hallway light is Ray. He steps into the room, smiling like a fucking creep. "Forgot to thank you for the dinner," he says, walking himself over and sitting next to me on my bed. He's close enough that I can smell the beer on his breath.

"You're welcome," I say, moving away. If he tries anything, I will claw his goddamned eyes out.

The light snaps on. I'm blinded momentarily.

"Thought you were waiting in the car," Damon says tightly, talking to Ray but looking me over. "I miss anything?"

Ray laughs, messing my hair up with his hand as he stands. "Nothing worth writing home over," he says. "C'mon. Let's go."

"Go where?" I ask, fixing my hair and thinking I need a shower to get rid of Ray's touch.

"We ran out of beer," Damon says. "Back in five."

I wait until they're gone, watching the taillights out the window. *Where do you get beer at this time on Thanksgiving?* Once I'm sure I'm alone, I check all the locks in the house before jumping into the shower. With a kitchen knife on the shower sill and a chair up against the door, I shampoo my hair until the crawling sensation goes away, using every bit of hot water in the tank. Then, after I'm dressed and warm, I get into my bed, pull the covers over my head, and pass out.

I dream about Leo. About the dog barking and dirty well water and Karen. About a snowstorm and two cars and death.

I wake with a start again around three. Rox is going crazy outside, barking up at my window. Ray's truck is back in the driveway, but the house is dark. I go downstairs and let her in even though Damon forbids animals in the house, leading her upstairs by her collar. When we get to the landing, she lunges for the attic. I'm not surprised—last time she was up there she found an entire family of mice living in a spot inside the drywall. I shudder at the thought that another rodent family has taken up residence for the winter.

"Come on," I whisper gently. "Silly old girl you are."

I let her sleep on the end of my bed until morning.

I'm up early, shortly after the sun rises, to sneak Rox outside. Damon despises the dog, makes her stay out in the yard. In winter he (very begrudgingly) lets her sleep in the garage, but the older the poor dog gets, the more she just wants to be with me. Sometimes she still disappears for a day or two, back down to Leo's I suppose, and when she comes back she smells of campfire and rain.

Downstairs, Ray is passed out on the couch. I almost shit my pants when I stumble into the living room and see him there. I hurry Rox outside and close the door again, making sure it's locked.

"Morning, sweetheart," Ray says, sitting up on the couch. He's still wearing his jeans and sweatshirt, his shoes neatly placed beside the couch end, his dark hair mussed up at the sides.

"Morning," I reply, suddenly feeling self-conscious in my thin cotton pajamas and the way my nipples are poking against the fabric, bemoaning the cold. I cross my arms over my chest, smiling briefly. "I'll make some coffee."

I brace myself for more awkwardness with Ray, but he simply asks to borrow a towel and takes himself off to the bathroom. I hear the shower start a moment later and breathe a sigh of relief. The coffee starts to drip into the pot, a reassuring sound to my sleep-addled brain. I'm flicking through the local newspaper when I spy something on the kitchen table, among a bunch of empty beer bottles.

A milk carton. I don't remember leaving it there after I cleaned up. Maybe the guys had some milk after they finished their beers. Damon occasionally likes that rum you mix with milk.

Glancing around to make sure I'm still alone, I cross the kitchen, picking up the carton. It feels strange in my hand. Waxy. Old.

It is old, I realize, as I turn it over in my hand. It's barely held together by the plastic coating that's started to peel away from it. I put it to my nose and sniff it. It smells unbelievably sour. I make a face.

"Whatcha got there?" a voice calls out behind me. I drop the carton, turning around to face the noise.

It's Ray, dripping wet, a towel wrapped around his waist as he makes a puddle on the floor I just mopped yesterday.

He has a kitchen knife in his hand. "Which one of you showers with a weapon?" he asks, clearly amused. Oh, shit. The same one I took into the bathroom last night. I laugh it off, pretend like it's no big deal, going back to the counter and pouring the now-finished coffee with a steady hand. Three cups, one for each of us, and then I pray that Ray goes home. I push one of the mugs toward him and he smiles, "Thank you, sweetie pie," as he places the kitchen knife down on the counter between us.

"I'll just take this up to Damon," I say, picking up the third coffee and going to walk past Ray. He catches my wrist, and some of the hot coffee splashes onto my hand. I wince but don't move. It's the hand that got burned in the accident. The nerves have never really settled and it hurts like a bitch.

"He's getting something from the attic for me," Ray says. "What's for breakfast?"

I put the coffee down on the counter and start pulling plates full of leftovers out of the refrigerator. When I turn back to the table, Ray and the milk carton are gone.

Damon knows his brother is a creep just as much as I do. So when he comes down from the attic, a black trash bag in his hand, he makes a beeline for me. I can tell he's looking for Ray at the same time.

"Morning," I say, handing him fresh coffee. When he's nice to me, I'm nice to him. We get into a rhythm like this, and we can go for weeks without him turning into a demanding asshole. The only good thing about Ray coming to visit is that it makes Damon and I get along. I know how much he wishes he could "divorce" his brother and never see him again—he tells me every Thursday night after Ray leaves. Every Thursday night, for the past almost-decade, we've had the same conversation. But not this week. Because this Thursday night, *Ray didn't leave.*

Ray's never stayed overnight before. It's weird. He's never worried about drinking and driving before—ironic since his brother is a police officer. Still. Our delicate schedule has been altered, and it makes my skin crawl. I like predictability. I like routine. I like not having a fucking creep on my sofa in the morning.

"Where's Ray?" Damon asks, sipping at the coffee. His blue eyes close when he takes that first sip, like he's in heaven or something, and it makes me unreasonably satisfied that my coffee-making skills do that to somebody. At least I'm good for something.

"Smoking," I say, pointing at the back door that leads from the kitchen to the backyard.

Damon nods, leaning against the counter beside me. He's dressed in his tan-colored sheriff's uniform, gun holstered snugly on his hip. All he's missing is the hat.

"He give you any grief?" he asks quietly.

I shake my head. "No. He was fine."

No use upsetting Damon unless his brother actually does something. Being born creepy in itself isn't a crime. Should be in his case, but still.

"He'll leave, soon," Damon says, and I'm not sure if he's trying to reassure me, or himself.

Ray swaggers back into the kitchen, reeking of burnt tobacco.

"You should put on a bra, young lady," he says, staring at my chest. "Somebody might get the wrong idea."

I feel blood rise in my cheeks, my arms crossed as tightly as possible. "OhmyGod," I mutter under my breath. Seriously?

"Ray!" Damon says. He glances at me before fixing his eyes on his oblivious brother.

"If I had a daughter like Cassie, I sure as hell wouldn't let her run around like that." He sips his coffee like talking about my tits is the most casual thing in the world. I look down at my pajamas, then at

Damon, with a look that says, "*Help me*." "I didn't know you were here," I say slowly.

Ray chuckles. "So if I wasn't here, you'd be fine wearing a see-through shirt with your titties on display for my poor brother here to try not to stare at?"

"Ray!" Damon yells.

An edge develops across Ray's expression. "What. She's the spitting image of her poor mother. What do you want me to say?"

Jesus Christ. I need to get out of here. I back up until I'm at the base of the stairs. "You're absolutely right. I should get dressed."

"And we should get going," Damon says tightly.

"See you next week, Ray," I call over my shoulder, climbing the stairs to my bedroom and closing myself in there. Fuck you, Ray! I take my shirt off, my eye catching movement in the yard at the same time. Ray's back outside, smoking again as he stands by his truck. He's looking up at the house, though I doubt he can see anything from this angle. I close the curtains properly and then get naked, searching through messy drawers for something to wear. After I drag on clean clothes, I flip Ray the bird through the thick drapes as I hear the rumble of his truck starting. He can't see my obscene gesture, but somehow it makes me feel better.

CHAPTER ELEVEN

Leo

On Friday, the day after Thanksgiving, Pike and I load the kids up in the backseat of his shitty Honda and drive into town. I don't want anyone seeing me, but in this Podunk town, that's easier said than done.

Especially when Pike is driving around slowly, almost leisurely, with me in the passenger seat. Like a fucking Sunday drive with Miss Daisy.

"Dude, step on it," I say with gritted teeth.

"*Dude*, this is as fast as we go with five of us," Pike replies. "Fix your fucking Mustang and we can talk about stepping on it."

I glare at him. "I crashed the Mustang, you idiot. Remember?"

"It's in Lawrence's yard, bro. You're a mechanic. Figure it out."

My chest tightens as I remember the corner of Lawrence's Auto Repair where old cars go to die. I guess I've never really thought about where my car went after the accident. I've blocked it from my memory, just like the accident itself. Suddenly I'm antsy, wondering if the wreck might be salvageable. I could never drive it around here, but maybe one day, when I finally get my license back and leave Gun Creek. . . .

Speaking of. I wanted to come out by myself, but I'm not allowed to drive, a condition of my early release. Guess that's fair when you almost kill somebody with your car.

Eventually, we get to the garage next to Dana's Grill. I've come to beg for my old job back. I expect my former boss to chase me out of the place with his old sawn-off, but when Lawrence sees me he drops everything and shakes my hand.

"You're back," the old man says as if I didn't almost kill somebody last time I saw him. As if I've been gone for the weekend, instead of almost a decade. "I've got a sticky one for you. . . ."

And he shows me Mrs. Lassiter's old Buick on the hoist, pointing out bits of rust and parts that need replacing, and eventually I have to stop him talking so I can get the kids home before they freeze to death in the car outside. He won't let me go until I promise to come back and start work on Monday morning.

While Pike is getting bread in the store, Sheriff King walks right by our car. He stops dead when he sees me, and I don't think I've ever seen someone look so full of hate.

I can't say I blame him. Pike does odd shifts as a patient care assistant at the hospital sometimes, with Amanda. Apparently she's the night nurse for Teresa King, and she told Pike once that Cassie's mom is the saddest patient she has ever had to deal with.

I can't help myself.

After Pike drives us all home, the kids set up in front of the TV and watch cartoons. Pike leaves, for what I don't ask. The less I know about the shit he's up to, the better.

In the time I've spent at home, I'm going crazy. Crazier than when I was locked up. And now that I've seen Damon, I want to see Cassie. It's like seeing him has confirmed that she exists. I go full psycho, or at least full armchair stalker, camped out in an old rocking chair by the window, binoculars in hand. I don't think about Jennifer, about what I did to her, and that's a terrible thing, isn't it? I should be sorry for what I did to her, but I'm just . . . not. Maybe the feelings will come later. Maybe the image of the way I left her will stop making my balls ache, and instead make me feel guilty.

Binoculars in hand, I search all day for Cassie. I cast my magnified gaze along the windows that line the front of her house on the hill, but I don't see anything. She keeps the blinds drawn. Almost like she's afraid of catching a glimpse of this old place and remembering me. But in the evening, just as I hear Pike's car in the driveway, I finally glimpse her.

It's just for a second, and it's so fleeting I'm not even sure she's real, but there she is: curtains flung open, looking out into the orangey dusk as it rapidly turns black. My chest hurts when I see her. I think about going up there, to her place, breaking in, taking her away. She'd struggle, but Jennifer struggled, piece of cake. I'm stronger than Cassie. I'm stronger than ever. I could have her in the back of Pike's car in under a minute, some rope around her wrists, duct tape to seal her protests away. I could drive her somewhere far away, somewhere out in the mountains where nobody would ever find us. Keep her there until I could make her understand how much I still love her. Keep her there until she loves me back.

Rage courses through me. I ball up a fist and slam it into the side of my skull, hard enough that I see stars for a second. *Don't you ever think about hurting her,* the good part of me commands. I hit myself again, in the fleshy part of my temple. *Don't you ever show your face to that poor girl again.*

I won't. I will stay away from Cassandra Carlino, even if it kills me. Even if I have to kill myself to keep my greedy heart from trying to have her.

She will not be my vice. She will not be my forgiver. She will not be my redemption.

These are the promises I make to myself. These are the lies I cannot bear to admit.

Old habits die hard; old addictions, even harder. Because sometimes, no matter how hard you try to slay your demons, they just won't stay dead. Like a moth to a fucking flame, I find myself standing in front of the refrigerator, the door flung open, my mouth watering as I look for my favorite poison. My eyes light up as I spy a six-pack of Budweiser, my tongue already wet and bursting with the flavor of something I haven't tasted in nearly a decade. I grab at the glass bottles feverishly, the balm that will ease my suffering, the thing that will wipe away the scent of Jennifer, the memory of Cassie, the taste of Karen and the well. I put the six-pack on the counter and rip a bottle from the rest, the twist-top popping away neatly in my palm like a sharp blade in butter, like a shovel in wet soil. It's that easy, *clink*, and then I'm lifting the bottle to my lips, ready for froth and hops and cold relief.

I'm excited, but I'm afraid, as well. My hand shakes from the anticipation, from the knowing of what comes next.

"Leo."

I'm so deeply entranced by the beer in my hand, I almost have a fucking heart attack and die, on the floor of the kitchen in my mother's shitty trailer. I startle violently, spilling beer all down my shirt, my jeans, onto the floor, the hypnotic spell broken. Now, I just feel embarrassed. And sticky. And cold.

"Hannah." She's standing in the doorway that separates the living space from the bedrooms, and she looks like she's been crying. I set the beer down, worry for my sister eclipsing my dirty drink cravings—for now, at least. I reach out to her, noticing the way she's holding her swollen stomach, the fear in her eyes. "What's wrong, kiddo?"

"I can feel something," she says. "Here." She takes my hand and places it on her stomach. Something inside my sister's stomach hits me square in the palm and I jerk my hand away, staring at her. It takes me a split-second to realize what I'm feeling, and then I let out the breath I've been holding.

"See?" she says, starting to cry again. "What's happening to me?"

I put my hand back on the same spot, a smile just for my sister. "Hannah, that's your baby. Your baby's kicking. It's saying hello."

I guide her hand back to the spot where her baby is currently holding a boxing match of one. She's awestruck, and I can understand why. I remember so many times, when I was tiny, *Leo, give me your hand.* When Ma had good days. When she was pregnant with Hannah, and she'd take my little-boy hand and place it on her stomach and say, *Leo, your sister is saying hello. Can you feel her saying hello?* And I'd always marvel at the way you could love somebody before they existed, when they didn't even know the world yet. I'd marvel at the way my mother was, all at once, so cruel, so kind, so in love with her children from the moment she learned she was pregnant, yet so determined to destroy us.

"It's okay?" Hannah asks uncertainly, her big eyes searching mine for reassurance. I nod, swallowing back the lump in my throat. Because she's fourteen. And she's my sister. And this shouldn't have happened to her.

"Get some sleep, kiddo," I say, giving her shoulders an affectionate squeeze.

"Thanks, Leo," she replies, wandering off. That's the beautiful thing about Hannah—you tell her something and she accepts it. I know she won't worry now. She'll probably spend the rest of her pregnancy poking her stomach, saying hello back.

I turn back to the beer. My sweet poison, the destroyer of worlds. Whatever runs through my veins, it calls out to the alcohol cells suspended inside the wheat-liquid brew, begging. *Come back to me.* Disgust holds me tight and slams me down, again and again. *You are pathetic.* I open the other five bottles and upend all of them at once, watching blankly as beer froths up and pours down the sink.

I hear movement behind me and look over my shoulder. It's Pike. "Hey," he says.

I make a sound in the back of my throat. I would say hey back, but my eyes are burning and that lump's in my throat and I can't speak, so I just stare into the sink instead. The smell of the beer makes me want to vomit.

"Glad you're back," Pike says, edging closer. "You okay?"

I gulp down a breath. Nod.

"You've always had this way of looking after everybody," Pike says. "You know? I never had that."

I brace myself over the sink.

I nod again.

CHAPTER TWELVE

Cassie

It storms on Friday.

Damon has to work during the day, and when he finally comes home, he disappears upstairs without so much as a hello. I don't try to find him.

Sometimes he likes to be with people, and other times, he demands to be left alone.

I hear him shower and close his bedroom door around eleven. Once I know he's asleep, I double-check all the locks in the house and turn in for the night.

Thunder wakes me. Thunder and frantic barking. I throw the covers off and reach for my thick robe and boots, slipping them on before I hurry downstairs.

I unlock the back door, expecting Rox to barrel past me into the house, but she doesn't. "Rox!" I coax. "Hey!"

The wind is fierce. It's raining, cold little ice pellets that remind me of the night of the accident. I feel sick thinking about it.

I hear movement upstairs, a door opening. Shit. If Damon has to come downstairs, he'll be pissed. He loves other dogs, but this one used to belong to Leo. A painful reminder of what happened to Mom.

But she's my dog now, and she's one thing I won't let him take away from me. I don't have any real friends anymore, apart from Rox, and I think that's the only reason he lets me keep her around.

I call the dog's name a few more times, but she totally ignores me. Jesus. I go outside, holding on to the railing as lightning flashes close by. Stupid dog. "Come here!" I yell at her. She's not even looking at me, transfixed on the house. It's like she's barking directly into the bedrooms to get our attention.

I'm halfway to the dog when I feel someone behind me. Damon's on the top step.

"Get inside," he snaps at me, over the noise of the weather.

I ignore him, approaching Rox.

"Cassie! Jesus Christ, girl." He follows me.

"She doesn't like the weather," I say. "She's old and senile, Damon."

He shrugs. "And?"

"Let me bring her inside."

He shakes his head. He hates her. "No."

"The garage."

He opens his mouth as if he's going to say something but changes his mind halfway. "One night," he says. "One goddamn night and then I'm taking that mutt back down to their property. She's not even yours."

He's threatened that countless times before; I don't even argue. He won't take her back. Or he will, and she'll bound back up here to me before he's even driven his car back to the road from Leo's property.

Can't keep a dog like that chained up or tell her where to stay. She's a free spirit, probably why I like her so much.

Damon reaches down to grab her collar, and Rox, poor old cataract-riddled Rox, jumps in fright, her teeth snapping at the bit of flesh between Damon's thumb and index finger.

He doesn't even hesitate. Almost like he knew this was going to happen. Like he was prepared.

Damon takes his gun out of his waistband and shoots Rox right between the eyes.

I scream.

She's dead before she hits the ground.

Everything around me dulls, slows down. I feel like I'm in one of those carnival rides that spins so fast it actually feels like you're moving in slow motion.

"Shit," Damon says, as I sink to my knees, one hand on the last piece of Leo that I could touch. I can't form words. I can't even think. He shot my dog. My dog is dead. How am I going to tell Leo?

And then: Oh, right. I'm not going to tell him. Anything. Ever again.

"Y-you shot her."

He looks around with an air of impatience, and his casual manner terrifies me.

"I better not get rabies from that cunt dog," he says, studying the bite on his hand like his arm's been amputated or something. The killing of an innocent animal doesn't bother him. Not in the slightest. I never would've picked him as the kid who burned ants with the magnifying glass, the boy who threw a sack of kittens in a lake. The man who shot a dog for barking.

"Get up," he says. "Now."

My shock gives way to panic, coupled with disbelief. I start to cry. I'm shaking all over, from the cold and from the adrenaline.

"Why?" I whisper. "Why did you do that?"

He makes a noise in the back of his throat, something akin to annoyance. Fuck him. I'm not leaving my dead dog out here to the elements. My chest hurts as I watch dark blood pool on the frozen ground beneath her still body.

"Fuck you," I say. "I hate you!"

"For Christ's sake, Cassandra," he says, fisting a hand into my hair and yanking me to my feet. "Come inside."

He drags me into the kitchen, despite my protests, despite my tears.

I break away from him; seeking comfort, seeking numbness and warmth. My eyes land on a bottle of vodka, my absolution in a bottle of Absolut. I twist the cap off, taking a slug of the good stuff and biting the inside of my cheeks as it burns all the way down. My eyes sting; my stomach reacts angrily, but I swallow it down. I drink as much as I can, *onetwothree*, and then Damon tugs the bottle from my grasp.

We stare at each other as I grip the metal Absolut lid in my palm, hard enough so it cuts into my skin and blood springs forth.

"Cassie," he says, and his gun is still in his hand. "That bitch bit me. I'm sorry. Okay?" And he really does look sorry.

I start sobbing again. Not okay. I fall to my knees. There are splinters in the wooden floor, and it hurts when they dig into my flesh.

"Come on," he sighs, holding out a hand. "Let's get you upstairs. I'll run you a warm bath and get you some milk. You'll catch a cold if you stay on the floor like that."

"I don't want to go upstairs," I say, drawing my knees to my chest.

Damon kneels, taking my arm and looping it over his shoulders. He pulls me to my feet, bearing most of my weight, and steers me to the hallway on reluctant legs. "I wasn't asking," he replies, pulling me upstairs.

The bath is hot. The milk is warm. Outside, I imagine Rox's body is already cold. As cold as Damon's gaze as he watches me shiver in a cast-iron bathtub full of scalding water, as I wash bits of blood and dog fur from my skin.

Damon's phone rings while I'm washing blood from the ends of my hair; at the same time, I hear the crackle of his two-way radio downstairs. He looks at me as if torn between staying in the fogged-up bathroom and answering the call. He answers after three rings, his eyes trained on me.

"Chris."

Chris speaks loud enough for me to hear; Damon and I hear the news at the same time. Jennifer Thomas is missing. She went to work, she left her shift right on time, texted her mother to say she'd be home late, and she hasn't been seen since.

That was last night.

There's another girl missing in Gun Creek. It's been nine years since Karen, but the feeling in my stomach is the same as it was the moment I laid eyes on her in that well. It's the feeling of a knife blade floating in your gut, waiting for you to move, waiting to cut you to ribbons from the inside.

CHAPTER THIRTEEN

Cassie

On Saturday, we eat breakfast in silence. I'm not hungry, but I get cereal served again anyway, Cinnamon Toast Crunch this time. I swear Damon only buys cereal so he can get the free toys. A grown man, and he collects shit from cardboard boxes and fast-food meals. They're like trophies for him, lined up on top of the refrigerator, above the fireplace, on the windowsill that looks out from the kitchen into the yard.

Damon was gone all night. Missing girls tend to demand the presence of the town sheriff, especially when her family is high profile like Jennifer's. He looks exhausted, his blue eyes rimmed with red, his clothes creased. He's only here to change his shirt and take me to the diner, fifteen minutes of calm in a case that could last days. Weeks. Months. Maybe they'll find her today. Maybe she ran away. Maybe she's dead in a well. Maybe she's gone forever.

"I'm not leaving Rox out there all day," I say, my words level and clear despite the panic bubbling up inside my stomach. I can't face her body. I can't face my fucking life anymore. I can't face the shit show I know I'll be walking into at the diner. I need a shot of vodka or a handful of pills, or both.

Damon turns his bleary eyes to me. "Well, then, you've got about three minutes to go and bury her," he snaps.

A small portable television sits on the kitchen counter, switched on to the local news filling the room with static-edged chatter. I hear the words *missing girl* and my ears prick up, something to take my attention away from this kitchen and the unbearable tension that fills it. I pick dry squares of cereal out of my bowl and crunch them between my teeth slowly, at least giving off the appearance of trying to eat something.

The news. It draws me in, greedy moth to overhead light. MISSING GIRL. A picture of Jennifer flashes up, her bleached-white smile dazzling, dressed in her cheerleading uniform. I have a matching outfit upstairs, though I haven't worn it in years. The reporter keeps talking about Jennifer, how she vanished after her shift at Dana's Grill on Thursday evening, how there are no suspects yet. The police aren't sure if it's a kidnapping or a runaway teen. She'd been fighting with her parents on Thanksgiving morning, took herself off to work in the afternoon, and then she was just *gone*.

"They used to put missing kids on milk cartons," Damon says, gesturing at the television. "Now everybody's got a TV and a cell phone."

He's right. I imagine everyone in Gun Creek will be glued to their phones today, refreshing the local news websites, sending frantic messages. *Did you see Jennifer on Friday?* She will be revered, her cheerleading photo plastered across town. I already know this—I've lived it once before when Karen went missing.

There are so many people passing through our tiny town each day that Karen's death was blamed on a passerby, a trucker, probably. It made everyone feel safer when all we had to do was watch out for the people we didn't know. Nobody wanted to believe that one of our own was capable of such a horrific crime. But now, nine years later, it's happening again.

Predictably, the reporter shifts to talking about Karen's case— Karen Brainard, seventeen years old, dead before she'd ever lived.

They gloss over the real Karen. The deeply flawed Karen.

She fucked anything that moved, including the entire football team.

She got high more days than not.

Karen Brainard wasn't a very nice person, truth be told. She was kind of an asshole.

But she had a pretty face, a newsworthy face, and so in death, she is a hero, she is tragic, she is *perfection*.

People will be talking about Karen Brainard today.

The report switches back to Jennifer, urging the public to call a special hotline if anyone knows anything. 1-800-JENNIFER. I feel sorry for the operators. I feel sorry for Karen. Karen didn't come from a rich family. Karen didn't get a hotline. Karen didn't even get a poster with her face on it until she'd already been missing for days, and by then it was too late.

"Are you looking for her?" I ask Damon.

He scowls at me. "What do you think? I'm the sheriff. Of course, I'm looking for her. Whole town's looking for her. Where have you been?"

He looks me up and down. "You keep doing you, darlin'. The rest of us'll look for your friend Jennifer." He reaches across and pushes the off button on the TV, the screen going black as a familiar silence settles around us once more.

She's not my friend, I want to say, but I don't, biting down on the tip of my tongue instead.

I lick my chapped lips and drink more coffee.

"Do you think she's dead?" I ask.

Damon gets up, deposits his empty bowl in the sink, and turns to me as he collects his keys from the counter.

"We'll be late," he says. "Get your things."

I make the mistake of using the rear door to leave the house, and that's where my worst nightmare springs back to life. My dog is still dead. It wasn't a dream, it really happened, but I can't bury her myself and I've got nobody to help me. I stop beside her stiff body, kneeling to pat her snow-dusted fur. I choke back a sob as I embrace her stiff form, and if my sorrow was enough to bring her back to life, she would stand up now and wag her tail. It's not enough, though. The aching grief at her passing only seeps into my bones like a cold, cruel poison.

"Hey," Damon calls out, already in the car.

I have to swallow down another sob and walk away from her, to the car.

In the passenger seat of Damon's police car sits a stack of colored posters. Jennifer beams from her yearbook photo, high-definition and full of pep.

I pick up the stack of posters and balance them across my thighs as Damon drives through the snow littering our driveway, my eyes only for Jennifer, the worst parts of me imagining how she died, what they did to her first, and by whose hand. I do not look up again. I don't want to see the outline of my dog, her blood frozen in patches around her, a hole in her skull the size of a nickel.

CHAPTER FOURTEEN

Cassie

The center of town is teeming with reporters when we arrive. The mood is somber, self-conscious even. Can an entire town be collectively self-conscious? They're shy, that's for sure. We don't get a whole lot of visitors in Gun Creek. Certainly not ones who stick microphones in your face and blast you with questions while you're still half asleep.

Damon parks the patrol car right across the front doors of the police station, his face drawn and tense. It must be a fucking nightmare, being in charge of an entire town like this. Especially when something like this happens.

I can only imagine how bad things are going to get at home if they don't find this girl soon.

"These people are fucking vultures," he mutters, and I make a noise signaling my agreement. He gets out, then opens my door for me, taking my purse from my lap before I can stop him.

I muster up a plastic smile as Damon holds out my purse, the strap dangling on his outstretched finger.

"Thanks," I say, taking the bag and slinging it over my shoulder. I put my oversized dollar-store sunglasses on my face, the day already too bright for me to bear.

"You okay?" Damon asks.

"Always," I reply, walking away from him before he can say anything else. I should ask him if he's okay, but that would mean pretending that I care.

I'm an asshole because I know I should be concerned about the fact that a girl I've grown up with is missing, but I have more pressing personal matters. I have something important that I need, something immediate.

I need to take care of myself first. I head for the diner, fifty feet away, already late for my shift. I push past reporters, hanging around eagerly at the doors they're forbidden to cross. They have to hover outside in the snow for their pound of flesh, their sound bites, their newsworthy quotes from Jennifer's distraught friends and family.

I see Casey Mulligan, a girl I went to school with, twirling a strand of long blond hair around a finger as she works up a couple of fat tears for a news camera, and it strikes me, just like last time, that the people who get the most attention in this world are the ones who least deserve it.

Still, I'm glad it's not me. Last thing I want is a camera in my face. I slip by, unassisted, unseen, an invisible girl with a hollow spot inside her. I notice the crates of milk that get delivered to Dana's every morning are still stacked out front and I grab one as I approach, throwing my purse on top and bracing my stomach muscles to carry the thirty-odd pounds of liquid weight. One of our regulars holds the door open for me and I smile in thanks, lugging the milk crate inside.

I'm making my way past rows of tables and customers talking feverishly about Jennifer, my arms full of milk bottles, when it happens.

I see him. *Him.*

I stop.

My arms stop functioning. I drop everything: the milk crate, my purse, my practiced neutral expression. The purse wafts to the floor, the milk bottles hurtle down with an unceremonious crash, and blue plastic lids burst off and go skittering in every direction.

I sink to my knees, in shock. People are looking at me, but I don't pay attention to them. I'm too busy fixated on the green-eyed ghost standing in front of me. The splinters in my knees sting like fire-ant bites, and I curl my legs to the side, coming to a sitting position.

"Shit!" Leo says, dropping to his knees and crouching in front of me. "Cass. Cassie. Are you okay?"

My entire body is alight, little pinpricks along my skin that make me dizzy. The feeling spreads like wildfire, across my chest and through my limbs until I'm overwhelmed and frozen on the spot, sitting on my ass in the middle of the diner, voices and whispers all around. I almost forgot how he looks, how he really looks. My memories of him have been filed down to a dull edge, a blurred flashback, but here he is, flesh and blood in front of me. He's older, but his lips are still full and wide. There are tiny lines at the edges of his green eyes, etches in his skin, years gone by. Growing older suits him. It's as if he's grown into himself, into his broad shoulders and big hands, his strong chin, his sharp jaw. It's as if I'm seeing Leo Bentley for the first time, and I cannot tear my eyes away.

I watch in fascination as milk spreads in a puddle in front of me, like spilled blood. It rushes at me like a miniature tsunami as a painful buzz begins in my head.

"You're gonna pass out," Leo says, his words sounding far away as he reaches out a hand to help me up. "Jesus, Cassie, you're white as a sheet."

I hold my hand out, the conviction in my reach laughable, and it's like that moment of electricity that people talk about.

I can feel it build in my fingertips, that arc of some invisible thing that wants to join with his invisible thing, but then a hand wraps around my wrist and yanks my arm away before I can make contact with the boy—no, with the man—I thought was still in prison.

"Did he hurt you?" Damon's voice in my ear breaks my dream-like state. I open my mouth to say something and decide against it, swallowing air instead. I shake my head.

"How'd you get on the ground?" Damon asks, shaking me a little.

"She fell down," Leo says, his arm no longer outstretched. He takes a step away from me and, Jesus, it hurts. He looks anguished. "She dropped the milk and fell down."

I can't stop looking at him.

I can't *bear* to look at him.

The milk has reached me. It seeps across my right knee, curled underneath me; the backs of my thighs, my palms. It's ice cold, and I can feel myself shaking.

Damon is crouched next to me, his hand on my cheek, diverting my attention to him. "Are you all right, Cassie?" he asks, helping me to my feet, his tone gathering more urgency with each question I don't answer. Amanda is picking up the milk bottles beside us, piling them high in her arms as I continue to stare at Leo. He's . . . different. He has tattoos now. He looks exactly the same but entirely reconstructed. He's eight years older, I realize. A third of his life, gone. A third of *mine*. It feels like it's been forever. It feels like it's been no time at all.

Deputy Chris appears, looking between me and Leo with uncertainty. *Why didn't anyone tell me? How the hell did Leo just materialize from thin air in the Grill?*

"Cassie," Damon snaps, and I know he means business.

I nod. "I'm fine. I'm okay." I think of where I was going before I saw fucking Leo. *Purge. Pills.* "I need a minute."

"I'll take you home," he says, his hand on the small of my back as he starts to guide me toward the front doors.

I panic, pushing him away. "You have a missing girl to find," I say quickly. "I'm fine, really. I just need some aspirin." And a fucking gun, so I can put myself out of my misery.

"I'll walk you to the back room," Damon says, ever the hero. *If they only knew,* I think, as Amanda opens the staff room door and ushers us inside.

"Give us a minute." Damon gives Amanda a concerned look. She nods, closing the door as my stepfather draws the blinds and twists the lock on the door.

"Didn't think he'd have the balls to show his face in public," Damon says, and that's when I understand.

I feel the blood drain from my cheeks as I realize. *He knew. He knew Leo was back in town.* I ask him with my eyes, searching, imploring. His expression tells me everything.

"You should have told me he was back," I whisper.

His eyes narrow. "I considered it. Figured it was better you didn't know in advance." He pauses. "Didn't expect you to fall to your knees in front of him."

"Fuck you," I seethe.

Damon's jaw twitches. "I'm sorry," he offers, almost as if he's suggesting an apology rather than delivering one.

I reach for the lock, twisting it and cracking the door open. The temporary quiet we've had is pierced by the excited noise of a diner that's just witnessed the tragic reunion of two star-crossed lovers, or maybe they're all just gossiping about the missing girl with the football-star brother.

"Jennifer," I spit at Damon. One word. It works. He shakes his head, his blue eyes fucking burning with anger, but he leaves.

Holy shit. As soon as he's gone, I close the door again. I don't bother locking it—who's going to find me in here? My head throbs under the bright lights. Rubbing my temple, I switch them off, plunging the room into near-darkness. *Better.*

Leo's long gone if he's got any sense, and as much as I don't care about anything, the thought of Amanda having to mop up the milk I spilled makes me so fucking guilty I can barely breathe.

Purge. Pills. *Yes.*

I go into the staff bathroom, a small tiled square off the main staff room, and start to throw up as soon as the door is closed. I don't even need to stick my finger down my throat—I'm so full of adrenaline from seeing Leo, I just open my mouth and everything comes out. It's the kind of vomit that gets in your nose and burns behind your eyes and makes you cry with the way it chokes you.

When I've emptied my stomach and I stop gagging, I clean myself up, my head feeling like it might split in two. I'm so hot I think I might burst into flames. I take off my cardigan, my fingers clumsy and damp, and use it to wipe my face.

Pills. I go back out to the dim staff room, seeking whatever pharmaceutical bliss I can rummage up from my locker. The only illumination comes from the slightly ajar bathroom door and the fluorescent strips that line its ceiling.

The staff room is empty. Except . . . it's not.

Leo. He's here. Somehow, the only person here with me is the one person I shouldn't be anywhere near.

He looks at me with eyes that have seen violence since I last gazed into them. I know because I recognize the hardness inside his soul; it matches mine.

My face is a blank canvas, but inside I'm screaming.

Not with fear. With *longing.* I want the boy who destroyed everything to pick me up and take me into the bathroom and put his hands all over me. I want him to erase every trace of the last decade. Under my shirt, my nipples stiffen, and shame pools in my belly.

I shouldn't want to be anywhere near this boy after what he did, but I do.

"I'm sorry," Leo says. His voice. Oh, God. I don't remember his voice being that fucking beautiful. It's deep and full and if it were a food, it'd be honey. *He's not a boy anymore.* He's a man now. A stranger.

His face falls as he gestures to my stomach, concerned. "You have blood on your shirt," he says, pointing from a safe distance. "Did you cut yourself when you fell?" Shit. I look down at my shirt as I remember hugging Rox. How do I tell Leo? He looks so remorseful. Like he thinks the blood is his fault.

My heart sinks. I shake my head tightly, tears springing to my eyes.

"Not my blood," I say, my voice coming out like a squeak. Leo looks confused.

"The dog," I stammer. "Rox. She—she—"

"I saw her yesterday," Leo says, his eyes wide as he looks from my eyes to my shirt. I didn't even realize the blood was there until he pointed it out. I'd been wearing my sweater until I took it off just now.

"She's dead," I say. "I'm sorry."

Leo takes a step back. Something passes over his face, a darkness, a fleeting suspicion. "How?" he asks.

I don't know how to answer that. So I don't. I push past him and start walking to the kitchen, as fast as I can, because I don't have an answer for him. My shoulder burns from where I grazed his arm on the way out of the staff room. He might have ruined my life, destroyed my family, taken my future in one careless night—but Leo Bentley still makes me burn like hellfire.

CHAPTER FIFTEEN

Leo

"Bentley."

I know that voice. *Fuck.*

I'm working in the garage beside Dana's, fixing up a transmission that decided to fall out of a car and onto the 95 highway a few miles up the road. It's in pieces on the workbench in front of me, grease is all over my palms, and I have a wrench in my hand. I turn around, keeping the wrench at my side. I'm not sure why. Maybe it's just that I feel threatened by the both of them showing up like this. I shouldn't. *I'm* the fuck up. I'm the killer in this town.

"Hey, Sheriff. Chris," I greet them.

I nod politely at each of them, but my singular focus is Damon King. What I feel when I look at him can't even be adequately conveyed. It's somewhere between intense fear and crippling shame, an uneasiness that burns in my chest and leaves me feeling like I want to start punching myself in the head.

Damon and I spent plenty of time together, before. He's a good guy, and that somehow makes it worse. He coached the football team before, back when I played, and he's the fucking sheriff of a shithole town that most people want to get out of, not get into. He's a nice guy. I would have called him a good friend, before.

Yeah. Damon and I were close before I killed his wife. And I know she's *technically not dead*, but I'm pretty sure being dead would have been better than the way I left Teresa King.

And Chris. Man, we grew up together. We played football together.

"How can I help you?" I ask, not sure what to do with my hands.

Damon casually unsnaps his gun holster, the noise deafening in the quiet of the garage. Hands on his hips, he surveys the garage, taking in every little detail. I blanch for a moment when I realize there's a photo of Cassie and me still tucked into the back of my toolbox. The lid's open, and when I look past Damon, I can see Cassie's smiling face in the photograph, a fragmented moment of days long past. Chase took the photo one day at the lake in the months before we found Karen. We'd spent all summer on the lake's dirt shore, parked in our folding picnic chairs, or when it was really hot, just sitting in the shallow waters, trying to keep cool.

"You know Jennifer Thomas?" Damon asks, coming to a stop in front of me. His smile seems genuine, friendly, even, but it's the eyes that have me gripping the end of my wrench so tight my fingers start to go numb. His eyes look fucking crazed, and I think he knows it.

My heart sinks when he mentions Jennifer. Of course. *Of course.*

"Yeah," I say. "Her brother and I went to school together. Before— well, you know."

"Before you killed my wife?"

I wince because he's right. "Yes, sir."

Damon nods. I glance at Chris, behind him, blending into the scenery like he's not even here. He's an unassuming guy, and I guess that's the point. Can't have two alpha dogs competing for control. Chris McCallister's meek and mild temperament makes him the perfect second-in-command.

"Seen her lately?" Damon presses.

"No, sir." Do I answer too quickly?

I glance at the toolbox again. It's in my eyesight, but unless he turns around to face away from me, he won't see it. Somehow, I don't think he'll be letting me out of his sight.

"You look nervous," Damon says. "You want to think about your answer a little harder?"

It feels suffocating being under his microscope. I'm prideful and full of kickback when somebody chats me up, but in this case, I can't say a damn thing, because he's justified.

"You nervous because you're hiding something?" he asks.

I shake my head. "No, sir. Just—I've been meaning to come around to your house and talk, is all. To apologize."

Damon's jaw tightens. "Don't do that. Bad idea, kid."

I haven't been called a kid in a very long time.

"Yeah," I agree, letting my eyes drop to the floor.

"You mind if we look around?" Damon asks, glancing about the workshop again. "I mean, we can get a warrant, but that's a lot of paperwork, and I hate paperwork. Caring for my wife doesn't really allow a lot of extra time for paperwork, you know what I mean?"

I put the wrench down, picking up a rag as I wipe my oil-soaked hands. "Sure," I say, a nervous feeling spreading in my chest. "Look at whatever you want. Nothing to hide here."

I think about the last time I saw Jennifer. Shit, it was so recent, they'd probably still find traces of her DNA on the shirt I was wearing when she pulled off the road and asked me if I thought she was pretty. Jesus, fuck. I could have saved myself a lot of shit by just telling her to put the car back in gear and fucking drive.

"Anything we might find?" Damon asks, gesturing to Chris to start moving, too. I trail after them, keeping my eye on my toolbox, praying like hell that Damon doesn't notice the photograph.

"A lot of oil and busted car parts," I reply, glancing outside.

"What about out back?" Damon asks, following my eyes.

I shrug. "A lot of rusted-out cars."

My old Mustang is out there. *Shit.* They towed it out back here straight after the accident, and it's never moved from its spot. I only know this because Pike told me, because old Lawrence has been stripping it for spare parts for the better part of a decade.

Damon makes a beeline for the back door, sliding it open and stepping outside. It's not snowing today, but the cold air that snakes inside is frigid. I want my jacket, but I don't want to leave the police officers alone in my garage. Before, I would have had no such qualms, but these days I don't trust anybody.

I forgo a jacket, stepping outside in my overalls, thankful at least that they've got long arms to cover my skin. It's going to be a real bitch here when summer rolls around, and I have to expose my scarred arms, burned in the accident, for all the world to see. The cold bites at me; the cold, and the reality of my situation.

"Would you look at all these cars?" Damon says, almost like he's impressed by the junkyard afforded by cheap land and a hoarding boss. Most of these heaps are completely useless, should be crushed for scrap, but try telling Lawrence that. Sometimes I think he was deprived of having any toys as a child and he's making up for it now with this auto graveyard.

"The things you could hide in a place like this," Damon says, and there's a painful stab in my gut. It feels like the time I got stabbed in the yard, almost bled out, and spent two weeks in the infirmary while my wound healed. Only there's no blood this time. Just the sharp realization that I am *fucked*.

They think I took Jennifer.

They think I killed Jennifer.

I want to tell them I didn't, that they're looking at the wrong guy, but I don't. Because they haven't actually accused me of anything. The more I say, the guiltier I'll look. Then again, if I say nothing, am I making myself look uncooperative?

Fuck.

"I don't have anything to hide, Sheriff," I say, my hands shoved in my pockets to ward off the chill. I trail behind him as he pokes his head into old, beat-up car bodies. I start to head back toward the garage, hoping he'll follow me, but, of course, he sees exactly what I don't want him to see.

"Ahh," he says, his words edged with glass, "the infamous Mustang. It survived, huh?"

"If you call that survived," I say to the ground. "Yes, sir."

Damon chuckles, picking up a crowbar that I've been using to beat the dents out of the car so I can get on to replacing the twisted chassis.

"The goddamn car that killed my wife," he says, one hand trailing along her hood, the part that escaped the fire and the impact.

I don't say anything. Not when he touches the car, his fingers almost tender as they skate along her polished curves, and not when he lifts the crowbar up and smashes it down onto the metal, leaving a deep dent and taking layers of paint off.

He smashes that crowbar down, and I flinch, imagining it's my skull. I know that's what he'd prefer.

A few more hits and he throws the crowbar to the ground at my feet, no hint of congeniality in his expression anymore.

"We'll bring the cadaver dogs from Reno," he says, wiping his hands on his pant legs. "If you've got a body in here, you can move it, but we'll still find the trail."

"I don't have a body here—you don't even know if she's dead!"

"You got her stashed away in that shithole you call a house, then?"

"I don't have her," I snap. "I don't know what happened to her, okay?"

Damon winces, looking down at his hand. It's swathed in a thick bandage, and I can see fresh blood rising through the white gauze.

"Are you okay?" I ask. "Your hand."

He frowns, wiggling his fingers beneath the bandage. "She was a sweetheart, that dog of yours," he says, and I notice the faint shape his blood forms under the bandage, a half-crescent between his thumb and forefinger that looks like a nasty bite. A deep one. "Somebody ran her over, so sad. Can you believe they didn't even stop? She was on her way down to your place. Must have known you were back."

I'm not sure whether to believe him.

"Somebody smashed their car *right* into her." He pauses. "She was in such a bad way. I had to put a bullet in her to end her suffering. You ever seen a dog die? They're survivalists. Dogs are so fuckin' stubborn. Takes forever for them to stop fighting."

My eyes are burning, and there's a lump in my throat. I loved that dog. I loved her and he shot her. I killed his wife. I have no right to be pissed.

"Sad, isn't it? Cassie was beside herself. Christ, I had to sleep next to her all night. Cried so hard she wouldn't let go of me. You remember how she can be."

The image of Damon sleeping beside my Cassie is a punch in the face; rage blossoms inside me, and it must show on my face, because Damon laughs, resting his hand atop his gun holster. "Hey, whoa, don't go getting the wrong idea. She's like a daughter to me." His smile dries up. "She's *everything* to me."

Something in his words disturbs me, but I can't figure out what. Maybe I'm just jealous as fuck that he got to wipe away her tears while I slept alone.

"Be seeing you, Bentley," Damon says, walking back inside like he didn't just bust my car up. "Let's go check that well," he says to Chris, who's just standing there like a goddamn mute, his hands folded neatly behind his back. *Let's go check that well.* I don't even bother to address that statement. We live on state land, modern-day squatters in our own town. Damon can search the well, hell, he can move into the well, and there'd be nothing I could do about it.

I follow him through the workshop, but before I can cut him off, he's at my toolbox, staring down at the photo, the only thing in the world I have left of Cassandra Carlino.

He plucks the photograph out of my toolbox and holds it up to me. "I'll be taking this," he says, stuffing it into his pocket. "Guess you'll have to find something else to jerk off to, huh?"

His tone is light, but his eyes are fucking incinerating me, they're full of so much hate. He climbs into the patrol car, only taking his eyes off me when he's driving onto the shoulder, signaling to get back onto the highway.

I make a mental note to go home and burn the clothes I was wearing when I last saw Jennifer in the woods.

"Bentley!" a voice barks about an hour later as I'm working underneath a car in Lawrence's garage. *Jesus, what's with all the visitors?*

I almost drop my wrench on my face. I know that voice. Hal Carter. *Mayor* Carter. I don't want to see his fat ass today. I pretend like I haven't heard him and keep tightening the nut on the bolt I've just affixed to the underside of old Mrs. Lassiter's Buick.

This damn car may as well be held together with Band-Aids and honeycombed rust, but the old lady owner is practically a fossil, and she knows I'll only charge her for the cost of the parts.

Seems wrong to charge folks for things when they don't have any money to begin with.

"Hey, kid," the voice shrills again, "my car's got a dent in it. I need it fixed. *Today.*"

I grip the wrench tightly. It takes everything inside me not to roll out from underneath the car and punch Mayor Carter's face until it caves in, so I hold on to my rage, letting it disperse and settle back into my veins like dirty coffee grounds in the bottom of the pot.

"Busy!" I yell, continuing with my task. Knowing my luck, the engine in this car will fall on my face and crush me if I'm under here too long. "Try Tonopah."

The fucker kicks my boot. Kicks it! It's like a hot shot of rage-spiked adrenaline to the heart. I squeeze the wrench in my hand so tight my fingers start to tingle and go numb.

"I let you stay in this town because you're the only one with a fucking clue about new cars with those computerized things in them," he says, crouching down to talk to me. He's so close I can smell the coffee on his breath, can see the way his ruddy face perspires in the sun. My eyes travel down to his meaty hands, as I imagine them pawing at my mother. I blink several times, trying to will away the thought, trying to stop myself from murdering this literal motherfucker where he stands—or squats, in this case.

"I've got a mind to call the sheriff and search your property, son. We might just find us something of value."

I don't bother telling him that the sheriff is probably already at my place right fucking now.

"Well, you already found my mother," I reply, trying to keep a lid on my anger. "What else you need?"

"I was thinking, the other day when I was fishing in the creek," Mayor says, all cocky. "Seems a little odd that you find one dead girl in your well, right next to your bedroom, and then another one goes missing just as soon as you blow back into town."

I snort, sliding out from under the car with my wrench still in my fist. I stand up so that I'm taller than Mayor Carter, my frame towering over his. I was always tall, but prison changed me. It's not the sinewy muscle from all the pushups I did beside my bed in the narrow cell I shared. I didn't actually get any taller. It's the way I stand. I don't stand in front of someone like Carter anymore, I stand *over* them. For all the shit that happened there, prison made me ten feet tall and fucking invincible.

"Seems a little odd that I'd call the police if I killed a girl and put her in my well," I reply, using my tongue to shift the wad of mint-flavored gum around my mouth. "Don't you think?"

He stares at me with those beady little eyes, those fucking eyes that look at young girls when he thinks nobody's looking.

"Shit, Carter," I say, "maybe you're the one who butchered Karen up. I mean, maybe she knew something she wasn't supposed to, right?"

"She was my cousin's girl, you fucking cocksucker," he spits, jabbing a finger into my chest.

The rage particles rise again, like piranhas in a tank swarming toward human flesh, frenzied. I want to hit him. *I can't fucking hit him.* Especially not now with Hannah needing me here.

"Kindly remove your finger from my shirt before I *rip* your goddamn arm off," I say in a calm voice. I enunciate every word clearly and slowly. A deadly voice. I wonder if he hears the rage that I feel. I wonder if he knows how close he is to being fucking *murdered* by a kid wearing overalls.

"You gonna fix the car?"

I count to five in my head like the jail psych taught me to. Onetwothreefourfive.

"You said it was dented?" I ask.

Mayor turns around and starts walking back to the car, a newer model Caprice with leather seats and wood trim. I know the car because I've been in one like it before. The mayor sure does like his leather-trim sedans. Pike and I used to sit in the backseat of one just like this and play with the electric windows while Carter visited our mother. When Hannah was born, he stopped coming around, made Mom go to him instead. The inconvenience of seeing your bastard handicapped child was too much for him, I guess. Hannah stayed with Pike and me, and we made sure she was safe while my mother climbed into his car and left her little kids alone, unsupervised, next to a fucking *creek*.

I can't hit him.

Instead, I drop the wrench, selecting a claw hammer from the tools hanging on the wall as I follow him outside. Maybe I'll cave his fucking chest in with the claw-tip.

He points to a small dent on the driver's door. It's so tiny you'd need glasses to see it if you were any older than me. Shit, maybe I do need my glasses. I never wear the things unless I'm trying to read engine numbers or order parts from one of those stupid supply catalogs where everything is printed in size zero font.

"Looks like someone opened their door against it," I say. "What do you want me to do about it?"

He raises his eyebrows. "I want you to fix it, you stupid oaf. Jesus, what that Carlino girl saw in you I'll never know."

Cassie. He's talking about Cassie. Now I know why I brought the claw hammer with me. I smile at Carter, and he looks taken aback. "Maybe you're right," I say. "Here, I'll fix it for free."

And I know I shouldn't because I've been home, what, a week?

But they think I've got something to do with Jennifer, I just know it, and something tells me I won't be in Gun Creek for long before either Sheriff King or Mayor Carter find a way to push me back out.

And I've been in jail for all those fucking years, so violence is the answer to everything for me now.

So, yes. I know I shouldn't allow myself to be provoked. Try telling that to the shark who smells blood in the water.

A look of confusion passes over his face as I pull the hammer back and swing as hard as I can, turning the tiny dent into the size of a small suburb.

"Shit!" he says, stepping back. "You wait till I tell your momma about this."

I swing again and find purchase. It feels fucking good. "Don't talk about my mother," I growl, moving my aim to the driver's side window and shattering the glass in one motion. I hope he sits his fat ass on the shards and bleeds out through his femoral artery.

"You're gonna pay for that, Bentley," he says, backing up another step.

I can't hit him.

"Get the fuck out of my garage," I say, even though it's not my garage at all. "I told you, we're all booked up."

"Maybe I'll just take it off your momma's bill next time I visit her," he says, his eyes flashing with something akin to menace again.

I can't hit him.

I hit him.

Luckily it's with my fist and not with the claw hammer, because if it were the hammer, he'd be dead at my feet right now and Sheriff King would be on his way to gleefully escort me back to prison for the remainder of my natural life.

"Listen, you piece of fuckin' shit," I say, taking him by the scruff of the shirt and pinning his fat ass to the car. His nose is bleeding and I have to be careful that it doesn't get on me. "I know you're Hannah's daddy. Ain't nobody ever said a word about it, but I *know*."

He doesn't say anything. His face pales a little, but he doesn't say a thing.

"Did you really think it wouldn't catch up with you one day?" I ask. "Maybe I should tell your wife. Hell, maybe I should tell the whole fucking town, Hal. I bet they'd love that. A man who can't even cough up child support for his disabled child, much less acknowledge her existence."

Hal leans to the side, spitting a mouthful of blood on the ground. "I'd have you back in prison before you could even get a DNA sample," he sneers. "I got rights. All you have is a ticking bomb called *parole* that's going to blow up your entire life the minute you step one foot wrong."

I chuckle. "I forgot to tell you, Hal. I got a real nice lawyer from LegalAid. Some hotshot from a big law firm in Reno who grew up in these parts. Tough as hell, this woman. She's the only bit of luck I've had in this sorry-ass fucking life. And she'll get your DNA, even if she has to come and bleed it out of you herself. So you stay the fuck away from me and my family, unless you want her to come knocking on your door. You hear?"

He mumbles something unintelligible as I loosen my grip on him.

"What's that?" I snap. "Go on, say it."

His face blanches. "I said, 'You'll be back in prison soon one way or another, you little bastard,'" Carter says, holding his broken face. "And it won't have anything to do with me. It'll be all you, because you're nothing but a useless piece of shit."

I lick my lips, grinning as I run my fingers along the sharp tip of the hammer's claw.

"You still got dogs, Hal?" I ask.

He raises his eyebrows. "What?"

"Yeah, I've seen them before. Yappy little poodles, right?" I stare him down with every ounce of intimidation that I can call up from inside me. "I bet this hammer would take the head clean off a dog that size."

I'm bluffing, of course. I'd never touch a dog. Never hurt an animal. People are an entirely different story.

"Are those dogs good security, though, Hal?" I ask. "Seems they wouldn't provide a wealth of protection. I mean, the teeth on this hammer are bigger than the teeth on a lap dog." To prove my point, I press the tip of the hammer into the center of my palm until I break the skin. Blood wells up and I hold my wound up for the mayor to see. He balks. He probably thinks I'm completely fucking crazy, but that's not a bad thing. You don't mess with crazy people. You leave them well enough alone. You definitely, absolutely do not threaten their mothers or abandon their sisters.

"Seems this wound wouldn't take down an intruder, would it, Hal?"

He swallows, his Adam's apple bobbing in his liver-spotted throat. He sickens me. Everything about him sickens me, and I have to remind myself that at least I know for certain he's not *my* father. That Hannah is simple enough to be kept away from the reality of the man she came from.

"You still live out near the lake, Hal?" I ask pleasantly.

My question makes his eyes pop even wider out of his stupid face. He takes a handkerchief from his pocket and mops the sweat from his head, his hand trembling slightly. Just like a little dog. All bark and no bite.

"You ain't ever getting out of this town, boy, unless it's a one-way ticket back to Lovelock," he says, using the handkerchief to wipe away the blood under his nose. "You remember that."

I stare at the back of his balding head as he gets into his wife's car and imagine how much better it would look if I shattered it with my wrench into a mess of pulpy blood.

CHAPTER SIXTEEN

Cassie

"I need your help," Damon says, cutting through my daydream.

I'm drawing up Mom's evening tube feed into a large plastic syringe, making sure everything is sterile, making sure everything is lined up right. On the other side of the kitchen counter, Damon drops a stack of paper in front of me.

The posters. Jennifer stares out from her yearbook photo. I never noticed before how similar she looks to her brother. They have the same eyes, the same slight upturned noses. Their front teeth are the same shape.

"Cassie."

"Yeah," I reply, setting the syringe down and wiping my hands on my jeans. "You need my help?"

"Can you put these up for me?" He taps his finger on the stack of posters. "And ask your friends to help, too."

I don't have any friends, I want to say to him.

"Sure," I reply.

The next morning, I find my old school backpack in the back of my closet, still adorned with stickers and full of holes. I swallow down a lump in my throat, wipe away the memory, and stuff the pile of Jennifer posters inside. A staple gun from the garage, a roll of duct tape, and I'm set. Damon drives me to the diner where the rest of the volunteers are meeting to go over the plan.

When we enter, the place is full. I hold the door open while Damon knocks his boots against the wall, shaking off the snow and dirt. Amanda is running around like she's possessed, yelling breakfast orders into the kitchen, balancing plates up and down her arms.

I guess pretty girls disappearing is good for business.

Shelly and Chase are here; no kids this time. Shelly looks like she's going to squat and pop out their baby on the diner floor. Everyone is looking at Chase while pretending not to. I scan the place, looking for any sign of Leo, feeling equal parts disappointment and relief when I see he's not here.

Damon ushers everyone to a corner and hands out more stacks of posters. Shelly and Chase have been crying; their eyes are red, their faces lined with stress. I imagine what it would be like if my sister went missing. If I had a sister.

After everyone has their posters and their little maps, Damon takes me aside. I've been assigned the diner and surroundings, most likely so Damon can keep tabs on me.

"Don't go near that fucking garage," Damon murmurs in my ear. "I mean it, Cassie."

I nod. "I won't."

It's cold outside. Snow fell pretty heavily last night, and the place is blanketed in white. I wonder, briefly, if someone should have had the posters laminated to stave off the weather. I grit my teeth, setting my focus on getting this done as quickly as possible. It's not that I don't want to find Jennifer; I just don't see how posters help anything. Maybe it's because I'm used to seeing the glass half empty. Completely empty, if we're being honest. That Jennifer is missing tells me one of two things has happened: Either she has run away from this shithole, or she is dead. Posters don't help either of those things.

I do what I'm told, anyway. I plaster Jennifer's beaming sixteen-year-old face to every store window, every bare brick wall, every pole

I can find. It doesn't take long—the place is pitifully small. When I'm done, I look around the parking lot of the Grill, my heart heavy, Jennifer's eyes following me from the posters I've already attached to every solid surface.

I'm about to staple a poster to the base of a wooden power pole when I notice the remnants of an old poster in the very same spot. Most people wouldn't even see the tiny slivers of paper caught underneath two staples, all that's left of a poster that rotted away eons ago. My blood turns to ice as I realize this is the exact same spot where Leo and I stood nine years ago and stapled a poster of Karen Brainard. This exact spot.

I throw the rest of the Jennifer posters into a nearby trash can.

HAVE YOU SEEN THIS GIRL? No, I haven't. Nobody has. That's the whole fucking point.

CHAPTER SEVENTEEN

Leo

The next day, I skip my shift at the garage. Hannah's been complaining of pains in her stomach, and I need to make sure she's okay. I want to take her to see a proper doctor, but she's terrified of hospitals. She had medical problems when she was little, part of her condition, and now you can't get her into one of those places unless you basically drug her first. Even to take her to the dentist when she had an abscess, Pike and I had to hold her down and make her take some of Mom's strong painkillers to calm her down enough.

The girl's had a lot of trauma in her short little life.

I could drug her now—only I can't drug her—she's pregnant. So I get Pike to drive us to the diner and once most of the breakfast crowd has cleared out, I lead her down the hallway to Amanda's office. Part of me hopes I run into Cassie again. Another part makes sure I pull my baseball cap down low over my face so that even if she were here, we could pretend we didn't see each other.

I've already briefed Amanda on the situation. She's a good person, and she gets us the help we need, sitting Hannah on an old sofa in the corner and speaking to her gently. She has a little thing called a Doppler that she got from Craigslist after I told her about Hannah a few days ago, and she slides it along Hannah's stomach, searching.

There it is. A *clip-clop-clip-clop*, a horse's gallop, over and over. I don't think Hannah understands what it is, or even the notion that there's a real, live baby inside her. After Amanda checks her over, she gives her a menu, tells her to order whatever she wants, and sends her to one of the booths out front.

We step into the hall and watch as Hannah walks, or waddles, past the kitchen pass and slides into a booth. She could be hours—a poor trailer kid being given a free meal is akin to a junkie being given a spoon and a baggie full of pharmaceutical-grade heroin. She's grinning from ear to ear, and I make a mental note to take her to do something like this—the diner visit, not the rest—more often.

"This last year's been tough on your sister," Amanda says. "I try to check in when I can, but your mother hasn't let me past the front door these past months. Now I can see why."

Hannah doesn't go to school. She spends her days in the trailer, watching TV, hanging out, coloring. There's no school that could take her around here, and none of us want to send her away to one of those facilities. I guess I thought by keeping her home, she was more protected.

Guess I thought wrong.

I chew on the inside of my cheek as I mentally berate my mother. "I appreciate that," I say, smiling at Amanda. "Thank you."

"Of course," she replies, as we both watch Hannah slide her finger along the plastic menu, taking her time to look at the image beside each item carefully. "Your brother tried, I think, but he's not you."

"Pike's always needed someone to tell him what to do."

"Must be a lot to have on your shoulders, that burden of responsibility. Especially at your age."

"Honestly, I feel like I'm about a hundred years old these days."

"Have you started drinking again?"

"Most people are too scared to ask that," I say, amusement lifting one side of my mouth into a smirk.

"Leonardo Bentley, I used to change your diapers when you were a baby. I'm not scared of you."

I chuckle at that. I haven't heard someone say my full name in God only knows how long. It's a closely guarded secret. I'm not sure a name like Leonardo would have helped me back in Lovelock.

"Besides, I know your real name. I have currency."

I look around, making sure we're not in earshot of anyone. The back tables are clear.

"The sheriff came digging around the garage yesterday," I say quietly. "I think he thinks I've got something to do with Jennifer's disappearance."

Amanda's momentary smile vanishes, replaced by a deep frown. "Jesus, Leo."

"Yeah."

"Be careful what you say. Be careful who you talk to. You have a lawyer?"

I nod.

"Good. Make sure you warn them. It's a packed-lunch trip from any other town to here."

That hangs in the air between us for a while as Hannah finally makes her selection from the menu, humming a song as she waves at us. Amanda waves back, diverting one of the waitresses I don't know over to the table.

"Have you spoken to Cassie since you've been back?" Amanda asks, her tone tentative. I shove my hands in my pockets, suddenly feeling about two feet tall.

"Nope," I say. "Well, that day with the spilled milk, but not since then."

"You never answered my question before. Have you been drinking since you got out?" she asks me.

"No," I reply evenly, wanting to be angry but knowing that it's a perfectly legitimate question. I kick at the floor with the tip of my sneaker. "No, I haven't had a drop."

We watch Hannah order with the waitress.

"Your sister needs to go to see a real doctor at a medical center," Amanda says as Hannah approaches us.

I shake my head, putting my finger to my lips. "She hates hospitals. We'll have to trick her. Don't let her hear you."

Amanda nods, smiling broadly as Hannah gets within earshot. She takes her back to her booth and gives her an iPhone to play with. We don't have one, don't have anything like that at our place, so she's instantly enthralled by a YouTube video of people unwrapping various toys and figurines. She's completely captivated, some annoying high-pitched voice narrating all of the videos, and Amanda comes back to join me.

"Have you asked her who the father of the baby is?"

I shake my head. "I already know. It's Derek Jackson, the guy who used to do janitorial stuff at the hospital until he got fired. Remember?"

Amanda frowns. "Are you sure?"

"Pretty sure. I mean, I walked in on them in the bedroom—"

"How long have you been home, Leo?"

I count the days. "A little over a week."

"Well, I'm sorry to break it to you, but judging by your sister's measurements, she's anywhere from five to seven months pregnant."

"And?"

"And Derek Jackson wasn't fired. He was arrested. Outstanding warrant for unpaid fines. That was . . . Christmas. He only got back to Gun Creek a few weeks before you did. If he was the father, Hannah would be about eleven months pregnant right now."

I feel fucking stupid all of a sudden. "How do you know all this?" I ask, alarm bells ringing in my head. Because if Derek isn't the father of Hannah's baby, who is? I mean, it could literally be anyone. She's so damn trusting, and all she wants is attention, and she can't tell good attention from bad.

"I work weekend shifts at the hospital," she says. "Derek broke into the drug store and stole a heap of pharmaceutical-grade morphine."

Probably shared it with my mom, I think wryly. "I saw them arrest him. That's how I know what happened."

"Shit," I say. I don't know what to think. Just that now I have to kill two people for laying their hands on my baby sister. Derek, because I know he's one of them, and whoever else it was who did this to her.

I'm going to run out of places to bury all these bodies.

I hope to God it's a kid Hannah's age. Somehow, that would make it less bad. I'd still smash the little punk's face in, and she's still mentally not old enough to be having sex with *anybody*, but at least if it were another fourteen-year-old kid, I could *begin* to understand how this happened.

"I need to know who the father is," I say.

Amanda gives me a look. "Let me guess—so you can kill them?"

"Something like that," I mumble. Yeah, something very fucking similar to that.

"Let's see if we can talk to her, get any information," Amanda says. "If you promise me you won't do anything bad with the information."

I think about that for a moment. "Then what's the point of *having* the information?"

This woman is so patient, she must be a fucking saint. "We tell the authorities if we need to, and we let them deal with it. If he's an adult, we make sure it's reported to child services."

"What if they try to take her away?" I snap, my whole body going rigid. "No. NO."

"Okay, then, we don't tell anyone. Unless we both agree. Okay?"

I nod. "Yeah. Okay. Yeah."

Amanda goes over to the booth and talks with Hannah for a moment. I edge closer, just within earshot, but I have to focus very carefully, and I'm missing every second or third word that Hannah says.

"—sent him away. Now I'm sad," Hannah says, pushing something on the iPhone. *Derek. She must be talking about Derek.*

I smile to myself when I hear Amanda tell Hannah how special God made her, and how important it is to find the special father of her special baby. I don't know how, or why, but my sister starts talking, and I wish to hell that I hadn't asked.

"Mom's friend says I'm special, too," I hear Hannah say. "He used to bring me presents until I started getting fat. Now he just comes and picks up Mom and he won't talk to me."

I look at Amanda, and I can see the alarm bells on her expression. "What friend, sweetie?"

Now he just comes and picks up Mom. Jesus. Don't let it be him. Anyone but him.

"Mr. Carter," Hannah chirps up.

Fuck, no.

"He'd bring me presents, and then we'd have special time. I'm not supposed to tell anyone."

I clench my teeth, my fists, my entire body, to stop myself from rushing over to Hannah and shaking her until she tells me everything. I count to five in my head as I continue to listen to my sister speak.

Amanda asks her when he started visiting. Hannah doesn't know how to reference time that well, so Amanda helps her describe the weather.

It was hot because the AC was broken and Ma asked him to pay to fix it. He started "visiting" Hannah at the same time.

Did my mother know what was happening?

Hannah says the leaves crunched when Carter stopped visiting her. Fall.

He was visiting her in summer, the very time she would have gotten pregnant.

The guy who fathered Hannah fifteen years ago is the same guy who fathered Hannah's baby, while I rotted in a jail cell and Pike sold meth in Reno.

Hannah.

I was always so careful with her. She never had any fear as a baby, the way she'd toddle around, her hair in pigtails and her eyes never quite managing to focus on anything. She would have walked straight into that goddamned creek and drowned if it weren't for me keeping tabs on her twenty-four hours a day. She was my sister, but she was *mine*. I fed her bottles in the night. I changed her diapers. I brushed her hair and tied her shoelaces.

I thought I'd protected her. Now, I can see how woefully inadequate my quasi-parenting was. I didn't protect her at all. I left her, a lamb among wolves, and as soon as I was gone she was fair game.

All I can see is red, all I can feel is this yawning chasm sucking me in. I'm going to kill him. I'm going to die in prison because I have to kill him for what he did to my sister.

Hannah goes back to the iPhone—a pair of headphones over her head this time, snug from ear to ear—and Amanda guides me into her tiny office, closing the door behind us. Her expression is grave, like the hole I'm about to dig for Hal Carter. My hands are shaking.

"Leo," she says, just as I punch my fist into the wall. It hurts, but I do it again, and again. Amanda grabs my arm and I don't struggle. I struggled once when Ma grabbed me, and I ended up giving her a black eye by accident when I swung my elbow around to push her away. I was only a kid when that happened, but it scarred me, the way she grabbed her face and screamed. When you're raging on an inanimate object and a woman grabs you, you freeze.

I go rigid, staring down at my knuckles as blood swells up and drips down my wrist, down the arm of my shirt where it forms a wet, sticky puddle between cotton and flesh.

"Leo. Please look at me."

I do. I look her straight in her bloodshot blue eyes, and she doesn't flinch.

"We can figure this out," she states, and suddenly it's like someone has given me a dose of Percocet, a hit of weed, something that makes me sag against the wall I was just assaulting. The fight's out of me. My eyes are burning, there's a hard lump in my throat that no amount of swallowing can will away. I don't think anyone else has ever taken charge like Amanda is, even if it's just for a moment. Nobody except

Cassie, that is. She was always the problem-solver, always the one who fixed everything, but aside from her, it's been me. Just me. Trying to make sure nobody gets hurt, or dies, or worse.

"If what Hannah's saying is true, we will get him arrested. Okay? But we can't do anything until we're sure. Do you understand, Leo? You cannot go and see that man until DNA tests are conducted, until we have proof. Because Hannah is beautiful, and she is special, but we cannot take her word as gospel."

I shake my head; she has no idea about Hannah. About where she came from.

"Hannah doesn't look like our mother," I say, in a voice barely above a whisper. "And she didn't look like my father, either. You know who Hannah looks like?"

She stills; I can see the connections firing in her eyes.

"Hannah looks like *her* father. Her *real* father."

"You're not saying—"

"I am."

"The mayor—"

"Hal Carter is Hannah's real father. He's a sick, mean old bastard. And if she says he did this to her? I take her word as fucking gospel."

Amanda's face is ashen; she keeps doing this thing where she holds her hand to her mouth. Her fingers are shaking. I think mine are, too. Shaking and bleeding. *Fuck.*

"What are you going to do?" she asks me. "You can't go back to prison, Leo. Your sister needs you, now more than ever."

She's right. I hate it that she's right. I hate it that no matter what I do, I'll always be the lowest common denominator. I hate that if I do something to Hal Carter, he'll get off scot-free and I'll be the one who gets punished.

"It's not fair," I mutter.

"Life's not fair," Amanda says. She might as well have poured napalm on me.

"FUCK!" I yell, kicking the wall. "FUCKFUCKFUCK!"

Somebody knocks on the office door. I throw the door open, feeling sorry for whoever it is because now I have to kill them, too, for interrupting my boxing session.

Cassie. When she sees me, she steps back as if she's been burned.

"I heard yelling," she says.

"Everything's fine," Amanda says dismissively.

Cassie looks at the small puddle of blood my knuckles are creating. "You sure?"

Amanda nods. "Sure as sure can be. I think table twelve needs their check." Subtext: *Go away.*

Cassie looks almost disappointed as she walks back to the front of the diner. Once she's gone, Hannah makes a beeline for me, snowballing into me, hugging me around my waist as hard as she can. "You miss her, don't you?"

"Who?" I ask.

"Cassie," she says, pressing her ear to my chest. And that's the thing about Hannah. She doesn't even understand that this is all because of what's happened to her.

"Yeah, sis," I say, messing up her hair. "That's why I got mad. I'm sorry."

Before we leave, Amanda gives me some sleeping pills that are safe to take in pregnancy and the address of a clinic in Reno. And she makes me swear on Hannah's soul that I won't do anything to Hal Carter.

CHAPTER EIGHTEEN

Cassie

Amanda drives me home after we close up the diner. When we pull up, there's an ambulance parked out front.

The lights aren't on.

And there are more cars. Damon's patrol car. Chris's SUV. I've never seen so many people here at once. The light in the den is on; it's too bright. We only ever use soft lamps for my mother's makeshift hospital room. Through the kitchen window, I can see Damon sitting at the table, his head in his hands.

And I know, before I've even opened my car door, that my mother is dead.

CHAPTER NINETEEN

Leo

I can't kill Hal Carter, at least not yet. Not until Hannah gets some proper medical care. After I spoke to Amanda, I got Pike to take Hannah home. I couldn't go there, not until I'd found a way to deal with my rage. Because if I walked into that trailer and saw my mother? I would have killed her on the spot with my bare hands for what happened to Hannah. What she let happen.

So I'm here, at midnight, sitting in the empty garage with nothing but the old car bodies out back as companions.

I've been sitting here all day. I watched the sun rise high into the midday sky, and then drop below the horizon until inky darkness claimed the night again. And I've been sitting here, freezing my ass off, shaking with the fiery anger that's burning me from the inside.

I need to hurt something. I think of Jennifer, her bent neck and spread thighs. I think of the way I hurt her. If she were here, I'd do it all again, and I'd feel better for it. But she's not here. She's missing. And I can already read the writing on the wall. Sheriff King wants to pin her disappearance on me. I've got days, at best, before I'm back in lockup.

I can't run. I'll violate my parole, and besides, who would take care of Hannah then?

I can't tell the truth about Jennifer. If I do, I'll get the death penalty.

It doesn't even matter if I killed her or not. All that matters is that if they find her car, it'll probably have my DNA all over the fucking thing. And if they find her body . . . well, then, it really is game over for me.

At one a.m., I finally stand up. My legs are numb from the cold, from sitting for so damn long. I flick my lighter to get some illumination. I find a crowbar. I take it out back to where the Mustang is, turn on the floodlights so I can see, and I beat the absolute shit out of the car my daddy left for me all those years ago.

I'm beating it so hard, I start to bleed. At least, that's what I think I see. Red splashes of something on the bumper. I drop the crowbar and it clatters to the asphalt beneath me. I study my arms, my hands, my face—no blood.

Confused, I kneel in front of the car—or what's left of it—and run my thumbnail across what, upon closer inspection, looks like specks of red paint. I've never seen them before; I mean, I haven't seen this car up close in years. I scrape a little of the red and it comes away under my fingernail. It's definitely paint. And it's sparking a vague memory of something long buried inside me.

I call Chris McCallister. It's the middle of the night, but he answers. He's on duty, just a few doors down at the sheriff's office. I ask him to come over to the garage, and to my surprise, he's standing beside me before I can so much as hide the crowbar.

He's holding two cups of coffee, his uniform looking a little worse for wear.

"You look like shit," he says, offering one of the Styrofoam cups.

"Could say the same about you," I reply, accepting the coffee and gesturing my thanks with a tip of the cup.

"Missing girls mean lots of overtime," he says, swigging his coffee.

I take a sip of mine and make a face; it's watery and bitter, but at least it's hot enough to warm me. "Your boss is gonna try and pin Jennifer on me, you know."

Chris shrugs. "Is that why you asked me to come over here? You know I can't talk about that shit with you unless you've actually got some information for me."

I shake my head, watching as my breath turns into thick fog in front of my face. "No. I actually wanted to show you something. Can you keep it to yourself? Just for now?"

Chris looks dubious.

"It's not about Jennifer Thomas. It's about the red paint I found on the hood of this Mustang." I point to the wreck.

Chris blanches; clearly this is not something he was expecting. "This is your car from the accident," he says.

It's not really a question, more a statement, but I nod in confirmation anyway. "Yeah. I was beating the shit out of it just before, and I noticed the red. I thought it was blood, but it's the wrong consistency. See?" I scrape a little off with my nail and shake it into my palm. "It's metallic paint. From another car."

"Why were you beating the shit out of a car you crashed eight years ago?" Chris asks suddenly.

I clear my throat awkwardly. "My sister's pregnant to a guy old enough to be her father, and I'm not allowed to beat the shit out of him."

"Right," Chris replies, his eyebrows rising in disbelief. "So, you wanted to blow off some steam, you decided to take it out on your car, and that's when you saw these paint chips?"

I nod.

"How do you know they didn't get here recently?" Chris asks. "This car's been sitting in a scrapyard for almost a decade, Leo. Even if we did find something . . ."

"Please," I say. "I think I'm remembering shit. I think somebody ran me off the road that night. We used to be friends, didn't we?"

Chris scrubs his hand along his clean-shaven jaw.

"You remember that night, man. You were the one who took me away in cuffs."

"Even if somebody did run you off the road," Chris says solemnly, "you could never prove it. It's been so long. You've already served your time, Leo. Just let it go. Do your parole, and then leave this town and don't ever come back."

"Please," I beg him, and I fucking hate having to beg. "Please just test the fucking paint and see if you get a match. Just tell me what kind of car it comes from. I know you can do that with forensics. That's all I need to know."

I just need to know I'm not completely fucking crazy here. I'm afraid that if Chris doesn't take these paint chips right now, they'll disappear, like Jennifer disappeared.

"Stay here," Chris says. "Don't go anywhere."

"Where the hell am I gonna go?"

He shakes his head as he walks off.

When he comes back, he's holding one of those plastic evidence bags in his now-gloved hand. I watch on as he takes a single-use razor blade from a package and scrapes as much of the red paint from the car bumper as he can get off.

"I'm only doing this because we have history," he says, sealing the bag up and stuffing it into his jacket pocket. "If I find something, I'll let you know. Until then, don't say anything to anyone about this, you hear?"

I nod. "Thank you," I reply, and I really fucking mean it.

"Why are you doing this, man?" Chris asks. "Is it because she's dead? Is that it?"

My heart leaps into my throat. "Who's dead?" I demand. "What do you mean?"

"Teresa King," Chris says. "She died a couple hours ago."

Fuck. She's dead. I killed her. And I know I just spent most of my adult life locked away for what I did to Cassie's poor mother, but there's a vast chasm between almost dead and *actually* dead.

My eyes are stinging. Even after all these years, the first person I think of calling is Cassie.

CHAPTER TWENTY

Cassie

My mother isn't even dead forty-eight hours before we bury her. It happened so suddenly, and yet so slowly—how can both of those statements be true? I can count on both hands the years it took for her to finally die after the accident that should have killed her instantly. And yet, I went to work in the morning, and she was alive, and I served food and wrote checks and took money and processed credit cards while my mother's heart stopped inside her paper-thin chest. As she took her final breaths.

My mother died, and nobody was there with her.

Maybe it's better that way. Maybe she waited until she was alone to pass. Maybe we tried too hard to keep her around in the prison that her body had become.

We travel to the Gun Creek Cemetery in the back of a funeral car, just Damon and I. Ray drives behind us in his truck. In front, the hearse carries my mother's body to its final resting place, in the dirt. I stare out of the window during the short drive. I don't talk. There's nothing left to say.

"It'll be okay," Damon murmurs beside me. Our eyes meet for the briefest of moments.

He puts his hand on my knee. I look down to where his flesh touches mine; and I can't, for some reason, take my eyes away from the bandaged bite mark between his index finger and thumb that continues to seep blood.

CHAPTER TWENTY-ONE

Leo

I f Damon King knew I was stalking him right now, I think he'd shoot me dead on sight.

I have to admit, I look like a goddamn psychopath. I'm dressed entirely in black, a balaclava covering my face in case anyone should glimpse me in my vantage spot underneath the old chestnut tree in Cassie's yard.

But goddamn it, I just want to see her. Get a glimpse. Know that she's okay after her mother died and was buried.

I look up into the window, *her* bedroom window. The shades are open just a crack, and I can see movement. Bodies. Two people, joined together, moving as one.

I should look away, but I can't. I know immediately what I'm looking at—hell, the window is fogged up—but I don't look away. I can't be with her, but I can stand here and look up and watch as Cassie presses her palm against the windowpane as somebody else makes the girl I love feel things she will never let me give to her as long as I live.

I'm so busy looking at her face that I don't notice his at first. Could it be Chase? Pike, even? Chase was close with Cassie many years ago, and he probably hates me along with everyone in town for what I did to Cassie's mom, so I don't see him filling me in if he is seeing Cassie behind closed doors.

No. It's not skinny enough to be Pike. The shoulders aren't bulky enough for it to be Chase. But something about the guy looks . . . familiar. I can't get a good enough look to make out either of their facial features, but I'd know Cassie anywhere.

I've got those binoculars in my pocket. I don't want to get them out, but if I can see her better for just a moment, I'll do it.

I don't take my eyes off that spot she's touching on the window as I take the binoculars from my pocket and hold them up to my eyes.

I focus again, still standing behind the chestnut tree, thankful for its size and position. With my spare hand, I run my fingers along the rough bark, remembering the way my palms broke and bled when I pressed Cassie up against the trunk of this very tree and fucked her. Now, my palms are scarred from the accident, and she's up there in her house on the hill with some other guy.

I turn a little dial on the binoculars and everything comes into sharp focus.

Suddenly, I can see the guy who has his hand around her throat, pressing her up against the window as he fucks the shit out of her.

It's . . . oh, *shit*.

Her hand is pressed against the glass, and he's got one hand on her hip, rutting into her like . . . well, like I want to. Like an animal.

It's not Pike.

It's not Chase.

It's *Damon*.

CHAPTER TWENTY-TWO

Cassie

The morning after my mother's funeral is . . . quiet. Everything is deathly still. There's a buzzing in my ears, a static hiss that the sound of her medical equipment used to fill.

It's been so long that, even though I know she's dead, that she's buried in a shiny black coffin six feet under at the Gun Creek Cemetery, I still shuffle downstairs, get her liquid nutrition mixed, and am standing in her empty room with the syringe in my hand before I realize what I'm doing.

The bed is gone already. The room is devoid of the medical equipment that used to crowd around the bed. It's just an empty room that smells like bleach.

I wonder who cleaned it out. Part of me wishes they hadn't touched it. Another part is grateful that I don't have to deal with the aftermath. It's like it never happened. There's not a trace of my mother here. Except for the scars on my heart, the reflection in the mirror whenever I see myself and recognize her, the burns on my wrist. They'll never go away.

It's been snowing again. The curtains are open; it's so beautiful out there. So empty. From the window, I can see the spot in the far corner of our yard where Damon dug a hole and buried my dog.

"Good morning," Damon says behind me.

I turn away from the snow, my retinas pulsing and blind in the center of my vision from the stark white light outside. It's like someone has set off a camera flash right in my eyes.

"Sleep well?" Damon asks, sipping from the mug of coffee he's holding.

I'm so tired. I can feel my eyes, puffy and red from all the crying I've done in the past forty-eight hours.

"Like the dead," I reply. Ha. I barely slept at all.

"Come out of there," he says, his eyes flicking around my mother's dying room with clear discomfort.

I try to blink away the blind spot in my eyes. It persists. I decide I can't really fathom a fight right now and follow Damon into the kitchen. The pot of coffee is still there, and I pour myself some. I sip it and almost gag. He really cannot make coffee to save his life.

Damon smiles lazily from across the counter, his eyes still puffy from sleep. "I can see the cogs turning in your brain, Cassandra. What are you daydreaming about?"

I lean my elbows on the edge of the counter. My legs are tired and my head hurts. I don't have it in me to lie.

"This novel I read about a sociopath."

"Oh, yeah?" He drains his coffee and rounds the counter, setting the empty mug in the sink. Turning to me, he reaches out, tucking messy blond hair behind my ear. And he leaves his hand there, his palm against my jaw, the pad of his thumb just below my bottom lip as he gazes down at me. "Enlighten me."

The snow outside reflects off his blue eyes and I feel *so heavy*.

"A sociopath is . . . somebody who's empty inside. Somebody who needs to take from everybody else to fill them up. Because they were born wrong. Because there's nothing inside them."

Damon smiles; his lazulite eyes crease up ever so slightly at the edges. I imagine how beautiful he would have looked as a young child; how his mother would have melted whenever he smiled up at her. Because his eyes deceive. They don't look empty. They're beautiful, full of the souls of everyone else he's sucked dry and left in his quest to find that something, that perfect *thing* to fill him up.

In my head, I imagine opening a can, pulling away the lid to reveal a mass of writhing worms. The lid cuts me, and some of my blood drips down onto the worms so that their beige bodies are mottled with red.

This is what happens when you open a can of worms and show it to Damon. You end up with blood, and it's almost always your own. But blood isn't always a bad thing. Sometimes, it's the one thing that reminds you you're still alive.

I can see myself in his eyes. My soul. *He's taken it from me.*

"Do you feel empty, Damon?" I whisper.

He rests a hand at the base of my throat, all trace of his smile gone as he matches his fingers, *onetwothreefourfive*, to the brand-new bruises he left on me in the night, in the dark. *"Not when I'm inside you."*

CHAPTER TWENTY-THREE

Cassie

ache between my thighs. I'm reminded of last night. Of how Damon crept into my bedroom after my mother's wake and fucked me until I hurt. Of course, it wasn't enough that she was dead. That we'd just buried her. It wasn't enough that he shot my dog. Once he'd had a taste of my pain, he had to come back for more.

The man I've been fucking for the past eight years, or rather, the man who's been fucking me—his eyes gleam in the harsh sunlight that casts a brightness over the kitchen, bathing it in some macabre stage lights that scream: *Action!* But this isn't make-believe, and the curtains won't fall at the end of our grotesque little act, and after we're done here, I won't be able to peel my mask off and toss it on the ground as I exit the stage.

I swallow thickly. I wish he'd get tired of me.

"I heard you in the shower last night," he says, his fingers squeezing into my flesh. "Did you think you could just wash me off like nothing happened?"

My cheeks burn as I try to twist away from him; Damon tightens his hold on my throat, crushing my windpipe as he pulls my face to his.

"You need to learn," he says, through gritted teeth, "that I know everything about you, Cassie. You can sit here and try to psychoanalyze me, but I know what you think. I know where you are. And I know exactly where you're going."

It hurts, this familiarity. This incessant pain.

"My wife just died. Say sorry," he says, loosening his grip.

"I'm sorry!" I wheeze, my throat burning as tears stream from my eyes.

"Not like that," he says, one hand moving to his belt buckle. "Show me how sorry you are."

I do what I'm told. I show him just how sorry I am. How sorry I am that he ever came to this godforsaken town and ruined my life.

CHAPTER TWENTY-FOUR

Leo

Taking Hannah to see an obstetrician in Reno is like a covert fucking CIA mission. We don't tell my mother. She will freak. She will worry that we won't come back, or that we are trying to take Hannah away for good. My mother is nothing if not a ball of narcissistic anxiety and paranoia with a streak of nasty for good measure.

We drive Hannah to the hospital under the cover of darkness. We tell her we're going on a vacation, and she gets so excited, she ends up packing a bathing suit, all of her coloring books, and every stuffed toy ever made.

The doctor's smile fades as he takes more measurements and calls more doctors in. Hannah is doing so well. I'm so fucking proud of her. I keep giving her candy, so distracted by keeping her calm that I don't notice the two doctors in the room have given way to ten different people, squinting at the screen.

Hannah notices, though, because she starts to freak out a little bit. I manage to keep her calm long enough for the doctor to send them all out and bring in a new sticker book for her. It's got all the Disney princesses, and she gets to work on it while the doctor and I talk in the hall.

Always shutting her away while we talk about her. I feel a brief flash of anger at my mother. She did this. Hannah would be so smart, so capable, if Mom hadn't poisoned her. It would have been better if she'd been shooting up heroin during her pregnancy—at least then detox as a newborn would have been the worst of Hannah's struggles. But alcohol has effectively ruined her chance of ever growing up, stuck in a body that gets older as she stays a little child. As it grows a child.

The news is bad. Very fucking bad. "Incompatible with life" is what they say, but what they actually mean is that if a disabled girl has a baby with her own biological father, things are generally going to fuck up. We don't tell the doctors the Daddy Carter part, of course. I haven't even told Pike that part yet. It's a knowledge I carry in my chest like a delicately balanced grenade with a faulty pin, waiting to explode.

Child Protective Services shows up at the hospital, two of the motherfuckers, and it takes some very fast talking to get them to back off. They won't let Hannah come home with us, though. She's a minor who has been raped and is in her third trimester. Not only that, she's got something called preeclampsia, and she's one bad day away from multiple organ failure. From death. My baby sister is teetering on the brink of dying because of what that bastard did to her.

She needs to be induced. But first, she needs a legal guardian. And since neither Pike nor I are legally her parent, that leaves one particular bitch who needs to fix this situation.

Yes, in the end, the only way to save my sister from the system is to go home with Pike to collect our useless fucking *mother*. It means a four-hour round trip to Gun Creek and then back to Reno. Time is against us—if Hannah's situation worsens, CPS will step in and make her a ward of the state. They'll decide what happens to our sister. And we'll never see her again.

That cannot happen.

Pike speeds the entire way home. It'd be much easier if we were in the Mustang, but sadly we're relegated to his piece of shit Honda. As soon as we arrive, Pike locks the car doors before I can open mine. I glare at him, a fist in his face and a growl in my throat. I am fucking homicidal. I will kill everyone I lay eyes on, family or not, to get my sister fixed and back home where I can keep her safe.

"Unlock the fucking door," I growl at my brother.

He stares at me with eyes that have seen the weight of the world and have been crushed beneath it. "You can't kill her yet," he says flatly. "Not until we get Hannah back."

"I know that," I fume. Yet. You can't kill her *yet*. Not, *You can't kill her.*

"She's not going to come with us," Pike adds.

"I know that, too," I reply. "You got a gun?"

I expect my brother to yell at me, to tell me I'm crazy. But he doesn't. It's been a long eight years while I've been locked up. He nods. "In my bedroom," he says. "Underneath my bed. You want me to get it?"

I shake my head. "You keep the car running. Those social workers won't wait around long. They'll have Hannah in the system and shipped off to a fucking foster home if we're not back in a hot minute."

"Yeah, okay," Pike mutters.

"The gun. Is it loaded?"

He nods.

"Well, all right then. If you see her running, fucking run her over and throw her in the trunk, will you?"

I burst into the trailer like a man possessed. If I were an action hero right now, I'd be Hulking out. But since I'm just a human, and an average one at that, I go for the gun. It's exactly where Pike said. *Thank you, little brother.* A sawn-off shotgun—perfect. I'm almost sad that I need my mother alive right now. Blowing her head clean off with a double-barrel would be poetic at this point. I stand in the kitchen and holler.

"Mommy!" I yell mockingly. "Where are you?"

I hear movement in the main bedroom and stalk down the hallway like a fucking panther on the hunt. She's there, sitting up in bed in her pajamas. A cigarette burns between her lips. She barely gives me a glance but doubles back to me when I pump the shotgun in one hand and aim it at her head.

"What—what are you doing, baby?" she slurs.

Great. The bitch is high as a kite. I bite down on the insides of my cheeks. "Get up," I spit.

She closes her eyes. I glance at the bedside table—sure enough, she's got all the ingredients for a one-person smack party. There's a syringe caked in dried blood, a length of rubber tubing, a dirty spoon, a lighter. It's the middle of the afternoon on a weekday and my mother is high. Go figure.

I pour a glass of water over her head and she sputters to life. She can barely talk. It's okay—we have a long drive ahead. It's almost easier that she's all soft and rubbery from the heroin. In the end, I simply grab a fistful of her dirty hair and drag her to the car.

I throw her into the backseat, triumphant when her head hits the opposite window. I hope it bleeds. I hope it fucking clots and kills her.

Two hours later, we arrive back at the hospital with one sober, pissed-as-fuck mother. I try to push her outside as soon as she's signed the consent forms, but the bitch insists on staying with us.

Hannah's vitals have crashed in the four hours we've been collecting Mom, and they're preparing to perform an emergency C-section as we arrive. The doctor—who is highly suspicious of all three of us—reluctantly tells us that Hannah is sedated but is allowed one person in the operating room with her. "I'll go," my mother volunteers. "My baby would want me to be there with her in case she wakes up."

I smile at the doctor. "Give us a second," I say, taking my mother's elbow and steering her out of earshot. Pike follows.

"Let go of me," she says. "Listen to your mother."

I stare directly into her bloodshot eyes, well aware that my fingernails are digging into her arm hard enough to break the skin. "You listen to me, you useless cunt," I whisper, in a voice loud enough for just her and I. "Hannah's in here because of you. Her baby is going to die because of you. She's pregnant with Hal Carter's deformed baby because of *you*. Hannah's *father*. Did. This. To. Her."

All the blood drains away from her sunken cheeks; she starts to cry. "W-what?"

"*I* will be going into that surgery with her," I say, towering over my mother. "And *you* will be sitting out here, thinking about how you should kill yourself when we get home."

"Leo . . . ," she whimpers.

"You're not a mother," I continue. "You're a whore. A whore who should have been sterilized at birth."

She slaps me across the face with all the feeble strength a skinny junkie's arm can muster. And it stings; not so much physically, but deep in my chest. And then, she leans against the wall, her face in her hands, and begins to sob.

I glance at Pike. "Go," he says, waving me away. "I'll keep her here in case she needs to sign anything else."

Hannah is already sedated and unconscious on the table when the nurse ushers me into the theater, clad in surgical scrubs, plastic bags over my boots. She leads me to the head of the bed, a green cotton sheet separating Hannah's head and shoulders from the rest of her body. On the other side of the bed, an anesthetist watches her closely, glancing at a screen that displays heart rate and blood pressure. And her blood pressure is through the fucking roof. Poor Hannah. This baby is literally killing her just by existing. I stroke her hair. She might not know what's happening, but it makes me feel better to lay my hand on her head and remind her she is loved.

Later that night, when Hannah is out of the recovery ward, Pike and I sit beside her hospital bed while our mother hovers silently at the foot. I called Amanda and asked her to pick up the younger kids from school. Everyone is safe, for now.

"My baby's gone," Hannah says, putting her hand on her stomach.

It's still swollen, which I wasn't expecting, but the doctors warned me she'd be pretty banged up for a while after they removed her uterus to stop the bleeding.

Yeah. In the end, the decision was out of my hands. She almost died on the table when they went in to take the baby out. It was a boy. He looked all wrong, but he was still a baby. It still broke my fucking heart that he'd had to be conceived and suffer because people are cruel and vile and evil. He was alive for thirteen minutes, and Pike held him that whole time. I couldn't bear to hold him, knowing that he was going to die in my arms.

We named him after my grandfather, my mother signed the paperwork, and then a nurse took him away.

I asked Hannah if she wanted to see him, but she said no. I was relieved.

No kid should have to endure something like that.

CHAPTER TWENTY-FIVE

Cassie

I was fall-down drunk the night it happened. The night Damon—well, you'll see.

My eighteenth birthday. I'd been at the Grill, eating and sneaking beers on the side with Chase and the rest of the football boys. I think they pitied me in the aftermath of the accident, took me under their protection, and made sure I was "taken care of," in a way.

Chase had driven me home around eleven after we'd all stopped at the football field and had some more to drink. It had started raining while we were lying on the grass, drinking and passing around a joint that made my head spin every time I took a drag.

The porch light had been the only one still on, and I'd tried to unlock the front door as quietly as possible but ended up making about the same amount of noise as a feral cat stuck in a trash can. Suddenly, the door opened from the inside, yanked unceremoniously, and I fell flat on my face beside two bare feet. I watched, mesmerized, as droplets of water began sliding off my rain-soaked arm and dripped onto the floor, puddling beneath me.

"Fuck," I muttered, my cheek buzzing from where it had hit polished wood. It'd hurt once the alcohol in my system burned up. I was grabbing at the floor with clumsy fingers, trying to rise, when I was hoisted to my feet.

Damon was bleary-eyed as he glared at me as though he'd been sleeping. He was still wearing his police-issued shirt and pants, and the tan clothes were wrinkled, adding to that "slept in" look.

"What do we have here," he said, but it wasn't really a question. He sighed, resting his forehead against the door momentarily. "A drowned rat. A drunk rat."

I giggled. He slammed the door shut and ushered me to the kitchen as I dripped all over the floor.

"Are you . . . stoned?" he asked, grabbing my chin, forcing my eyes to meet his.

"No, Sheriff!" I replied, mock-saluting him. I dissolved into another pile of giggles because suddenly, everything was so fucking funny. I heard him mutter "Jesus Christ" under his breath.

"If your mother saw you—"

"Yeah, she's not going to see me," I cut him off, sobering a little. The giggles were gone, replaced by an intense sadness, a loneliness inside me that stretched as wide and as empty as the prairie surrounding us. The feeling sucker punched me in the gut, and I wrapped my arms around myself, shivering.

"Cassie—"

"She's dead already," I said. I started to cry. Big, heaving sobs and fat tears that rolled down my cheeks, mixing in with the rain and blurring my already less-than-stellar vision.

"Cassie." Softer this time. Sympathetic. Arms went around me, even though I was soaked from the rain and probably smelled like stale beer. I rested my ear against his chest, and it was almost like somebody loved me for a moment. I closed my eyes, melting into Damon's chest, listening to his heart beat evenly under flesh and bone.

"Hey," he said, leaning back a little. He tipped my face up with his finger. "We'll get through this. It's going to work out. Okay?"

I shook my head, utterly miserable. "Not okay. It's not okay."

"Cassie, stop," he said quietly, his arms stiffening around me so I couldn't breathe. *"Stop."* I was a chatty drunk, an emotional drunk, and I didn't heed the warning signs that signaled his turning mood.

"We have to turn her off," I whispered against his chest. "We have to let her die."

His fingers squeezed into my arms; the first time Damon ever left bruises on me.

"Shut up!" he yelled, and now he was really angry. He shoved me away from him and my back hit the kitchen counter.

"Don't you ever talk like that," he said, blue eyes ablaze, a finger in my face. "You don't just give up on your own mother. Do you know how many people don't even *have* a mother? And you just want to let yours die?"

I stared at the floor, my hands gripping the counter behind me. I despised confrontation. I hated yelling. *I hated the fact that I wanted my mother to hurry up and get better or hurry up and die.*

My heart started to race. An uneasy feeling began to drip into my veins and spread like wildfire through my body. Something very bad was about to happen, and I couldn't for the life of me figure out what it was, or how to stop it.

I tried to walk past him to the stairs, but he blocked me. Blue eyes stared me down as a hand shot out and pressed me back against the counter.

"Damon—" I started.

A hand went over my mouth, another at my tank top pulling it down so that my breast was exposed. The sudden cold air on my flesh shocked me out of my stupor, and I slapped him across the face as hard as I could, pulling my top back up to cover myself. Something flashed in Damon's eyes—anger?

We stared off for a moment. I was stone cold sober in the space of about thirty seconds. In my head, above the drunken chatter and buzz, there was a realization: *We can never go back from this.*

"I heard what you said about me," he said, his sudden neutral tone disarming. The flip of a switch. The edge of a blade. *There you are.*

"What?" I edged to the side, thinking that if I could just keep him talking long enough, he'd calm down.

"When I first moved in here. You were on the phone to that friend of yours. I heard what you said."

My stomach twisted painfully. "What?" I repeated. Somewhere in the edges of my consciousness, a thought gnawed at me, a memory. I'd joked about the hot sheriff to one of my friends. But that's all it had been. I wasn't serious. He was marrying my mother, for Christ's sake.

Damon stepped forward without warning, his hips trapping me against the counter.

"I was sixteen!" I said, pushing at his chest. "I was joking!"

He shook his head, one hand around my throat as he dragged me to the ground and trapped me underneath him. "And now you're eighteen. And I'm not joking."

I tried to fight him, to get him off me, but it didn't matter. He was stronger. He'd always been stronger than me.

It hurt. I remember it hurting.

I remember begging him to stop.

I remember him ignoring me.

I'm sorry, Damon said to me after. He kissed me on the cheek. Hugged me tightly, so tightly I heard my neck crack from the pressure. I didn't reply. I couldn't. I was too busy trying to breathe.

While I was still on the floor, too terrified to move, he got up and sat at the kitchen table, right next to my head. After a few minutes, he picked me up, cradled me to his chest like a baby, and put me in his car.

I'd thought that maybe he was going to kill me. I was terrified. I kept looking at the gun on his hip, the shiny silver metal glinting each time we passed under a streetlight. We drove all the way to Tonopah and into a drive-thru in complete silence.

A cheeseburger and fries, and a little kid's toy for me on the side of my meal. I was shaking, my entire body having some kind of fit, and I threw the bag of food back in his face, punching him for effect.

He broke my nose for that.

He won, in the end. Made me eat every single bite of that meal, choked down, *washed down* forcefully with the giant Pepsi he'd ordered for me. It was his way of apologizing, I realized much later. His way of trying to make things right between us. A fucking kid's fast-food meal. *I'm sorry for raping you, have this collectible action figurine.*

When I'd finished eating, he drove home. We sat in the driveway for a long time, the engine idling as the pain between my thighs grew hotter and more fierce, bruises blossoming across my skin as the stupor in my brain increased. A large Pepsi, filled with fucking sleeping tablets that I watched him crush up and drop in. The bitterness at the back of my throat. I tried to hold on to the dashboard of the car while Damon put his head in his hands and cried.

The next morning, I woke up in my bed. He'd put me there, my thighs and the mattress underneath me still damp from whatever else he'd done while I was drugged and unconscious.

I took the Volvo—the car Damon drove when he had a day off and his patrol car was needed—and I drove all the way to fucking Reno. I didn't stop for food. I didn't stop to pee. I drove and drove and when I got there, I flirted for a moment with the possibility that I had gotten away.

He found me, of course. He was five minutes behind me the entire time. The GPS in the car was synced with his cell phone. He'd already anticipated that I'd flee after what he'd done.

The second time, a few nights later, I barely resisted. I fought him at first, sure. But once he had me pinned, I just kind of gave up and let him do what he wanted.

I think I disappointed him, in a way.

I think he liked it better when I was fighting him the entire time.

A couple months later and I'd become entirely complicit. You could even say I was eager. Twisted, sure, but in my own sick way, I'd quickly come to enjoy the attention I'd been starving for all those months.

I know what you're thinking. You're disappointed in me, aren't you? I was supposed to be different. I was supposed to get out and make something of myself.

Yeah, and Leo was supposed to, too, but look at how that turned out. *Look at what he went and did.*

By the next summer, I'd finally snapped to my senses. I'd seen my reflection in the window one afternoon, naked and panting, Damon behind me, and I had been horrified. It was like I was waking up for the first time since that night and really *seeing* what I was doing. What *we* were doing.

"I don't want to do this anymore," I'd said to him. "This is *wrong*." Mom was home by then, packed away in the den, her breathing machine hissing in the quiet of the night.

He'd just laughed. A sound that was pure reflex. A sound that contained no joy.

The same way my laugh sounds now.

"I mean it," I'd said, my palms slick with sweat, my voice unsteady. "We can't do this. Even without all the other fucked-up stuff, I don't love you. I don't even like you."

He gave me this look, and it made me feel so fucking cold inside. The way snow looks upon a field of flowers every winter and says, "I will smother you from the sun's rays until I destroy you."

"You'll learn," he'd said, his voice far too calm for all that fury that raged in his eyes.

"To what? To love you?"

He'd chuckled bitterly. "No. You'll learn that it doesn't matter if you love somebody or not. They'll still love you. *I'll* still love you."

CHAPTER TWENTY-SIX

Leo

It isn't until we bring Hannah home, three days later, that I tell Pike the truth.

It's dark outside, and all I can think about is Jennifer. How they clearly think I had something to do with her disappearance. How, if I don't act now, I may never get another chance at making things right.

Not that they could ever be right. Hannah will bear the scars of this for the rest of her life. She will live forever knowing that her child died and almost killed her, even if the chances of her understanding that knowledge are almost nonexistent. She will carry the trauma of being cut open and stitched shut by strangers.

We are in my room, Pike and I. I've told him to dress in black, and he doesn't disappoint. We look like we're about to go rob a bank.

In reality, we're about to do something much worse.

"We're going to make this right," I say to my brother. "We're going to fuck him up, and we can never talk about it again. Do you understand?"

Pike nods. "Now?"

I pick up the tire iron from the bed in one arm, Pike's shotgun in the other. I hand him the gun, then fish a black ski mask out of my pocket for him. "No time like the present, right?"

"Right."

Hal's house is less than ten minutes from ours, but the area is much nicer. The houses have shutters and manicured lawns and white picket fences. Hal's house is particularly grand, set over two levels, a three-car garage and a yard that backs onto a small lake. Pike parks down the block and we skulk down the empty sidewalk, two grim reapers armed with crude weapons. Once we're positioned in front of Hal's back door I look at my brother, his balaclava-clad face staring back at me, and I smile, baring my teeth. He grins back. I take his shotgun for him as he jimmies the door open with his lock pick and busts the fucker wide open.

Hal has his TV up so loud, he doesn't even hear us. He's eating a TV dinner, alone, the smell of fake mashed potatoes and string beans hanging on the warm recirculating air the heater is pumping out. I think about telling him why we're here, why this is happening, but I figure he'll realize soon enough. He doesn't even have time to swallow his mouthful of food before I lay the first blow into the side of his skull.

The entire time I'm bludgeoning Hal Carter on his living room floor, I'm thinking of poor Hannah. Of her baby. Of Cass and Damon fucking in the window. Hal's wife is at her weekly card game with the rest of the old bitches she calls friends, and that's a good thing because the poodles go fucking mental in the laundry room as we smash their owner apart. Hal begs for mercy as I beat his head in with the tire iron, but his pathetic pleas aren't the reason for us sparing his life. I stop just when I think one more blow might kill him, tossing the tire iron to one side, taking my gloves off and shoving them in my back pocket before I pull a plastic package from inside my jacket. I tear the package open, carefully extracting the long, slim cotton tip inside and bending down over Hal. He chokes on his blood, making a sickening gurgle noise. Huh. I wonder if DNA kits work when they're tainted with blood. Whatever. I force Hal's mouth open, running the swab roughly against the inside of his left cheek. When I'm satisfied I have enough of his saliva coating the swab, I slide the cotton tip back into its packaging and seal it.

"Wh-what are you doing?" Hal manages to croak as I put the sample of his DNA back into my jacket pocket for safekeeping. I grin down at him, alive with the thrill of violence in my veins, and I lay a sharp kick to his ribs.

"I'm punishing you, Hal." I kick him again. "Though honestly, I can't even think of a punishment good enough for a man who got his own daughter pregnant."

He whimpers.

"Can you think of a good punishment, Hal?"

Hal tries to crawl away from me, but there's so much blood that he ends up slipping. It's pathetic, really, watching as he flails about, like a pig being bled out in a slaughterhouse.

"You won't get away with this . . . ," Hal says feebly. "You moron, you've got my blood all over you. Kill me and you'll get the electric chair."

I kick him one last time, for good measure. "Jesus Christ, you idiot, they don't use the chair anymore. They've never used the chair in Nevada. But you know what they do in the prison I was in?"

I rest my boot on Hal's throat.

"If you're a pedophile, they rape you, Hal. Every fucking day, they rape you in there. *Imagine that.* All those men with nobody to fuck, and all that anger, and all the time in the world. So you come near me or mine again, and this DNA of yours? It goes straight to the police, who will throw your sorry ass in prison for what you did to Hannah."

Hal sobs. "I'm sorry, okay? I'm fucking sorry!"

I pick up the tire iron again, focusing on his left knee. "I know you are, Hal." *Whack!* His kneecap shatters as he hollers in agony. "I know."

CHAPTER TWENTY-SEVEN

Cassie

I was right. Nobody finds Jennifer. A month passes, then two. Christmas passes. New Year's. By the end of January, the rain and snow have ruined all of the Jennifer posters. I don't see Leo again; not once in all that time. In a town as small as this, that has to be deliberate. But that's okay, I suppose. He's got enough to worry about. Being the prime suspect in a missing persons investigation can't be fun. Especially when it's not the first time he's been suspected of such a thing. One place we know Jennifer isn't is inside the well on Leo's property—Damon made a huge deal of searching the entire property, top to bottom. No trace of Jennifer.

I, for one, hope she ran away. I hope she changed her name, dyed her hair, and got as far away from this place as possible. It's a fairy tale, mostly, a fragile longing for a different life.

In my heart, I know she's probably dead in the bottom of a lake somewhere. This place, it takes from you. It takes from everyone. If you're young and beautiful, like Jennifer was, the price of existing in a place like Gun Creek is impossibly high to bear.

Sleep is my refuge in this life.

A solace.

If I could sleep forever, I would. It's the only time when I can relax, loose-limbed and buzzing from whatever chemical stimulant is helping me to slumber, the artifice something I don't worry about anymore. Whether it's vodka or sleeping pills, I know all I need is something to nudge me along and give me some blessed relief from the cruel light of my winter days.

I do not wake up for anyone. Damon's tried before on a few occasions when mom's breathing machine flipped out and he needed me to help him set it straight. I slept through. She lived anyway. And then she died while I was at work. Funny how these things happen. But tonight, when a voice pierces my cotton-wool wrap of drugged sleep, I sit up in bed like I'm on fire.

I'm not; on fire, that is. I feel like I am, though. I've been bunched up in a thick duvet while the heat's been blasting. I'm so hot my hair is damp from sweat, a thin sheen of moisture prickling on my forehead. There is movement above me, in the attic?

I know something sharp and loud woke me, but now that my eyes are open and I'm rubbing my face I can't for the life of me remember what was so urgent that I snapped awake, alone, in the dark.

Until it comes again. "CASSIE!"

It's Damon. He's screaming my name. I haven't heard somebody scream my name like that since they were trapped in a well with a dead girl.

Mom.

Is it my mother? Is she dead?

No, that's right—she died already.

"CASSIE! HELP!"

Damon's voice is definitely coming from upstairs. From the attic. Has he hurt himself? What could he have possibly done to himself in the attic? There's nothing in there except my father's ghost and some old shit I keep meaning to box up and sell, or burn. Old family photos and my mother's wedding dress are about the only things I would keep from the piles of junk up there.

The drugs make my brain slow. He's called me three times now, and I'm still sitting up in my bed, sweat pouring off me, my feet tangled in sheets. I extricate myself from the mess of blankets and feel the sudden urge to pee, but there's no time. I shuffle over to my door, fling it open, and head for the attic. The hallway light is on and it burns my eyes. I squint as I make my way up the rickety stairs, marveling at the way they don't creak anymore.

The attic door is open when I reach the landing, a lone lamp illuminating the low-ceilinged space where old things go to die.

It's different than I remember. It's tidy; devoid of clutter, everything pushed against one wall and itemized thoughtfully. I see clear plastic boxes full of vinyl records; the front cover of Fleetwood Mac's *Rumours* presses against the side of the closest container, begging to be let out.

The smell of dust and must that is usually present is gone, replaced by a thick metallic odor that makes my stomach twist.

On top of the stack of neat containers sits the heart-shaped box that holds my mother's wedding dress—her first dress, the one she wore when she married my dad.

Away from the window, there is a large pine box, its lid ajar; built for storage but a box that looks eerily coffin-like in its shape and dimensions. Above me is the thick wooden beam that my father used to hang himself from.

Beside the pine not-coffin box is Damon, still in his uniform, blood on his palms as he kneels on wooden planks that are full of splinters.

And in front of Damon there is a horror I cannot fully comprehend.

"She's dying," Damon chokes, his blue eyes bloodshot and wild, her blood all over him. I open my mouth to speak but no words will come, so it just stays open like that, a shocked O as I try to blink away the bloodbath in front of me.

I look at the dead girl cradled in Damon's arms and that's when everything slams into place. I meet her eyes; she's not dead after all, just dying. Her eyes beg me for help; eyes I've seen before. She is the spitting image of her older brother, even down to the shape of their lips, their straight white teeth, the color of their eyes. This is what the dog was barking at incessantly. This is why Damon shot her.

"Jennifer," I choke.

I look back to Damon. *"What did you do?"*

CHAPTER TWENTY-EIGHT

Cassie

Jennifer Thomas is no longer missing, at least not to me.

She is no longer a smiling face printed on a stack of posters that I left in the trash. She is flesh and blood, emphasis on *blood*, and she is breathing in a way that suggests she is gravely ill.

I look Jennifer over, but I can't see any wounds. "Where is all the blood coming from?" I ask breathlessly, kneeling beside Damon. He puts a hand on her stomach—her swollen stomach—and that's when I realize she is pregnant.

"She's having a miscarriage?" I ask.

Damon runs a bloody hand through his hair. "No. Maybe. I don't know."

I touch Jennifer's hand; it is drenched with blood, warm and slippery. She hasn't uttered a word yet; as my eyes adjust to the dim light, I can see why. Tape on her mouth. Tape around her wrists. This poor girl isn't just bleeding to death; she's doing so completely unable to move or speak.

"I'll call an ambulance," I whisper, realizing I've got my phone in my hand. I must have carried it up here. I stand as I unlock it and start to dial, nine, one, but I don't get to punch in the third digit. Damon follows my movements, snatching the phone out of my hand with his wet fingers, Jennifer's blood streaking across my palms like angry lashes of a cane.

"Damon," I say urgently, glancing down at Jennifer. "She's bleeding everywhere. We have to call an ambulance. *Now.*"

"No." He takes my phone and throws it down the stairs, all the way to the kitchen where I hear it land on the floorboards. I bite my lip and try not to cry as I look around the attic for a weapon, for *something*.

"Damon," I try again. I keep glancing at Jennifer because I want to make sure she's still alive. She is. She's hyperventilating, her skin lily-white, her breaths dangerously shallow.

"No!" Damon roars.

I slap him across the face, so hard that my wrist goes numb and fresh blood beads along Damon's bottom lip. Good. "I don't know what the fuck is going on, but she's going to die."

Damon takes a step back. "We need to call Ray."

"Call an ambulance," I urge him. "Or don't. We can dump her in front of a hospital and leave. Damon, if you don't get her to a hospital, she's going to die."

Jennifer Thomas is in my attic, dying. Damon was getting me to put up posters of her beaming face in the cold, in the snow, *while she was in our fucking house.*

I kneel beside her, ripping away the tape that binds her wrists until my fingernails break, unsure what else I can do. Damon has a gun. I have nothing but a pair of threadbare pajamas and a full bladder. Damon dials his brother and hands the phone to me. "Tell him to hurry."

He's in Reno, I think. Or possibly Vegas. How is he going to hurry?

I press the phone to my ear. Ray answers almost immediately. "Ray," I begin before he can start.

"Oh, hey, little lady," he replies, his voice taking on a predatory edge that I don't like. "I was just thinking about you."

I'm sure you were.

"Ray," I rejoin. "Listen. You have to call us an ambulance—"

His tone changes immediately. "Is my brother all right? What's happened?"

I roll my eyes, patting Jennifer's shoulder with my free hand. "Damon is fine. Jennifer and her baby are not fine."

Damon rips the phone from my hand. "No ambulances," he barks, pacing the length of the attic. "You need to get here, now."

I can't hear what Ray is saying anymore. I look down at Jennifer, realizing she's quiet because of the duct tape across her mouth. Wincing, I locate an edge of it and pull it from her mouth in one swift rip. She's in so much pain already, she barely reacts.

"Jenny," I whisper. "What happened? Who did this to you?"

Her eyes dart to Damon momentarily before looking back at me.

"You did this to yourself, Jennifer," Damon mutters.

Jennifer cowers beneath my hands as Damon addresses her.

"Do you think you can walk if I support you?" I ask.

Jennifer shrugs, tears streaming from her eyes. I've never seen so much blood in my life, and *why won't Damon call an ambulance* for this poor girl? I can't even fathom how she came to be up here. I can't bear the thought that she might have been above me as I slept this entire time; that I could have somehow saved her before this.

Suddenly, Jennifer squeezes my hand hard enough that my bones hurt, a wail coming from her mouth. She's bearing down, her face scrunched up, her eyes closed as a wave of something paralyzes her.

"Contractions," I mutter. "Damon. She's having contractions. It's too early for this baby to be born." I'm no doctor, but her stomach, although clearly protruding, is tiny. She's barely in her second trimester.

"We have to call the police," I say to Damon.

He grits his teeth so hard, I think they might shatter from the pressure. "I *am* the fucking police, you stupid girl."

The cogs in my sleep-addled brain are starting to turn. But I barely have time to voice my suspicions because Jennifer is screaming. I look to Damon, who responds by slapping his hand over her mouth to drown out the noise.

"Be quiet," he says between clenched teeth. She shrinks away from him, terrified. I know that feeling. Something tells me that Jennifer knows it much more intimately than me, though.

Jennifer's contraction subsides, and Damon takes his hand away. She tries to sit up, balanced on her elbows. "I can f-feel something," she whispers. "I need to push. Oh, God." Her hands are tied but her legs are free, and she's trying to open them wider.

I look at Damon for a moment, before my instincts propel me. I scoot around so I'm in the juncture created by Jennifer's legs, the dim light only showing me a vague outline. She screams once more, and something wet and dark slides out of her.

"Oh, Jesus," I stammer. Jennifer's elbows go out from under her, the sound of her skull hitting the floorboards sickening. A rush of dark red blood surges from between her legs, pooling beneath her.

"I think the baby came out," I whisper. Jennifer isn't moving anymore; her knees fall together, her eyes glazing over. Damon, wide-eyed and probably in shock, shoves me aside.

"No," Damon whispers. "No, no, no." He sits back on his heels, the tiny baby in his hands, Jennifer's blood all over him, all over me, all over the attic.

Jennifer's eyes are still open, staring at the ceiling, unseeing. I put two fingers to her neck to check for a pulse. Nothing. I use those same fingers to press her eyelids shut. I'm not a religious person, but I put my palms together and say a prayer for Jennifer Thomas anyway, because if I don't, nobody will.

Ray is soothing. Ray is kind. To his brother, he is these things.

While Damon refuses to let go of the tiny baby Jennifer birthed—while Damon *loses his fucking mind*—Ray speaks softly to him. I have never heard the kindness in him but he possesses it, in his own way. He takes the baby in his hands and gives it to me, even though I don't want it. I take it, anyway, fresh shell shock running up and down my limbs as I stand in the middle of the attic.

Ray takes Damon away, out of the attic, and I am left alone with Jennifer and her baby. I hear the shower turn on, and a few moments later, Ray reappears in the attic. I place the baby on its mother's chest, looking to Ray for—what? Permission? Instruction? My own ending?

I knew the moment Ray arrived that he might kill me. Damon might love me, but Ray doesn't. I see the indifference in his eyes, the calculations. *I am a loose thread.* He is figuring out how to tie me up.

"Are we going to have a problem?" he asks me.

I shake my head emphatically.

"I didn't hear you."

"No," I reply. "No problems. I swear."

"Good," he says, apparently satisfied. "Find a box for that." He jabs a finger toward Jennifer.

"For Jennifer?" I ask.

He looks impatient. "For the kid."

"Oh."

He leaves the attic again and I look around properly for the first time. My whole focus has been on Jennifer and her baby, but now I look past them, to the large pine box she was obviously locked in, the padlock hanging loose, the lid flipped open. I peer inside the box to see ordinary things, things you wouldn't equate with death and dying. A pillow. Blankets. An iPod, ear bud headphones still attached. Gingerly, I lift one of the buds to my ear. It's blasting music. I don't listen long enough to hear what's playing.

I search the room for a box. My eyes land on a stack of milk cartons in the corner, meticulously stacked, almost as tall as me. Making sure I'm still alone, I take one of the cartons from the pile.

It's old and waxy, just like the one I found downstairs months ago, when Ray interrupted me the morning after Thanksgiving. But this carton is different. The picture on the side hasn't been rubbed out.

HAVE YOU SEEN THIS BOY?

Every hair on my arms stands on end as if I've been electrified. *They used to put missing kids on milk cartons.* Isn't that exactly what Damon said to me in the kitchen the morning Jennifer's disappearance broke on the news? I study the grainy black-and-white image of the kid pictured. Daniel Collins, age ten. Went missing from the sidewalk outside his house on August 26, 1987.

It was his tenth birthday. He'd been checking the mailbox, and then he was just gone.

I memorize the date and the name, putting the carton back in its spot and selecting another one. It's identical. I check three cartons, then five, ten. They're all the fucking same. *Daniel Collins, born 1977, disappeared 1987.* I don't recognize the face on the photo, it's so grainy and blurred, but I store it in the recesses of my mind for future reference.

I hear movement downstairs and leave the milk cartons, spying a heart-shaped box I know I can use. My mother's wedding dress from when she married my father, something I thought Damon would have insisted she throw out after he moved in. I gently take the lid off, aware that my bloody fingerprints are now all over it. I'm a part of this now. I am an accomplice. I am *complicit.*

Better to be an accomplice than dead, I suppose.

Inside is a smaller box, of identical heart-shaped cardboard, among the stiff old silk. I take the inner box out and lay it on the floor beside Jennifer, mindful to keep it away from the blood pooled beneath her body. This box contains my mother's veil; the most beautiful French lace, material she found at a thrift store and sewed herself while I grew in her belly. I take Jennifer's tiny baby from her chest and place it in the pile of lace, covering it as best I can, before replacing the lid.

"Cassie!" Ray's voice cuts through the buzz in my ears. I leave the heart-shaped box and follow the sound of my name downstairs to the bathroom beside my bedroom.

It's easier to cope with the sheer volume of blood upstairs, in the dark; here, it is lit up in Technicolor. Damon is sitting in the bottom of the bath, his face in his hands. He did not shed a single tear when my mother died, apart from the few fake ones he squeezed out at her funeral, but here, in the wake of Jennifer and her baby—he sobs like a broken child. Ray hears me enter the small space and steps back, his bloody hand immediately fishing a cigarette from his jeans pocket and lighting up.

"Come on, brother," Ray says quietly.

Damon is shaking violently; covered in the blood of his child's life and death, in the bottom of the empty bath. I look to Ray; he gestures with the cigarette in Damon's general direction as he wanders off down the hallway. There are no words exchanged but his meaning is clear: *Fix that.*

So I do what comes via instinct; I undress Damon as best I can, blood-slicked fingers fumbling with the buttons on his uniform, the tan stained a red so dark it's almost black. I get his socks off, his shirt, his boxer briefs, and the key from around his neck that hangs on a thin chain. I've never seen it before, but I don't have time to study it. I set it all beside the bath in a pile, and then I turn the faucet on, warm water shooting down and slowly, ever so slowly washing Jennifer's blood from his skin.

I scrub the red from his body as if he's a child muddied from playing in the rain instead of a murderer bloodied from keeping a girl tied up in his attic. His blue eyes stare at the wall at the end of the bath, unfocused, unseeing. He is somewhere else. When he's finally clean, I shut off the water and wrap a towel around his shoulders.

I can't breathe properly. My chest hurts. I realize I no longer have to pee. I have too many questions. The blood is gone and I need something to drink. Maybe I'll tip a bottle of bleach down my throat and end it all before something like this happens to me.

I stand on shaking legs and walk toward the hallway. As I'm about to step out of the bathroom, Ray steps into the doorway, his bulk blocking my path. He looks me up and down, fixing his eyes on mine. The message is clear: *You're not going anywhere.*

Ray smokes. Damon stares. I stand between the two brothers, biting the insides of my cheeks until I taste blood.

CHAPTER TWENTY-NINE

Cassie

I f I thought watching Jennifer Thomas die was bad, it's nothing compared to how I feel when we bury her in the yard.

Damon is sitting at the kitchen table where Ray can both dig and keep an eye on him at the same time, numbed into a semi-calm state by whatever pills Ray tipped into his mouth before he dragged me out here and handed me a shovel. We've been digging for what feels like hours in the spot under the huge chestnut tree that flanks the back of the house.

Jennifer's body is wrapped in plastic sheeting. Her baby is inside the heart-shaped box. I have blisters all over my hands from digging.

Ray and I work silently, the smell of his cigarette smoke turning my already delicate stomach. I want to throw up every time I look at Jennifer, her bare feet sticking out of the sheeting like a bad joke.

We're maybe four feet deep in black dirt when Ray stops and leans on his shovel, lighting a fresh cigarette off the butt of his old one. I think about asking for one, but I can't speak.

"He hasn't said a damn word," Ray says, looking up and into the house at Damon, still mute and staring into space.

"He's in shock," I reply.

"He needs to see a doctor."

I make a sound at the back of my throat. "Jennifer needed to see a doctor."

Something flashes in Ray's eyes. I don't even see his hand go to his hip; there's just his hand on the back of my neck, and the cold barrel of a gun digging into my throat.

"You don't ever talk to me like that, do you understand?"

I try to nod but it makes the gun barrel dig in harder.

"Do. You. Understand?" Ray repeats.

"Yes," I whimper.

"Don't give me a reason to put you in this hole and bury you alive."

"I won't."

He lets go of me and I put my free hand to my throat, massaging the spot where the gun was.

"My brother's pretty shaken up by this."

No shit, asshole. I look at the shovel in my hand and wonder if I could bring it up and smash Ray's temple in before he could get off a shot. Probably not. And if I try and fail, I'll be dead in this hole and under four feet of dirt before sunrise, with Jennifer and her baby as my eternal company.

"All right, this is deep enough," Ray says, changing tack. He takes my shovel and his and throws them out of the hole. He motions for me to get out of the way and I do, hoisting myself back onto firm ground as he rolls Jennifer toward him, into the hole. Her body drops heavily at his feet, and he swiftly steps back inside the hole so her dead weight doesn't crush his toes. He leans past her, picking up the heart-shaped box next, making a move to drop it on top of her, but I stop him at the last second.

"Let me," I say quietly, taking the box from him. I slide back down into the hole on my ass, the box in my hands, and place it as gently as possible in the middle of the plastic-wrapped lump that used to be Jennifer. I stand, and as I turn around Ray is sitting on the edge of this makeshift grave, the barrel of his gun just touching my forehead and *did I just dig my own fucking grave?*

"We already did this," I say. "If you're going to shoot me, just do it."

Nobody says anything for a moment. I see his finger on the trigger, my eyes crossed and aching as I try to focus. I wonder if I'd feel the bullet rip through my skull and bed into my brain. Maybe for just a millisecond? Or would it be a loud noise and then: *lights out.*

Finally, Ray laughs. "You are a stone-cold bitch," he remarks, lowering the gun and handing me a shovel.

I am so fucking grateful that I can't see Jennifer's face as I pile dirt on top of her until she disappears into the earth.

CHAPTER THIRTY

Cassie

There are things you think you know about a person, about a place, about life.

And some of those things will remain true. But others are lies we tell ourselves, constructs designed to keep us safe.

But I'm not safe anymore.

I never really was.

I'm complacent. That's the thing that has kept me here all these years, with Mom down the hall and Damon in my bed. Complacency is the drug I swallowed the night Leo went to prison. Complacency is the price I have paid for the illusion of my own survival.

Ray spends the rest of the night at our house, pinning me with his watchful eyes. When he leaves the next morning, I am surprised. Surprised that, in the end, he didn't kill me. I know he wants to. For once, it seems, I can be grateful that Damon loves me to the brink of insanity. Ray tried to convince Damon that they'd be better off killing me, too, but Damon refused. What a lucky girl I am. *What a good stepdaddy I have.*

Ray leaves.

I am alone with Damon.

Finally, he tells me what happened in the attic with Jennifer Thomas.

Sitting at the same kitchen table where he watched us bury her, Damon tells me the truth. At least, his version of it.

"Jennifer was pregnant," he says, looking anywhere but at me. His eyes are red.

"With your baby," I add.

Damon nods.

I don't even bother asking what a forty-year-old man is doing screwing a sixteen-year-old girl, let alone getting her pregnant. I've lived this life already. I was eighteen, not sixteen, but I take my birth control as religiously as a priest takes confession.

Seems Jennifer was not so zealous. Jennifer got pregnant.

"Jennifer wanted an abortion," he says. "She wanted to kill our baby. I promised her I would take care of things. Of everything. She didn't even have to stick around once it was born." He takes a deep breath. "I would have done anything."

I'm unimpressed. "And so you took her, and you tied her up and you locked her in a box in the goddamned attic."

He slams his fist on the table.

Now Jennifer is dead, their baby, too, and the whole town is still searching for her. There's still the stains of blood on the attic floor to scrub out, and I still need to find a way to figure out who the hell that missing boy on all those milk cartons was. Neither Damon nor Ray has asked me about whether I saw them, too fixated on Jennifer. Their ignorance is my ammunition.

As soon as I can retrieve my phone—thankfully unharmed after Damon threw it down the stairs—I lock myself in the bathroom and google *Daniel Collins*.

No wonder I didn't recognize him from the milk carton. The photo was so grainy, it was barely distinguishable. The color version is much easier to decipher.

The eyes. Lazulite blue, the color of the ocean in places you'd rather be. Daniel Collins, missing age ten, presumed dead, but a body was never found. Daniel Collins, found in my house, in my bed, in my nightmares. Daniel Collins—he goes by Damon King, now.

The most heartbreaking part of all? His mother never stopped searching for him. She lived three hours away from us, across the border in a little town in California. She had the same blue eyes as her missing son. She's dead now. The obituary, dated two months ago, says she died of a broken heart.

I go back to work the following day as if nothing has happened. As if there isn't a teenage girl buried next to my house, the freshly dug soil of her final resting place visible from my bedroom, her voice crying out to me when I try to fall asleep.

Ray calls me from Reno, promising he will come back and kill me if I tell anybody about Jennifer and the attic.

Damon goes back to work and pretends to search for the girl he had stashed away the entire time.

CHAPTER THIRTY-ONE

Cassie

There is an empty grave in Lone Pine, California, for Daniel Collins. I would know; I've spent every waking moment searching for anything and everything related to the boy on the milk carton. I know the time he was born, his mother's maiden name, the first place he went to school.

I know where his mother placed a headstone, ten years after he disappeared. Right beside his father, her late husband, who died of a heart attack less than twelve months after Daniel was taken from the front of his house. His mother rests there now, in the family plot that bears Daniel's name but is missing his remains.

I have no money, no car, no freedom—and yet, I have this burning desire to go to Lone Pine, California, and see the place where Daniel Collins grew up. It's only three hours away. I could be there and back before Damon even notices I'm gone.

I think of the handful of people I know. Damon's out, obviously. I doubt Deputy Chris would do something for me without telling Damon all about it. I don't even know if Pike's still in town, but either way, when he did see me he wasn't exactly enthused. And Amanda; well, she's far too busy running a diner and working weekends at the hospital. She would ask too many questions. And I need her to cover my shift at the diner anyway.

This is the thing about living with a madman, being kept away from the world you were once a part of. The people you love become strangers, ghosts of a time long gone, and though you might still pass each other on the street, there's nothing really there anymore.

There is one person, though, who always said he'd do anything in the world to make up to me what he did. I'm betting he's the same person who wouldn't tell a soul.

Damon makes things infinitely more difficult for me with his paranoia that I'm suddenly going to disappear into thin air. A legitimate worry, I suppose, when you kidnap your stepdaughter's co-worker after knocking her up and said co-worker ends up dead and buried in your yard. His solution? He visits the diner every chance he gets, right on cue. He's never absent for more than three hours, and my drive will take at least six. Somehow or another, he's going to find out that I'm gone. I just need to get where I'm going before he catches me.

He comes into the diner at 10 a.m., stands at the back of the restaurant with Amanda, and chats, casting glances my way every so often. He makes her laugh and I almost puke. He's way too good at this charade.

After he finally leaves, back to his office just feet away, I go back to work. Fifteen minutes later, on *my* break, instead of sitting in the staff room or making myself vomit in the bathroom, I beg off the rest of my shift and tell Amanda I'm getting a ride home to sleep. Then, before she can try to mother me, I take two Styrofoam cups of coffee, slip out of the diner's rear emergency door, and trudge through dirty snow to the old garage where Leo works.

CHAPTER THIRTY-TWO

Leo

Every time someone approaches the garage, I'm convinced it's the cops, here to haul my ass off for killing Hal Carter. There's nothing quite like having your entire body slid under a car, waiting for some bastard to grab your ankles and yank you out so he can cuff you.

Especially when the particular bastard who would be arresting me is Damon King. I can just imagine the goddamn gloating he'd do, carting me off to lockup on a murder charge. I'd be put away for real this time. It's anxiety like that that makes you want to drown in a case of fucking beer.

Old Lawrence isn't around much.

The cold messes with his arthritis, and now that I'm back and on minimum wage, he can spend more time eating pie at the diner and shooting the shit with his old-timer friends.

It doesn't bother me; I like being alone. But I make sure, whenever I get under a car now, I lock the doors first.

So when I hear her voice in the garage on a day when all of the doors should be locked—"Leo?"—I nearly piss my pants. Instead, I try to sit up, purely on reflex, and smash my face into the chassis I'm working on.

I wheel myself out from under the car, my face fucking throbbing. It's probably a good thing I smacked myself because otherwise my dick would be throbbing in my pants at the sight of Cassandra Carlino standing in the middle of my garage with two cups of coffee.

Is this a fucking dream? What's happening right now? I can feel the blood rising to my cheeks.

"Sorry if I scared you," Cassie says.

I wave her apology away, flustered. What is she doing here? Why is she talking to me? "It's fine. How'd you get in?"

She gestures to the back door with one coffee-laden hand. "It was open."

Great. I'm fucking losing my mind here and I left the back door open.

She holds one of the coffee cups out to me and I take it awkwardly, not sure what to do. We stare at each other for a long moment, soaking each other in. I saw her at the diner, yeah, but everything was so rushed and I'd clearly scared the living piss out of her by appearing after eight years, in the middle of her workplace, covered in prison tattoos.

"Do you need help with your car?" I ask finally.

"I don't have a car," she says slowly.

"Oh." What the fuck is even happening right now?

"Is this a bad time?" she asks, her eyebrows gathering into a frown. "You're bleeding." She puts her hand to her cheek, and I mirror her action, my fingers coming away wet with blood. Great. "Here," she says, setting her coffee down on the workbench and producing a tissue from her purse. She steps closer, erasing the void between us as she reaches up and presses the tissue against my cheek.

I can't fucking breathe. All I can smell is her perfume—oranges and flowers—all I can see is the tiny worry lines at the edges of her green eyes, the ones that weren't there when she was seventeen and I went away. I left behind a girl, and now that I'm back, that girl is gone. She's a woman now, with pain in her eyes that I put there.

"I'm sorry about your mom," I blurt out before I can think. "I wanted to go to the funeral, but I didn't think—"

"It was a good idea to stay away," Cassie cuts me off. "From the funeral, I mean."

She's still pressing the tissue to my face. Without even thinking, I bring my hand up, letting my fingers curl around her wrist. I'm not sure if I'm taking hold of her because I want to get her hand away from me or keep it there. Her skin is cold from the chill outside, but I'm on fire just having her in my presence.

"I need something," she says, her voice breaking ever so softly. Somebody else wouldn't even notice, but I know Cassandra Carlino.

"Anything," I say.

She tugs her hand away and I let her wrist go, wiping my face with the tissue. I watch as she walks over to the first-aid cabinet hanging from the wall; it's been there forever, but I'm surprised she remembers. I hold my breath as she opens it and takes out a multi-pack of Band-Aids, tipping a pile into her palm and selecting one before coming back to me.

"Here," she murmurs.

I lean down toward her, letting her affix the bandage to my cheek. Her cold fingers are like ice against my hot skin; hot for no reason, other than the fact she's flesh and blood and here, touching me.

"What do you need?" I ask.

She takes a step back, biting on the inside of her cheek. "I need somebody to drive me to Lone Pine, California," she says.

California. "I'll drive you," I say, a little too quickly. Then I realize how crazy that might sound—the guy who crashed his car and killed her mother, offering to take her on a road trip. "I don't drink anymore," I add quickly. "Eight years sober."

"I'm not worried about your driving skills," she says softly.

I killed your mother. Maybe you should be.

"I didn't think you were allowed to cross state lines," she adds.

"I'm not," I reply. "But I would. For you."

I'd burn this whole fucking town down for her. "When do you need to go?"

She looks around the mostly empty garage. "Now."

"*Now?*"

Her face falls.

"Forget it," she says, turning toward the back door of the garage. "It was a stupid idea to ask you."

"Whoa," I say, rushing to the door before she can open it. I cut her off, blocking her way to the handle, and she just *looks* at me.

For some reason, I thought she'd be afraid of me. But she's not. She waits patiently for whatever I'm about to say.

"Let me lock up," I say. "Five minutes."

Her whole body seems to relax. Again, somebody who didn't know her probably wouldn't notice. But I know Cassie. I love Cassie. And I'd drive her to the gates of hell and bust on through if that was where she wanted to go.

CHAPTER THIRTY-THREE

Cassie

Twenty-five years on this earth, and I've never been out of Nevada. It's sad, really. The border is so close to Gun Creek. Up the mountain pass, back down the other side, and through miles and miles of old ghost towns and bare fields. Somewhere along Route 268, Nevada turns into California, a tiny sign denoting the border crossing, so small that if you blinked, you'd miss it.

I do not miss it.

We're in Pike's car, an old sedan that's seen better days. I kind of wish we were in a giant truck where the center console separates the driver and passenger so wide you have to yell to hear each other. In this car, we're so close that Leo's arm brushes against mine every time he touches the gear stick between us.

We don't talk, except about the directions; which road to turn onto, how many minutes left. I don't have my phone; too paranoid about Damon tracking the GPS, I've left it at home, underneath my pillow, along with a bunch of clothes assembled in a rough body-outline that could be mistaken for my sleeping form in the dark.

"This thing go any faster?" I ask at one point.

Leo smirks. "You sound as thrilled as me about this piece of shit," he replies, eyes firmly on the road ahead. "I'm sitting on ninety. I get pulled over across state lines, your stepdaddy'll be hauling me back to Lovelock before sundown."

My stomach sinks. I'm acutely aware of the risk I'm putting Leo at by asking him to go to California with me. I'm a selfish fucking bitch. *It's going to be fine*, I tell myself. *We won't get caught.* By the time Damon even notices I'm gone, if he notices at all, we'll be well on our way back to Gun Creek, and nobody will be the wiser about our little road trip to Lone Pine.

"So," Leo says, as if reading my mind, "remind me where we're going again?"

"Nowhere special."

"Nowhere special," he echoes. "Okay. You think they have food and a gas stop in Nowhere Special?"

I look at him, and for the briefest of moments it's like we're teenagers again and the last almost-decade didn't happen.

"We're going to Lone Pine, smart-ass. And, yes, they have food and gas there."

"Good," Leo says, a small smile remaining as he focuses on the road. "I'm starved."

Three hours later, Leo is sitting in a restaurant on Main Street that boasts the best burgers in town and a life-sized cardboard cutout of John Wayne. I leave him there with a promise to come back in thirty minutes, and drive his car down the street to the place I'm actually intending to go.

Mount Whitney Cemetery is easy to navigate. Most of the place is dedicated to a mass grave from a colossal earthquake that leveled the town over a hundred years ago. If you didn't look properly, you'd assume it was just a grassy field. I head for the individual gravestones on the opposite side of the road, already knowing which plot I'm searching for. The things you can find online these days—they have maps of cemeteries that show exactly which plot each body is buried in, right down to the satellite coordinates. It's like a dead person GPS.

The Collins family plot is smaller than I expected but covered in more ornaments and trinkets than my eyes can take in at once. The whole space is only big enough for two coffins to rest side by side, but I guess they stack them in the ground these days.

And besides, I remind myself, there might be three headstones, but there are only two people buried here—Richard and Adelie Collins, two people who somehow created the man who has been my singular nightmare for eight years.

I think of Jennifer as I stare down at the family plot, at each gravestone. I look around, making absolutely sure nobody is looking at me, and then, like the psycho I have become, steal every little ornament and trinket from the empty grave marked *Daniel Collins*, shoving each piece in my bag as I struggle to hold back vomit.

Nobody ever talks about it, but cemeteries have this particular smell. Bodies, in various stages of decomposition, all rotting in their pine boxes under six feet of hard-packed dirt. People pretend that smell isn't there, but I'm hardly one to shy away from the practicalities of death.

Beneath me, the ground rumbles, and I immediately wonder if the next earthquake is just now hitting this tiny town. Wouldn't that be ironic, if I fell into this grave and was buried alive in the resting spot meant for Damon? I close my eyes briefly, partly because the sun is so bright, and partly to wait and see if the ground will split open to swallow me up, but when I open them again, the rumble is just an earthmover driving past me on its way to dig a fresh grave.

I don't stay to pay my respects. There's nobody to pay my respects to anyway because Daniel Collins isn't buried there. He isn't even dead. He's a grown man, living in my house, sliding into my bed, making bruises on my pale skin.

CHAPTER THIRTY-FOUR

Leo

Cassie's gone for forty minutes, and for most of that time, I'm convinced she isn't coming back. I don't know why. It's just this uneasy feeling that spreads through my limbs, that voice in my head that says, *Why the fuck would she want anything to do with me after what I did to her?*

Maybe she hates me so much she's led me here, so I'll break my parole and get sent back to prison. Her mother's dead now, maybe this is her way of trying to make things right.

I mean, I probably deserve it.

So when she does finally come back, her expression unreadable, her green eyes stark against the black scarf she's got wrapped around her neck, I almost cry with relief.

She doesn't tell me where she's been and I don't ask. It's enough to be here with her, to be able to look at her sitting across from me, to be within grabbing distance of her. I'm halfway through a burger and fries when her food arrives. I watch her mouth open, the way she loads her pink tongue with ranch-dressed lettuce, and I almost come in my jeans at the sight of her doing something as innocent as eating a fucking salad.

"You okay?" she asks, chewing slowly.

I nod, picking up my bacon burger and shoving it in my mouth before I can say anything stupid.

Something suddenly occurs to her. "Hey, when did you get your license back?"

I swallow. "About a year from now."

She shakes her head, but the expression on her face isn't disapproval. It's . . . amusement. I don't argue when she reaches her hand over the table and slides the keys away from me.

Once we're back in Nevada, Cassie, the girl who used to tell me to slow down whenever I was driving, puts her foot flat to the fucking floor and wipes fifteen minutes off our previous journey. Speed demon. I kind of like that she's driving; it gives me a chance to steal glances at her for three hours while she bites on the insides of her cheeks and searches through the radio stations incessantly, *clickclickclick*. Her hands grip the wheel tighter the closer we get to her house, and at the last minute, she turns down my driveway, not hers.

"I can take you to your door," I say, looking back at her empty driveway as she comes to a stop beside my container room. I can't fucking breathe, she's so all-consuming.

She shuts the car off and hands me the keys. "I don't think you showing up at my door is a very good idea," she replies. "Especially not with me."

"Right," I say. "Why didn't I think of that?"

"I guess you're a little preoccupied, huh?"

"It's been a strange day," I say. "A good day," I add quickly. "Just . . ."

"Not what you expected?"

"Right," I agree.

We sit there in silence. I don't want to say goodbye and watch her walk up to her house. I mean, I'm still not sure that today actually happened. Maybe I'm hallucinating. Because I'm sure as shit not convinced that I just drove to California and back with my ex-girlfriend *whose mother I killed.*

"Well, aren't you going to invite me in?" she asks finally.

The pressure inside my chest releases like a hot wave of lava. "You want to come in?"

She just looks at me. "You forget your manners in prison?"

"I'm sorry. It's just—I didn't think you'd ever want to look at me again."

I look at the floor, at the creek line in front of us, anywhere but at her.

"Leo," she says softly, putting a hand on my arm.

I cringe at her touch. It's entirely foreign to me. I pull my arm away and open the door. "Come on," I say gruffly, a lump in my throat the size of Nevada. "You'll catch a cold out here."

Inside it's warm, and I don't know what the fuck to do. It's not like I have beer or vodka or a goddamn soda to offer Cassie. Having her walk into my shitty little home and sit down on the unmade bed reminds me of how much I don't have.

"What's prison like?" Cassie asks, kicking her shoes off and crossing her legs on the bed.

I snort, sitting on the other end of the bed, as far away from her as I can get. "You'd know if you read any of my letters."

I'm staring at my feet, but that doesn't stop me from catching the way Cassie freezes in the corner of my eye. I glance at her. "What?"

She lets out a long breath. "Letters?"

I've got that sinking feeling again. I don't like it. I wish it would go away. "I wrote you, like, every week I was gone."

"Bullshit," she says, her eyes shining with tears. "Bull. *Shit.*"

Sinking, sinking. Everything is sinking.

I'm drowning in the impossibility of reality. *Damon.* Of course. I killed his wife. Of course he'd hide the letters. He was fucking his stepdaughter while I rotted in prison. Of course he'd intercept any communications from me. What a fucking idiot I am, thinking that I'd been writing her for eight years without a single goddamn reply, not even a "return to sender."

"He got to them, didn't he?" I say. "He fucking got to them."

Neither of us speaks for a long time. Cassie is crying, her mascara running in twin black rivers down her face. All I do is make this girl cry.

"What did they say?" she asks in a tiny voice. She sounds like a sad little girl. I didn't mean this for her. I don't want to make her despair like this.

I don't answer. She slides off the bed, and for a moment I think she's going to leave. She doesn't. She stands in front of me, pressing insistently against my knees until I part them and she melts into the space between my thighs. She's crying so hard, I bet she can hardly see me. "Cassie," I say sadly.

I cup her chin with one hand and use the fingers on the other to wipe away her tears. My fingertips are rough, her skin like velvet, and I hope I don't hurt her.

"They said sorry," I whisper, putting my fingers to my mouth and tasting the salt of her tears. "That I wished I could trade places with her. And that I loved you. That I *love* you."

She puts her hand on my shoulder and I almost recoil. *Almost.* I don't know what to do with her touching me. It's enough to drive a man to the brink of insanity, the way she touches me. It's like our minds know the things I've done, but our bodies have forgotten. My head throbs. My dick throbs. *I need air.*

I stand, putting firm hands on Cassie's shoulders and moving her to the side. I've got my sights set on the door and the cold air beyond, but Cassie doesn't care about that. She cuts me off, staring up at me with eyes that dare me to try that again. I step to the opposite side, again trying to get around her before I do something stupid, and what do you know? She cuts me off again. She reaches up, coiling her hand behind my neck and pulling me down to her. Our faces are almost touching. I can feel her breath against my lips; fast, almost anxious. My heart is fucking hammering in my chest, my resolve like a finely stretched elastic band about to snap.

I'm breathing so fast I feel like I'm going to have a fucking heart attack and die right here. My skin is crawling from being this close to another person. After eight years without being touched by a woman, the night with Jennifer notwithstanding, it's almost unbearable to have affection. At the same time, it takes every fiber of my being to stop from grabbing Cassie and throwing her down onto my bed because that's all I want to do.

Desire and avoidance are like opposing magnets inside me, making me flinch as Cassie brings her hands down to my shoulders, her breath on my mouth, steely determination in her glassy eyes.

She lunges, her mouth devouring mine. Sharp pain stabs behind my eyes as I kiss her back, hungrily. Our hands fumble lower, to belt buckles and shirt buttons as we try our hardest to rip off the material that separates us. It's so good it hurts. I want to tear my fucking heart out of my chest and give it to her to make the pain go away.

I pull at her scarf, flinging it across the room somewhere; at the same time, she unzips her jeans and kicks them off, naked from the waist down. I grab her hips and pull her toward me as I fall onto the edge of the bed, Cassie straddling my lap. She grabs the front of my shirt and pulls, our faces inches apart, and then she kisses me so hard it rips the breath from my lungs and makes me think I'm on fire. Her cunt is resting against my cock and it's so wet if I moved the right way I'd probably be able to slide in. I kiss her tits, suck a nipple into my mouth and bite down until she moans, trail my mouth up her neck— and that's when I see the bruises.

"Cassie," I say. I hear the hard edge my voice has taken on; the worry. She is bruised black and blue from the top of her neck all the way down her sternum. I place my hand against the bruises and it fits; somebody did this to her with their bare hands.

"Who did this?" I ask, even though I already know. I know because

I saw them. The night of the funeral, *I saw them*. Some girls like it rough, but this is more than that. This is terrifying.

"It's nothing," Cassie breathes, jerking my face back up to hers, kissing me as her hand finds my cock and guides me into her.

She's so tight . . . so hot . . . it's almost unbearable. I am burning alive inside her.

If I could choose a death, it would be this one right here.

Cassie lifts her hips up and back down, the friction fucking intense. Electric.

It takes every ounce of my concentration not to blow my load in her. But at the edge of my mind, those bruises linger. I mean, *fuck*. They're right in front of me. I'm practically fucking hyperventilating as she bounces on my cock, her little moans only making it harder to hold off, her tits warm as they press against my chest.

"I saw you with him," I murmur. She barely slows. I didn't imagine having a conversation like this while I was inside her. *Jesus*.

"What do you mean?" Cassie asks breathlessly.

"I saw you with Damon," I pant. "In the window. You were fucking him."

"It's not what you think." She pauses for the briefest of moments as I'm buried inside her, up to the hilt.

I should shut up. I should know better. "What are you doing with him? What *happened to you?*"

"You were gone for eight years," she says angrily. "And then you came back"—the anger fades—"and I tried so hard to be the girl you left behind."

"He's your—"

Out of nowhere, Cassie hits me in the jaw with her fist, so fast I don't see the movement of her hand until my cheek's already on fire. "Shut up," she insists, lifting her hips and falling down onto my cock again. "Shut up and fuck me."

I am buzzing and shocked and her violence only makes my need for her burn hotter. Look at her. *She's an animal.* We both are. And I decide I don't care what she was doing in the window, not now. I force all thoughts of Cassie and Damon out of my mind. I'll care about it again after we're done here.

Some girls like it rough. The Cassie I left all those years ago didn't like it rough. She liked flowers and sweet nothings and soft, tender lovemaking. The Cassie I have returned to wants none of those things, not now, at least. The Cassie I have returned to demands something far darker.

"I'm close," I mutter against her mouth. I lift her up, trying to pull out of her before it's too late because I'm not wearing a condom and it's the right thing to do, but she clamps her thighs tight and continues to rock deeper on my lap.

"I want you to come inside me," she breathes, and I'm so fucking turned on that I dig my nails into her arms and blow right there.

CHAPTER THIRTY-FIVE

Cassie

When I wake up, it's pitch-black outside. I float on the blissful ignorance that accompanies waking up for the briefest of moments; then, reality slams into me like a sledgehammer.

Damon.

Home.

Fuck!

I scramble to my knees on Leo's bed, knocking into him as I try to find my clothes. Jesus Christ, I can't see a damn thing. I don't even know where the light is in here.

Leo rouses as I feel around the bed, locating my bra and T-shirt, my scarf, throwing them all on as fast as I can.

"What's wrong?" Leo asks, his voice thick with sleep.

"I can't find my pants," I mutter, sliding off the bed and feeling around on the floor. Leo sits up, flicking on a flashlight and offering it to me. I take it, for a second jolted back to the morning when he found Karen Brainard in the well.

"Thanks," I say, finally grabbing my jeans. I can't find my panties. I guess Leo can have them as a souvenir.

"You're going?" Leo asks as I hand him the flashlight.

"Yeah." He can't hear the way my heart's about to explode from anxiety. "What's the time?"

He rustles around in the bed, probably looking for his phone. A moment later, he answers me. "It's six twenty-three."

Fuck. "In the morning?"

"At night."

"Oh, thank Christ." We were only asleep for a couple hours. I was scheduled to work a double today—my shift normally wouldn't finish until six thirty. I've got seven minutes to get up to the house before Damon gets to the diner expecting to pick me up after work and realizes I'm not there.

I grab my bag, loaded with stolen memorabilia from Lone Pine, thankful that my eyes have adjusted to the dark.

"Cassie," Leo says, but I don't turn around.

"I have to go," I say quickly, locating the door and opening it. I gasp as cold air slams into me. I pull the door shut behind me and start power walking toward the road, and beyond, to my house. My eyesight isn't terrible but it's not perfect, either; I think the driveway is still empty, but in this darkness, it's impossible to know for sure. I think of the way Damon casually lined Leo's place up in the crosshairs of his riflescope more than once, and cringe inwardly as I imagine him shooting me as I fumble my way home.

"Cassie!" Leo's voice rings out behind me, more insistent this time. "Wait!"

I stop in my tracks, turning toward him. *Oh, my God, Leo, you're going to get me killed.*

I break into a run away from Leo. I don't think he'll follow me home. I don't think he's that stupid. My bag is falling from my shoulder, heavy with secret grave-robbed gifts, the freezing night air burning in my lungs. I make it to the road and stop, catching my breath, almost screaming as I hear footsteps behind me.

"Cassie," Leo says, stopping beside me. "What are you doing?"

I push him, hard. "You're going to get me into deep shit, Leo! You need to go back down there and stop fucking following me."

Leo stumbles back when I push him, but he's a giant, and it's not as if I'd ever be able to push him over.

"What kind of shit?" Leo probes, tugging on my scarf, exposing the bruises at my throat. "He gonna do this again? You don't have to go back there—"

"Oh, my God," I cry out, yanking on my scarf and putting it back over my neck. "You have no fucking idea what you're talking about. Leave me alone. I mean it."

"If he's hurting you, Cassie, we can call the police—"

"Leo!" I push him again, acutely aware of how exposed we are on the shoulder of the road. "He *is* the police! Don't you understand? He could send you back to prison."

Leo's eyes are full of anger, full of unshed tears. "I can't let you go up there if he's going to hurt you," he says, his words taking on a hard edge.

Fucking fuck. Fuck! I glance over my shoulder, making sure there are no headlights driving in our direction.

"He's not going to hurt me," I say. "But if he sees us together, he's going to hurt you."

The first part is a lie; he's definitely going to hurt me at some point.

"I can take him," Leo says, his gaze hard as he stares up at my house.

"Can you take a bullet?" I challenge him. "Can you take being arrested? Can you take going back to prison?"

Leo's shoulders sag.

"Go home, don't go home," I snap. "Whatever. But for the love of God, don't fucking follow me across this road or it will be the last time we ever see each other. You get me?"

He gives a short nod, walking back a couple of steps. I check the road for any cars then run across it, along my driveway, up the front steps, and onto my porch.

I left the door unlocked on purpose this morning, part of my plan.

I don't even have a key to my own goddamn house, Damon's control over my every move is so precise. I can't come and go as I please if I don't have access to the place, a deliberate move on his part.

The door handle turns in my palm, I crack open the door, and I'm safe. The house is pitch black and silent, *thankyouthankyouthankyou*. I step across the threshold and close the door behind me, sagging against it as the adrenaline in my veins continues to throb.

I made it.

A lamp snaps on in the living room, the noise deafening in the silence, the light impossibly bright. I jump so violently I drop my bag, and its contents scatter across the floorboards like little traitors exposing me.

"Well," Ray smirks, a shotgun resting across his knees as he sits at one end of the sofa. *"Would you look what the fuckin' cat dragged in."*

CHAPTER THIRTY-SIX

Cassie

Ray sizes me up like I'm a piece of steak he's about to cut into. His eyes drift from my face, down my torso, all the way to my feet and back again, and when he's done I feel like he's painted an oil slick from my head to my toes.

"Ray," I say listlessly.

"*Ca-ssan-dra*," he mocks, the grin on his face a mile wide. He stands, the shotgun casually slung over one shoulder as he approaches me. I put my hand on the doorknob and twist, pulling it open an inch, but Ray is faster. He's in front of me, using his free hand to slam the door shut again, leaving it there so I'm caged in by his thick arm.

I swallow thickly. Fuck.

Ray wrinkles his nose up, the grin still cemented to his face. "You. Stink. Like. Sex."

My stomach drops. I want to throw up. The room spins around me as I look past the man who buried Jennifer's body, the man who held a gun to my head after I'd rolled her into the ground, the man who I've feared since the moment he shook my sixteen-year-old hand in his clammy palm and squeezed it a beat too long.

I'm so terrified, I can't even speak.

Smirking, Ray takes his hand away and pulls a cell phone from his jeans. He dials and holds it to his ear, pulling a face as he studies mine. He's entertained by my fear. He's . . . what's the word? He's triumphant. He thinks he's won, but I don't even know what game we're playing. I hear a voice on the other end of the phone, and really, who else would it be?

"Brother, you'd best get home," Ray says to Damon. "I found your girl. I think she's got some things she'd like to tell you about who's been sticking their dick inside her."

Damon says something that distracts Ray. I see it in the way his eyes glaze over, the way he turns away from me ever so slightly. I'm trapped against the door, but if I can just get past him, I'll be able to run for the kitchen.

Ray ends the call. Damn.

There are sharp things in the kitchen. Knives.

Fuck. Whichever way this ends, there's going to be blood.

I bring my knee up as hard as I can, hitting Ray in the groin. He's got an erection. I guess I shouldn't be surprised. All that excitement from trapping me in my own home without Damon to call him off. Ray doubles over, groaning. "You fucking cunt!" he roars, dropping the phone. He reaches out to grab me, but I twist out of his grip, elbowing him in the side as hard as I can.

I run to the kitchen, my arm throbbing, my brain screaming. Knife! Knife?

Knife. I find the sharpest blade in the block, the one I accidentally cut myself with when Chris visited, and brandish it in front of me. Ray charges at me, the shotgun still in his hand, aimed at the floor.

If I can just get the gun away from him.

If I can just get the gun.

If I can just.

Fuck.

"Give me that," Ray says, holding out his hand like I'm a petulant child who grabbed a second helping of chocolate ice cream after dinner. I feign surrender, letting my wrist go limp as I hand the knife to Ray. He chuckles, his wide palm in striking distance.

I don't hand him the knife. I slash the knife as hard as I can across his palm. *Fuck you, you psycho. As if I'd hand you the only weapon I have.*

Ray growls, his face scarlet. "Ffffuuuuck!" he rages, spittle landing on my cheek. I step back, but not fast enough. Ray is *biggerstronger-faster* than me, and his bloodied hand closes around my knife-wielding wrist so hard, I feel like the bone might snap. I gasp in a breath, fighting his vise-like grip as my wrist screams in agony. The pain is sharp, it's warm, it's coated in the blood that pours from Ray's deep laceration all down my arm.

"You fucking cut me?!" he rages.

The knife clatters to the floor and he lets go of my twisted wrist. I turn to run as he lifts the butt of the shotgun above my head. There's a sharp crack at the back of my skull, and a syrupy warmth that begins to ooze into my hair. It's almost a relief, the way the world blurs and fizzes. I sink down to my hands and knees, like I'm praying to this murderous God above me. My vision tunnels as I begin to crawl, black haze eating at the edges of my sight. Ray kicks me in the ribs, hard enough that I land on my back. He plants his feet on either side of me, the leather of his boots warm through my jeans as he holds me in place, and he's all I can see in the pinpricks of my sight.

Ray. He's not smiling anymore. *What will he do to me?*

"So that's where you've been," Ray marvels, holding a Matchbox car up and spinning the wheels with his fingertip. "On a field trip. Looks like you got yourself some souvenirs." I stare at the little car, swallowed up in his big hand. The crude letters scratched into its underside are too far away for me to read, but I already know what they spell. *DANIEL.*

When I open my eyes, the pain in my head is so sharp I vomit a little. But I'm on my back, nowhere for the bile to go. I swallow it back down. It burns.

I'm cold. My arms are stretched above me, bound together and aching, and when I try to move them nothing happens. I tug again, harder. Fuck. I'm tied to the table, but worse than that, there's a length of rope or something equally strong running underneath the table, reaching from my wrists to each of my ankles. When I pull my wrists, the rope around my ankles tightens. If I try to kick my feet away from the table legs, it only drags the rope tighter around my wrists.

I tug at them anyway, twisting this way and that, but it's useless. Every tug makes the rope a little tighter. I am bound, trussed up like a roast turkey ready to be carved for Thanksgiving. Above the refrigerator, Damon's bobblehead toys and collectibles mock me with their unnaturally large eyes, their plastic grins, their ridiculous irony.

Ray appears at the edge of my vision. I turn my head just as he sits down on a dining chair and scoots toward me.

"You got me *good*," he murmurs, staring down at his palm. "You're a fucking bitch, you know that?" He laughs, but then his laughter turns to rage. He reaches his hand over and presses his bleeding palm to my mouth. Before I can clamp my lips together, warm blood breaches my mouth. It tastes like I just licked an ashtray full of pennies and dirt. I retch, trying to twist my head away as Ray digs his fingernails into my cheeks.

"You taste that?" he growls, standing, causing his chair to fall behind him with a crash. "You crazy bitch. That's on you. That's on *you*."

He shifts his grip, pinching my nostrils together and covering my mouth at the same time. I gasp against his hand, vacuum-sealed to my face, searching for air where there is none.

"You want me to take my hand away?" he asks, his dark eyes crazed, the pupils stretched wide open. It's as if I'm looking into hell when I look into those pupils, vast and empty and midnight-black.

I nod furiously, pleading with my eyes. *Please let me breathe.* He applies more pressure with his hand, digs his fingernails deeper. It's like having a fucking bear trying to claw my face off. He waits patiently as I struggle against his grip, as my whole body starts to shake uncontrollably, desperate and hungry for just a sip of oxygen. The room starts to spin, the edges turn dark. If I black out again, I don't know if I'll wake up. Maybe I'll just be dead. Maybe this is it.

I don't want this to be it. Not here. Not now. Not with Ray.

My lungs start to pulsate in my chest. I must look like a fish out of water when it spreads out its gills as it drowns in air.

"If I take my hand away, you're gonna behave. Okay?"

I nod some more. He takes his hand away and I turn my head from him, gasping in a breath. All I can taste is blood. All I can feel is the lactic acid screaming in my locked-up arms, the dead weight of my legs slung over the edge of the table, the burn in my lungs where air was gone for too long.

"I fucking *told* my brother you'd be a problem," he says, grabbing a roll of paper towels and wrapping a thick makeshift bandage around his hand. "I fucking told him. You think he'd listen?" He's muttering to himself, and to me, and if he doesn't kill me I don't know who'll be more surprised.

"Where's the fucking PBR?" he demands, disappearing from view again. I hear the refrigerator door open and slam shut. Seriously? I'm hog-tied to a table and he wants a fucking *beer*?

I hear him stomp out to the garage. The moment he leaves the kitchen a strangled sob floats out of me, unbidden and unexpected. I blink back tears, biting the insides of my cheeks. Crying is ammunition to people like Ray. Every tear shed is like handing him a nail for your coffin.

I wonder if I will get a coffin, or if I'll be rolled into the dirt beside Jennifer.

I wonder if he'll kill me first, or bury me alive.

So many details to ponder.

And he's back. He slams a six-pack of Pabst bottles on the table beside my head, making me jump. He gazes down at me as he tears a bottle from the pack and opens it, a predator sizing up his prey as he takes a slug of beer. He sets the bottle down, the condensation from the glass soaking through his makeshift bandage and turning the kitchen paper red. "Fucking useless," he mutters, unwinding the paper towel from his palm and tossing it aside.

"Now," Ray says, scratching the stubble on his chin. "What are we going to do with you?"

CHAPTER THIRTY-SEVEN

Cassie

What are we going to do with you?

His grin tells me. He's already decided what he's going to do with me. He's just waiting to see if I catch up.

"What happened to you to make you like this?" I whisper.

Ray stops for a moment, his grin shrinking. He pulls the Matchbox car he held earlier out of his shirt pocket and tosses it at me. It lands on my chest, and if I crane my neck I can see all of the tiny bits of rust on its metal frame.

"What happened to me? *What happened to me.*" He takes a pair of paramedic shears from his jeans pocket and steps into the space in front of me, pressing his thumb and forefinger into my thigh until I yelp. I know they're paramedic shears—metal scissors with the end kicked out at an angle to run along clothed skin without slicing somebody by accident—because I watched them cut off my mother's clothes in the hospital after her accident.

I crane my neck harder, watching as he reduces my jeans to ribbons of denim in seconds. "What are you doing?" I whimper.

"It's not what I'm doing that you need to worry about, darlin'," he says, finishing his handiwork. "It's what I'm about to do."

He chuckles.

I hyperventilate.

The air is cold, I am naked from the waist down, and he is right—it's *what he's about to do* that has me shaking. My whole body, trembling on the table like I'm having a seizure, the little Matchbox car on my chest bouncing every time I drag in a shallow breath. Ray takes his beer and sips it casually, grinning as he glances down at me. As if we're at a bar, on a date, and he isn't about to rape and murder me.

I'm cold and I'm half-naked, and *this cannot be happening*. I buck like a wild animal when Ray's fingers find their way to my thighs and push them wider like it's nothing, like I'm a piece of paper he's tearing in half. I scream so loud, I put Jennifer's death wails to shame.

"Don't!" I scream. *Fuck.* I scream as loud as I can, blood-curdling and shrill, and even though I told Leo to never come near this house again, I hope he didn't listen. "Please. *Please.* Don't."

I didn't want to beg but I beg now. *Please don't.* It doesn't matter, though.

Amused Ray is suddenly furious, raging Ray. He smacks me across the face, hard enough that I see stars. Before I can lift my head again, he's shoving a wadded-up bunch of denim into my mouth, a crude off-cut from what used to be my jeans. I gag, trying to dislodge the material with my tongue, but it won't budge, conforming to the shape of my mouth and making me retch.

"You shouldn't have done that," he says angrily. "You think lover boy down there is gonna save you? Huh? You think my brother's gonna bust through that door and stop me?" He drains the last of his beer and leans over me, spitting the liquid right into my face. I try to draw back but there's nowhere to go, and all I manage to do is smack the back of my head against the table. Beer, warm from Ray's mouth, dribbles into my eyes and nose and down the sides of my face, into my ears.

"Stay still," he demands, spitting into his hand and slapping his palm against the spot where my panties should be. Where they *would* be, had I not lost them somewhere in Leo's bed. "Stay still or you'll get what you deserve, just like your mother got what she deserved."

My mother? I don't stay still. I struggle. I fight. Ray's trying in vain to get himself inside me, but he can't. It's like trying to get that last scoop of ice cream from the bowl. It's slippery and you chase it but you can't quite get it on your spoon.

There is blood and beer and saliva and Ray can't quite get the ice cream on his spoon, can't quite get his dick wet. Not with me thrashing like a wild animal. He punches me, and I don't stop struggling. He screams in my face, "Lie! Still!" and I don't stop struggling.

Clearly agitated, he takes a kitchen towel and presses it over my face, which is not so bad. I can't see, but it doesn't hurt. Then he pours cold beer all over the cloth, making it stick to my mouth and nose so that when I try to take a breath, all I get is burning liquid. He grips my chin with one hand and pushes my face up so that the liquid easily flows into my nostrils. It's waterboarding for rednecks. It's like being plunged headfirst into Gun Creek in the middle of winter, and held there. But it's worse. Because I can't stop the beer flooding my nostrils, from pouring into my mouth through the cloth that vacuum-seals to my face the moment I try to take a breath.

I'm going to drown inside my house, without a single drop of water, and there's nothing I can do to stop it.

"I got no problem fucking you when you're dead if that's what it takes," Ray says, pulling the wet cloth from my face as I retch. "Lie. Still."

I lie still.

"Good girl. You're learning." Ray pushes into me, the awful sound of his teeth grinding matched only by my stifled sobs. It hurts. Ray grunts as he ruts, back and forth, like a blunt saw trying to fell a tree. Back and forth.

Back and forth.

I *lie still.* Beer burns lines of fire inside my sinuses, in my chest. Rope burns at my wrists, around my ankles, biting tighter into my skin every time Ray pushes deeper, everywhere is fire.

I surrender to the pain. I let it take me, like a wave, like a tsunami. Drowning isn't peaceful, but it is easier once you stop resisting it.

I've left my body, taken it off like a dirty dress and left it puddled on the floor while I float along the ceiling and watch. And wait.

Please hurry. Hurry for what, I'm not sure. For him to finish. For him to kill me. Or for somebody to open the front door.

Brother, you'd best get home. Ray's words, when he called Damon. How long ago was that call? Ten minutes? An hour? I have no sense of time. I don't know how long I was blacked out on the table while Ray tied my limbs and watched over me. I don't know how long he's been on top of me. All I know is Damon should have been home long ago.

Never thought I'd be wishing for my worst nightmare to turn up and rescue me.

Then again, I never thought I'd be tied to my own kitchen table, the one where I sit and eat cereal that tastes like lies and sour milk every single morning, while my not-uncle rapes me to death.

Some things you just can't imagine until they're happening.

And then he's . . . there. Here. Standing in the kitchen, his blue eyes wide and bright, hand on his gun holster.

"Ray."

You would think that Ray would stop.

He doesn't.

"Ray!"

Ray. Doesn't. Stop.

I want to scream out to him, but I can't.

Help me. Please help me. Save me from this man.

But he doesn't. He just fucking stands there, looking like he might cry.

Ray stops his rutting long enough to address his brother, to take a slug of beer. What a multitasker, our Ray. I moan through the cloth stuffed into my mouth, vying for the attention of a seriously fucked-up police sheriff who should be shooting Ray right now, if he had any moral compass.

"I caught her sneaking in the front door," Ray says, panting from exertion. "Stinking like a dirty cum bucket, weren't you, darlin'?" He jabs a finger into my stomach, hard, enough that I scream. "She came straight from that little shit's trailer down there. No panties and a nice little cream pie to remember him by." Ray glances down at me. "What, you think I didn't check you out before I started to fuck you?"

Pleasemakehimstop.Damon!Youhavetohelpme.Please.PLEASE.

My words are one long unintelligible tangle, muffled through my gag. I beg with my eyes. But Damon doesn't hear.

"Pull up a pew, brother," Ray says, rearing back and driving into me so hard I scream again. "Grab a brew. We're gonna use this bitch up before we bury her."

Ray takes the paramedic shears and cuts through my shirt and bra, throwing scraps of material on the floor, everything gone now. My nipples tighten in protest against the cold, my body shivering even more violently without any cover.

I am as naked as the day I was born, and probably just as bloody.

I stare at Damon in disbelief. My fear blossoms, it becomes anger, it becomes rage, warm and thick in my veins as my heart beats vicious and fast. I watch as he takes a seat. As he scrubs his hand across his stubble, his anxiety palpable. As he looks at the spot where Ray is violating me, over and over, and does *nothing*.

He finally looks at my face again, and that's when I understand: This is my punishment. This is my lesson. I broke the rules. I went to Leo. And now, I'm going to wear the consequences.

Damon looks sick. I wonder what I look like. I'm covered in blood and beer, and the side of my face is swelling rapidly from Ray's fists.

"Remember, Danny?" Ray says, panting heavily as he continues to thrust into me. "Remember how good we used to be together? I bet we could both take this one at the same time. Just like old times."

He called him *Danny*.

"Shut up, Ray," Damon snaps.

Ray doesn't let up. "We haven't shared a girl since that junkie Creek bitch," he says, wrapping his hands around my throat and squeezing tighter. The part of me that's left in my body—that tiny sliver of Cassie—looks at Damon, pleading with her eyes as she starts to smother. "Remember?"

We haven't shared a girl since that junkie Creek bitch. Something about that statement hits me, and I mentally catalog it so I can study it later. Assuming there is a later for me.

I see Damon reach behind him for something. I'm on the ceiling again. Floating. I can't hear and I can't feel. All I can do is float, and wait until it's over. Suddenly, I miss my snowflakes. Miss having something to count. Ray has stamina, that's for sure. I thought for sure he wouldn't be able to last more than a minute or two. But he just keeps going and going, relentless, back and forth, his fingers around my throat stealing my breath, stealing my life.

And then, just like that, I am brutally thrust back into my abused, naked body, as the whole room explodes.

At least, that's how it looks. Something makes a dull bang-hiss beside my ear. Ray's head explodes like a watermelon under a jackhammer, bits of blood and slush splattering a 360 where he was standing just a second ago. I feel him pulled from inside me, and then a crash as what's left hits the hardwood below.

Ray has disappeared—he's just *gone*—and Damon is standing beside the table, a gun in one hand, complete with a silencer screwed onto the barrel. No wonder the noise wasn't louder. But could Leo have heard it from his place? I doubt it. Damon looms over me, the knife suddenly in his hand, brandishing it above my face.

I'm covered in wet stuff—in what's left of Ray—and now Damon is going to stab me to death?

"I'm not going to hurt you," he spits out, taking the knife and freeing my wrists. They're still bound together, but no longer attached to the length of rope that runs under the table and secures my ankles. The rope tears loose under the blade and I instinctively curl my arms back down and around myself, the pain in my shoulders indescribable. It's as if someone has cut off my arms with a rusty butter knife and then stapled them back on.

Damon circles to the end of the table and frees my ankles as well; I draw my knees to my chest, slipping on the blood and beer coating the table, and then I'm falling, landing hard on my side on something wet.

I'm on the floor, my arms wrapped around my knees, and I'm resting on warm, bare flesh. I turn my head to the side and scream into my gag, feeling my eyes practically bug out of my head at the sight of Ray's half-missing skull. There is blood *everywhere*. I'm lying in it, it's splattered against the side of my face, all over my arms, I'm lying in Ray's blood and brains.

I'm lying in *what's left of Ray*.

Damon scoops his arms under my shoulders and gets me to a sitting position. "You gonna be quiet?" he asks.

I nod feverishly, and he sticks his fingers into my mouth, scooping out the cloth jammed inside. As soon as my mouth is free, I lean over and throw up. My hair is loose and I'm pretty sure I get vomit in it, but I don't care. I don't care about anything.

On hands and heels, I crawl away from Ray, backward, never letting him out of my sights lest he should spring back to life and murder me. He makes a move and I can no longer see him. I feel hands behind me, yanking me up on shaking knees, and the soft *knick* sound of Damon cutting my wrists free.

My back is against his chest, and I sag into him as he holds me off the floor. My head lolls against his shoulder, and I can't find it in me to try and run, even though he's probably going to shoot me now. Even though I know he's a murderer. *I must be in shock*, I think. I'm frozen, and not just from the bitter cold. I can't get my limbs to work. Can't get my brain to kick into gear and tell me what to do next. Can't stop looking at Ray, at the top of his skull, the way it just smashed apart like a piñata full of watermelon slices.

"I have one question," Damon murmurs, his mouth so close to my ear I can feel the graze of his teeth on my earlobe. "Was he telling the truth about Leo?"

My silence is enough of an answer for him.

"Oh, Cassie," he says sadly. "I try so hard to make you happy. And you are *such* a disappointment to me."

His gentle hands turn hard. One stays on my arm, his fingers like a vise. The other threads into my messy hair, fists a bunch of bloody strands, and rips me to my feet.

"Wh-what are you doing!?" I shriek, trying to get his hand away from my scalp. It feels like he's going to pull my skin off right down to the bone, peel off my mask and leave me just a faceless skull.

My entire body starts to shake violently. Because I thought this was over. I thought I was safe. But I'm not safe, am I? I've traded one monster for another. There's a reason they pretended to be brothers. Somebody took Damon all those years ago, put him in their car, and drove away, and something so bad happened that Damon *never went home*. Never went to the police and told them he'd survived.

Survived what? What happened to that ten-year-old boy to turn him into this? What was so bad that he'd rather have a gravesite for himself instead of admitting that he lived?

He drags me to the upstairs bathroom by my hair. It hurts more than you'd think, being dragged by your hair. I'm still covered in pieces of Ray, blood and skull, and sticky from having taken facefuls of Pabst. A bright red line paints my forced ascent up the stairs, onto stark white tiles, and into the small shower stall where Damon shoves me. I land awkwardly, pain shooting through my knees and up my body. *It can always get worse,* I remind myself, as freezing cold water erupts from the shower and douses me. So cold. So, so cold. It's winter—a few degrees cooler and the pipes would freeze over in our house.

I try to scream, but barely a whisper comes out. I'm so cold. So stunned. So weak. I can barely make a sound. I gasp as Damon reaches in and shoves my head under the steady stream of ice-cold water, panting as I watch Ray's blood wash off me and circle around the drain.

"Look at me," Damon snaps.

I look at him.

Everything is pale in here; white tiles, white ceiling, white towels.

Even the whites of Damon's eyes. But it's the irises that fix me to the shower floor, the same way a pin might fix a dead butterfly inside a glass case. So blue. Blue used to be my favorite color. That was before. Now, I hate the color. Now I want to forsake the sky, the ocean, because they remind me of Damon King. *Daniel Collins,* I correct myself. His real name is Daniel Collins.

"I should take you outside and hose you down in the snow like a fucking animal," Damon breathes. "That's all you are. A fucking *animal.*"

He shuts off the water and leaves me there, on the tiles, shivering, my arms wrapped around my knees. I hear water running and realize he's filling the old claw-foot bath that sits beside the shower. A moment later, he's picking me up like I'm a feather and lowering me into the bath.

I find my voice when my bare ass hits hot water. I scream. After the cold of the shower, it's as if he's dropped me into a vat full of acid. Maybe he has. Maybe this is how he kills me. Damon claps a hand over my mouth. I hold the sides of the tub as if it's a lifeboat and I'm being tossed around in the middle of the ocean, instead of being boiled alive in my own bathroom. *Onetwothreefourfive,* and the burning sensation recedes ever so slightly.

Damon takes his hand away from my mouth, handing me a bar of soap and a washcloth. "Clean yourself up," he says, his jaw set. He takes a step back and watches intently as I shake and scrub the blood from my skin. I should be crying, shouldn't I? Crying or having a breakdown or something. Instead, I'm thinking about Ray. About Jennifer. About Karen.

"Are you going to bury Ray with Jennifer?" I ask suddenly.

Damon glares at me. He's starting to look a little worse for wear, my philandering stepdaddy. His clothes are covered in blood, his eyes are bloodshot to hell, and the black circles under them weren't there when I met him. It must be hard to keep your youth when you're busy stealing it from everyone else.

"What kind of question is that?" he snaps. "Of course not." And then, "Sometimes I worry about you, Cassie."

There's a dead man missing half his skull downstairs, a teenage girl and her stillborn fetus buried in the yard below this window, and *this is what makes him worry about me?* The ridiculousness of his thought process makes me laugh in my head at first, and then my whole body is taken by a convulsion that brings tears to my eyes and a cramp to my stomach. Laughter is so close to crying, that pretty soon my cackle is a full-blown sob, strips torn off my soul, my eyes bleeding salty tears that burn my eyes.

I bring my knees up to my chest and hug my arms around them, just a small ball of a girl, naked and waiting to die.

I break.

I cry and cry, cracked open, falling apart, or just plain falling.

This is not a fairy tale and there is no happy ending, no prince to ride in on his horse and save me.

It's just me and my monster, just us in our house built out of bones and lies.

"*Cassie,*" Damon says, his tone softer this time. Almost like he's pleading. For what, I don't know. There's a longing in his tone, a need. He puts his hand on mine, squeezing gently. I would recoil, but there's nowhere to retreat to.

"I went to Lone Pine today," I whisper.

His entire demeanor changes. He squeezes my hand harder, and when he speaks, there is fear in his voice, incredulity. "*What?*"

Now he knows that I know. Now he knows that I have his secrets. Maybe this will be my end. Maybe he'll thread his hands through my hair and hold my head under water until I suck in a watery last breath.

Maybe that would be the very best thing for him to do.

"I went to your grave," I say sadly, crying again. I don't know why I'm crying for him, because he's never caused me anything but darkness. But as I look at Damon King, a person who doesn't exist, a boy from a milk carton, I cry. His grip on my hand is so tight now he's crushing my bones. "That's where I went. I found your milk cartons in the attic. I needed to know. *I needed to know.*"

When his words come out, he sounds like a little boy. "Did you tell anyone?"

I shake my head. "There's nobody left to tell."

He lets go of me, sagging to the floor. He starts to cry, too. All these years and I don't think I've ever seen him cry.

CHAPTER THIRTY-EIGHT

Cassie

One bath, two shots of bourbon, three extra blankets. I can't get warm. I can't stop shaking. My teeth chatter along to the beat of my heart, a hummingbird trapped in my ribcage desperately hitting against my bones in an effort to break free. There are water stains on my ceiling, dark brown patches with irregular edges. They remind me of blood. If they hadn't been there for so long I could mistake them for Jennifer's blood seeping through the attic floor, through the ceiling, dripping onto my face as I slept.

All these thoughts of blood, of course, because I still itch from it, from Ray. He's still downstairs, what's left of him, and Damon is dressed in a blue plastic crime scene suit, ready to battle the carnage and make everything disappear.

"Open," he says to me from his spot on the edge of the bed. I open my mouth obediently. Usually he would be sliding something else in at this point, but tonight it's a little white pill on the end of his finger. He presses it deep enough that I almost gag, forcing the pill down dry. This isn't the first time he's drugged me, but usually it's crushed up in a glass of milk, like he thinks he's tricking me. Tonight he's dropped the pretense.

"You'll be out in a few minutes," he says, like I don't already know.

We've danced this dance a thousand times. More than a thousand. How many days since I turned eighteen? That's how many nights, give or take. That's how many pills. He gets up to leave just as the pill is threading its way through my limbs, down my chest, deep into my core.

I catch Damon's hand with loose fingers. He looks back, confusion on his face, irritation.

"I have to go," he says.

I start to cry again. "*Idontwantyoutogo.*"

I won't remember most of this in the morning. The pill will leave me with a thankful case of near-amnesia. I will recall flashes of things, single words picked out of the fray, but that's it. That is the greatest mercy and the biggest lie of all. *I will not remember.* But now, encased in the thick rush of euphoria, of whatever he's given me frothing in my veins, I need him to stay.

"Please, don't go," I beg, my words slurring under the sedative effect of the drug. I beg him! I am a sick girl. I am ruined. I will take my captor because he is the only person left in the world. I see the hesitation in Damon's eyes, the hard reality of what's to come when he reaches the foot of the stairs and steps in his brother's blood. He can't stay, but he doesn't want to go, either.

He relents. He strips off the plastic blue overalls he was wearing, naked underneath, and slides into the bed beside me. His hands are hot on my cold skin. Despite my hot bath, two shots of bourbon, and three extra blankets, I am as cold as Jennifer's bones in the icy ground. The moon casts an eerie sliver of light into the room through the gap in my curtains, a sliver that illuminates Damon's face.

His head rests on the pillow beside mine, his hand under the blankets on my bare hip. He slides his palm down, cupping between my legs.

"Did it hurt?" he asks.

I nod.

"Do you want me to make it better?"

These damn pills and the haze they cloud you in. In ten minutes they can turn you from an unwilling victim into a begging slut.

Do you want me to make it better?

I do. I nod.

And then he's on me and *in* me and the room is spinning, my knees pressed wide, my hips protesting at the way I'm spread apart. But none of it registers as pain anymore, not when I'm flying high above Gun Creek in a hallucinatory daze. Damon uses me as I use him, as he scratches an itch deep inside me that nobody can ever seem to find. He takes and I take and no wonder we are all so empty, so barren, so dead inside. His thumb finds the magical spot, right above where he's pushing inside me, and I finally feel whole again.

I bite down on my tongue so I do not say Leo's name. I come quickly, loudly, and when Damon kisses the moan from my mouth, there is blood.

CHAPTER THIRTY-NINE

Cassie

The morning brings a blue tinge to the world, a fresh layer of snow, a kitchen and a staircase scrubbed clean of any crime. I want to ask where Ray is buried, or burned or submerged, but I don't. I make coffee instead, and sip it from my Disney mug like nothing ever happened. My body is humming pleasantly, thanks to the two Percocet I took before I got out of bed. The heat is blasting through the house, I can't feel the rope burns on my wrists and ankles through my buzz, and there's a gentle snow falling outside the kitchen window. The dining table Ray tied me to is gone, probably firewood now, and our plastic outdoor table sits in the spot where it once lived.

Damon hasn't slept by the look of him. I sit down at the new table, across from him, wincing as my bruised thighs make contact with the dining chair.

"Did you sleep?" Damon asks.

I return his vacant stare. "Like the dead."

"Are you fucking kidding me?"

"Too soon?"

"Just shut up and get me some coffee."

I mock salute him, standing up from my chair. My sweater is loose, and it drops down my arm, exposing my bruised shoulder. Damon looks at the bruises, then at me. I hold his gaze for a moment before I pour him a cup of coffee from the pot, slamming it down on the table in front of him.

I resume my spot, drinking my own coffee as I size up the man who thought it was a good idea to roofie and fuck me *after* his brother raped me.

"Cassie," Damon says sharply. "Say something."

Something, huh? *Okay.*

"What did Ray mean about that junkie Creek bitch?"

Damon's eyes cloud over and he looks at the floor.

"It was Karen, wasn't it?" I prod.

Damon looks at the ceiling and nods, his eyes glassy as he blinks. "Yeah. It was Karen."

Something inside my chest tightens so hard, I can barely breathe. "Did you kill Karen, Damon? Did you kill her and dump her body on Leo's property so it would look like he had something to do with it?"

He shakes his head tightly. "I didn't. I wouldn't."

"Did you rape Karen Brainard?"

He gives me a withering look. "You don't need to *rape* girls like Karen, Cassie. You just need the right currency. Hers was any kind of upper she could get her filthy little hands on."

"You're not supposed to speak ill of the dead."

Damon snorts. "I think we drove off that bridge a long time ago."

Something about the way he says that rattles me. I can't quite put my finger on it, but I'm deeply unsettled.

"Is that why you killed Ray? Because of what he did to Karen?"

He finally meets my gaze again. "I killed him because of what he did to you, Cassie. *You.* I thought . . . I didn't know how else to stop him."

You stopped him, all right. Stopped him all over the kitchen. Now there are pieces of his skull stuck in my hair.

"I hate you," I say plainly.

"I know that," he replies.

"You knew that, and you still killed your brother for me?" I should be thankful, but I'm just confused. "Your *brother*."

Damon looks at me and I see the little boy in his grown eyes. The fear. The dread. I didn't find Daniel Collins when I visited his empty grave, but I have found him now.

My skin breaks out in goose bumps as his words sink past my bruises, down into my bones, where they settle, heavy like lead.

"He wasn't my brother," Damon says, pushing his coffee away. "He was the one who made me get into that van."

CHAPTER FORTY

Cassie

Damon, sadly, has to work. Which means I am dropped off at the diner for my 10 a.m. start, just in time to walk into a fucking shit show.

The place is teeming with truckers, waiting out a snowstorm up north before they carry on with their loads. Everyone wants to eat, waffles and bacon and endless refills of coffee. I don't want to be here, and I'm limping more and more as the painkillers wear off.

Everything hurts.

Even the tips of my fingers feel bruised from where I tried to fight Ray off. I can't close my eyes without seeing the mess Damon's gun made of his face, the blood. I beg an easy task from Amanda, who directs me to a booth in the back to roll cutlery and fold napkins. She can tell I am sick with something. I wonder what she'd say if she knew I was sick with having almost been murdered in my own kitchen less than twelve hours ago. I'm folding a stack of napkins when he appears.

"Cassie," a low voice says, startling me to attention.

"Fuck," I mutter, knocking over the black coffee I just poured for myself. Hot liquid goes everywhere, all over the table and my stack of neatly folded napkins. I stare dejectedly at the scene in front of me, not bothering to clean up the mess.

"Shit, I'm sorry," Leo says. He fetches a wad of dish towels from the pass, mopping up the coffee as I watch impassively. "Cassie, are you okay?"

I jerk my head up to meet his gaze. God, he's like a fucking teddy bear. His eyes are soft and imploring. I just want to jump into his arms and beg him to take me away from all of this before Damon kills me, or worse, kills him.

"You're scaring me," he whispers, looking around the diner. We're alone in this little corner for the moment, but who knows how long that will last.

"*I'm* scaring *you?*" I say scathingly, staring up at six feet and three inches of muscle and flesh. My God, he survived prison, and he finds me frightening?

"You're not . . . *you*," he says, balling up coffee-soaked napkins and dropping them on the table between us. "What happened last night after you went home?"

"I can't do this anymore," I say. "I can't see you again."

"Bullshit," Leo says, sliding into the booth opposite me. "What. Happened?"

I stare out the window, into the forest, where the police and an army of volunteers searched three times for any trace of Jennifer.

"Did he hit you?" Leo says, reaching across the table, his hand cupping my jaw as he studies the swollen left side of my face, bruises and swelling that my bangs and a thick application of concealer only half hide.

"I walked into a door," I say vacantly. I can't tell him the truth. I can't open that can of worms. It will ruin everything. If Leo provokes Damon, Leo will end up back in prison, and this time, it might be for good.

"Cassie, just tell me what to do, and I'll do it."

Take me away. Hide me. Love me. Save me.

All perfectly acceptable responses for the way I'm feeling. For the violent brutality I've been subjected to. I just want to go somewhere dark and safe and silent with Leo, bury my face in his chest, and sob.

"Tell me what to do," he repeats, his tone more urgent this time.

I look up at him, wiping my face of emotion as if it were a blank slate. It has to be.

If Damon thinks Leo has anything to do with me, he'll kill him.

"You've already done enough," I say coolly.

I think of Ray's face. I think of Damon's hands. I think of the way I punched Leo as I fucked him. Something breaks inside of me. I wonder how many days—no, how many years until Damon grows tired of me and lets me leave.

I think of how peaceful Ray was after he died, leaving only a broken, empty vessel.

How I was so horrified at the time. How now, I'm not horrified; I'm jealous. Furious, filled with the envious truth that he got to die and I had to stay.

And I decide, very calmly, very matter-of-factly, that I'm done. Finished. *I quit.*

I stand, not bothering to collect my apron and order pad, both now covered in coffee. I won't be needing them. I won't be back here tomorrow.

Leo stands, too, blocking my path, and I take the opportunity to reach out and press my fingers flat against his chest, right above his heart.

"I know it was an accident," I say, smiling sadly. "I know you waited for me in that prison, all those years. I know you love me. Okay?"

Leo's jaw clenches, his eyes darken. Anguish. Oh, how well I know that feeling.

I wish it could be different. This is my greatest unanswered wish, the thing that burned in some tiny part of my soul all these years. That someday, things might be different. But as I look at Leo, the boy I used to know, the man I still love, I search for that flame that burned quietly.

It's not there anymore. It's gone. Just like Jennifer, it has disappeared. The love is there, but the hope—the hope has been smothered.

"I'm so sorry, Leo," I say softly. "You waited all that time to see me again. And I was *such* a disappointment to you."

"Cass, wait—" he says, but I don't stop. I keep walking, through the kitchen, past the office, through the back door, and outside.

It's cold, so very cold, but it doesn't matter. I walk around the side of the building, until I get past the dumpsters and into the parking lot, and then I start to run.

I make it home in record time. Thirteen minutes—I don't think I've ever run so fast. I slow only when I reach our front driveway, checking for signs of Damon.

He's not here. I saw his car parked in front of the sheriff's office, and there's no way he'd come back on foot. I still don't have keys to my own fucking house, not that it matters.

I go around back and find a suitable piece of firewood in the stack that leans up against the house, using it as a club that I swing into the kitchen window. It breaks on the third hit.

Momentarily, I stare at the spot where Jennifer is buried and feel a pang of jealousy stab at me. I think, for a long moment, about how peaceful it must be under all that dirt, then I drop the piece of wood, hoisting myself up on a couple of old cinderblocks and into the kitchen.

Cold air billows into the house, but I ignore it. I collect my supplies with military precision; a razor blade, a fifth of vodka, a chair, the bottle of Percocet I've had hidden beneath a loose floorboard in my bedroom. I take it all up to the bathroom, where not twelve hours ago Damon was scrubbing Ray's blood from my burning skin.

I hope he finds me, dead and bloodless.

I hope he cries.

I hope it rips him to shreds that his love, his darkness, was the thing that killed me.

I take the pills while the tub fills with warm water, three at a time, washed down with vodka that burns as I gulp it. I can't take so many pills that I start throwing up, but enough that it won't hurt so much when I slip off, or under, or whatever the fuck it is that comes before my final sleep. I catch sight of myself in the mirror as I'm throwing pills down my throat, and the girl staring back at me makes me so fucking angry that I ball my hand into a fist and smash the mirror to pieces. My knuckles start to bleed, the pain sharp and hot. *Good. Very good.*

I strip down to my underwear, the bruises and cuts littering my body telling a tale that I'd never be able to voice. I sink into the tub, steam rising from the water's surface, taking the razor and pressing it into the flesh at my left wrist before I can think, before I can hesitate. Oh, fuck, it hurts. Even with the painkillers starting to take effect, it still hurts enough that I gag. Blood spurts from my radial artery like syrup, thicker than I expected, and faster. The room spins. *Holy fuck.* Maybe I won't have to cut the other one after all.

But *Damon.* He could come home at any moment. Find me. Save me. And then spend the rest of my life making sure I'm never alone again.

Cut the other wrist, the dark voice inside me urges. It's so hard to grip the razor in my left hand, what with the blood gushing from my left wrist and all, but I manage. I repeat the action on my right wrist, not getting quite as deep, but deep enough that this shouldn't take long.

I drop the razor somewhere in the water, letting my head loll back against the edge of the tub. I hold my wrists up in front of me, laughing, and then it all goes blissfully, beautifully black inside. It was a nice life, before Damon. *It was such a lovely life before him.*

CHAPTER FORTY-ONE

Leo

She explicitly warned me against going to her house. But something's not right. Something is very fucking wrong. I don't know what happened last night after Cassie got home. I watched as she got inside and flicked on the light. I watched as Damon arrived home. I watched as the bathroom light went on, and Cassie's bedroom, and finally as the house went dark. There was no noise, no struggle, no signal that I was desperately seeking. And so I went back to bed, Cassie's panties in my hand as I jerked off and came all over the sheets where we'd just fucked for the first time in eight years.

But the girl I watched run up to her front door last night was not the same girl I frightened in the diner this morning. Something happened. Something *bad*. And I'm going to find out what he did to her.

If only she'd open the goddamn front door. I knock and knock, pounding my fist on the door to no avail. I ring the bell. Something is wrong. There's an anxiety gnawing at me. I need to get inside this house. I need to see for myself that Cassie is okay. When she left, there was a look in her eyes that scared the absolute shit out of me. A look I've never seen before, not even after the accident all those years ago.

I go around back, trudging through melting snow to the rear door. I'm about to try it when I notice the kitchen window has been smashed.

Shit. If she's in there, alone, and someone has broken in, I have to get in there and save her. I'll kill them if I have to, to keep her safe. I don't care if I end up on death row if it keeps her from harm.

I climb up into the window quietly, shimmying through the gap and dropping over the kitchen counter and to the floor as silently as possible. I check the bottom floor before creeping up the stairs, taking them two at a time, flinching when the boards creak halfway up.

I can hear water running, and that's where I go—to the bathroom. I try to open the door, but it's jammed with something. "Cassie!?" I yell. Now that I know she's in the bathroom, I'm not worried about an intruder—I'm worried about what a beat-up girl is doing in the tub at midday on a Friday. If she's taking a bubble bath after a grueling work shift, if she's listening to her iPod and can't hear me, I will replace the door and apologize a thousand times over.

But I know in my bones that Cassie isn't relaxing or listening to music or having a fucking bubble bath. I saw the haunted look in her eyes before she took off running; I've known that feeling myself a time or two. In the days after I found Karen in the well. In the nights after I drove off the bridge and ruined Cassie's mother. In the long years I spent in Lovelock prison, everything blurring into one long nightmare. I saw that look in her eyes. The look that said: *I don't know if I can go on.*

"Cassie!" I yell one more time, just in case. Nothing. I smash my shoulder into the door as hard as I can, again and again. On the third go, it opens slightly, just a crack, enough for me to see my beautiful girl lying pale and motionless in a bathtub full of water and blood.

"Oh, shit," I mutter, kicking the door until I've created a hole big enough to reach my arm into. I discover the chair propped underneath the door handle and unwedge it, opening the door and rushing to the bath. I hit the tiles with my knees, the shock vibrating up my body as I look down at Cassie. She's so fucking pale, dressed in a bra and panties, cuts and bruises littering her entire form. But it's not those I'm worried about now. It's the deep gashes in her arms that are pouring with blood, blood that starts bright red and diffuses to a pinkish color in the water she floats in. With her hair fanned around her shoulders, she looks like an angel. She looks dead.

"No," I whisper, reaching in and lifting her out of the tub, setting her on the tiled floor. I grab at the towels hanging on the rack, wrapping one around each of her bleeding wounds and holding her arms above her body, trying to use gravity to help stem the thick pulsing of blood from the identical deep lacerations on her wrists. I hold her wrists in one hand, searching for a pulse at her neck. It's so faint I can barely feel her heart, struggling to pump whatever blood is left in her body to keep it going.

"Cassie, can you hear me?" I fish my phone from my jeans pocket and dial 911. I know that by doing this, I'm inviting the wrath of Damon King upon me, but I don't care. I would walk through fire to save this girl. I would open my chest and bleed my heart's blood into her if it would save her right now. I would kill everyone in the world if it brought her back, if it woke her up. The ambulance is dispatched. I hear sirens wail in the distance. I keep checking her heartbeat because I'm terrified that if I take my fingers away from her neck, she will die right here in my arms.

CHAPTER FORTY-TWO

Cassie

I didn't die.

I couldn't even get that right.

What I did do was ensure that I'll never be alone long enough to try it again. I don't remember Leo finding me in the bathtub, or the ambulance arriving, or Damon riding in the back with me. I don't remember them tapping his vein to transfuse more blood into me after their stock ran out.

I do remember waking up in the hospital, though, strapped to a bed with leather restraints, my wrists stitched up and bandaged heavily and my pumped stomach full of charcoal, my poor, concerned step-daddy sitting beside my bed.

I remember the drive home, two days later, after Damon had signed me out with a promise to watch me like a hawk and never leave me alone. I remember the way he pulled up on the side of the road when we were halfway home, pointed at a clearing in the thick pine trees, and told me that's where he'd bury Leo's body if I ever pulled a stunt like that again.

That was three weeks ago.

Now, Chris McCallister sits across from me, his fingers drumming restlessly along the arm of the sofa. I had to rearrange this room, move the floor rug to cover the large stain that Ray's blood made. Ironically, not from the shot that killed him—apparently, that blood came clean off the floorboards in the dining nook. But in here, in the living room, the wooden boards lining the floor aren't glossy, but dull and sanded back, waiting for a fresh coat of varnish.

Instead, they got a fresh spray of blood when I slashed Ray's palm with a carving knife.

Damon says we'll need an industrial sander to get the stain out, so in the meantime, my mother's Turkish rugs and some clever furniture repositioning will have to suffice. Thank God it didn't seep under the piano—he'd probably make me lug it myself. The only reason I don't want anyone to find out what happened to Ray is the same reason I don't want anyone to find out what happened to Jennifer—because Damon will, undoubtedly, be able to pin the crimes on Leo and send him to prison for the rest of his life.

Nevada has the death penalty.

That's not going to happen.

Chris is here because Damon had to go into Reno and meet with a new task force. They're taking over the investigation into Jennifer's disappearance. And since I can't be alone, I have a babysitter here.

I doubt Damon would have chosen Chris had he known our history. Still. He doesn't have any real friends, and he killed his own so-called brother to save me. So I guess Deputy Chris is as good as it gets as far as babysitters for suicidal stepdaughters.

"You want something to drink?" I ask, breaking the silence.

Chris shakes his head. "No, thanks. I'm good."

I wander into the kitchen, looking at the view through our brand-new kitchen window. Safety glass. Unbreakable. Another lock on my tomb.

I pour myself coffee and replace the pot, turning to see Chris has followed me into the kitchen. "Thank Christ you followed me in here," I say. "I almost killed myself getting this coffee."

Chris rolls his eyes, circling the counter. "I know you don't want me here," he says, looking at me across the kitchen. "But nobody wants you to hurt yourself, Cassie."

I take a deep breath. It's not myself I want to hurt right now. It's everyone else. I've got this boiling rage inside me, this frustration. I can't even pee without somebody standing outside the bathroom door, talking me through it. I need to escape, but I can't. I need to see Leo, but I *can't*.

"Have you seen Leo lately?" I ask Chris. Suddenly, his presence isn't so annoying. Suddenly, I can see a way to find out what's happening.

Chris nods. "I saw him at the hospital," he says. "After you—well, after they brought you in. He was pretty messed up. Kept asking all the nurses if you'd made it, but they wouldn't tell him a thing. Damon told them not to talk to him about you."

I nod. "I hope somebody told him I'm alive," I murmur.

"I told him," Chris says, looking guilty.

"Thanks," I reply, surprised. Chris is loyal to Damon, but I guess he's only human, too.

"Why are you still so worried about him?" Chris blurts out. "I mean, after everything. Why?"

I frown. "It was an accident," I say slowly. "It was a fucked-up thing that he did, but he didn't go out there that night intending to kill my mother."

"I'm not talking about the accident," Chris says.

Fear spikes along my spine, thick and cloying. "What are you talking about?"

"Cassie. I'm talking about Jennifer. It looks pretty fucking bad, don't you think?"

Panic rises in my chest and I push it down. I wish I had a drink right now. "He didn't do it, Chris."

Chris says nothing, but his jaw flexes like he's debating whether to talk more. Like there's something he's dying to say to me.

"I thought you were Leo's friend," I say, shocked. "I thought you were *my* friend. If you know something, tell me."

"I could lose my job," Chris protests.

"Leo could get the death penalty," I snap. "But sure. You worry about your job."

"You've been working in a diner since you finished high school while I worked my ass off looking for dead girls," Chris says, stabbing his finger in the general location of the diner. "Don't pretend this is nothing. I can't tell you anything. This is an active investigation!"

"Oh, my God," I say, clutching the counter. "You think he did it, don't you?"

Chris is visibly agitated. "Come on, Cass. They found Karen next to his house! On his property! And then Jennifer's just gone right after he gets back to town? After he's seen with her every goddamn day from the time he got back until the night she disappeared? How am I supposed to trust him when he tells me he didn't do either of these things? Huh?"

Angry tears are burning my eyes. "You don't seriously mean that. I was with him when Karen was murdered."

"Well, maybe I don't trust you either," he says.

Imagine if I told him that he was standing on top of the bloodstain that belongs to the dead man who slaughtered Karen. Imagine if I told him that Jennifer was outside the window, dead and buried. Imagine if I told him *everything*.

He probably wouldn't believe me.

Nobody ever believes you when you try to tell the truth.

"I want to show you something," he says.

"I don't want to see your dick, Chris."

"Cassie!"

"Sorry. Jesus. Ever heard of a joke?"

Chris pulls his phone out, hits a few keys, hands it to me.

"We can joke later. I want you to tell me if you know this car. If you've ever seen it. Who it would belong to."

I look down at the photo and a deep unease spreads in my belly. "I don't think so," I say slowly. "Why?"

"Look again."

I pretend to look again, even though I don't need to. "Nope. What's so special about this car?"

Chris sighs, pocketing his phone again. He looks disappointed. "Nothing. Leo came to me a while ago, asked me to look into some paint chips on the side of his Mustang."

"His Mustang from the accident? I thought that car was crushed or scrapped or whatever."

Chris nods. "We all thought it was. Turns out old Lawrence couldn't bear to part with it, covered it with a tarp, and hid it in the corner of his lot."

More unease. More head-numbing stuff. Suspicion is rising within me, hot and fierce, but I can't show Chris that. "And the paint chips?"

Chris shrugs. "Probably from the guardrail from a previous accident. Or from the scrapyard. Honestly, it was clutching at straws anyway."

"Wait," I say, still utterly confused. "So Leo was trying to say the paint chips were from the night of the accident?"

Chris nods uneasily.

"From another car?"

Another nod. "Hypothetically, of course. Because I sent the chips off to a private lab, and they're the ones who matched it to this make and model, but I can't find a single car in the state of Nevada that has ever been registered in this color."

"But if there were a car this color. Hypothetically. You're saying this person may have caused the accident?"

Chris sighs. "Yeah. It's possible this other car pushed Leo's car off the bridge. At that angle, at that speed, it'd have to be somebody who knew what they were doing."

I change the subject. I don't want to appear too eager. I also don't know if I trust Chris as far as I can throw him, even if he does seem like a lovely boy. He's fiercely loyal to Damon, and so I cannot let him too close.

I have the information I need.

Now, I just need him to leave.

Sure enough, a 911 call comes in about an hour later. Chris tries to get me to accompany him, but I flat-out refuse. He calls Amanda and asks her to come over, and speeds off, sirens blaring. I know I have about three minutes before Amanda and her pitying fucking eyes arrive, and I use those three minutes wisely.

I make my way into the garage, quietly and efficiently sidling up to the car Damon still hasn't gotten rid of. Well, I say car, but it's a truck. Ray's truck. I circle around to the front of it, still parked in the spot Ray left it when he ambushed me, the night Damon blew a hole in his head.

I skate my hands along its metallic paint, looking for something.

It's the right make.

It's the right model.

It's the exact color of the truck Chris showed me on his phone.

The elusive pickup with the dark red paint.

I remember Ray's warning to me: *Stay still or you'll get what you deserve, just like your mother got what she deserved.*

At the time I'd thought it nothing more than an empty threat, but maybe that threat was full and overflowing.

My brain does all sorts of calculations as I study the hard corners of Ray's pickup.

I run my hands along its front edges, and at the corner, I can feel these tiny raised spots as if someone has fixed up the paint job.

Usually you'd paint over rust spots, but these don't feel like that. These are long strands, like gouges, but raised instead of indented into the metal.

Using my fingernail, I dig at the dark red paint. Whoever patched the car did a great job of matching the paint; it's invisible until you're looking specifically. I scratch at the little raised parts, the dark red flaking away in my palms. Midnight-blue paint glints at me from underneath.

Oh, God. Oh, God, oh, *God.*

I stagger back, glancing at the license plate. Registered in California. Of course you'd never find this car on the Nevada database.

Ray made sure to register it out of state to cover his tracks.

But the bastard kept the truck, he kept the weapon he used to push Leo's Mustang off the road.

He kept it as a trophy.

Because it wasn't an accident at all, was it?

Damon wanted me, and Mom was obviously in the way. Leo was in the way. So they got rid of them both in one fell swoop. One side-swipe on an ice-covered bridge. One old car with no airbags, no roll cage, no safety.

Ray is the one who killed my mother.

Ray and Damon.

Brothers without blood.

Accomplices.

Murderers.

I hear Amanda's car pull up in the driveway and blink back tears, abandoning the truck investigation for now. I'm pulling the garage door shut and heading for the front door just as Amanda knocks.

I open it and she's there, smiling, such a kind fucking smile. She must see the look on my face, utterly bereft, trying to unravel a decade of secrets and lies while trying not to fall to the floor.

"You look like you need a hug," she says, closing the front door behind her, pulling me into her, holding me tight.

She smells like the cherry pie my mom used to bake, and I fucking lose it. I bury my face in her neck and cry. "Hey, come on," she coos, stroking my hair. "It's all right. Everything is all right."

Everything is not all right, Amanda. Everything is not fucking all right.

CHAPTER FORTY-THREE

Cassie

G rief is seasonal. Disbelief comes and goes, and leaves an aching pit of sadness for you to somehow carry around while you smile and nod and pretend you're not dead inside.

Grief is useless. It's like drowning in a sea of your own despair because you won't grab on to the rope being offered to you. So you let yourself be sucked under, you let the rough waters invade your nose and your mouth and your ears and your eyes until you're dead on the inside, hollowed out, a walking corpse. Grief makes you weak.

But rage . . . rage is useful. It is the tiny seed that sprouts inside you and spreads like tendrils on a vine. It weaves itself around your veins, sticks in its barbs, and reminds you that you are still alive. It burns in your blood, that blood passes through your heart, and over time you fill up your hollow with something else. Rage. . . . And purpose.

I can thank Damon for my rage. A hard kernel of hate that passed from him to me, a metaphorical transaction, the grit from which a pearl forms. It rests inside my belly like a bullet, smooth and hidden, and with it I find a strength that comes only from surviving something utterly catastrophic.

The accident wasn't Leo's fault. The accident wasn't an accident at all.

In my rage, I find my solace. In my rage, I vanquish my despair.

CHAPTER FORTY-FOUR

Cassie

The next morning, I make coffee, just like I always do. One cup for me and one cup for him, fresh and black and bitter, just the way we like it.

Damon's cleaning his gun when I sit at the table across from him, sliding him his cup. He glances up at me, our eyes catching for the briefest of moments before he goes back to brushing imaginary dust out of his gun parts. The guy is obsessed with military cleanliness. And while I enjoy living in a tidy house, I do not understand why he cleans so compulsively.

I bear the time patiently, watching him as he works in between sips of coffee.

"What?" he finally asks.

So he's noticed my sudden interest in him. Good. I have a few things I'd like to ask him. "Did your mom used to clean a lot? Your real mom, I mean."

He freezes, his right eye twitching the tiniest bit. You'd miss it if you weren't watching, but I *am* watching. Intently.

"I don't remember," he says. "Why?"

"My mother used to tell me I was made of glass," I say, smiling as

I remember her in happier times. "You remember? She had this way of knowing what I was thinking. She always knew if I had lied to her."

He frowns. "I don't want to talk about your mother."

"I think you're made of glass," I continue. "I see right through you, Damon. I know what you're doing."

He smiles then, a smirk that drags up one side of his wide, sensual mouth. "Oh, really?" he says. "Enlighten me."

I wait for a moment, watching as he fiddles with a tiny brush and some clear oil.

"I think you're trying to pin Jennifer's disappearance on Leo."

His expression goes blank.

"You promised me that if I stayed away from him, you would let him be. And yet, he's your only suspect in her disappearance."

Damon's jaw tightens; his grip on the little brush in his hand threatens to snap the thing in two. "*Are* you staying away from him?" he asks.

I always look down at the ground when I'm lying. Mom always told me lying would send me straight to hell, so when I lie, that's probably why my eyes go down.

"Yes," I reply, a flawless lie, and my eyes don't waver from his. "I am. And so should you. Find somebody else to blame Jennifer's disappearance on."

He doesn't say anything for a while, his eyes on the gun, his body language telling me that he's mad. One wrong word and he could snap.

"Damon," I press. "Promise me you will leave him alone."

He pretends like I'm not even here.

In my mind, I sharpen my knife. I stare at the vein in his neck, the jugular, and I imagine slicing through it like a surgeon of death.

"*Daniel.*"

He drops the gun like it's made of fire; if it had bullets in it, the thing would probably fire from the force at which it hits the tabletop. *There it is.* I have cut him open and now I'll watch him bleed out.

And I've got to say, I expect something more in his reaction. Something indelible, something violent. I expect him to tackle me down to the floor, maybe stick a bar of soap in my mouth and make me choke on it until I promise never to say his real name again. But he doesn't.

He doesn't do anything.

I say his name again. His real name, the one his mother gave him. "*Daniel?*"

I look at his hands; they're trembling. Damon King—*Daniel Collins*—doesn't move a goddamn inch.

I grab those hands, pulling them, jolting him out of his daydream and toward me. Though the table separates us, I kneel on my chair, draping my top half across the table so our noses are almost touching, his blue eyes to my green, and that's how we stay for a long moment, while I imagine the horrors of his childhood, the events that created the monster.

I whisper my secret, his secret, a handful of murmured words that tear everything apart. "I know who you are. And I know what you did."

I push back, getting off my chair and getting the fuck out of the kitchen before his violent tendencies kick in. I go up to the attic, the heavy bolt removed, something that took me all of five minutes to pry off while Damon showered earlier. Damon's laptop is up there already, part of my plan, and I've moved the stacks of milk cartons so all the photos face out.

"Come back here!" Damon yells, barreling up the stairs. *There he is.* The little boy I glimpsed in the kitchen is gone, and the man full of darkness and rage is back.

I reach for the laptop's smooth keys and hit play, turning the volume up. I set the laptop on the closed pine box that housed Jennifer; Damon's mother's voice fills the room; his real mother, the one who birthed him and nursed him and sent him off to school. The one who tended an empty grave that bore his name, the one who waited for thirty years for him to come home, and then died of a broken heart when he never, ever did.

Damon comes through the doorway, slamming his coffee cup

down, charging at me until he sees the milk cartons, the face on the video. *"Daniel was such a loving boy,"* his mother says, her devastation ringing clear in the same attic where Damon's own child lived and died for the briefest of moments. I fix my gaze on the bloodstain on the floor, the one beside the now-empty box where Jennifer bled out, because I can't bear to look at Adelie Collins as she talks about her missing son.

"What is this?" He's horrified, tears pooling in his eyes.

"It's your mother," I say. "Don't you remember her, Damon? Daniel?"

"Stop it."

I turn the volume higher.

"Daniel was such a beautiful boy. His eyes, they were so blue."

Damon grabs the laptop and throws it at the ground as hard as he can. It shatters into a million tiny pieces, and the sound of his mother's anguished voice is gone, replaced by an ugly silence that promises terrible things.

I think about Leo. About how, by doing this, I'm protecting him from every evil thing Damon has planned for him. For both of us.

"I'm going to beat the shit out of you," Damon says, his eyes blazing.

I nod. "Yeah," I say, my voice resigned. "I thought you might say that."

A weird look passes over his face. He steps to the side, holding on to the pine box for balance. He stumbles.

"What's wrong?" I ask him. "Cat got your tongue?"

He rights himself. "Nothing. I'm fine." A fine sheen of sweat has broken out on his forehead.

"You don't look fine," I say. "You look like you're about to pass out."

He stumbles again, his eyes sparking with recognition. "You . . . ," he manages, before falling to his knees. "What the fuck did you give me?" He swipes madly behind his back, probably looking for the gun in his waistband, but it's not there anymore. It's in my hand.

I start to laugh as he sways on his hands and knees in front of me. "Just a little bit of the medicine you've been giving me all these years, Daddy-O."

He lunges for me drunkenly, but I step back, away from his foolish grip.

"You *cunt*," Damon utters between clenched teeth.

I'm so fucking proud. He grabs my ankle and tugs. *I don't think so.*

"Watch it," I say, kicking him in the face with my Doc Martens boot. Blood explodes from his nose as he goes down, hard.

"Cassie . . ."

"Shhhh," I whisper. I imagine my words circling around in his addled mind as the last bit of light fades from his vision, but Damon's a big boy, and he's not going down with just a handful of ground-up Percocet. He gets up on one arm and drags himself closer to me again, within grabbing territory. He's fast with his hands, but I'm faster. I raise the gun in my hand and smash the butt into Damon's face, sending him to the floor in a limp pile. Before he can move, I take his own police-issued cuffs and fasten his hands behind his back, as tight as the metal links will go around his wrists.

I roll him over and he's still conscious, but barely. His blood-spattered face is clammy and warm, his eyes struggling to focus on me as they roll around in his head. I sit on his chest, the gun in one hand, his half-empty cup of coffee in the other. I press the gun into his cheek, forcing his mouth open, and tip the rest of the drugged coffee into his open mouth. He starts to thrash his head to each side, but I'm quicker, and I'm not drugged to the eyeballs. I slap my hand over his mouth and lean in real close, so our noses are almost touching.

"Swallow, bitch," I whisper.

He chokes and splutters, but he swallows the rest of my coffee cocktail. I wonder if I gave him enough to sedate him. Maybe it will kill him. I have five morphine-filled syringes hidden in my mother's room if I need to take him down again.

"Cass," he slurs, and I'm equal parts disturbed and fucking impressed that drugs and a pistol whip haven't knocked him out yet.

"I always wondered how you got there so fast," I say. "I was fifty feet away from the creek when they crashed, and you were there within seconds of me getting to that car."

His eyes roll and flutter; it won't be long now. "Cassie, what did you give me?"

More urgent. More desperate. I wish I could freeze time so that I could press my lips to his and taste his despair the way he has tasted mine all these years. I bet it tastes like orange Life Savers and cotton candy. I bet it tastes like a bright-red candy apple that sick old men use to lure ten-year-old boys into vans and whisk them away from their mothers.

"I hope you enjoyed ruining my life," I say to him. "Because I'm about to end yours."

I am a girl with a coal-black heart beating inside my chest and a murderer underneath me. The first one I can't do anything about, but the second I can.

Because there's no other way around this: Damon has to die for what he's done to us, and nobody can ever know it was me.

I curl my hands underneath his arms and drag him into the now-open pine box where he stuffed Jennifer, his dead weight backbreaking. I drop him in the middle of the box, and his head makes a thick sound as it connects with the wood.

I gather my supplies: plastic sheeting, rubber gloves, Leo's hunting knife, Damon's gun.

You're not gun-shy, are you?

I look down at the man who destroyed my life and I feel nothing. Nothing except the first butterflies of excitement. Of relief. Because this is the part where I take my life back. This is the moment when I grab the wheel and correct course.

This is where Damon King—Daniel Collins—says his final goodbye.

ONE YEAR LATER

CHAPTER FORTY-FIVE

Leo

Spring came early this year. All the flowers in the garden are blossoming. Cassie is blossoming, with a baby. *Our* baby.

Yeah. We're having a baby. It still sounds weird when I say it. Good weird. I never thought I'd see the day. Cassie, literally barefoot and pregnant in the kitchen of her house, our house.

It's strange to think how much has changed in one year.

Since Damon lost his shit and went on emergency stress leave, right after Cassie's suicide attempt, everything has changed. I haven't seen or heard from the guy since the day I found Cassie in the bath, bleeding and drugged from her almost-suicide. Cassie says he still calls and writes her periodically. Sounds like the guy just couldn't take it anymore, handed in his badge and gun, and high-tailed it out of town. Which I didn't believe at first. Didn't think he'd ever let Cassie out of his house, out of his sight, out of his clutches.

She was all he had, but now she's mine, and if he ever comes back, he can't have her, because she belongs to me.

I keep waiting for him to come back. But it's been a year now, a year since that night when Cassie ran down to my place in the freezing snow and told me he'd gone for good, that we could finally be together. My parole is almost finished, I've got the girl, and now she's having my child.

We didn't plan that. About three months after Damon left, as the twin scars on Cassie's wrists had just started to fade a little, two other lines showed up. Not planned, not ideal, but probably the best thing that had happened for either of us since we were kids. Now she's nine months pregnant and she should let me cook while she rests, but she insists.

"You want bacon?" she asks, breaking me out of my thoughts as she holds a pan above the dining table. The engraved key she always wears on a chain around her neck glints against her skin, the word *Nomad* etched into it, an ironic thing for a girl who's never been anywhere farther than Lone Pine, California.

"Do I want bacon?" I echo, pinching her ass. She squeals, dropping a pile of burnt slices on my plate, her baby belly brushing against my arm as she heads back to the sink with the empty pan. She comes back and sits next to me, her plate looking much healthier than mine, covered in slices of avocado and scrambled eggs and broccoli. Mine looks like a heart attack in comparison, but I'm sure I'll be working it all off straight after we're done.

Sure enough, we don't even make it five minutes before Cassie's sitting in my lap, her food untouched. "You know," I say in between her fevered kisses, "if you want my bacon, you could just take it off my plate."

She laughs, her fingers making quick work of my zipper and boxers. I sink my fingers into her round ass cheeks as she pulls her panties to the side and slides down on me, her eyes rolling back as I sink into her. She's fucking insatiable now that she's past the morning sickness and she's finally got some weight on her. She looks healthy, instead of gaunt. Her cheeks are rosy, instead of pale. And she wants sex all the damn time, so much that I can barely keep up with her. Not that I'm complaining. We have all those years I was gone to make up for. And I fully intend on making it up to her.

After we're done, with the food and the fucking, I wash up the dishes while Cassie showers. She heads downstairs a few minutes later in an oversized striped sweater and leggings, her hair in a loose knot atop her head.

"You coming?" she asks.

"Coming where?"

"The midwife appointment," Cassie says breathlessly. "She's going to do that stretch and sweep thing, see if we can't get this baby out. The sex obviously isn't working."

"Maybe we're not trying hard enough," I reply.

She looks stressed. "I'm having this baby at home," she says stubbornly. "I'm already three days overdue. If I go much more, they'll induce me in the hospital and that's not going to happen."

I dry my hands on a kitchen towel, heading over to the bottom of the stairs where my pregnant-to-bursting girlfriend is fighting back tears. The fucking hormones, man. I love this girl, but she's psychotic with the hormones.

"I asked Pike to help me fix the fence this morning," I say, putting my hands on her belly as I lean down to kiss her forehead. "He'll be over in a minute."

She looks like she might murder me, or fall on the floor in a pile of tears. Murder would be easier for me.

"The fence is a quick fix," I say. "Half an hour, tops. Why don't I just meet you there? They always make you wait for hours, anyway."

She weighs her options silently as I watch her face. "C'mon," I say to her. "You were right. You don't want the induction unless it's the absolute last resort." I rub her back. "I promise I'll be there before they get all up in your business."

She chews on her lip. "Okay," she says. "Okay. But you'll meet me there, won't you?"

"I promise," I say, kissing her again.

She drives off in the new pickup she bought with her mom's insurance money, a cruel twist of fate that something I did paid for that car.

It makes my skin crawl every time I think about it, so I try not to think about it. Cassie says she forgives me. I'm not so sure I forgive myself.

But I have to keep my shit together, and keep sober, and work my ass off because I'm going to be a father in the next week, Cassie's induction date looming on the calendar like Christmas.

I'm just about to call Pike and ask where the fuck he is when there's a knock at the door. I open it, expecting Pike, but there's a very somber-looking Chris McCallister standing on the porch instead, looking all official-like in his tan-colored police uniform.

"Chris," I say, opening the door wider. "Come in, man. How are you?"

"Thanks," he says, taking off his hat and sidestepping past me. We end up in the kitchen.

"You want coffee?" I ask. "Pot's still hot."

He declines, hovering awkwardly on the other side of the counter. I pour one for myself and wonder where Pike is. "Everything okay?" I ask.

Chris puts his hat down on the counter and pulls a piece of paper from his pocket, unfolding it. The air between us develops a heaviness.

"What's wrong?" I ask, my tone sharp this time.

Chris pushes the piece of paper over to me. "Your last drug test was positive," he says, unable to meet my gaze. "I haven't told Sheriff Anderson yet."

Sheriff Anderson was brought in to replace Damon after he left with his fishing rods, a backpack of clothes, and a harried email citing extreme stress as the reason for his sudden departure. Sheriff Anderson is exactly the kind of guy you'd expect to be installed in a town like ours—ruddy-faced from drinking, generally useless, and counting down the days until his retirement.

I grab the paper, scanning the words. A lot of it is police speak and codes that I don't understand, but the words POSITIVE FOR OPIATES stand out against everything.

"This is a mistake," I say, rage creeping up my chest. "I haven't taken anything. I don't even take fucking aspirin!"

I slam my cup down on the counter, and coffee splashes over the sheet of paper. A weird desperation bubbles underneath my skin, like acid eating it away, layer by layer.

"I caught it before it was sent off," Chris says. "I know Cassie's about to pop any day now. It must be stressful. Anyone would understand if you felt like you needed something to take the edge off."

I stare at Chris like he's fucking stupid. "I. Didn't. Take. Anything."

Chris clears his throat. "Well, I'm here to tell you to definitely not take anything in the next week. Like I said, I caught this early. We'll retest in a week."

I nod.

"I'll lose my job if anyone finds out about this," Chris adds. "I only did this because Cassie's been through enough shit. She doesn't need you back in prison while she's about to give birth."

"Thanks, man. I appreciate that." I'm trying to be grateful, but I'm fucking raging. I definitely didn't take anything. I don't need to take anything, ironically, for the first time in years. I have Cassie.

"I'm telling you, man, it's a false positive," I insist. "Tell me again all the shit that can cause opiates to show up on a test."

Chris shrugs. "I mean, there are all sorts of things that can give a false positive. Cold and flu tablets. Does Cassie use poppy seeds when she bakes? They show up as opiates if you eat enough of 'em."

"Like I said, I don't take anything. Poppy seeds? Maybe. Shit. I'll ask her when she gets home."

Chris looks unconvinced. "You'd have to eat bags of poppy seeds to get a result that high."

I can see it in his face; he doesn't believe me. He thinks I've sunk back to the lows of my family. And nothing I say is going to change his mind.

"If you really didn't take anything, you might want to check who you've been hanging out with. Wouldn't be the first time I've seen someone slip their friend something in a beer. Your brother?"

"I don't drink beer!" I exclaim. "I don't drink anything! I'm a boring fucking mechanic who's about to be a father. And my brother would never do that, not in a million fucking years. The test is *wrong*."

Chris takes the piece of paper back, folds it, and slides it into his pocket. He pinches his hat between his fingers and sticks it back on his head, a silent gesture that says, "We're done here."

"Next week," he says. "I won't be able to hide that one if it's positive. And if you tell anyone I hid this for you, I'll fuck you up, Bentley."

I lean against the sink and bite on the insides of my cheeks, waiting for the front door to close as Chris shows himself out. I listen for the sound of his engine, the crunch of gravel where the driveway meets the road, and then I search for fucking poppy seeds.

I don't find them.

But I do find something else. Packets and packets of pills, very powerful sedatives, hidden under a floorboard in our bedroom. I turn one of the packets over, skimming all of the words, looking for the ingredients. I find the name of the drug—the opiate—and all the blood in my veins turns to ice as I carefully put the pills back, and the floorboard, and get the hell out.

Something is wrong.

Something is very, very wrong.

Pike speeds like a hell demon with me in the passenger seat, but I'm still late to the appointment. Cassie is already trying to shimmy up the bed as a midwife sticks her fingers up her.

I hold her hand as the midwife finishes fingering my girlfriend and snaps off her latex gloves, tossing them in the trash as she says words like "membranes" and "breaking waters." It's all so primal, this baby-birthing business. It's all so messy.

But Cassie seems sated by the reassurance that she'll most likely go into labor any moment now that her cervix is soft, that she's already looking a little bit dilated.

She insists we pick up McDonald's on the way home, giant sodas and hot fries and dirty double cheeseburgers. I want to tear into the food as soon as it's passed to us in the drive-thru, but Cassie insists we eat on plates at home like civilized humans.

In fact, the more I think about it, Cassie's very insistent about what we eat and when. I've passed it off as pregnancy and her trying to be a good housewife, but after Chris's bombshell, there's a deep feeling of worry starting to spread in me.

It's like a cancer in my blood, snaking down my limbs and around my heart, and by the time we get home I'm reeling.

I'm starting to think about all the nights I've passed out on the couch, too tired to even make it up to bed.

All the mornings waking up to Cassie's sweet face, laughing at me because *I fell asleep again.*

"Go wash up," Cassie says, bumping my hip with her belly as she takes the tray of sodas to the kitchen. I wash up in the bathroom, looking at myself in the mirror. *You're crazy,* I think. *The test is at fault. You're fucking paranoid.*

I head back into the kitchen and the table is all set; our dinners placed neatly in the spots where we always sit. Me at the head of the table and Cassie tucked off to the side, next to me, her back against the wall.

"Damn," I say, picking up my Coke. "I thought I ordered Sprite. You wanna swap?"

Cassie pulls her Sprite closer to her. "I'm not supposed to have caffeine."

"Oh," I say. Perfectly logical explanation. *You're paranoid,* the little voice in my head repeats. *You're freaking out because of the baby.*

I pick at my food, suddenly not hungry. When Cassie goes to pee, I throw half of my food away and cover it with other trash. Then, I tip my Coke down the sink before taking it back to the table. Cassie reappears just as I'm sitting back in my spot, stopping short when she sees my face.

"Are you okay?" she asks. "You look like there's something wrong."

I shake my head. "I think I've finally realized that we're having a baby."

Her face falls.

"No, no, not like that!" I say, putting my hand up in protest. "I mean the hot water heater and the induction date and the fucking birthing pool. I can't even blow the damn thing up, let alone figure out how to get enough hot water to fill it up."

"Oh," she says, visibly relaxing. "Don't worry. There's an air pump that blows up the pool. We'll have hours to get it full of water. You can use the stove to heat water if we run out."

"Good," I say, smiling, trying like fuck to appear like everything is normal. "I just want everything to be perfect for you. I know how much you want to have this baby at home."

She smiles, sliding onto my lap. She's so big that her belly sits between us, swollen and ready to burst. "We should go to bed," she says, her hands on my chest. "Make up for the fact that we won't be able to do it for, like, a month after he or she is born."

"We should," I agree.

We go to bed. We do the deed. But unlike this morning, when we were laughing and I was trying not to choke on my mouthful of bacon at the same time, tonight I flip Cassie over, onto her hands and knees, and try to get done as quickly as possible. I'm almost about to come when I remember this is exactly how I saw her and Damon in the window, over a year ago, the night of her mother's funeral. Before I can stop myself, I come inside Cassie, but with that image in my head, it feels fucking horrific.

Normally I would fall asleep immediately, as soon as my head hit the pillow. But tonight, I'm wide awake. I feign sleep, aware that Cassie is still very much awake beside me, the glow from her phone illuminating the room slightly. I breathe slowly, I wait it out, and after about forty minutes, Cassie shakes me.

"Leo," she whispers. "Are you awake?"

I stay "asleep." She tries to rouse me once more, and I waver. What if she's having labor pains? What if she needs something?

Before I can think anymore, she's up and out of bed. It's probably nothing. She's so hugely pregnant that she can barely get comfortable, let alone get to sleep with the baby pummeling her with kicks. I listen intently, hearing her shuffling about in the kitchen. She's always hungry. It's nothing.

I close my eyes again as I hear her coming up the stairs. I wait for her to get into bed, but her footsteps continue past our bedroom.

And up to the attic.

Huh.

I don't hear anything else, and she's only gone for ten or fifteen minutes. I spend the time listening in vain for anything, but it's dead silent.

When she comes back, she slides into bed. Nothing amiss. She probably went to find something. All her medical records are stored up there, and her old baby clothes. She probably just went to get something. I'm being paranoid.

"Leo?" She shakes me again. I know I should respond, but something in me tells me to stay still. She lies down beside me. The bed starts to rock slightly. Oh, my God, is she doing what I think she's doing? She is. She's touching herself. My dick immediately gets hard, and I have to shift onto my side to stop it from being mashed into the mattress.

Beside me, Cassie stills. "Leo?"

This time, I groan in response. Moments later, hands are pulling my boxers down, my extremely pregnant girlfriend crawling up on top of me before I can crack an eye open. We don't speak. She takes my hand and places my fingers against her clit as she guides me inside her, and it's mere seconds before she's coming against my touch.

CHAPTER FORTY-SIX

Leo

Cassie is showering the next morning when I go up to the attic. It's locked, no surprise there. No problem. I've got a power drill, and it takes me about three seconds to remove the lock and open the door. I'm not sure what I'm expecting to find. Maybe nothing. Maybe a whole lot of dust. But something in my gut tells me I'm going to find something.

The room looks just like you'd expect an attic to look. Low, sloping ceiling. Things stacked in the corner in neatly labeled bins and boxes. Oddly, there's a high stack of old milk cartons. And in the middle of the room, a plain pine storage box.

I want to know what's in that box.

But it's locked, another padlock that prevents me access. No matter. I study the lock, looking for a weak spot, and then I smash the whole thing off with the tire iron I brought up with me. It takes two or three hits, and I hope to fuck that Cassie's shower drowns out the noise.

I drop the lock and open the latch. I don't know what I'm going to find, but suddenly, I'm terrified. I open the lid before I can talk myself out of it, and what do you know, I've been sleeping under a box with a dead body inside it for an entire year.

CHAPTER FORTY-SEVEN

Leo

I recoil from the box, stumbling back until I find the wall. I lean against it, trying to breathe, my palm mashed against my mouth as I try not to scream this entire fucking house down.

Did I just see what I think I saw? A pine storage box in the attic that's now somebody's coffin. I bite my fist to stop myself from yelling, edging back to the box.

Damon King.

My lovely girlfriend was lying about the letters she got from him, unless she handed him the paper and pen herself. Because her stepfather hasn't been fishing in early retirement or taking stress leave in the Ozarks. No. He's been in our fucking attic *this entire time.*

I peer over the edge of the makeshift coffin, and just when I think things can't get worse, I'm sorely proven wrong. Dead Damon opens his eyes and stares straight at me, his bright blue eyes the only thing I recognize about before. But this isn't a horror movie, folks. He's not a vampire waiting to rise from his casket and drink my blood. He's a man who's been starved until his skin stretches painfully over his skeleton, his cheekbones sharp and jutting, his neck bulging with veins, an array of chains and handcuffs restraining him. He's got duct tape over his mouth, to keep him quiet I suppose, and without thinking, I rip that tape off.

If it hurts, he doesn't show pain. No, the captive who's been imprisoned in our attic opens his mouth and fucking laughs.

There's something about his laugh—hollow and throaty and maniacal—that terrifies me almost to the point of a goddamn heart attack. I slam the lid of the box shut, but he's still fucking laughing, the sound drilling into my brain like a sledgehammer. I open the lid again, just long enough to slap the tape back on his mouth, and then I slam it shut again.

I look around the dark attic, noticing things I hadn't seen before. There are chains drilled into one wall, heavy metal cuffs on the ends. It doesn't smell great in here; a plastic bucket full of what looks like piss is tucked behind the pine box, and there are stacks of men's clothes folded neatly on the ground. Some of them I recognize as mine, shirts I haven't seen in months, and other things I don't recognize. A gauzy white dress hangs in one corner, a box of records beside it. An empty McDonald's paper bag, crumpled up by the door. My mind pieces together what's been happening in this room full of horrors before I can stop it. I don't want to know; I can't bear the knowing. He's been up here this whole time. Existing. Living. Eating—a little, at least—*and I've been completely fucking oblivious to the entire thing.*

"Leo!" I hear Cassie yell from downstairs.

Damon's in our attic. He's in our fucking attic! I must be in fucking shock, my head swimming in a sea of what the fuck as I exit the attic and head down to the bathroom.

"Yeah?" I say, my voice sounding foreign, what the fuck has she done? Cassie doesn't notice me, one hand on the shower wall as steam billows around her.

"Oh, shit," I say, noticing the way she's hunched over, her face scrunched up in pain. "Is this it?"

What the fuck have you done?

What the fuck have you DONE?

But I can't ask her to please stop being in labor so she can explain to me why the FUCK there is a dude tied up in our attic, a man who looks like he's been starved within an inch of actual death. If it weren't for the eyes, I wouldn't even recognize him, because he'd surely fit right into a concentration camp in wartime Nazi Germany.

"This is it," Cassie breathes, straightening, as what I'm assuming was a contraction passes. And then she's fine, normal, standing in the bath smiling at me. "We should start filling that birthing pool."

Sure thing, Cassie. Whatever you want, babe. *Whatever the fuck you want.*

I help Cassie dress—yoga pants and a sports bra—and then we head downstairs. She has to stop halfway as another contraction rips through her, and holy shit I thought it would happen more slowly than this. Isn't it supposed to be a gradual thing at first? Maybe my super semen burst her cervix open last night when she climbed on top of me and went to town. Who fucking knows. I help her down to the sofa, sit her down, and take a spot across from her.

"You should start timing my contractions," she says.

I nod. "In a minute. I need to talk to you about something."

She raises her eyebrows, pissed. "I'm in *labor.*"

I glimpse the key dangling around her neck, the one I've since learned is a rip-off of those keys you buy that are engraved with ta-glines. You know, chicks wear these keys that say *Love* or *Trust* or *Strength* as some kind of fucking totem to remind themselves. I always thought Cassie's said *Nomad.* I'd tease her for it—You can't be a nomad if you've never been anywhere—and she'd laugh.

But I guess the joke's on me.

Because Nomad spelled backward is *Damon.*

THE BOY IN THE BOX

CHAPTER FORTY-EIGHT

Damon

That fucking bitch.

That's the first thing I thought when I woke up in here, my head pounding and the room still spinning from whatever it was she put in my goddamn coffee.

Just when I thought she was starting to come around. I mean, yeah, I know, she tried to kill herself, but that was because of Ray. Fucking Ray. I always knew I'd have to kill Ray one day. I just didn't expect it to go down like that.

I certainly didn't expect to have to seal him up in a barrel of acid and dump him into an abandoned mine shaft three hours away.

The first thing I saw when I woke up in that attic? Wood. Pine. *I'm in the box.* Fuck. I'm in the box. That cunt fed me poison and kicked me in the face and now I'm locked in a coffin.

I don't know how long I'm in here for, but I bide the time patiently. I could rage and kick and scream, but I know she'll be back. My little bird wants answers. And answers she shall get. Besides, I need to conserve my strength for when I beat her to fucking death for pulling this stunt.

She eventually comes back, the lid to my box opening with a thunk. She's found the key to the padlock, and it shines in the overhead light against her skin.

"Have a nice nap?" she asks.

"Delightful," I reply. "What'd you give me?"

She shrugs. "A little bit of this, a little bit of that. A cocktail. To be honest, I wasn't sure you'd wake up at all."

That makes me mad. I've spent the hours after I woke up studying my situation. Cassie's smart—she's cuffed my hands behind my back, so I can't reach out and grab her when she leans her smug fucking face over the side of the box. My legs are shackled, too. I can feel thick chains around my ankles. Maybe this is my karma for putting Jennifer in here.

Then again, I don't believe in karma. I believe we make our own fate.

"How'd you do it?" she asks tonelessly.

I laugh. "How'd I do what?"

She rears her fist back and punches me in the face so hard, her knuckles start to bleed. The force rings in my ears, and I can feel new blood on my cheek. Baby girl's angry. She's so pretty when she's angry.

She's stupid, too. Because she climbs into the box and straddles me, her knees draped across my hips. "Careful, sweetheart," I say, forcing my hips up suddenly. "I might get the wrong idea."

She hits me again, in the mouth this time. She smashes her fist hard enough into my head that I hear a tooth crack in the back of my jaw. "You're gonna break a finger," I mutter around a mouthful of blood. "And you'll have to be more specific. How'd I do *what*?"

She watches, mesmerized, as I turn my head to the side and spit a bloody molar onto the box's wooden floor.

I settle back, giving her my full attention. Somehow, I'm betting she thought this would go differently. She probably thought I'd be begging for my life.

"If you're trying to scare me, sweetheart, you'd better try harder than this." I rattle the chain that loops around my ankles for effect.

She blinks heavily. Once. Twice. This is not going as she planned.

"I'm not trying to scare you," she blurts out. "I want to know what you *did*."

I roll my eyes. "Okay, Cassie. Where do you want me to start?"

"At the beginning."

"Which beginning? There are so many."

"Did you kill Karen?"

Wow, straight to the point. I look at the ceiling, the time for joking over. Karen left a bad taste in my mouth, almost as bad as the taste she must have left in Leo Bentley's mouth when he drank the dirty creek water that she rotted in until he found her. "No," I say quietly.

"Bullshit."

"I tried to cut contact with Ray when I moved to Gun Creek. He killed Karen to send me a message."

She looks almost relieved, if a little dubious. "How do I know you're not lying to me?"

I shrug. "I've got nothing to hide from you anymore, Cassie. I'll give you a list of the people I've killed. Karen's not on it, though."

She looks tired. "Tell me about the accident."

"Are we still calling it an accident?"

She just raises her eyebrows.

"Okay, fine," I concede. Something squeezes inside my chest. I deserve this. And she should know the truth.

Tears well up in her pretty eyes, and if my hands were free I'd brush them away. I'd lick my tongue along her cheek and soak them all up.

"I already know what you did. Got Ray to drive up alongside Leo's car and push it over the guardrail."

"How'd you figure it out?" I ask her. "I mean, now, really? Took you long enough."

Her eyes burn with hatred. It's sad that she hates me. I've only ever tried to keep her safe.

"Paint chips," she snaps. "Paint chips and motive."

It's probably a terrible idea, but I tell her what she wants to know. All of it. Maybe if she knows the truth, she'll finally understand why I had to cut her mother out like a cancer all those years ago.

CHAPTER FORTY-NINE

Damon

*T*he heart wants what the heart wants.

That's what Ray told me when I confessed my feelings for Cassie to him. I knew I shouldn't have told him almost as soon as the words came out of my mouth, but it was too late by then.

I wanted Cassie from the moment I laid eyes on her that morning at the Bentley property.

Karen Brainard's mutilated corpse, sawn in half with the precision of a High Street butcher.

One half in the well—*plop!* And the rest in the creek—*splash*. I knew as soon as I got the call on the radio that it was Karen.

I'd had my dick in her mouth only days earlier, thanks to Ray, and now I'd be leading an investigation into her murder, also thanks to Ray.

A parting gift when I tried to evade him. *Brothers stick together*, he'd reminded me when he showed up at my door as if nothing had happened.

Karen Brainard was a warning.

You can never run away from your past. It will chase you through the night, and all into the next morning.

But I digress. Cassie. She looked older than sixteen, but not by much. Everybody wants the young, don't they? I mean, that's why

Stephen Randolph took me when I was ten. Because everybody loves the young. Soft and pliable and ready to be warped into shape.

I couldn't have her, could I? I was a sheriff. I was old enough to be her father. And I was supposed to be upholding the law, not breaking it to satisfy my dark desires.

But then I learned she had a mother. A mother who was only a little younger than me. A mother who was beautiful, just like her.

Teresa Carlino was funny. She was generous, she was kind. She was the sort of person who really listened to you when you talked. And she was such a good mother. And later, she was such a good wife.

Until she wasn't.

It's my fault. I shouldn't have been spying on Cassie as she showered. And I definitely shouldn't have had my cock in my hand while I was doing it. But it was hardly hurting anyone, was it?

Then Teresa came home early from work one day, and the sound of the shower drowned out the noise of her footsteps.

My wife caught me peeping on her daughter like a dirty pervert, and I had to do something. She started saying words like *underage* and *divorce*, and I wasn't about to lose my life a second time.

I always knew I'd kept Ray around for a reason. After Teresa kicked me out of the house, I drove straight to Ray's place. He'd know what to do. He always knew what to do.

"I need to do something before she outs me," I said, pacing the length of Ray's tiny kitchen in Reno. Ray leaned against the counter, drinking Pabst, watching me wear a hole in the linoleum.

"You think you can convince her she imagined it?" he asked slowly.

I shook my head. "No. Nope. She's too sharp." I tapped my head with my index finger. "She's too fucking switched on."

"So you got to get rid of her," Ray said. "Simple. Just you and the kid, like you always wanted."

I stared at him, disgusted. "She's not a kid. Don't call her a kid."

Ray made a face, seemingly amused by my disgust as he put his hands up in surrender. "What are you gonna do about the boyfriend?

By the sounds of it, those two are fucking like rabbits in that damn car of his every second they get."

I stopped pacing. "Fuck. I don't know. One death I can explain. Two is gonna be fucking impossible."

Ray shrugged. "Well, you know what they say about two birds and one stone. Or two birds and one car."

"I'm listening," I replied.

Ray was excited; Ray wanted to help me get rid of Leo and Teresa. And I wanted to let him.

CHAPTER FIFTY

Damon

Two birds and one stone.

That's how Ray and I approached the problem with Teresa and Leo. Except neither of them fucking died, did they? It was always a risk, doing something so messily. But Teresa's survival was probably a good thing, in the end. It kept Cassie locked to me, to the house, to her mother. She was too guilty to leave, even after all the things I did to her. I would say *with* her, but it was pretty apparent that she was not a willing party to our relationship. Not at first, anyway.

We managed to get rid of Leo for eight years, though. God, was that fucking blissful. By the time he was up for parole, I was dealing with another problem: a problem with a tight pussy and a mouth like a Hoover.

Jennifer Thomas.

What an injustice. Getting out after less than half of his sentence had been completed? Before I'd managed to get Cassie pregnant with my baby, ensure she'd never leave? I mean, eight years goes past in the blink of an eye, and I should have moved faster, focused on the task, hell—even moved her and her vegetative mother out of town where Leo Bentley could never find us. But I was greedy. I wanted it all. I wanted my town and my stepdaughter and Jennifer's golden pussy.

And I never, not in a million years, thought that Leo's parole would go through so soon.

Leo fucking Bentley. I should have killed him the first chance I got. I should have worked harder to pin Karen's murder on him. It was all set up so damn perfectly. She was in his well! He would have gotten death row, or at the very least, life without parole.

But I was soft. I faltered. I saw how much Cassie loved him, the way her eyes sparkled every time she looked at him. Like he was the sun.

I should have blacked out the sun and kept her in the dark, with me.

I use peoples' weaknesses against them.

Leo's was alcohol. Cassie's, her mother.

Everybody has a weakness waiting to be exploited.

I tried to do it to Jennifer, but it doesn't work on everyone. Sometimes people aren't damaged enough to fall for the bait, and other times, they're too far gone. I should have known that when Jennifer sat on my desk, spread her legs, and told me she'd always wanted to be fucked by a police officer, she had me wrapped around her little finger. *Bitch.*

Occasionally, people just can't be blackmailed. Most of the time, though, they can. I should know. I was taught by the best. My self-proclaimed father, the one who raised me from perdition. His words, not mine. The one who stole me from everything I'd ever known and then turned me into the thing that I am.

"I need five hundred dollars," Jennifer had said to me, and then I finally had a weakness to exploit.

Jennifer, sixteen-year-old Jennifer fucking Thomas, needed five hundred dollars.

Because she was pregnant.

With my baby.

And she needed me to pay for an abortion.

Ray was there, as always, his thirst for bloodletting second only to his loyalty to me. I told him my problems, my two threats, and he sat back in his recliner. "Two birds and one stone," he said.

The thing is, I don't even *like* brunettes.

But Jennifer fucking Thomas swore black and blue that she was a natural blonde, and when I wouldn't believe her, she sat her ass up on my desk and spread her legs, no panties, cheerleading skirt hitched up around her hips, and that girl was telling the truth. She used dye to make the hair on her head a glossy brown, mascara to turn her blond eyelashes a plump black, and my desk to prove that she was lying about it all. I always found it strange; I mean, the girl was smart. I think that was her whole problem with being blond, though. She knew she was smart, and she wanted everybody else to notice, too. Hence the L'Oréal dye and the Max Factor mascara. I know the brands because she had them both with her when I took her. Who packs a box of hair dye to touch up their roots when they're going to get a fucking *abortion*?

I had some giant fucking warning flags when it came to Jennifer fucking Thomas. I didn't choose her. She chose me and pursued me, and that should have been my first warning to stay away. I should have known better. But the cock wants what the cock wants, and when what the cock wants is presented on a silver platter—or a Formica desk, as it turns out—the cock takes.

She was a virgin. That surprised me. I didn't find that out until I was balls deep in her and she started crying. That really pissed me off, you know? You want your first time to be special. My first time with Cassie was special. My first time with Jennifer was decidedly *not* special.

Warning signs. Fucking neon signs. The girl was unhinged. But she was persistent. *She chose me*, is what she'd said. I already had Cassie, but I could see that Cassie was struggling, and I'm not a total asshole (even though you think I am). I fucked Jennifer on the side, it gave Cassie some breathing room, and things were going swimmingly well.

But here's the problem with someone pursuing you. When someone chooses you, it inevitably ends up on their terms. That's why I chose Cassie, see? I chose her.

My rules.

My terms.

My needs.

My wants.

Jennifer fucking Thomas.

Pregnant. The bitch told me she was on birth control, and of course I believed her. Another warning sign. I came in that girl so often, I'm surprised there wasn't a whole litter of babies up in there. I think that thrilled her a little bit, to have that power over me. To have a part of me inside her. If we're talking about sociopaths, let's talk about this baby sociopath, this teenage fucking dream. Let me tell you right now: she sucked dick like a champion, but not enough to make me forget that she was not the girl I really wanted.

Don't get me wrong, she was a beautiful girl. You think I'm a monster, but I cried when I watched Ray pour dirt over her dead body, down the throat of the girl who was broken and bleeding but who might've been saved if she'd gotten a good doctor, a hysterectomy, and about ten bags of blood. Yeah. I know all about that miscarriage stuff. My own mother nearly died once, when I was four years old. She was almost dead when I found her in bed because she wasn't up and pouring my Cinnamon Toast Crunch when I woke up. I went to her room to find her, my stomach growling with hunger, her hands and the blankets all covered in red. Her blood had soaked through the sheets, and there was a blue tinge around her lips. I thought she was dead, but she wasn't. A good doctor, a hysterectomy, and about ten bags of blood saved my mother, and at the same time, ensured I would be the only child she ever had. But that was different. It was so very different.

Jennifer fucking Thomas. She had to get pregnant, didn't she? Pregnant and sixteen, and the bitch insisted on getting an abortion.

I pretended to concede to her wishes if she'd only let me take her to the clinic myself.

She wanted to let a stranger stick a cold metal speculum inside her womb and murder my unborn child so she could forget about it and go off to fucking college. *I don't think so, honey,* is what I said to her when I dragged her up to the attic and threw her inside my wooden box, the same one I'm in now, bound and gagged and bleeding from where I'd punched her in the nose.

An abortion. That was never going to happen. As if I'd just let some punk kid throw my baby away like it was trash.

I mean, I know, it was less than ideal. I'm not an idiot. The town sheriff knocking up a little sixteen-year-old cheerleader is bad fucking news. It's technically not illegal—age of consent is sixteen in Nevada, don't think I didn't google that shit to double-check as soon as I'd fucked her that first time—but a *cop* and a high school student? She could have ruined me. I'd lose my badge, my job. I'd lose my town, and, most of all, I might just lose my Cassie.

Two birds and one stone. This time it was Jennifer and Leo. I promised Jennifer I'd give her the five hundred dollars for an abortion if she'd just do one small thing for me first.

Okay. Not that small. All she had to do was get some of Leo Bentley's DNA. Not that hard for a girl so pretty, so seductive, so manipulative. Walk in the park. Or a drive in the forest, in her case.

"What'd you do with him?" I asked her, still stinking of sex after I'd picked her up from the road in front of her house.

Jennifer shrugged.

"Jenny."

She squirmed. "I did what you said."

I thought of Leo Bentley putting his dirty hands on the mother of my child and I felt nothing. I thought about Leo Bentley putting his dirty hands on Cassie and I wanted to smash the whole world until everything bled.

"You know I have to ask—"

"My panties," she said dully. "I wiped his . . . stuff on my panties. There's enough DNA there for—Jesus, I don't know. There was a lot."

"Mmm," I said. "Eight years' worth."

She scrunched her face up. "You think he hasn't come in eight years?"

I couldn't believe I used to think she was smart. "Not inside a sixteen-year-old's cunt, no."

She leaned back; she seemed stressed. "You're not going to do anything bad with it, are you? His DNA?"

"Why?" I asked slowly. "Would that upset you?"

"Damon!" she said sharply. "You told me it was just to keep him away from Cassie."

"Exactly," I grinned. "Very far away."

"But . . . how?"

Fucking idiot still hadn't connected the dots. For a moment, I wondered if I wanted my offspring to have half her DNA, because how could she not understand what was happening?

"Never mind about the details," I said, leaning across the center console of my car to press my forehead to hers. "What can I do to thank you for your hard work tonight?" And Jennifer didn't melt into me like she always did, a girl with daddy issues as far and wide as the days she'd been alive. No, this time she gave me the look. I knew that look. It was the look that said I'm done with you.

I knew that look.

I'd seen it on my father's face.

I'd seen it on Teresa's face.

I've seen it on Cassie's face.

I'd been expecting the look from Jennifer, but I can't say it didn't hurt.

We'd spent many a night in my car, my fingers in her pussy, her mouth on my dick; but she'd never turned away from me before.

"You can thank me by giving me my money," she said quietly, looking straight ahead. Her casual indifference—give me the cash so I can pay for our baby's murder—made my eyes ache. But I had to make sure I didn't scare her. There was still some small shred of me that believed, even then, that I could talk her into doing the right thing and carrying that baby willingly to term.

I know; I was a fool. A blind fool.

"Why are you even asking me?" I snapped. "Poor little rich girl. Your daddy would carry more than that in his wallet any day of the week."

She glared at me. "Because he didn't come inside me after he promised to pull out."

I snickered. "Oh, your daddy pulls out every time?"

"You did this to me," she accused, ignoring my jab. "You said you'd pull out. You didn't. I'm pregnant. *Asshole.*"

"You said you were taking birth control," I replied.

"I-had-a-fucking-stomach-virus! How was I supposed to know throwing up makes the pills useless?"

It seemed perfectly logical to me how throwing up a pill could make it ineffective, but again, I was starting to realize how stupid my pretty little Jennifer was.

"And what happens if I don't give you the money?" I asked, feigning boredom. In reality, my blood was simmering, my eyes bloodshot. I regretted getting into this conversation before I got my dick sucked. I tried to forget that, to focus on the fact that I now had everything I needed to cover my tracks, to kill two birds with one stone. Make Jennifer disappear, pin it on Leo, and kick back with Cassie while the chips fell. I still hadn't figured out how I would explain the brand-new baby that would arrive in about six months' time, but I had plenty of time to start constructing an elaborate story. I'd invent a long-lost sister, or maybe a cousin, somebody who was sick or drug-addicted or just a fucking mess. I would "rescue" their child from them and everyone would think me a hero, and I'd be the best daddy there ever was. Cassie would finally forget about Leo Bentley because my child would steal her heart instead. She'd be a good mother. We would be a family. Jennifer could have had this, but Jennifer was a selfish cunt.

I knew I'd have to kill her once the baby was born. It's so sad; I had a real affinity for the girl, but I had a far greater affinity for my own son or daughter she insisted on holding hostage inside her womb.

"You can't ever come back from a decision like this," I said to her. I already knew in my heart that Jenny was too far gone. She didn't want to be a teenage mother. She didn't want to let her family down. She didn't want to shame her famous football star brother.

"I stole one of my brother's credit cards," she said. "If you don't give me the money like you promised, I'll take it from his account. He won't even miss it."

"There's nothing I can do to change your mind, is there?" I was merely verbalizing the fact but she felt the need to argue anyway.

"You think I wanted this to happen?" she yelled, tears in her eyes as she slapped my hand from her shoulder. "You did this to me, Damon. You told me it would be okay. And now look what you've done. I'm ruined. You ruined me. And I'm not having a baby so I can be like every other girl in this town. I'm not going to give my life for some ungrateful fucking kid to destroy. I'm not going to live and die in Gun Creek because you're too much of an asshole to wear a fucking condom. This is my life. Don't you care about my life?"

I ground my teeth so hard my jaw ached. Black dots swam in my vision. I wanted to beat her fucking skull in, and I would have, were she not carrying my child.

She pulled out her midnight black Kate Spade purse, the one her daddy bought for her sixteenth birthday, and I thought it so ironic; that I gave her a human being for her sixteenth birthday and he gave her this bag and she hated the thing I gave her but the piece of dead animal, the shiny leather, is what made her eyes light up every time she took the damn thing out and stroked its slick surface.

I thought of all the times I'd politely smiled and nodded along with women's rights protests—of course women should be able to choose—because I lied. I'm not pro-choice at all. I'm pro-me. I'm pro don't fucking abort my kid, you stupid little girl.

I'm so sorry, Jenny, but that was the end of the line for you and your tight mouth and your expensive little purse.

Never choose somebody who worries about their appearance more than the things that matter. It's impossible, isn't it? Because we all want the beautiful.

We all want the young.

But in that moment, staring at the mother of my unborn child as she held her perfectly manicured hand out for five hundred dollars, I realized how inherently ugly Jennifer Thomas really was. Peel away the surface and I could see her skull and her bones and the way she'd fit neatly into the earth when it came time for me to bury her.

I smiled because at the end of it all was blessed relief. I'd take her home and put her away and make her do as she was told. I had regained control. I was the hero. I would rescue my son—I was so sure it was a boy. She would push him from her body with no painkillers, no doctors, just a towel to bite down on and rope to keep her from trying to run. And when I finally murdered that bitch I'd spend the five hundred dollars she so desperately wanted on a fucking pine box to bury her in.

"Fine," I said, reaching into my pocket. She calmed instantly—here comes the money—but it wasn't money that I took out of my pocket. It was a rag covered in chloroform, and I shoved it over her nose and mouth before she could so much as draw a breath.

She bit me. Hard, in the soft spot between my thumb and index finger. The pain was sharp and jolting; I bit down on my tongue in reflex and the taste of copper filled my mouth as I slammed Jenny's pretty face into the passenger window. "Cunt!" The blow stunned her long enough for me to grab hold of the back of her neck and seal the rag over her face properly.

That's enough for you, little bitch, I thought, as she struggled under the chloroform-soaked rag in my hand. Sorry, babe. I don't care about your life. I only care about the life I put inside you. The light in her eyes dimmed to a flicker as she writhed underneath my grip. She was terrified, and this was what you got when you threatened me. Silly girl. She should have known better.

Once she was passed out I lay her down on the seat beside me. Jennifer thought she'd kill my kid and go on to have a life away from here. Cassie thought she'd get to leave town eventually. Leo thought he'd get out of prison and continue his life, get to put his greedy hands on the people who belong to me.

I flashed my lights at Ray, his truck idling fifty feet from where we were parked, and he flashed his back. We were a team, me and my psychotic not-brother. Water is thicker than blood. Pine boxes are thicker than the lies we tell ourselves. The lines on a pregnancy test are things to be revered. And the lines we should never cross are thicker than any redemption we might think we deserve.

Damon

Did you love her? Cassie asked me once. *Did you love my mother?*

Of course I did. I just decided somewhere along the way that I loved Cassie more.

Damon

Starvation.

That's how Cassie pulled the truth of my childhood from me, like strands of runner grass ripped out of the dirt. Telling her what I did to her mother, to Leo, to Jennifer. That wasn't enough. That sated her reasoning for revenge, that drove away her doubt about locking me up, but it did nothing to quench her rampant curiosity.

My little Cassie was a voyeur, just like me. She wanted to dig around in people's chest cavities, searching for the weak points, stealing all the secrets.

I didn't want to give her my secrets. I didn't want to ever think about them. But starvation is a cruel way to suffer, and so I gave her metaphorical bread crumbs in exchange for real ones.

I was having my daily time outside of the confines of that damn box, my chains just long enough to allow me to climb out and sit in front of my living tomb. Cassie tossed the empty Happy Meal box at my feet, and I was so hungry, I would have eaten her whole if she'd just come close enough. Not in a sexual way—by that point, I was so hungry I would have literally bitten into her pale flesh, chewed, and swallowed. She would have tasted good, too. She always ate my favorite foods. She put a golden french fry in her mouth, and in the dark, my eyes could see the way the oil on that fry fucking shimmered. Those marketing people at McDonald's would have been salivating over such an exquisite french fry.

Cassie settled in, cross-legged, just out of my reach. One day soon, I was going to get thin enough that my wrists would slip out of those damn cuffs, and then I'd rip her smug fucking face off with my fingernails while I laughed and she screamed.

She always ate in front of me. Cunt. A burger and fries, and then a caramel sundae. My favorite. I wanted to kill her. I should have killed her when I had the chance. But she was smart, too. Knew the only way to get me back into the box once I was out was by enticing me with food, like a fucking pet. It is what it is. Human animals need to eat, too, and we can be trained just like dogs.

"You look angry," she said, opening those gloss-covered lips long enough to deep-throat five french fries at once. Five. Greedy bitch. I only wanted one. One!

"This isn't supposed to be fun," she added, chewing noisily. "This is punishment, Daniel."

I was going to kill her. She used that name and it was more painful than somebody peeling my fucking foreskin off with tweezers. I'd tie her down, good and proper on the kitchen table, and play a very messy game of Operation. I'd start with her fingers and toes first. Maybe her tongue next. It'd be a shame to never feel that tongue on mine again, though. Maybe I'd save her mouth until last, and take all the teeth so she couldn't bite me.

She finished her own meal and turned back to the brown paper bag. Dear God, if there is a God, I'm fucking sorry, okay?

"Are you praying?" Cassie asked, tilting her head back and laughing, a noise that I used to enjoy before. When I was starving, I'd prefer if she stuck a cockroach in each of my ears and let them race to see which one could claw through my eardrum and burrow into my head first.

I must have been muttering. I did that sometimes. I'd been locked in this room for an undetermined length of time. Give a guy a fucking break. She was a mean prison guard. At least I fed Jennifer and bought her as many audiobooks as she wanted. I knew Cassie had a little darkness in her, but I didn't know she was a fucking psychopath. If she weren't using her particular methods on me, I'd have a hard-on at how cunning she is. Liquid food replacement? She bought those meal replacement shakes that cancer patients drink, and I had to suck it through a straw.

"Don't think I'm going to let you die yet," she would always say to me. "How long did my mother live on a liquid diet, stuck in a bed? Get in the fucking box."

And I'd get in the box, and she'd toss me a couple fries, or a single Chicken McNugget, and I would almost die from how good the salt tasted on my tongue.

"It would be easier to just kill me," I'd remind her, as she force-fed me sleeping pills. And she would smirk as she ripped fresh tape from a roll and stuck it over my mouth, waiting for the drugs to knock me out as she brushed her fingertips across my forehead.

"It would have been easier to just kill my mother," she would always reply. "Eight years you kept her in that bed. Silly boy. You of all people should know, you reap what you sow."

That was the thing that frightened me. Not dying. Dying is easy. No, I was always terrified at how much longer she'd keep me alive.

CHAPTER FIFTY-THREE

Damon

"Tell me," Cassie insisted. "Tell me what happened."

She had one of the milk cartons in her hand, and she turned it over, studying the picture of little-boy me.

"Why?" I asked her. "Why does it matter?"

"Because I want to understand," she replied. "And you owe me that."

After what felt like weeks in the attic—what literally must have been weeks—I told her.

"I was checking the mail," I said, looking up at the ceiling. "It was my birthday. I would have been out there for thirty seconds, if that." My words were flat, no emotion in them. I'd recited this story in my head for almost thirty years waiting until I found the right person to trust with my secrets.

"It was so fast," I added. "Sometimes it feels like a dream."

Or a nightmare.

"You were ten?" Cassie asked.

I nodded. "I was ten."

I told her everything.

CHAPTER FIFTY-FOUR

Damon

It was Ray who lured me into the van, the van that would carry me to my death, to my rebirth. From my small front yard in Lone Pine, California, on my tenth birthday. My mother sent me to the mailbox. My grandmother had mailed me a package, she said, and I should check if it had arrived yet.

Ray was on the footpath. I never asked him what he'd been doing out there, in front of my house. He was just there, a kid about twelve, poking cards into the spokes of his bicycle so they'd make a noise when he pedaled.

He stopped short when he saw me. "Hey," he said, abandoning the bicycle as he walked toward me. "What's your name?"

I didn't answer. My mom always told me never to speak to strangers. I kept walking toward the mailbox, opening it with anticipation. My grandmother always sent me the most elaborate gifts, and they always magically appeared in our mailbox on my birthday.

"Daniel?" my mother called from inside.

"Coming!" I yelled back, closing the empty mailbox in defeat.

Ray shrugged. "You waiting for something?"

"A package," I said. "It's supposed to arrive today."

"Are you Daniel?" Ray asked.

"Yeah," I said slowly.

"My dad's delivering packages!" Ray said excitedly. "Come on, his van's parked right out here!"

I looked back at my front door, hesitant. Mom always said to never leave the front yard. But the van was right there. And it had my package from Grandma. I wanted that package.

"It's okay," Ray said, walking to the nondescript white van without looking back at me. He opened one of the doors and stepped in, offering me his hand. "See?"

I looked back at my house again, less than fifty feet away.

"Maybe I should get my mom," I said.

"If you're a little baby," Ray said. "We might be gone by the time you come back, though."

I puffed my chest out, offended. "I'm not a baby! I'm ten!"

I got into the back of the van. Ray pulled the door closed behind me. There were no packages. Just a man, a man whose face I didn't even see, and a sharp pinch in my neck as he injected me with something that made the world go away.

I woke up in a pine box. The irony. I didn't know where I was or how long it had been. I just remember feeling scared. I just remember calling out for my mom.

Stephen Randolph.

That was his name. The man who took me was a very sick man, a man who should have been in a mental hospital for life. He saw things and heard voices that had convinced him he was a prophet of God, that it was his job to save the children of the world by delivering them to heaven.

I thought it was all a load of shit, but I was ten years old. I had no power. I had no currency. I did what I was told.

Ray and I were Disciples of God. That's what Stephen Randolph told us when he beat us in the night. When we cried for our mothers. When we begged to go home. He didn't like it when we begged to go home. He would hold our heads down in a bucket full of ice water when we begged to go home.

We were the only boys. I wasn't even supposed to be there—it was just Stephen and Ray—but Ray begged for a brother. I was Ray's new brother. He named me—Damon—and Daniel Collins was never seen again. Stephen became my new father. And we were a family of three, moving from place to place, stealing souls all along the way.

It was our job to lure other children in. Girls, always girls. Pretty girls with shiny hair and little dresses that were edged with frills and lace. Father would choose the girls from the safety of the van, and we would have to scoop them up like little tadpoles in our net.

The girls never lasted long. We always needed to replenish the stock.

Once we got a little older, Ray and I used to play this game.

Father would take us to the park and wait in the van while we scoured the place for potential targets.

We'd see who could convince a girl to get into the van first.

I always won.

CHAPTER FIFTY-FIVE

Damon

We killed Father when I was sixteen and Ray, eighteen.

He'd become spooked. He was paranoid, delusional, and he was convinced that the police were on to him. He had three girls at the time, locked away carefully in their little boxes, mouths taped over so they wouldn't make a noise. We lived in a house on the Mississippi, and one by one, Father carried them down to the river and drowned them.

I'd watched him load his gun with three bullets, and I knew what he intended—one for me, one for Ray, and the final one for him. But Ray and I, we didn't want to die. We were older and wiser, and we'd started to talk about how to get away.

We killed Father the same way he killed those girls. Ray knocked him out with a fry pan. We loaded him into the biggest box, the one Ray had first slept in when Father took him. We locked the box up, nice and tight, and as our Father screamed at us to let him out, we dragged his makeshift coffin down to the riverbank and pushed him in.

We had a choice: Go to the police and tell them everything. Or pretend that we'd died along with those poor girls, along with our kidnapper, and start our lives again.

Ray wanted to go to the police. I was the one who refused.

All I could think about was my mother's face if she knew the things I'd done. I'd have to tell her everything. I'd be in so much trouble for leaving the yard that day.

I'd have to tell her about leading all those girls to their deaths, about how good I was at it, about the way I beamed under Father's praise.

I'd rather die than tell her what I did. Ray showed me another way. We became new people. And we never saw our families again.

CHAPTER FIFTY-SIX

Damon

I t's not the hunger that will kill you.

It's the thirst.

Thirst will drive you to madness, but I'm already mad. I made my peace with my insanity a long time ago. I've known for a long time that I was never meant to exist.

I've been in this box, in this room, for so damn long I don't even have words to quantify it anymore. I know when Leo isn't in the house—because that's when Cassie comes up here to let me out, to take me to the bathroom, to force-feed me more pills that knock any inkling of energy out of me.

That's when we talk. And other things.

And then the nosy fucker found me in here. I bet Leo got the surprise of his goddamned life when he saw me, locked in a box like a goddamn corpse. I haven't seen myself in a mirror, but I know I must look hideous. I'm skin and bones, I haven't shaved in what must be months and months and months. And I'm crazy. Batshit fucking crazy. I have moments of clarity, but those are the worst. Those are when all the pain comes back. I prefer the crazy.

I heard them talking outside the attic door, hushed voices. He was angry. She was screaming. A few hours later, a drill, right outside the door. *He's replacing the lock*, I realize. He's locking me in. He's locking her out.

I panic, briefly, but I've already been up here for days without food and I'm too far gone. The only sounds I hear after that are the guttural battle cries of a woman bearing down, the intensity and the volume increasing through the long, dark night. I cry then, but no tears come out.

I think of the girl downstairs, with the straw hair and the green eyes, and I wish that I'd been born a different person, for her. I loved her. I *still* love her. And that's the thought that gives me peace as I feel myself drift into a blackness only a boy in a box would be acquainted with as he rubbed his fingers down splintered wooden sides and sang the song his mother used to sing to him at night. I'm too weak now to sing anything, too weak to even cry real tears, but that's okay because I can still hear my mother in my mind. I can see her in the distance in my mind's eye, a tall glass of water in her hand, outstretched to me, and I run toward her. It is my tenth birthday again and I am strong, and I don't get in the van with Ray, and I run to my mother as fast as a boy has ever run before. And when I get to her she's beautiful, and the glass of water has transformed into a carton of milk, and the carton of milk has nobody's face on it because this is heaven and nobody is snatched into a van in heaven and milk cartons do not come with the faces of missing children printed on the sides. I drink from the carton of milk and it tastes better than anything I've ever tasted in my life, and my mother watches me with a smile and hands me a slice of rainbow birthday cake, and everything is perfect.

It's not the hunger that will kill you, Stephen Randolph used to say to me.

It's the *thirst*.

CHAPTER FIFTY-SEVEN

Leo

If you'd asked me where I would have ended up in the world, the answer wouldn't have been where I am.

I mean—I was never going to get out of this town, that much is clear to me now. It became clear somewhere in the moments between finding Damon King in a box in Cassie's attic and holding my newborn daughter just a few hours later. If the truth about Damon's existence, about what he did, was the pile of bricks that weighed me down to this place, then baby Grace was the cement that filled up the hollow spaces and made sure I stuck.

I wanted to run away after she was born. I'm not proud to admit that.

I work at the garage most days, changing out oil filters and jump-starting cars for weary travelers who've left their headlights on too long while they grab a meal at Dana's. The irony of where I work doesn't escape me; smack-bang in front of the spot where the accident happened. Hell, I could throw a rock and it'd clear the stretch of highway where Damon tried to kill me—where he virtually killed Cassie's mom—but that's life in a town like Gun Creek. Everything and nothing happens on the same two-mile stretch.

I work because it's something to do, because I need to keep my hands busy and my mind occupied, because it's too quiet in that house.

The night Grace was born, man, something flipped a switch inside me. Cassie was so fucking brave. So much pain to bring a baby into the world, so much anguish and all I could do was watch helplessly as she breathed and moaned and doubled over in pain in the bath, fetching her ice chips and massaging her back until my fingers went numb and the homebirth midwife told me to take a breather. Cassie was born to be a mother. I saw glimpses of it when she was pregnant, the way she spoke to her stomach as I rubbed oil into her stretching skin. I saw the sheer determination on her face even when the birthing pool turned a deep red wine color and the midwife paled, insisting we call an ambulance. Cassie almost died, she lost so much blood trying to bring our daughter into this world. But when she finally bore down and gave that final push in the safety of hospital walls, when she reached down and pulled that baby from her own body, dragging the tiny thing up through her legs and onto her bare chest, I watched Cassie be *reborn*. It made me love her in a way I can't even describe except to say that I'd tear the entire world down to keep her and Gracie safe.

Sometimes I think of what Damon did to her. How being in that accident and going to prison was nothing compared to what she had to endure, on her own, for all those empty years. I'm not a murderer. But I am a killer. I'd kill for my girls. I'd do anything to keep them safe. Including having Cassie involuntarily committed on a 72-hour psych hold after she begged me to take her home against medical advice. I didn't have to ask why she was so eager to return home. Damon. She wanted to make sure I didn't hurt him, and though I couldn't understand why, I did know that she wasn't in her right mind.

Most often, though, I think of the way she sobbed when we buried Damon in the yard, under the chestnut tree. I told her I'd do it myself, that Pike and I would be able to dig the hole down faster while she stayed inside, but she insisted that she be a part of it. Of *all of it*. In the end, my brother was the one watching from the warmth of the living room window, little Grace in his arms, while Cassie and I lowered Damon King into his final resting place; the hollow in the earth where, as I'd found out only days earlier, Jennifer's body rests.

CHAPTER FIFTY-EIGHT

Cassie

There's an old chestnut tree outside our kitchen window.

When I was a girl, I'd sit in that tree and survey my kingdom, the fields that stretch out in every direction.

We've made love against it, Leo's hands pressing my hips into the weathered bark until it cut the skin on my back.

Jennifer is there, bones now, wrapped in plastic and laid to rest without fanfare, without a headstone, without a priest to give her any last rites.

The ground was hollowed after we buried her, no matter how much dirt I piled on top of her final resting place. No matter how many hours I knelt in that dirt and prayed for her soul. No matter how many nightmares she visited me in, her big eyes imploring me to save her.

The ground never let me forget that she was there. Their baby rests there, too, in a heart-shaped box that used to hold my mother's wedding veil, a soul too small to have ever survived the violent way it entered this world.

It's cold tonight. This winter was just as harsh as the last one, but spring is here, now. Soon it will warm up. Luckily we have the money from Mom's life insurance policy, something that keeps the heat going twenty-four hours a day and lets us pay for firewood instead of stealing it.

Leo's stretched out on the couch, his big hands looking huge as he pats our baby girl on the back.

She's only a month old. A baby isn't something we had planned for, but she is so beautiful, so *perfect*, it's made me happier than I could have ever imagined on those lonely nights when it was just Damon and I between these four walls.

I could stare at these two my whole life, the way her ear rests on his chest, the slow breath that they've somehow managed to synchronize. I might have carried our daughter in my belly for nine months, but she belongs to her father.

We've talked about moving, but we both agree that it's better to stay here. To keep an eye on things. We wouldn't want anybody else digging around the property and finding things that are best left buried.

Leo moved the old piano away from the window, but I made him put it back. He thought I wouldn't want to stare at that spot below the chestnut tree as I played, but he's wrong. Apart from my baby girl and my Leo, that spot fills all the empty spaces inside me. It comforts me on those cold nights when they're asleep and the memories come flooding back. We spend most of our nights like this; Leo holding little Grace while I play for them. He told me once how it wasn't the noise he feared in prison, but the quiet. He doesn't like the numbing silence, so I try to fill it for him. Between my fleeting music skills and the way Grace cries for food every few hours, we have him covered.

Sometimes I lie on top of the spot where they're buried, in the night, in the weak yellow light the porch lamp casts off. Now that it's spring, the snow has melted, and the grass on top of them is thick and healthy. The ground does not hollow anymore with the weight of Jennifer. Now it is smooth and flat, and Damon is with her.

All I ever wanted was somebody to love. To love me.

Leo thought I was crazy when I insisted on digging right down until I hit bone. What did a year in the ground do to somebody's body? Would the flesh be gone? Would they just be shiny white bones?

Please don't leave me here, Cassie.

There was nothing shiny about Jennifer Thomas and her year-buried body. It was just dirt and bones and a little flesh and the dark remnants of the outfit she'd been wearing when we put her in the earth. Leo wanted to shove Damon's body into the hollow and be done with it, but I couldn't bear the thought of the three of them spending eternity separated by dirt and rocks and a thin sheet of plastic. So I unwrapped her, and we put her next to him, the tiny heart-shaped box on top, and when Leo saw what was left of Jennifer, he cried.

All I ever wanted was somebody to love. To love me.

You're probably wondering why I went to any effort to bury them together. Why I cried. Why I loved him in my own strange way. I didn't love the man who killed my mother and sent Leo to prison, no. It was the man he could have been; the man he would have been if he hadn't stepped into that van. If he hadn't been a boy on a milk carton. I think I would have loved that boy very much if things had been different.

More than anything—even in death—I didn't want him to be alone. He should be with his child, with the girl he loved in the only way he knew how. With violence, and with a finality that was as brutal as it was unwavering.

But I can't think about Damon anymore. I can't think about my mother or Ray. I can't think about Adelie Collins and the way she died of a broken heart. I have to think about my family now. My husband. Our daughter. Everything I've ever done has been for them, for us, for *this.*

I didn't know the depth of love until I stared into my daughter's brilliant eyes. The color of the ocean, the color of hope, the color of everything I ever dreamed of having. Her eyes are so bright it makes me want to cry.

What big eyes you have, Gracie. Leo swears they're turning green like his, like mine, but when I look at her, all I see is lazulite blue.

CHAPTER FIFTY-NINE

Leo

"You sure I can take the car?"

Pike's standing beside me, the weight of every terrible secret we share in the air that hangs between us. He looks how I feel; older, hollowed out, a husk of everything he used to be. I wish for a moment that I could unsee all the things we've been privy to these past years, but that would be like wishing away our lives and settling into the same death that has already claimed so many people.

"Yeah, 'course. It's not exactly a family car."

Pike snorts. "Got that right. You sure you'll be okay with the Honda?" he presses, as we look out the kitchen window at Cassie and her picnic companion. We both know he's not asking about the fucking Honda, he's asking about Cassie. Will I be okay with the woman who lied for a year and more, who kept a grown man, a murderer, in our attic right above the spot where we slept every single night? Will I be okay with the woman I promised to love for better or worse, in sickness and health, knowing what she was capable of? Pike was devastated when we eloped, a few weeks after Grace was born. A few weeks after we buried Damon beside Jennifer.

I know my brother, and I know that the weight of his concern for me hangs around his neck like a noose.

"I'll be fine. The farthest I need to drive is the pharmacy in Tonopah." Our mother is on methadone again—at least until she manages to fuck her life up again—and I insist on driving her every morning to get her dose of the stuff that might just save her life. It's self-preservation as much as anything—while she's clean, I don't have to worry about CPS calling me and asking me to take in all my siblings. While she's clean, I can convince her to stay far away from Mayor Carter. For the moment, at least, the situation is controlled.

"You don't need to worry about Mom," I add.

"It's not her I'm worried about," Pike replies.

"Pike," I say quietly. "You go. I'll be fine here. Better than fine. I'm happy here."

"Happy."

"Cautiously optimistic?"

"I don't trust her," Pike says, heat in his words as his eyes narrow at Cassie, outside. "You can't tell me you trust her, Leo."

I shrug. "Don't have to trust somebody to love them."

"Really? Is that what she said when she told you she loved *him*?"

Blood rises in my cheeks at the mention of Damon. I count to five in my head as I breathe in. *Onetwothreefourfive*. I hold for two. Exhale.

"She didn't love him."

Pike shakes his head, hands stuffed in his jeans. I know what he wants to say. He wants to remind me about the way Cassie cried and pleaded and screamed when I found Damon and refused her any more *visits* upstairs. When I coaxed the truth out of her, in between contractions that had her doubled over and vomiting from the pain. When I filled the birthing pool and she begged me to take some water up to him in the attic so that he wouldn't die. And me, the bastard I am, refused.

I let that motherfucker starve in a pine box with nothing but air to fill his empty stomach, with nothing but the salty sweat on his palms to chase away the thirst. I let him die up there, alone, and the only thing I regret is that I wasn't able to torture him first. He took everything from us. *Everything.* So when Cassie was pushing and pushing and screaming his name, pleading for me to help him, she didn't mean it. She couldn't possibly have meant it. Pain does strange things to a person.

Pike opens his mouth as if to speak. Closes it again. *Good choice, brother.*

He wants to run away from here, I can tell. He's not just edgy, he's terrified. He's scared of this house, of what lies just outside, of Cassie. He's scared of the straw-haired girl we grew up with, the girl who cried when we caught butterflies in jars and insisted on freeing them; my baby brother, all six-five of him, is scared of the tiny girl outside who used to steal his cigarettes and flush them down the toilet to save him from getting lung cancer.

I mean, I get it. If I didn't know her so well, I'd be scared of her, too.

Cassie's on a picnic blanket on the grass, her legs curled around to the side as she coos over Grace. Our little daughter is kicking her legs clumsily, her bright eyes focused on Cassie as she pulls faces and chatters away. I've never seen Cassie so happy, so full of life.

"That baby's got her daddy's eyes," Pike says quietly beside me. We're standing at the kitchen counter, the fields green and stretching out for miles beyond our property. I hesitated to call it mine for so long, but I've been here for over a year now, and my name is on the title deed, so I suppose it's mine. Ours.

Unlike our daughter, who might be *ours*, but is definitely not *mine*.

Pike's words are like a stab in the heart, a rip through the careful web we've spun all around us. Besides Cassie and me, Pike is the only one who knows the truth. And even though I know Cassie would never do anything to hurt him, the fact that he knows so much makes my skin crawl. I don't ever want him to say the wrong thing to her. I don't ever want him to get mad and threaten her. No, what I want—what I need—is for him to be gone. I want him to have a chance. A life. Away from here.

"All kids are born with blue eyes," I reply, but my words lack any real conviction.

"That's not your kid, bro," Pike says. "You know that, right?"

"Of course I know that."

Pike scoffs. "You're gonna raise his kid in his house while he's buried in the *fucking* yard?"

I turn and stare at my brother, in his bright green eyes, eyes that match my own. He must see the intent in my gaze, the absolute conviction that I have to protect these girls from the world because he takes a step back and nods. "Okay, man, whatever. But don't get complacent, okay? Don't you ever forget what she's capable of."

I won't forget. I won't be fooled again. "Thanks for looking out for me, bro. You think you don't have it in you, but you do."

A small smile threads across Pike's face. Until he looks back to Cassie and the baby, who are done outside and are headed right for the house, and us.

"Your wife is a dangerous woman," Pike says softly, plastering a proud uncle smile on his face as Cassie opens the door and he holds his arms out for Grace. She beams, handing Grace over to my brother and curling herself into my side. I let her, wrapping my arm around her small frame, my skin hot against hers.

"Did you tell your brother?" Cassie asks, poking me in the ribs with the tip of her finger. It tickles and I pull away, giving her a playful swat on the arm.

"I was waiting for you," I say, my face smiling and my heart racing.

Cassie takes that as an invitation, disappearing into the living room and coming back with a photograph in her hands. She hands it to Pike, who seems a natural at holding babies while juggling other items. His face goes blank, and I can tell he's struggling.

"We just found out," I say, taking Grace from him so he can study the picture properly. "Two babies in less than a year. Can you imagine?"

"Irish twins, just like you two," Cassie adds.

Pike feigns excitement. "Congratulations, guys," he says, handing me the ultrasound picture of my son, the son currently the size of a peach and growing like a weed inside my crazy wife's womb. The son who was conceived well after we buried Damon, the son who is my child by DNA, not just by my complacency.

We make small talk for what seems like an acceptable amount of time and then it's time for Pike to leave. I'm excited for him, and sad, so sad, like it's the end of an era. I know it won't be, he's only going as far as Reno, and then who knows from there. He'll be back. He's still bound to our mother by some invisible chain of guilt that I managed to saw off a long time ago; *he'll be back.*

I watch him flinch minutely when Cassie hugs him. If she notices, she doesn't show it. She has become the master of storytelling, of make believe, playing the part of Cinderella after the slipper has been fitted. We live in another man's castle and we make believe that this life is something we can bear; we make believe that we are normal people with a normal child, that there are no bodies buried beneath the hollow where my wife enjoys long picnics in the afternoon sun. I don't have to make believe that I love her more than the sun, though, and it's the ferocity of my love for her that makes all of the other things possible.

We stand out on the grass by the road and watch Pike drive my Mustang off into the afternoon, my eyes fixed on the white racing stripe I so meticulously restored. I watch until he's a speck in the distance. I blink, he's gone. I let out a breath I didn't know I was holding. Cassie turns to me and smiles, threading her fingers through mine. "I hope he finds somebody to love," she says dreamily, "the way you and I love each other."

I smile and nod, kissing her cool forehead. I hope Pike never finds somebody to love the way Cassie and I love each other. I hope he finds a normal kind of love, not one that drives you to do things you never dreamed you were capable of.

"Are you sad?" Cassie asks.

"About my brother, or about my car?" I joke, but my heart pinches at the thought.

I am not *sad* but I carry this sadness with me; the sadness of Jennifer and Karen and my sister and my brothers; the sadness of my mother and how nobody, none of them, *ever*, had a chance. I carry the sadness of Cassie. Of *her* mother. All these people, I am sad for, and if I think about their sadness too long, I start to drown in it.

I take a sleepy Grace from Cassie and carry her to the porch. Together we rock in the old chair and I stare down at her face, utterly detached, willing myself to love her. She's *my* daughter. For better or worse. I will love her. I have to.

Later, when Pike's long gone and Grace has passed out in her bassinet after a breast milk binge, Cassie finds me in the bedroom. I'm freshly showered and naked, save for the thin top sheet I've pulled over myself while I read.

"This is really fucked up," I say, holding up the book she's been reading to Grace, *Where the Wild Things Are*. "It's about a kid who runs away because his mother doesn't feed him? And then these monsters love him so much they'd rather eat him than let him go?"

She laughs, taking the book from my hands and setting it on the nightstand. "It's just a book," she says, crawling into my lap. "Besides, it's a classic."

I raise my eyebrows. "Really? It's old and it smells like wet dog."

"Mr. Bentley," she says, one hand on my throat, "I don't want to talk about kids' books right now. I want to talk about what's under these sheets."

"Anything for you, Mrs. Bentley," I say, moving the sheets away, pulling her against my cock. I'm ready for her and she's ready for me, no panties under her summer dress for me to contend with. She lets out a small sigh that sounds like happiness when I enter her, as she starts to ride me. I have to be gentle with her. She's only just given birth, less than three months ago, and now she's carrying my son. Some girls like it rough, but I can't be rough with my pregnant wife.

I thread my hands into her hair and pull her face to mine. I close my eyes and kiss her and she tastes like strawberry yogurt and summer rain. She tastes like all the things I never thought I would have again.

Your wife is a dangerous woman. Pike's words come back to haunt me. My wife might be a dangerous woman, but I love her anyway. None of this was her fault, not really. At least, that's what I tell myself as Cassie takes my hands and places them on her waist, her dress gone somewhere while my eyes were closed, her eyes locked on mine. My thumbs find the slight swell of new life in her belly as I grip her hips, her milk-filled breasts pressed against my bare chest, and I wonder how anyone could ever call her dangerous. And then I remember the bodies in the yard, and I close my eyes again.

CHAPTER SIXTY

Cassie

wish Stephen Randolph had just killed me, Damon said to me once. His delivery was stunning, a blow to my chest, a bruising punch right in my blue-black heart.

I scrubbed the box and the attic as best I could after we buried Damon. The attic of lost souls, I thought, as I knelt on knees that were still tender from all the hours I knelt and panted and cried in labor just days before.

Afterward, I sat in the box up in the attic, cross-legged, no light except the thin slice of weak sunlight that filtered in through the high window.

I held one of Damon's milk cartons in my hands, turning it over and over.

HAVE YOU SEEN THIS BOY? it screamed at me.

Yes. I have seen him. It took me a long time, a year and more, but I broke the man into enough pieces to reveal the child.

I have seen this boy. Lazulite eyes and a dimple in each cheek when he smiled.

He was *beautiful.*

I thought back to all the nights we spent in there. Nights when Leo was deep in a drugged sleep, safely downstairs, nights when I would pull more secrets from the man who almost broke me completely. How intimately I got to know him, to understand him, to hate him.

How sorry I felt for him.

How much I wanted to taste his pain the way he had tasted mine, how fucking heartsick he'd made me.

He'd already tasted of his own death when I kissed his mouth, dry lips and sunken cheeks, but his body still worked just fine. It still longed for me, hard and rigid as I unbuttoned his dirty jeans and reached inside. His eyes went wide as he shrank back from me. I think he was expecting violence. Maybe expecting that I'd come good on my threat and was going to cut his dick off like I had promised so many times to do.

"Cassie," he breathed, muscles still sinew, eyes still full of violent love for me, all for me.

His eyes were wet as I took from him what he'd taken from me.

After, I locked the attic door and checked it twice. I took the stairs leisurely, still full of him. I went into the kitchen and drank a glass of milk.

I went upstairs and slept beside Leo, the sticky smear of my old lover still wet against my thighs.

Going mad doesn't happen all at once. It's a process. It's girls in wells and mothers in comas and boyfriends in prison. It's Damon King in your bed, in your head, and then finally, in the prison you constructed for him.

EPILOGUE

Cassie

"**S**weet creature!" said the spider. "You're witty and you're wise! How handsome are your gauzy wings, how brilliant are your eyes!"

I bet you thought that I was the fly, didn't you? All wide-eyed and frightened as the spider closes the gap.

But I am a girl with a darkness inside me.

Carefully placed. Cleverly concealed. A darkness that could devour you.

I am not the fly in this story.

Pray you do not wrong me. Pray you do not stick in my carefully threaded web.

I am a girl with a darkness inside me.

But I think you knew that already.

About the Author

Lili St. Germain is a USA Today bestselling author who has sold over one million books since her debut series shot to the top of the bestseller charts in 2014.

She is presently working on the Alex Black series, a collection of espionage thrillers involving the illegitimate daughter of the world's most famous British spy. Reluctantly recruited by MI6 in the wake of her mother's kidnapping, Alex is forced to work together with the very people she loathes—the same people who have kept her apart from her father—in order to find her mother, and save the world. The series is currently in development for film.

Lili lives in a small seaside town in Western Australia with her husband and children.

Join the mailing list for updates:

www.lilisaintgermain.com/level4

Lili St. Germain Collection

Espionage Thrillers

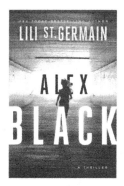

ALEX BLACK

ISBN: 978-1-933769-58-5

After twenty-eight years in the shadows, Alex Black, the bitter, estranged daughter of the world's iconic super-spy, is reluctantly recruited by MI6 to uncover the mystery of her mother's disappearance and, in the process, foil a vast conspiracy that threatens the world.

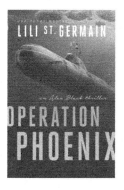

OPERATION PHOENIX

ISBN: 978-1-64630-002-0

Black strikes back. When a ballistic missile submarine goes missing, MI6 needs Alex to recover the sub before the U.S. is framed as a nuclear murderer. But this time around, Alex has a 10-year-old girl she is responsible for, opening painful scars she thought were in her past.

THE KING'S GAMBIT

ISBN: 978-1-64630-048-8

Book three in the series pits Alex Black against a pharmaceutical tycoon determined to reshape the human race genetically. Alex must infiltrate his organization and find a way to stop the plot.